THE RUTAB...
WALKED LI...

The girl lay in the rain by h... must help me," she whispered. "...... the Rhox!"

"What rocks?" Roger looked around wildly. "I'll go for a doctor!"

Her voice faltered. "No time . . . to explain . . . take . . . button . . . put it in . . . your ear. . . ." The green eyes held on Roger's, pleading.

"Seems like a funny time to worry about a hearing aid," Roger gulped, "but . . ." He held the button to his ear. Did he hear a faint, wavering hum, or was it his imagination? He pushed it in.

"*Drive to Pottsville,*" the girl's voice said in his ear. "*Start now. Time is precious!*"

There was the sound of a motor. The headlight of a second motorcycle was approaching. As it shot past, he saw the shape behind the handlebars: a headless torso, bulbous, ornamented with two clusters of tentacles. Through the single goggle, an eye as big as a pizza swiveled to impale him with a glance of utter alienness.

With a strangled yell, Roger leaped back and saw the motorcycle veer wildly, hurling its monstrous rider clear, then skid to a stop in the center of the highway. Roger could see that the rider's upper portion was smashed into a pulp.

"I should go to the police," he said. "But what can I say? That I was responsible for the death of a giant rutabaga?"

"*Time is of the essence,*" the girl's slightly accented voice said. "*Get going! Take the motorcycle!*"

"That would be stealing!"

"*Who's going to report it? Relatives of a giant rutabaga?*"

"You have a definite point there," Roger said . . .

—from *Time Trap*

KEITH LAUMER:
THE LIGHTER SIDE

EDITED AND
COMPILED BY
ERIC FLINT

Keith Laumer: The Lighter Side

This is a work of fiction. All the characters and events portrayed in this book are fictional, and any resemblance to real people or incidents is purely coincidental.

"In the Queue" was first published by Putnam in 1970 as part of the anthology *Orbit 7*, edited by Damon Knight. "The Planet Wreckers" was first published in *Worlds of Tomorrow*, February 1967. "The Body Builders" was first published in *Galaxy*, August 1966. *Time Trap* was first published by Putnam in 1970. "The Devil You Don't" was first published by Doubleday in 1970 as part of the anthology *Alchemy & Academe*, edited by Anne McCaffrey. "The Exterminator" (aka "A Bad Day for Vermin") was first published in *Galaxy*, February 1964. "The Big Show" was first published in *Galaxy*, February 1968. "Goobereality" was first published by Berkley in 1968 as part of the anthology of Keith Laumer stories entitled *It's a Mad, Mad, Mad Galaxy*. "Prototaph" was first published in *Analog*, March 1966. *The Great Time Machine Hoax* was first published by Simon & Schuster in 1964.

A Baen Books Original

Baen Publishing Enterprises
P.O. Box 1403
Riverdale, NY 10471
www.baen.com

ISBN: 0-7434-3537-0

Cover art by Richard Martin

First printing, May 2002

Distributed by Simon & Schuster
1230 Avenue of the Americas
New York, NY 10020

Production by Windhaven Press, Auburn, NH
Printed in the United States of America

Contents

IN THE QUEUE

✺

The old man fell just as Farn Hestler's power wheel was passing his Place in Line, on his way back from the Comfort Station. Hestler, braking, stared down at the twisted face, a mask of soft, pale leather in which the mouth writhed as if trying to tear itself free of the dying body. Then he jumped from the wheel, bent over the victim. Quick as he was, a lean woman with fingers like gnarled roots was before him, clutching at the old man's fleshless shoulders.

"Tell them *me*, Millicent Dredgewicke Klunt," she was shrilling into the vacant face. "Oh, if you only knew what I've been through, how I *deserve* the help—"

Hestler sent her reeling with a deft shove of his foot. He knelt beside the old man, lifted his head.

"Vultures," he said. "Greedy, snapping at a man. Now, I *care*. And you were getting so close to the Head of the Line. The tales you could tell, I'll bet. An Old-timer. Not

1

like these Line, er, jumpers," he diverted the obscenity. "I say a man deserves a little dignity at a moment like this—"

"Wasting your time, Jack," a meaty voice said. Hestler glanced up into the hippopotamine features of the man he always thought of as Twentieth Back. "The old coot's dead."

Hestler shook the corpse. "Tell them Argall Y. Hestler!" he yelled into the dead ear. "Argall, that's A-R-G-A-L-L—"

"Break it up," the brassy voice of a Line Policeman sliced through the babble. "You, get back." A sharp prod lent urgency to the command. Hestler rose reluctantly, his eyes on the waxy face slackening into an expression of horrified astonishment.

"Ghoul," the lean woman he had kicked snarled. "Line—!" She mouthed the unmentionable word.

"I wasn't thinking of myself," Hestler countered hotly. "But my boy Argall, through no fault of his own—"

"All right, quiet!" the cop snarled. He jerked a thumb at the dead man. "This guy make any disposition?"

"Yes!" the lean woman cried. "He said, to Millicent Dredgewicke Klunt, that's M-I-L—"

"She's lying," Hestler cut in. "I happened to catch the name Argall Hestler—right, sir?" He looked brightly at a slack-jawed lad who was staring down at the corpse.

The boy swallowed and looked Hestler in the face.

"Hell, he never said a word," he said, and spat, just missing Hestler's shoe.

"Died intestate," the cop intoned, and wrote a note in his book. He gestured and a clean-up squad moved in, lifted the corpse onto a cart, covered it, trundled it away.

"Close it up," the cop ordered.

"Intestate," somebody grumbled. "Crap!"

"A rotten shame. The slot goes back to the government. Nobody profits. Goddamn!" the fat man who had spoken looked around at the others. "In a case like this we ought to get together, have some equitable plan worked out and agreed to in advance—"

"Hey," the slack-jawed boy said. "That's conspiracy!"

"I meant to suggest nothing illegal." The fat man faded back to his Place in Line. As if by common consent, the small crowd dissipated, sliding into their Places with deft footwork. Hestler shrugged and remounted his wheel, put-putted forward, aware of the envious eyes that followed him. He passed the same backs he always passed, some standing, some sitting on canvas camp stools under sun-faded umbrellas, here and there a nylon queuebana, high and square, some shabby, some ornate, owned by the more fortunate. Like himself: he was a lucky man, he had never been a Standee, sweating the line exposed to the sun and prying eyes.

It was a bright afternoon. The sun shone down on the vast concrete ramp across which the Line snaked from a point lost in distance across the plain. Ahead—not far ahead now, and getting closer every day—was the blank white wall perforated only by the Window, the terminal point of the Line. Hestler slowed as he approached the Hestler queuebana; his mouth went dry as he saw how close it was to the Head of the Line now. One, two, three, four slots back! Ye Gods, that meant six people had been processed in the past twelve hours—an unprecedented number. And it meant—Hestler caught his breath—he might reach the Window himself, this shift. For a moment, he felt a panicky urge to flee, to trade places with First Back, and then with Second, work his way back to a safe distance, give himself a chance to think about it, get ready . . .

"Say, Farn." The head of his proxy, Cousin Galpert, poked from the curtains of the three foot square, five foot high nylon-walled queuebana. "Guess what? I moved up a spot while you were gone."

Hestler folded the wheel and leaned it against the weathered cloth. He waited until Galpert had emerged, then surreptitiously twitched the curtains wide open. The place always smelled fudgy and stale after his cousin had spent half an hour in it while he was away for his Comfort Break.

"We're getting close to the Head," Galpert said excitedly, handing over the lockbox that contained the Papers. "I have a feeling—" He broke off as sharp voices were suddenly raised a few Spaces behind. A small, pale-haired man with bulging blue eyes was attempting to force himself into Line between Third Back and Fifth Back.

"Say, isn't that Four Back?" Hestler asked.

"You don't understand," the little man was whimpering. "I had to go answer an unscheduled call of nature . . . " His weak eyes fixed on Fifth Back, a large, coarse-featured man in a loud shirt and sunglasses. "You said you'd watch my Place . . . !"

"So whattaya think ya got a Comfort Break for, ya bum! Beat it!"

Lots of people were shouting at the little man now: "Line-ine-ucker-bucker—Line   bucker,   Line bucker . . . "

The little man fell back, covering his ears. The obscene chant gained in volume as other voices took it up.

"But it's my *Place*," the evictee wailed. "Father left it to me when he died, you all remember him . . . " His voice was drowned in the uproar.

"Serves him right," Galpert said, embarrassed by the

chant. "A man with no more regard for his inheritance than to walk off and leave it . . ."

They watched the former Fourth Back turn and flee, his hands still over his ears.

After Galpert left on the wheel, Hestler aired the queuebana for another ten minutes, standing stony-faced, arms folded, staring at the back of One Up. His father had told him some stories about One Up, back in the old days, when they'd both been young fellows, near the end of the Line. Seemed he'd been quite a cutup in those days, always joking around with the women close to him in Line, offering to trade Places for a certain consideration. You didn't see many signs of that now: just a dumpy old man in burst-out shoe-leather, sweating out the Line. But he himself was lucky, Hestler reflected. He'd taken over from Father when the latter had had his stroke, a twenty-one thousand two hundred and ninety-four slot jump. Not many young fellows did that well. Not that he was all that young, he'd put in his time in the Line, it wasn't as if he didn't deserve the break.

And now, in a few hours maybe, he'd hit the Head of the Line. He touched the lockbox that contained the old man's Papers—and of course his own, and Cluster's and the kids'—everything. In a few hours, if the Line kept moving, he could relax, retire, let the kids, with their own Places in Line, carry on. Let them do as well as their dad had done, making Head of the Line at under forty-five!

Inside his queuebana it was hot, airless. Hestler pulled off his coat and squatted in the crouch-hammock—not the most comfortable position in the world, maybe, but in full compliance with the Q-law requirement that at least one foot be on the ground at all times, and the head higher than the waist. Hestler remembered an incident years before, when some poor

devil without a queuebana had gone to sleep standing up. He'd stood with his eyes closed and his knees
bent, and slowly sunk down to a squat; then bobbed
slowly up and blinked and went back to sleep. Up and
down, they'd watched him for an hour before he finally
let his head drop lower than his belt. They'd pitched
him out of Line then, and closed ranks. Ah, there'd
been some wild times in the queue in the old days,
not like now. There was too much at stake now, this
near the Head. No time for horseplay.

Just before dusk, the Line moved up. Three to go!
Hestler's heart thumped.

It was dark when he heard the voice whisper: *"Four
Up!"*

Hestler jerked wide awake. He blinked, wondering
if he'd dreamed the urgent tone.

"Four Up!" the voice hissed again. Hestler twitched
the curtain open, saw nothing, pulled his head back
in. Then he saw the pale, pinched face, the bulging
eyes of Four Back, peering through the vent slot at
the rear of the tent.

"You have to help me," the little man said. "You saw
what happened, you can make a deposition that I was
cheated, that—"

"Look here, what are you doing out of Line?"
Hestler cut in. "I know you're on-shift, why aren't you
holding down a new slot?"

"I . . . I couldn't face it," Four Back said brokenly.
"My wife, my children—they're all counting on me."

"You should have thought of that sooner."

"I swear I couldn't help it. It just hit me so suddenly. And—"

"You lost your Place. There's nothing I can do."

"If I have to start over now—I'll be over seventy
when I get to the Window!"

"That's not my lookout—"

" . . . but if you'll just tell the Line Police what happened, explain about my special case—"

"You're crazy, I can't do that!"

"But you . . . I always thought you looked like a decent sort—"

"You'd better go. Suppose someone sees me talking to you?"

"I had to speak to you here, I don't know your name, but after all we've been four Spaces apart in Line for nine years—"

"Go away! Before I call a Line cop!"

Hestler had a hard time getting comfortable again after Four Back left. There was a fly inside the queuebana. It was a hot night. The Line moved up again, and Hestler had to emerge and roll the queuebana forward. Two Spaces to go! The feeling of excitement was so intense that it made Hestler feel a little sick. Two more moves up, and he'd be at the Window. He'd open the lockbox, and present the Papers, taking his time, one at a time, getting it all correct, all in order. With a sudden pang of panic he wondered if anyone had goofed, anywhere back along the line, failed to sign anything, missed a Notary's seal, or a witness' signature. But they couldn't have. Nothing as dumb as that. For that you could get bounced out of Line, lose your Place, have to go all the way back—

Hestler shook off the morbid fancies. He was just nervous, that was all. Well, who wouldn't be? After tonight, his whole life would be different; his days of standing in Line would be over. He'd have time— all the time in the world to do all the things he hadn't been able to think about all these years . . .

Someone shouted, near at hand. Hestler stumbled out of the queuebana to see Two Up—at the Head of the line now—raise his fist and shake it under the nose of the small, black-moustached face in the green eye-shade framed in the Window, bathed in harsh white light.

"Idiot! Dumbbell! Jackass!" Two Up yelled. "What do you mean take it back home and have my wife spell out her middle name!"

Two burly Line police appeared, shone lights in Two Up's wild face, grabbed his arms, took him away. Hestler trembled as he pushed the queuebana forward a Space on its roller skate wheels. Only one man ahead of him now. He'd be next. But no reason to get all upset; the Line had been moving like greased lightning, but it would take a few hours to process the man ahead. He had time to relax, get his nerves soothed down, get ready to answer questions . . .

"I don't understand, sir," the reedy voice of One Up was saying to the small black moustache behind the Window. "My Papers are all in order, I swear it—"

"You said yourself your father is dead," the small, dry voice of Black Moustache said. "That means you'll have to reexecute Form 56839847565342-B in sextuplicate, with an endorsement from the medical doctor, the Residential Police, and waivers from Department A, B, C, and so on. You'll find it all, right in the Regulations."

"But—but he only died two hours ago: I just received word—"

"Two hours, two years; he's just as dead."

"But—I'll lose my Place! If I hadn't mentioned it to you—"

"Then I wouldn't have known about it. But you did mention it, quite right, too."

"Couldn't you just pretend I didn't say anything? That the messenger never reached me?"

"Are you suggesting I commit fraud?"

"No . . . no . . . " One Up turned and tottered away, his invalidated Papers clutched in his hand. Hestler swallowed hard.

"Next," Black Moustache said.

It was almost dawn six hours later when the clerk stamped the last Paper, licked the last stamp, thrust the stack of processed documents into a slot and looked past Hestler at the next man in Line.

Hestler hesitated, holding the empty lockbox in nerveless fingers. It felt abnormally light, like a cast husk.

"That's all," the clerk said. "Next."

One Down jostled Hestler getting to the Window. He was a small, bandy-legged Standee with large, loose lips and long ears. Hestler had never really looked at him before. He felt an urge to tell him all about how it had been, give him a few friendly tips, as an old Window veteran to a newcomer. But the man didn't give him a chance.

Moving off, Hestler noticed the queuebana. It looked abandoned, functionless. He thought of all the hours, the days, the years he had spent in it, crouched in the sling . . .

"You can have it," he said on impulse to Two Down, who, he noted with surprise, was a woman, dumpy, slack-jowled. He gestured toward the queuebana. She made a snorting sound and ignored him. He wandered off down the Line, staring curiously at the people in it, at the varied faces and figures, tall, wide, narrow, old, young—not so many of those—dressed in used clothing, with hair combed or uncombed, some with facial hair, some with paint on their lips, all unattractive in their own individual ways.

He encountered Galpert whizzing toward him on the power wheel. Galpert slowed, gaping, came to a halt. Hestler noticed that his cousin had thin, bony ankles in maroon socks, one of which suffered from perished elastic so that the sock drooped, exposing clay-white skin.

"Farn—what . . . ?"

"All done." Hestler held up the empty lockbox.

"All done . . . ?" Galpert looked across toward the distant Window in a bewildered way.

"All done. Not much to it, really."

"Then . . . I . . . I guess I don't need to . . ." Galpert's voice died away.

"No, no need, never again, Galpert."

"Yes, but what . . . ?" Galpert looked at Hestler, looked at the Line, back at Hestler. "You coming, Farn?"

"I . . . I think I'll just take a walk for a while. Savor it, you know."

"Well," Galpert said. He started up the wheel and rode slowly off across the ramp.

Suddenly, Hestler was thinking about time—all that time stretching ahead, like an abyss. What would he do with it . . . ? He almost called after Galpert, but instead turned and continued his walk along the Line. Faces stared past him, over him, through him.

Noon came and went. Hestler obtained a dry hot dog and a paper cup of warm milk from a vendor on a three-wheeler with a big umbrella and a pet chicken perched on the back. He walked on, searching the faces. They were all so ugly. He pitied them, so far from the Window. He looked back; it was barely visible, a tiny dark point toward which the Line dwindled. What did they think about, standing in Line? How they must envy him!

But no one seemed to notice him. Toward sunset he began to feel lonely. He wanted to talk to someone; but none of the faces he passed seemed sympathetic.

It was almost dark when he reached the End of the Line. Beyond, the empty plain stretched toward the dark horizon. It looked cold out there, lonely.

"It looks cold out there," he heard himself say to the oatmeal-faced lad who huddled at the tail of the Line, hands in pockets. "And lonely."

"You in Line, or what?" the boy asked.

Hestler looked again at the bleak horizon. He came over and stood behind the youth.

"Certainly," he said.

THE PLANET WRECKERS

In his shabby room in the formerly elegant hostelry known as the Grand Atumpquah Palace, Jack Waverly pulled the coarse weave sheet up about his ears and composed himself for sleep.

Somewhere, a voice whispered. Somewhere, boards creaked. Wind muttered around the loosely fitted window, rattling it in its frame. The pulled-down blind clacked restlessly. In the room above, footsteps went three paces; clank; back three paces; clank . . .

Drat the fellow, Waverly thought. *Why doesn't he stop rattling his chains and go to bed?* He turned on his other side, rearranged the pillow of the consistency of bagged sawdust. Beyond the partition, someone was whistling a strange, unmelodic tune. It was hot in the room. The sheet chafed his neck. Next door, voices muttered with a note of urgency. Waverly made out the words *magma* and *San Andreas fault.*

"Geology, at ten minutes past midnight?" he inquired of the mottled wallpaper. Above, bedsprings squeaked faintly. Waverly sat up, frowning at the ceiling. "I thought the clerk said he was putting me on the top floor," he said accusingly. He reached for the telephone on the bedside table. A wavering dial tone went on for five seconds, then cut off with a sharp click.

"Hello?" Waverly said. "Hello?"

The receiver was dead against his ear.

"If this weren't the only hotel in town," Waverly muttered.

He climbed out of bed, went to the high window, raised the roller shade, looked out on a view of a brick wall ten feet away. From the window next door, a pattern of light and shadow gleamed against the masonry.

Two silhouettes moved. One was tall, lean, long-armed, like a giant bird with a crested head and curious wattles below a stunted beak. The other resembled an inverted polyp, waving a dozen arms tipped with multifingered hands, several of which clutched smoking cigars.

"Trick of the light," Waverly said firmly. He closed his eyes and shook his head to dispel the illusion. When he looked again, the window was dark.

"There, you see?" He raised the sash and thrust his head out. Moonlight gleamed on a bricked alley far below. A rusted fire escape led upward toward the roof. Leaning far out, Waverly saw the sill of the window above.

"No lights up there," he advised himself. "Hmmmm."

Faintly, he heard a dull rattle of metal, followed by a lugubrious groan.

"True, it's none of your business," he said. "But inasmuch as you can't sleep anyway . . . " Waverly swung his legs over the sill onto the landing and started up.

❖   ❖   ❖

As he reached the landing above, something white fluttered out at him. Waverly shied, then saw that it was a curtain, billowing out from an open window. Abruptly, a feminine sob sounded from within. He poked his head up far enough to peer over the window sill into darkness.

"Is, ah, something the matter?" he called softly. There was a long moment of silence.

"Who's there?" a dulcet female voice whispered.

"Waverly, madam, Jack Waverly. If I can be of any help?"

"Are you with the Service?"

"I'm with ISLC," Waverly said. He pronounced it as a word "islick." "That's International Sa—"

"Listen to me, Wivery," the voice was urgent. "Whatever he's paying you, I'll double it! And you'll find the Service not ungrateful."

"No payment is necessary for aid to damsels in distress," Waverly returned. "Er, may I come in?"

"Of course! Hurry up, before one of those slimy Gimps steps out for a stroll up the wall and sees you!"

Waverly climbed quickly in through the window. The room, he saw, was a mere garret, cramped under a low ceiling. It appeared to contain no furniture other than a dimly seen cot against one wall. A vague form moved a willowy arm there. Waverly moved toward it.

"You don't have a molecular disassociator with you?" the melodious voice queried urgently. "There's not much time left."

"Ah . . . no, I'm afraid not. I—"

"They mean to strap me to my own twifler, set the warperators at two and a half busters and aim me toward Neptune," the feminine voice went on breathlessly. "Can you imagine anything more brutal?"

Waverly groped forward. "Now, now, my dear. Don't be upset."

As he reached the cot, his hand fell on stout links looped around the foot rail.

He fumbled, encountered the blocky shape of a hefty padlock.

"Good lord! I thought—that is, I didn't actually think—"

"That's right. Chained to the bed," there was a slight quaver in the voice.

"B-but—this is preposterous! It's criminal!"

"It's an indication of their desperation, Wivery! They've gone so far now that nothing short of the most drastic measures can stop them!"

"I think this is a matter for the authorities," Waverly blurted. "I'll put a call through immediately!"

"How? You can't get through."

"That's right; I'd forgotten about the phone."

"And anyway—I *am* the authorities," the soft voice said in a tone of utter discouragement.

"You? A mere slip of a girl?" Waverly's hand touched something cool, with the texture like nubbly nylon carpeting.

"I weigh three hundred and seventy pounds, Earth equatorial," the voice came back sharply. "And we Vorplischers happen to be a matriarchal society!"

A pale shape stirred, rose up from the rumpled bedding. A head the size of a washtub smiled a foot-wide smile that was disconcertingly located above a pair of limpid brown eyes. A hand which appeared to be equipped with at least nine fingers reached up to pat a spongy mass of orange fibers matted across the top of the wide face. Waverly broke his paralysis sufficiently to utter a sharp yelp.

"Shhh!" the sweet voice issued from a point high in the chest. "I appreciate your admiration, but we don't want those monsters to hear you!"

2

"Fom Berj, Detective Third Class, at your service," the creature soothed Waverly. "I'm not supposed to reveal my identity, but under the circumstances I think it's only appropriate."

"D—delighted," Waverly choked. "Pardon my falling down. It's just that I was a trifle startled at your, ah, unusual appearance."

"It's perfectly understandable. A neat disguise, don't you think? I made it myself."

Waverly gulped. "Disguise?"

"Of course. You don't think this is my natural look do you?"

Waverly laughed shakily. "I must confess that what with all this creeping around in the dark, I *was* ready to leap to conclusions." He peered at the massive form, more clearly visible now that his eyes accommodated to the dim light. "But what are you disguised as, if you don't mind my asking?"

"Why, as a native, of course. The same as you are, silly."

"As I am what?"

"Disguised as a native."

"Native of where?"

"Of this planet."

"Oh, of course." Waverly was backing toward the window. "Of this planet. A native . . . I take it you're from some *other* planet?"

The detective laughed a rippling laugh. "You have a jolly sense of humor, Wivery. As if a Vorplischer were native to this patch of wilderness."

"And the people who chained you up—are they

from, ah, Vorplisch, too?" Waverly made conversation to cover his retreat.

"Don't be absurd. They're a mixed bag of Broogs, Limpicos, Erwalts, Glimps and Pud knows what-all." Fom Berj rattled her manacles. "We'd better do something about these chains in a hurry," she added briskly.

As Waverly reached the window, an eerie, purplish glow sprang up outside, accompanied by a shrill warbling. Waverly retreated hastily.

"I think that's them arriving with my twifler now," Fom Berj said tensely. "It's a brand-new model, equipped with the latest in antiac gear and the new infinite-capacity particle ingesters. You can imagine what *that* means! My frozen corpse will be three parsecs beyond Pluto before my Mayday beep clears the first boost station."

"Frozen corpse? Pluto?" Waverly gobbled.

"I know it sounds fantastic, but disposing of an agent of the Service is a mere bagatelle to these operators, compared with what they're planning!"

"What *are* they planning?" Waverly choked.

"Don't you know? I thought you were working for Izlik."

"Well, he, ah, doesn't tell us much . . . "

"Mmmm. I don't know about that Izlik. Sometimes I wonder just how deep a game he's playing. By the way, where *is* he?"

"He was delayed by a heavy cloud cover over Ypsilanti," Waverly improvised. "He'll be along later." His eyes roved the room, searching for an escape route. "You were saying?" he prompted in an obscure instinct to keep the detective talking.

"They're making a Galacular," Fom Berj said solemnly.

"A . . . Galacular?"

"Now you see the extent of their madness. An open violation of Regulation 69723468b!"

There was a sharp series of bumping sounds above. "Better hurry with that molecular disassociator," Fom Berj said.

"What's a Galacular?" Waverly was close to the door now. He froze as something made a slithery sound beyond it.

"A multi-D thriller," Fom Berj was explaining. "You know, one of those planetary debacle epics."

"What sort of debacle?" Waverly recoiled at a sound as of heavy breathing outside the door.

"Floods, quakes, typhoons—you know the sort of thing. Audiences love them, in spite of their illegality. The first scene they're shooting tonight will be a full-scale meteor strike in a place called Montana."

"You mean—a *real* meteor?"

"Of course. According to my informant, they've grappled onto a cubic mile or so of nickel-iron that was parked in a convenient orbit a few million miles out, and nudged it in this direction. I would have stopped it there, of course, but I blundered and they caught me," the detective sighed. "It should make quite an effective splash when it hits."

"They're going to wreck an entire state just for a— a spectacle?" Waverly choked.

"I see you're not familiar with the Galacular craze. To be accepted by discriminating multi-D fans, nothing less than a genuine disaster will serve."

Up above on the roof, heavy feet clumped; something massive bump-bumped.

Fom Berj's voice was icy calm. "Now, Wivery, it's true we Vorplischers pride ourselves on our coolness in the face of peril, but WILL YOU GET THESE DAMNED CHAINS OFF ME BEFORE IT'S TOO LATE!"

Waverly darted to the window. "Don't go away," he called over his shoulder. "I'll be right back!"

❖   ❖   ❖

It took Waverly forty-five seconds to descend to his room, snatch up his sample case, hastily examine his tongue in the mirror and retrace his steps to the attic. He opened the case, lettered International Safe and Lock Corporation, took out a tool shaped like a miniature crochet hook, turned to the lock.

"Hmmm. A variation on the Katzenburger-McIlhenney patents," he muttered. "Child's play . . . " He probed delicately in the wide key slot, frowning as he worked.

"Hurry, Wivery!" Fom Berj cried.

Waverly wiped perspiration from his forehead. "It's trickier than it looked," he said defensively. "Apparently they've employed a double-reserve cam action."

Feet clumped on stairs, descending from the roof. A mutter of hoarse voices sounded in the hall, just beyond the door. The latch rattled. Waverly reached for his sample case, rummaged among the odds and ends there, came up with a cylindrical object. He sprang to the door, hastily engaged the chain latch just as the doorknob turned cautiously. The door creaked, swung open two inches, came to rest against the chain. A beaklike nose appeared at the opening, followed by a hand holding a gun.

Aiming coolly, Waverly directed a jet of menthol shaving cream at a pair of close-set eyes just visible above the nose. They withdrew with a muffled shriek. The gun clattered on the floor. Waverly snatched up the weapon, jammed it in his waistband, dashed back to the lock. Five seconds later, it opened with a decisive *spongg!* Fom Berj emitted a delighted squeak, rolled off the bed as the chains clattered to the floor. Waverly gaped at the cluster of supple members on which the bulky detective rippled swiftly across to the window. Outside the door, excited twitters, burbles and growls sounded interrogatory notes. The doorknob rattled. Something heavy struck the door.

"To the roof!" Fom Berj flowed through the window and was gone. The door shook to a thunderous impact. Waverly sprang to the window. On the landing, he looked down. A round, pale face with eyes like bubbles in hot tar stared up at him. He yelped and dashed for the roof.

Pulling himself up over the parapet, Waverly looked across an expanse of starlit roof, at the center of which an object shaped like a twelve-foot gravy boat rested lightly on three spidery jacks. The upper half was a clear plastic, hinged open like a mussel shell. Fom Berj was halfway to it when a small, sharp-featured head appeared over its gunwale. The monkeylike face split vertically, emitted a sharp cry and dived over the side. The boat rocked perilously as Fom Berj swarmed up and in; she turned, extended a long, three-elbowed arm to Waverly, hauled him up as something popped nearby. Pale chartreuse gas swirled about the canopy as it slammed down. The detective lurched to a small, green-plush-covered contour seat, groped for the controls. Waverly scrambled after her, found himself crowded into a restricted space which was apparently intended as a parcel shelf.

"Which way is Montana?" the detective inquired over a rising hum that sprang up as she poked buttons on the padded dash.

"Straight ahead, about a thousand miles," Waverly called.

"Hold on tight," Fom Berj cried as the little vehicle leaped straight up. "On optimum trajectory, the trip will take close to half an hour. I don't know if we'll be in time or not."

3

Level at 100,000 feet, the twifler hummed along smoothly, making the whispering sound which gave it its name. Its velocity was just under 1850 MPH.

"Hurry," Waverly urged.

"Any faster at this altitude and we'd ablate," Fom Berj pointed out. "Relax, Wivery. We're doing our best."

"How can I relax?" Waverly complained. "The headroom is grossly inadequate."

"Well, you know the Q-stress engine produces a lens-shaped field with a minor radius proportional to the reciprocal of the fourth power of the input. To give you room to stand up, we'd need a diameter of about half a light-year. That's unwieldy."

"Hmmm. I wondered why flying saucers were shaped like that. It never occurred—"

"It seems to me you're pretty ignorant of a lot of things," Fom Berj studied Waverly with one eye, keeping the other firmly fixed on the instrument panel.

"I seem to note certain deficiencies in your costume, when it comes to that," he pointed out somewhat acidly. He eyed the three padded foundation garments strapped around the bulbous torso. "Most local beauties consider two of *those* sufficient," he added.

"You don't know much about these locals. They're mammary-happy. And if two of a given organ are attractive, six are triply attractive."

"What are you trying to attract?"

"Nothing. But a girl likes to make a good impression."

"Speaking of impressions—what are you planning on doing about this meteorite? You *did* say a cubic mile?"

"I was hoping to disintegrate it outside the outer R-belt, if possible, but I'm afraid we're running a little late."

"A thing that size—" Waverly felt the sweat pop on his forehead—"will vaporize the crust of the earth for miles around the point of impact!"

"I hate to think of what it will do to the native wild life," Fom Berj said. "Their feeding and mating habits will be upset, their nests destroyed—" Fom Berj broke off. "Oh, dear, I'm afraid we're too late!"

Ahead, a glowing point had appeared high in the sky. It descended steadily, becoming rapidly brighter. Waverly braced his feet as the twifler decelerated sharply, veering off. The glaring point of fire was surrounded by a greenish aura.

"It's about three hundred miles out, I'd say," Fom Berj commented. "That means it will strike in about thirty seconds."

A faint, fiery trail was visible now behind the new star. Through the clear plastic hatch, Waverly watched as a beam of blue light speared out from the swelling central fire, probed downward, boiling away a low cloud layer.

"What's that?" Waverly squeaked.

"A column of compressed gases. It will be splashing up a nice pit for the actual body to bury itself in."

A pink glow had sprung up from the surface far below. The approaching meteor was an intolerable point of brilliance now, illuminating the clouds like a full moon. The light grew brighter; now Waverly could see a visible diameter, heading the streaming tail of fire. Abruptly it separated into three separate fragments, which continued on parallel courses.

"Tsk," Fom Berj clucked. "It exploded. That means an even wider distribution . . . "

With appalling swiftness the three radiant bodies expanded to form a huge, irregular glob of brilliance, dropping swiftly now, darting downward as quick as thought—

The sky opened into a great fan of yellow light more vivid than the sun.

Waverly squinted at the actinic display, watched it spread outward, shot through with rising jets of glowing stuff, interspersed with rocketlike streaks that punched upward, higher, higher, and were gone from view—all in utter silence. The far horizons were touched with light now. Then, slowly, the glare faded back. The silver-etched edges of the clouds dimmed away, until only a great rosy glow in the west marked the point of the meteorite's impact.

"Fooey," Fom Berj said. "Round one to the opposition."

Waverly and the Vorplischer stared down at the mile-wide, white-hot pit bubbling fifty thousand feet below and ten miles ahead.

"You have to confess the rascals got some remarkable footage that time," Fom Berj commented.

"This is incredible!" Waverly groaned. "You people—whoever you are—were aware that this band of desperadoes planned this atrocity—and all you sent was one female to combat them?"

"I'll disregard the chauvinistic overtones of that remark," Fom Berj said severely, "and merely remind you that the Service is a small one, operating on a perennially meager appropriation."

"If your precious Service were any sort of interplanetary police force, it wouldn't tolerate this sort of sloppy work," Waverly said sharply.

"Police force? Where did you get an idea like that? I'm a private eye in the employ of the Game and Wildlife Service."

"Wildlife—" Waverly started.

"Brace yourself," Fom Berj said. "Here comes the shock wave."

The twifler gave a preliminary shudder, then wrenched itself violently end-for-end, at the same time slamming violently upward, to the accompaniment of a great metallic *zonnggg!* of thunder.

"I shudder to imagine how that would have felt without the special antiac equipment," the detective gasped. "Now, if we expect to intercept these scoundrels in the act of shooting their next scene, there's no time to waste."

"You mean they're going to do it *again?*"

"Not the same routine, of course. This time they're staging a major earthquake in a province called California. They'll trigger it by beaming the deep substrata with tight-focus tractor probes. The whole area is in a delicate state of balance, so all it will take is the merest touch to start a crustal readjustment that will satisfy the most exacting fans."

"The San Andreas Fault," Waverly groaned. "Goodby, San Francisco!"

"It's the Sequoias I'm thinking of," Fom Berj sighed. "Remarkable organisms, and not nearly so easy to replace as San Franciscans."

4

The twifler hurtled across the Rockies at eighty thousand feet, began to let down over northwestern Nevada, an unbroken desert gleaming ghostly white in the light of a crescent moon. Far ahead, San Francisco glowed on the horizon.

"This gets a trifle tricky now," Fom Berj said. "The recording units will be orbiting the scene of the action at a substratospheric level, of course, catching it all with wide-spectrum senceivers, but the production crew will be on the ground, controlling the action. They're the ones we're after. And in order to capture these male-factors red-handed, we'll have to land and go in on foot for the pinch. That means leaving the protection of the twifler's antiac field."

"What will we do when we find them?"

"I'd prefer to merely lay them by the heels with a liberal application of stun gas. If they're alive to stand trial, the publicity will be a real bonus, careerwise. However, it may be necessary to vaporize them."

Decelerating sharply, Fom Berj dropped low over the desert, scanning the instruments closely.

"They've shielded their force bubble pretty well," she said. "But I think I've picked it up." She pointed. Waverly detected a vague bluish point glowing on a high rooftop near the north edge of the city. "A good position, with an excellent view of the target area."

Waverly held on as the flier swooped low, whistled in a tight arc and settled in on a dark rooftop. The hatch popped up, admitted a gust of cool night air. Waverly and the detective advanced to the parapet. A hundred yards distant across a bottomless, black chasm, the blue glow of the fifty-foot force bubble shone eerily. Waverly was beginning to sweat inside his purple pajamas.

"What if they see us?" he hissed—and dropped flat as a beam of green light sizzled past his head from the bubble and burst into flame.

"Does that answer your question?" Fom Berj was crouched behind the parapet. "Well, there's no help for it. I'll have to use sterner measures." She broke off as the deck underfoot trembled, then rose in a series of jarring jerks, dropped a foot, thrust upward again. A low rumble had started up. Brick came pelting down from adjacent buildings to smash thunderously below.

"Oh, oh, it's started!" Fom Berj shrilled. Clinging to the roof with her multiple ambulatory members, the detective unlimbered a device resembling a small fire extinguisher, took aim and fired. Waverly, bouncing like a passenger in a Model T Ford, saw a yellow spear of light dart out, glance off the force bubble and send up a shower of sparks as it scored the blue-glowing sphere.

"Bull's-eye!" Fom Berj trilled. "A couple more like that, and—"

The whole mountainside under the building seemed to tilt. The parapet toppled and was gone. Waverly grabbed for a stout TV antenna, held on as his feet swung over the edge. Fom Berj emitted a sharp scream and grabbed for a handhold. The vaporizer slid past Waverly, went over the edge.

"That does it," the detective cried over the roar of crumbling mortar. "We tried, Wivery!"

"Look!" Waverly yelled. Over his shoulder, he saw the force bubble suddenly flicker violet, then green, then yellow—and abruptly dwindle to half its former diameter. Through a pall of dust, Waverly discerned the outlines of an elaborate apparatus resembling an oversized X-ray camera, now just outside the shrunken blue bubble. A pair of figures, one tall and thin, the other rotund and possessing four arms, dithered, scrabbling at the dome for entrance. One slipped and disappeared over the roof's edge with a mournful yowl. The other scampered off across the buckling roof, leaped to an adjacent one, disappeared in a cloud of smoke and dust.

"Did you see that?" Fom Berj cried. "They've had to abandon their grappler! We've beaten them!"

"Yes—but what about the earthquake?" Waverly called as the roof under him bounded and leaped.

"We'll just have to ride it out and hope for the best!"

Through the dust cloud, they watched as the blue bubble quivered, swam upward from its perch, leaving the abandoned tractor beamer perched forlornly on the roof.

"Let them go," Fom Berj called. "As soon as the ground stops shaking, we'll be after them."

Waverly looked out toward the vast sprawl of lights, which were now executing a slow, graceful shimmy. As he watched, a section of the city half a mile square went dark. A moment later, the twinkling orange lights of fires sprang up here and there across the darkened portion. Beyond the city, the surface of the Pacific heaved and boiled. A dome swelled up, burst; green water streamed back as a gout of black smoke belched upward in a roiling fire-shot cloud. The moonlight gleamed on a twenty-foot wavefront that traveled outward from the submarine eruption. Waverly saw it meet and merge with the waterfront, sweep grandly inland, foaming majestically about the bases of the hills on which the city was built. The long, undulating span of the Golden Gate bridge wavered in a slow snake dance, then descended silently into the bay, disappeared in a rising smother of white. More light went out; more fires appeared across the rapidly darkening city. A deafening rumble rolled continuously across the scene of devastation.

Now the backwash of the tidal wave was sweeping back out to sea, bearing with it a flotsam of bars, billboards, seafood restaurants and automobiles, many of the latter with their headlights still on, gleaming murkily through the shallow waters. Smoke was forming a pall across the mile of darkened ruins, lit from beneath by leaping flames. Here and there the quick yellow flashes of explosions punctuated the general overcast.

"G-good Lord," Waverly gasped as the shaking under him subsided into a quiver and then was still. "What an incredible catastrophe!"

"That was nothing to what it would have been if they'd had time to give it a good push," Fom Berj commented.

"The fiends!" Waverly scrambled to his feet. "Some of the best bars in the country were down there!"

"It could have been worse."

"I suppose so. At least the San Franciscans are used to it. Imagine what that tidal wave would have done to Manhattan!"

"Thanks for reminding me," Fom Berj said. "That's where the next scene is due to be shot."

5

"The scare we gave them should throw them far enough behind schedule to give us a decent crack at them this time," Fom Berj said, staring forward into the night as the twifler rocketed eastward. "They only have the one production unit here, you know. It's a shoestring operation, barely a hundred billion dollar budget."

Waverly, crouched again in his cramped perch behind the pilot, peered out as the lights of Chicago appeared ahead, spread below them and dwindled behind.

"What do they have in mind for New York? Another earthquake? A fire? Or maybe just a super typhoon?"

"Those minor disturbances won't do for this one," Fom Berj corrected him. "This is the climactic scene of the show. They plan to collapse a massive off-shore igneous dike and let the whole stretch of continental shelf from Boston to Cape Charles slide into the ocean."

"Saints preserve us!" Waverly cried.

"You should see what they'd do on a Class-A budget," Fom Berj retorted. "The local moon would look quite impressive, colliding with Earth."

"Ye gods! You sound almost as if you approve of these atrocities!"

"Well, I used to be a regular Saturday-afternoon theatergoer; but now that I've attained responsible age, I see the folly of wasting planets that way."

The blaze of lights that was the Atlantic seaboard swam over the horizon ahead, rushed toward the speeding twifler.

"They're set up on a barge about five miles offshore," the detective said as they swept over the city. "It's just a little field rig; it will only be used once, of course." She leaned forward. "Ah, there it is now."

Waverly gaped at a raft of lights visible on the sea ahead.

"Gad!" he cried. "The thing's the size of an Australian sheep ranch!"

"They need a certain area on which to set up the antenna arrays," Fom Berj said. "After all, they'll be handling a hundred billion megavolt-seconds of power. Now, we'll just stand off at about twenty miles and lob a few rounds into them. I concede it will be a little messy, what with the initial flash, the shock wave, the fallout and the storms and tidal waves, but it's better than letting them get away."

"Wait minute—your cure sounds as bad as the disease! We're a couple of miles from the most densely populated section of the country! You'll annihilate thousands!"

"You really *are* hipped on conservation," Fom Berj

said. "However, you can't cure tentacle mildew without trimming off a few tentacles. Here goes . . . "

"No!" Waverly grabbed for the detective's long arm as the latter placed a spatulate finger on a large pink button. Taken by surprise, Fom Berj yanked the limb back, struck a lever with her elbow. At once, the canopy snapped up and was instantly ripped away by the hundred-mile-per-hour slipstream. Icy wind tore at Waverly's pajamas, shrieked past his face, sucked the air from his lungs. Fom Berj grabbed for the controls, fought the bucking twifler as it went into a spin, hurtling down toward the black surface of the sea.

"Wivery! I can't hold it! Vertigo! Take over . . . " Waverly barely caught the words before the massive body of the feminine detective slumped and slid down under the dash. He reached, caught the wildly vibrating control tiller, put all his strength into hauling it back into line. The flier tilted, performed an outside loop followed by a snap-roll. Only Waverly's safety harness prevented him from being thrown from the cockpit. He shoved hard on the tiller, and the twifler went into a graceful inverted chandelle. Waverly looked "up," saw a vast spread of dark-glittering, white-capped ocean slowly tilting over him. With a convulsive wrench of the tiller he brought the Atlantic down and under his keel and was racing along fifty feet above the water. He dashed the wind-tears from his eyes, saw the lights of the barge rushing at him, gave a convulsive stab at four buttons at random and squeezed his eyes shut.

The twifler veered sharply, made a sound like ripped canvas and halted as suddenly as if it had dropped an anchor. Waverly pitched forward; the harness snapped. He hurtled across the short prow, clipping off a flagstaff bearing a triangular pink ensign, fell six feet and was skidding head over heels across the deck of the barge.

❖   ❖   ❖

For a moment, Waverly lay half-stunned; then he staggered to his feet, holding a tattered strip of safety harness in one hand. The twifler was drifting rapidly away, some ten feet above the deck of the barge. He scrambled after it, made a despairing grab at a trailing harness strap, missed, skidded into the rail and clung there, watching the air car dwindle away downwind.

Behind him, a brilliant crimson spotlight blared into existence. Hoarse voices shouted. Other lights came up. The deck, Waverly saw, was swarming with excited figures. He ducked for the cover of a three-foot scupper, squinted as the floodlight caught him square in the face. Something hard was pressing into his hip. He groped, came out with the compact automatic he had jammed into the waistband of his pajamas. He raised the gun and fired a round into the big light. It emitted a deep-toned *whoof!*, flashed green and blue and went out.

"Hey!" a rubbery voice yelled. "I thought you boobs stuck a fresh filament in number twelve!"

"Get them extra persons in position before I put 'em over the side," another voice bassooned.

"Zero minus six mini-units and counting," a hoot came from on high.

The gobbling mob surged closer. Waverly clutched the pistol, made three yards sideways, then rose in shadow and darted toward a low deckhouse ahead. He rounded its corner, almost collided with an apparition with coarse-grained blue wattles, two-inch eyes of a deep bottle green, a vertically hinged mouth opening on triple rows of coppery-brown fangs, all set on a snaky neck rising from a body like a baled buffalo robe shrouded in leather wings; then he was skittering backward, making pushing motions with both hands.

"Hasrach opp irikik!" the creature boomed. "Who're youse? You scared the pants off me in that getup! Whaddya want?"

"Izlik s-sent me," Waverly improvised.

"Oh, then you want to see the boss."

"Ah, yes, precisely. I want to see the boss."

"You want the feeding boss, the mating boss, the leisure-time boss, the honorary boss, the hereditary boss or the compulsory boss?" The monster snapped a blue cigar butt over the rail.

"The, er, boss boss!"

"Balvovats is inside, rescripting scene two. Din't you hear what happened out on the coast?"

"As a matter of fact, I just got in from Butte—"

"How did the fireball routine go?"

"Very impressive. Ah, by the way, how long before things get underway here?"

"Another five minutes."

"Thanks."

Waverly sidled past the horror, made for a lighted doorway fifty feet away. Above, invisible behind banked floodlights, someone was gabbling shrilly. Two beings appeared at the entrance as Waverly reached it. One was an armored creature mincing on six legs like a three-foot blue crab. The other appeared to be a seven-foot column of translucent yellow jelly.

"Here, you can't go in there," the crablike one barked. *"Ik urikik opsrock,* you know that!"

"Wait a minute, Sol," the gelatinous one burbled in a shaky voice like a failing tape recorder. "Can't you see he's just in from location? Look at the costume."

"A lousy job. Wouldn't fool anybody."

"What you got, Mac? Make it fast. Balvovats is ready to roll 'em."

"Ip orikip slunk," Waverly said desperately.

"Sorry, I don't savvy Glimp. Better talk local like the style boss said."

"It's the rotiple underplump!" Waverly barked. "Out of the way, before all is lost!"

"I got to have a word with Mel about his runners, they're a little too uppity to suit me." Waverly caught the words as the two exchanged glances and moved from the doorway. He stepped through into a room dazzling with light and activity. Opposite him, a fifty-foot wall glittered with moving points of light. Before it, on high stools, half a dozen small orange-furred creatures bristling with multi-elbowed arms manipulated levers. On a raised dais to the left, a circular being with what appeared to be four heads shouted commands in all directions at once, through four megaphones.

"Okay!" Waverly heard the call. "We're all ready on one, three and four! What's the matter with two and five?"

"Here, you!" A scaled figure in a flowing pageboy bob thrust a sheaf of papers into his hand. "Take this to Balvovats; he's got holes in his head!" Waverly gaped after the donor as it turned away. The noise around him made his ears ring. Everything was rushing toward a climax at an accelerating pace, and if he didn't do something fast . . .

"Stop!" he yelled at the room at large. "You can't do this thing!"

"It's a heart-breaker, ain't it, kid?" a bulging being on his left chirruped in his ear. "If I would have been directing this fiasco, I'd of went for a real effect by blasting the ice caps. Now, *there's* a spectacle for you! Floods, storms—"

"Here, take these to Balvovats!" Waverly shoved the papers toward a passing creature resembling a fallen pudding. The bulgy being nictitated a membrane at him, snorted, said, "Okay, okay, I'm going, ain't I?" and pushed off through the press. At a discreet distance, Waverly followed.

6

The room the impressed messenger led him to was a circular arena crowded with screens, dials, levers, flashing lights, amid a cacophony of electronic hums and buzzes, all oriented toward a central podium on which was mounted a red and white, zebra-striped swivel chair, wide enough to accommodate triplets.

"Where's Balvovats?" The unwitting guide collared a jittery organism consisting of a cluster of bristly blue legs below a striped polo shirt.

"He stepped over to Esthetic Editing for a last-minute check," a piping voice snapped. "Now leggo my shirt before I call the shop steward!"

"Give him these!" The bulbous intruder handed over the papers and departed. Waverly faded back behind the column-mounted chair, looked around hastily, put a foot on a rung—

"Two minutes," a PA voice rang. "All recorder units on station and grinding."

"Hey, you, back outside on Set Nine! You heard the two-minute call!" Waverly looked down at a foot-high composition of varicolored warts mounted on two legs like coat-hanger wire.

"Mind your tone, my man," Waverly said. "Balvovats sent me. I'm sitting in for him. Is the, er, power on?"

"Cripey, what a time for an OJT! Okay, sir, better get on up there. About a minute and a half to M millisecond."

Waverly clambered to the seat, slid into it, looked

over an array of levers, pedals, orifices, toggle switches and paired buttons with varicolored idiot lights. "Don't monkey with the board, it's all set up," the warty one whined at his elbow. "I balanced her out personal. All you got to do is throw the load to her when you get the flash and push-field is up to full Q."

"Naturally," Waverly said. "It wouldn't do at all to push, say, this little green button here . . . ?"

"If you got to go, you should've went before you come in here. Better tighten up and wait. You only got fifty-one seconds and you're on the air."

"How about the big blue one there?"

"What for you want more light on deck? The boys are crying their eyes out now."

"The middle-sized yellow one?"

"The screens is already hot, can't you see 'em? Boy, the greenies they send out to me!"

"I know; this immense black lever is the one—"

"You don't need no filters, for Pud's sake! It's night-time!"

Waverly ran both hands through his hair and then pointed to various levers in turn: "Eenie, meenie, minie, moe . . ."

"Lay off that one you called 'minie,'" the instructor cautioned. "You touch that, you'll dump the whole load onto the left stabilizer complex—"

A door banged. Waverly looked up. A vast, white-robed being with arms like coiled boa constrictors had burst into the room, was goggling stem-mounted eyes like peeled tomatoes at Waverly.

"Hey—come down from there, you!" the new arrival bellowed. The snaky arms whipped up toward Waverly; he ducked, seized the forbidden lever, and slammed it home.

A shudder went through the seat under him; then the floor rose up like a stricken freighter up-ending for her last dive. A loud screech sounded in Waverly's ear as the warty being bounded into his lap and wrestled with the big lever. He rolled sideways, dived, saw the vast form of Balvovats cannon past and carom off the control pedestal, ophidioid members flailing murderously. Lights were flashing all around the room. A siren broke into a frantic, rising wail. Gongs gonged. Waverly, on the floor now and clinging to a cabinet support, saw an access panel pop open, exposing a foot square terminal block. "In for a penny, in for a pound," he muttered and grabbed a handful of intricately color-coded leads and ripped them loose.

The resultant cascade of fire sent him reeling backward just as a baseball-bat-thick tentacle whipped down across the spot he had been occupying. A dull *boom!* rocked the deck plates under him. Smoke poured from the ruined circuitry. He tottered to his feet, saw Balvovats secure a grip on a stanchion and haul his bulk upright.

"You!" the giant bellowed and launched itself at Waverly. He sprang for the door, tripped, rolled aside as the door banged wide. A gaggle of frantic spectacle-makers hurtled through, collided with the irate director. On all fours, Waverly pulled himself up the slanted deck and through the door.

In the corridor, the blare of gongs and sirens was redoubled. Buffeted by milling technicians, Waverly was spun, jostled, shoved, lifted along the passage and out onto the windswept deck. All around, loose gear was sliding and bounding down the thirty-degree slant. Waverly threw himself flat, barely avoiding a ricocheting cable drum, clawed his way toward the high edge of the barge.

"There he goes!" a bull-roar sounded behind him. He twisted, saw Balvovats winching himself upward in close pursuit. One extensible member lashed out, slapped the deck bare inches short of Waverly's foot. He groped for the automatic. It was gone. Ahead, a superstructure loomed up at the barge's edge, like a miniature Eiffel Tower. He scrambled for it, got a grip on a cross-member and pulled himself around to the far side. Balvovats' questing arm grabbed after him. He held on with both hands and one foot and delivered a swift kick to the persistent member; it recoiled, as a yell sounded from the darkness below. The deck lights had failed, leaving only the feeble gleam of colored rigging lights. Something struck the cross-bar by Waverly's head with a vicious *pwangg!* He clambered hastily higher.

On deck, someone had restored a spotlight to usefulness. The smoky beam probed upward, found Waverly's feet, jumped up to pin him against a girder fifty feet above the deck.

"A fat bonus to the one that nails him!" Balvovats' furious tones roared. At once, spitting sounds broke out below, accompanied by vivid flashes of pink light. Waverly scrambled higher. The spotlight followed him. Across the deck, a door burst open and smoke and flames rushed out. Waverly felt a shock through the steel tower, saw a gout of fire erupt through curled deck plating below.

"We're sinking!" a shrill voice keened.

"Get him!" Balvovats boomed.

Waverly looked down, saw white water breaking over the base of his perch. In the glow of the navigation lights, half a dozen small creatures were swarming up the openwork in hot pursuit. Something bumped him from behind. He shied, felt another bump, reached down and felt the hard contours of the automatic, trapped in the seat of his pajamas.

"Lucky I had them cut generously," he murmured as

he retrieved the weapon. Something *spangled* beside him, and a near-miss whined off into the darkness. Waverly took aim, shot out the deck light. Something plucked at his sleeve. He looked, saw torn cloth. Below, a red-eyed ball of sticky-looking fur was taking a bead on him from a distance of ten feet. He brought the automatic up and fired, fired again at a second pursuer a yard below the leader. Both assailants dropped, hit with twin splashes in the darkness below.

"Decks awash," Waverly said to himself. *"Dulce et decorum est, pro patria, et cetera."*

Another explosion shook the stricken barge. The tower swayed. A shot whined past his face. Another struck nearby.

"Get him, troops? Get hiburbleburble . . ." Balvovats' boom subsided. Waverly winced as a hot poker furrowed his shin. He saw a flicker of movement revealed by a blue rigging light, put a round into it, saw a dark body fall with a thin bleat. The spout of fire rising from the hatch on the high edge of the deck showed a white smother of foam washed almost to the survivors clinging to the rail. A gun burped below, chipped paint by Waverly's hip. He shifted grips, leaned far out and placed a shot between a pair of overlapping, egg-white eyes. They fell away with a despairing wail.

Abruptly, the fire died with a hiss as a wave rolled entirely across the deck. Waverly felt the tower shake as a breaker thundered against it, bare yards below where he clung. The lower navigation lights gleamed up through green water now.

There was a whiffling sound above. Waverly clutched his perch convulsively, looked upward.

"Fom Berj!" he yelled.

A dark ovoid shape settled down through the night toward him. He saw the cheery glow of running lights, the gleam reflected from a canopy.

"But . . . but our canopy blew away . . . " he faltered.

The twifler hove to, six feet above his head. A face like a plate of lasagna appeared over the edge. Squirmy hands, gripping an ominous-looking apparatus with a long barrel, came over the side, aimed at Waverly. A whirring sound started up. He brought up the pistol, squeezed the trigger—

There was an empty click.

"Superb!" the creature above exclaimed, extending a large grasping member over the side to Waverly. "What an expression of primitive savagery! Great footage, my boy! Now you'd better come aboard where we can talk contract in peace!"

7

"I'm afraid I don't quite understand, Mr. Izlik," Waverly said dazedly, trying not to stare at the leathery-hided bulk draped in a Clan Stewart tartan, complete with sporran and Tam o'Shanter. "One moment I was teetering on top of a sinking tower, with a horde of furry atrocities snapping at my heels—and ten minutes later . . . " He looked wonderingly at the luxuriously appointed lounge in which he sat.

"I left my yacht anchored here at two hundred thousand feet and dropped down to spy out what Balvovats was up to," the entrepreneur explained. "I confess I wasn't above purloining a little free footage of whatever it was he was staging. Then I saw you, sir, in action, and presto! I perceived the New Wave in the moment of its creation! Of course, I secured only about three minutes' actual product. We'll have to pad it out with another hundred hours or so of the same sort of action. I can already visualize a sequence in which you find yourself pursued by flesh-eating Dinosaurs, scale a man-eating plant for safety and are attacked by flying fang-masters, make a leap across an abyss of flaming hydrocarbons and, in a single bound, attain the safety of your twifler, just as it collides with a mountaintop!"

"Ah . . . I appreciate your offer of employment," Waverly interposed, "but I'm afraid I lack the dramatic gift."

"Oh, it won't be acting," Izlik handed over a slim glass of pale fluid and seated himself across from his guest. "No, indeed! I can assure you that all my productions are recorded on location, at the actual scenes of the frightful dangers they record. I'll see to it that the perils are real enough to inspire you to the highest efforts."

"No." Waverly drained his glass and hiccupped. "I appreciate the rescue and all that, but now I really must be getting back to work—"

"What salary are you drawing now?" Izlik demanded bluntly.

"Five hundred," Waverly said.

"Ha! I'll double that! One thousand Universal Credits!"

"How much is that in dollars?"

"You mean the local exchange?" Izlik removed a note book from his sporran, writhed his features at it.

"Coconuts . . . wampum . . . seashells . . . green stamps . . . ah! Here we are! Dollars! One Unicred is equal to twelve hundred and sixty-five dollars and twenty-three cents." He closed the book. "A cent is a type of cow, I believe. A few are always included in local transactions to placate Vishnu, or something."

"That's . . . that's over a million dollars a month!"

"A minute," Izlik corrected. "You'll get more for your next picture, of course."

"I'd like to take you up on it, Mr. Izlik," Waverly said wistfully. "But I'm afraid I wouldn't survive long enough to spend it."

"As to that, if you're to play superheroes, you'll naturally require superpowers. I'll fit you out with full S-P gear. Can't have my star suffering any damage, of course."

"S-P gear?"

"Self-Preservation. Developed in my own labs at Cosmic Productions. Better than anything issued to the armed forces. Genuine poly-steel muscles, invulnerable armor, IR and UV vision, cloak of invisibility—though of course you'll use the latter only in *real* emergencies."

"It sounds—" Waverly swallowed. "Quite overwhelming," he finished.

"Wait!" a faint voice sounded from the floor. Waverly and Izlik turned to the cot where Fom Berj was struggling feebly to sit up.

"You wouldn't . . . sink so low . . . as to ally yourself . . . with these vandals . . ." she gasped out.

"Vandals!" Izlik snorted. "I remind you, madam, it was I who took in tow your derelict twifler, which was bearing you swiftly toward a trans-Plutonian orbit!"

"Better annihilation—than help . . . from the likes of you . . ."

"I, ah, think you have an erroneous impression," Waverly put in. "Mr. Izlik here doesn't produce Galaculars. In fact, he's planning a nice, family-type entertainment that will render the planet wreckers obsolete."

"The day of the Galacular is over!" Izlik stated in positive tones. "What is a mere fractured continent, when compared with a lone hero, fighting for his life? When I release my epic of the struggle of one beleaguered being, beset by a bewildering bestiary of bellicose berserkers, our fortunes will be made!"

"Oh, really?" Fom Berj listened to a brief outline of the probable impact on the theatrically minded Galactic public of the new Miniculars.

"Why, Wivery—I really think you've solved the problem!" she acknowledged at the end. "In fact—I don't suppose—" She rolled her oversized eyes at Izlik. "How about signing me on as leading lady?"

"Well—I don't know," Izlik hedged. "With a family-type audience, there might be cries of miscegenation . . . "

"Nonsense. Take off your disguise, Wivery."

"To be perfectly candid, I'm not wearing one," Waverly replied with dignity.

"You mean—" Fom Berj stared at him. Then a titter broke from her capacious mouth. She reached up, fumbled at her throat, and with a single downward stroke, split her torso open like a banana peel. A slim arm came out and thrust the bulky costume back from round shoulders; a superb bosom emerged, followed by a piquant face with a turned-up nose topped by a cascade of carrot-red hair.

"And I thought I had to conceal my identity from *you!*" she said as she stepped from the collapsed Vorplischer suit. "And all this time you were really a Borundian!"

"A Borundian?" Waverly smiled dazedly at the graceful figure before him, modestly clad in a wisp of skintight gauze.

"Like me," Fom Berj said. "They'd never had hired me in my natural guise. We look too much like those Earth natives."

"Here," Izlik interrupted. "If you two are the same

species, why is it that she's shaped like *that*, and you're not?"

"That's part of the beauty of being a, um, Borundian," Waverly said, taking the former detective's hand and looking into her smiling green eyes. "Go ahead and draw up the contracts, Mr. Izlik. You've got yourself a deal."

THE BODY BUILDERS

❧

He was a big bruiser in a Gendye Mark Seven Sullivan, the luxury model with the nine-point sensory system, the highest-priced Grin-U-Matic facial expression attachment on the market and genuine human hair, mustache and all.

He came through the dining room entry like Genghis Kahn invading a Swiss convent. If there'd been a door in his way he'd have kicked it down. The two lads walking behind him—an old but tough-looking utility model Liston and a fairly new Wayne—kept their hands in their pockets and flicked their eyes over the room like buggy whips. The head waiter popped out with a stock of big purple menus, but the Sullivan went right past him, headed across toward my table like a field marshal leading a victory parade.

Lorena was with me that night, looking classy in a flossed-up Dietrich that must have set her back a

45

month's salary. She was in her usual mood for the usual reason: she wanted to give up her job at the Cent-Prog and sign a five-year marriage contract with me. The idea left me cold as an Eskimo's tombstone. In the first place, at the rate she burned creds, I'd have to creak around in a secondhand Lionel with about thirty percent sensory coverage and an undersized power core; and in the second, I was still carrying the torch for Julie. Sure, Julie had nutty ideas about Servos. According to her, having a nice wardrobe of specialized outfits for all occasions was one step below cannibalism.

"You and that closet full of zombies!" she used to shake her finger under my nose. "How could a girl possibly marry you and never know what face she'd see when she woke up in the morning!"

She was exaggerating, but that was the way those Organo-Republicans are. No logic in 'em. After all, doesn't it make sense to keep your organic body on file in the Municipal Vaults, safe out of the weather, and let a comfortable, late-model Servo do your walking and talking? Our grandparents found out it was a lot safer and easier to sit in front of the TV screen with feely and smelly attachments than to be out bumping heads with a crowd. It wasn't long after that that they developed the contact screens to fit your eyeballs, and the plug-in audio, so you began to get the real feel of audience participation. Then, with the big improvements in miniaturization and the new tight-channel transmitters, you could have your own private man-on-the-street pickup. It could roam, seeing the sights, while you racked out on the sofa.

Of course, with folks spending so much time flat on their backs, the Public Health boys had to come up with gear to keep the organic body in shape. For a while, people made it with part-time exercise and home

model massage and feeding racks, but it wasn't long
before they set up the Central File system.

Heck, the government already had everything about
you on file, from your birth certificate to your fingerprints. Why not go the whole hog and file the body
too?

Of course, nobody had expected what would happen when the quality of the sensory pickups and play-
backs got as good as they did. I mean the bit the
eggheads call "personality gestalt transfer." But it figured. A guy always had the feeling that his consciousness was sitting somewhere back of his eyes; so when
the lids were linked by direct hookup to the Servo, and
all the other senses tied in—all of a sudden, you were
there. The brain was back in Files, doped to the hairline, but you—the thing you call a mind—was there,
inside the Servo, living it up.

And with that kind of identification, the old type
utilitarian models went out of style, fast. People wanted
Servos that expressed the real inner man—the guy you
should have been. With everybody as big and tough
as they wanted to be, depending on the down payment
they could handle, nobody wanted to take any guff off
anybody. In the old days, a fellow had to settle for a
little fender-bending; now you could hang one on the
other guy, direct. Law Cent had to set up a code to
cover the problem, and now when some bird insulted
you or crowded you off the Fastwalk, you slugged it
out with a Monitor watching.

Julie claimed it was all a bunch of nonsense; that
the two Servos pounding each other didn't prove anything. She could never see that with perfect linkage,
you *were* the Servo. Like now: The waiter had just put
a plate of *consomme au beurre blanc* in front of me,
and with my high-priced Yum-gum palate accessory, I'd

get the same high-class taste thrills as if the soup was
being shoved down my Org's mouth in person. It was
a special mixture, naturally, that lubricated my main
swivel and supplied some chemicals to my glandular
analogs. But the flavor was there.

And meanwhile, the old body was doing swell on
a nutrient-drip into the femoral artery. So it's a little
artificial maybe—but what about the Orggies, riding
around in custom-built cars that are nothing but substitute personalities, wearing padded shoulders, contact lenses, hearing aids, false teeth, cosmetics, elevator
shoes, rugs to cover their bald domes. If you're going
to wear false eyelashes, why not false eyes? Instead of
a nose bob, why not bob the whole face? At least a
fellow wearing a Servo is honest about it, which is more
than you can say for an Orggie doll in a foam-rubber
bra—not that Julie needed any help in that department.

I dipped my big silver spoon in and had the first
sip just under my nose when the Sullivan slammed my
arm with his hip going past. I got the soup square in
the right eye. While I was still clicking the eyelid, trying
to clear the lens, the Liston jarred my shoulder hard
enough to rattle my master solenoid.

Normally, I'm a pretty even-tempered guy. It's my
theory that the way to keep a neurotronic system in
shape is to hold the glandular inputs to a minimum.
But, what with the big event coming up that night, and
Lorena riding me hard on the joys of contract life, I'd
had a hard day. I hopped up, overrode the eye-blink
reflex, made a long reach and hooked a finger in the
Liston's collar going away.

"Hold it right there, stumblebum!" I gave the collar a flick to spin him around.

He didn't spin. Instead, my elbow joint made a noise
like a roller skate hitting loose gravel; the jerk almost
flipped me right on my face.

The Liston did a slow turn, like a ten-ton crane rig, looked me over with a pair of yellow eyes that were as friendly as gun barrels. A low rumbling sound came out of him. I was a little shook but mad enough not to let it bother me.

"Let's have that license number," I barked at him. "There'll be a bill for the eye and another one for a chassis checkup!"

The Wayne had turned, too, and was beetling his brows at me. The big shot Sullivan pushed between the two of them, looked me over like I was something he'd found curled up in a doorway.

"Maybe you better kind of do a fade, Jasper," he boomed loud enough for everybody in the restaurant to hear. "My boys got no sense of humor."

I had my mouth open for my next mistake when Lorena beat me to it:

"Tell the big boob to get lost, Barney; he's interrupting what I was saying to you."

The Sullivan rolled an eye at her, showing off his independent suspension. "Shut your yap, sister," he said.

That did it. I slid my left foot forward, led with a straight left to the power pack, then uppercut him with everything I was able to muster.

My right arm went dead to the shoulder. The Sullivan was still standing there, looking at me. I was staring down at my own fist, dangling at my side. Then it dawned on me what was wrong.

For the moment, I'd forgotten I was wearing a light sport-model body.

2

Gully Fishbein, my business manager, Servo-therapist, drinking buddy, arena trainer and substitute old-maid aunt had warned me I might pull a stunt like this some day. He was a Single-Servo Socialist himself, and in addition to his political convictions, he'd put a lot of time and effort into building me up as the fastest man with a net and mace in show business. He had an investment to protect.

"I'm warning you, Barney," he used to shove an untrimmed hangnail under my nose and yell. "One day you're gonna get your reflexes crossed and miss your step on the Fastwalk—or gauge a close one like you was wearing your Astaire and bust the neck of that Carnera you wasted all that jack on. And then where'll you be, hah?"

"So I lose a hulk," I'd come back. "So what? I've got a closet full of spares."

"Yeah? And what if it's a total? You ever heard what can happen to your mind when the connection's busted—and I do mean busted—like that?"

"I wake up back in my Org body; so what?"

"Maybe," Gully would shake his head and look like a guy with dangerous secrets. "And maybe not . . ."

While I was thinking all this, the Sullivan was getting his money's worth out of the Grin-U-Matic. He nodded and rocked back on his heels, taking his time with me. The talk had died out at the tables around us. Everybody was catching an ear full.

"A wisey," the Sullivan says, loud. "What's the matter, Cheapie, tired of life outside a repair depot?"

"What do you mean, 'Cheapie'?" I said, just to give my Adam's apple a workout. "This Arcaro cost me plenty . . . and this goon of yours has jarred my contacts out of line. Just spring for a checkup and I'll agree to forget the whole thing."

"Yeah." He was still showing me the expensive grin. "I'll bet you will, pint-size." He cocked an eye at the

Wayne. "Now, let's see, Nixie, under the traffic code, I got a couple courses of action, right?"

"Cream duh pansy and let's shake an ankle, Boss. I'm hungry." Nixie folded a fist like a forty-pound stake mallet and moved in to demonstrate his idea.

"Nah." The Sullivan stopped him with the back of his hand against his starched shirt front. "The guy pops me first, right? He wants action. So I give him action. Booney." He snapped his fingers and the Liston thumbed a shirt stud.

"For the record," the Sullivan said in a businesslike voice. "Notice of Demand for Satisfaction, with provocation, under Section 991-b, Granyauck 6-78." I heard the whir and click as the recorder built into the Liston's thorax took it down and transmitted it to Law Central.

All of a sudden my mouth was dry.

Sometimes those Servo designers got a little *too* realistic. I tapped a switch in my lower right premolar to cut out the panic-reaction circuit. I'd been all set for a clip on the jaw, an event that wouldn't be too good for the Arcaro, but nothing a little claim to Law Cent wouldn't fix up. But now it was dawning like sunrise over Mandalay that Big Boy had eased me into a spot— or that I'd jumped into it, mouth first. *I'd hit him.* And the fact that he'd put my consomme in my eye wouldn't count—not to Law Cent. He had the right to call me out—a full-scale Servo-to-Servo match—and the choice of weapons, ground, time, everything was his.

"Tell the manager to clear floor number three," the Sullivan rapped out to the Wayne. "My favorite ground." He winked at Lorena. "Nine kills there, baby. My lucky spot."

"Whatever you say," I felt myself talking too fast. "I'll be back here in an hour, raring to go."

"Nix, Cheapie. The time is now. Come as you are; I ain't formal."

"Why, you can't do that," Lorena announced. Her voice tapes were off key, I noticed; she had a kind of shrill, whiney tone. "Barney's only wearing that little old Arcaro!"

"See me after, doll," the Sullivan cut her off. "I like your style." He jerked his head at the Wayne. "I'll take this clown bare-knuck, Nixie, Naples rules." He turned away, flexing the oversized arms that were an optional extra with the late-model Gendyes. Lorena popped to her feet, gave me the dirtiest look the Dietrich could handle.

"You and that crummy Arcaro." She stuck it in me like a knife. "I wanted you to get a Flynn, with the—"

"Spare me the technical specs, kid," I growled. I was getting the full picture of what I'd been suckered into. The caper with the soup hadn't been any accident. The timing was perfect; I had an idea the Liston was wired a lot better than he looked. Somebody with heavy credits riding on that night's bout was behind it; somebody with enough at stake to buy all the muscle-Servos he needed to pound me into a set of loose nerve ends waving around like worms in a bait can. Busting the Arcaro into a pile of scrap metal and plastic wouldn't hurt my Org physically—but the trauma to my personality, riding the Servo, would be for real. It took steel nerve, cast-iron confidence, razor-edge reflexes and a solid killer's instinct to survive in the arena. After all, anybody could lay out for a Gargantua Servo, if that was all it took; the timing, and pace, and ringcraft that made me a winner couldn't survive having a body pounded to rubble around me. I'd be lucky if I ever recovered enough to hold a coffee cup one-handed.

The Floor Manager arrived, looking indignant; nobody

had called him to okay the fracas. He looked at me, started to wave me off, then did a double take.

"*This* is the aggressor party?" The eyebrows on his Menjou crawled up into his hairline.

"That's right," I give it to him fast and snappy. "The bum insulted my lady-friend. Besides which, I don't like his soup-strainer. After I break his rib cage down to chopsticks, I'm going to cut half of it off and give it to the pup to play with." After all, if I was going to get pulverized, I might as well do it in style.

The Sullivan growled.

"You can talk better than that." I pushed up close to him; my nose was on a level with the diamond stick-pin in his paisley foulard. "What's your name, Big Stuff? Let's have that registration."

"None of your pidgin, Wisey." He had a finger all ready to poke at me, saw the Monitor coming up ready to quote rules, used it to scratch his ear instead. The big square fingernail shredded plastic off the lobe; he was a little more nervous than he acted. That cinched it: he knew who I was—Barney Ramm, light-heavy champ in the armed singles.

"Assembly and serial numbers, please," the Monitor said. He sounded a little impatient. I could see why he might. It was customary for a challenger to give the plate data without being asked—especially a floor-vet like Sullivan. He was giving the official a dirty look.

"Where's Slickey?" he growled.

"He doesn't come on for another fifteen minutes," the Monitor snapped. "Look here—"

"*You* look here, Short-timer," the Sullivan grunted. The Wayne moved up to help him give the fellow the cold eye. He glared back at them—for about two seconds. Then he wilted. The message had gotten through. The fix was in.

"Where's the men's room?" I piped up, trying to sound as frisky as ever, but at the moment my mind felt as easy to read as a ninety-foot glare sign.

"Eh?" The Monitor cut his eyes at me, back at the Sullivan, back to me, like a badminton fan at a championship match. "No," he said. He pushed out his lips and shook his head. "I'm ruling—"

"Rule my foot." I jostled him going past. "I know my rights." I kept going, marched across the dance floor to the discreet door back of the phony palm tree. Inside, I went into high gear. There was a row of coin-operated buffing and circuit-checking machines down one wall, a power core dispenser, a plug-in recharge unit, a nice rack of touch-up paints, a big bin of burned-out reflex coils, and a dispenser full of replacement gaskets with a sign reading FOR SAFETY'S SAKE—PREVENTS HOT BEARINGS.

I skidded past them, dived through an archway into the service area. There were half a dozen padded racks here, loops of power leads, festoons of lube conduit leading down from ceiling-mounted manifolds. A parts index covered the far wall. There was no back door.

"Kindly take (click) position numbered one," a canned voice cackled at me. "Use the console provided to indicate required services. Say, fellow, may I recommend this week's special, Slideeze, the underarm lubricant with a diff—"

I slapped the control plate to shut the pitch off. Coming in here suddenly didn't seem as cute as it had ten seconds earlier. I was cornered—and an accident on a lube-rack would save any possible slip-up on the floor. A little voice about as subtle as a jackhammer was yelling in my ear that I had half a minute, if I was lucky, before a pair of heavies came through the door to check me out . . .

It was three quick steps to the little stub wall that

protected the customers from the public eye. I flattened myself against the wall beside it just as big feet clumped outside. The door banged open. The Wayne wasn't bothering about being subtle. I wasn't either. I hooked his left instep, spun in behind him, palmed his back hard. He hit face-first with a slam like two garbage flats colliding, and started looping the loop on the tiled floor. Those Waynes always did have a glass jaw. I didn't stick around to see if anybody heard him pile in; I jumped over him, slid out through the door. The Liston was standing on the other side of the palm, not ten feet away. I faded to the right, saw another door. The glare sign above it said LADIES. I thought it over for about as long as it takes a clock to say "tick" and dived through.

3

Even under the circumstances it was kind of a shock to find myself standing there staring at pink and turquoise service racks, gold-plated perfume dispensers, and a big display rack full of strictly feminine spares that were enough to make a horse blush.

Then I saw *her*. She was a neat-looking Pickford—the traditional models were big just then. She had fluffy blonde hair, and her chassis covers were off to the waist. I gaped at her, sitting there in front of the mirror, then gulped like a seal swallowing a five-pound salmon. She jumped and swiveled my way, and I got a load of big blue eyes and a rosebud mouth that was opening up to scream.

"Don't yell, lady!" I averted my eyes—an effort like uprooting saplings. "The mob's after me. Just tell me how to get out of here!"

I heard feet outside. So did she, I guess.

"You—you can go out through the delivery door," a nice little voice said. I flicked an eye her way. She was holding a lacy little something over her chest. It slipped when she pointed and I got an eyeful of some of the nicest moulded foam-plastic you'd care to see.

"Thanks, baby, you're a doll," I choked out and went past her, not without a few regrets. The door she'd showed me was around a corner at the back. There was a big carton full of refills for the cosmetics vendor beside it, with the top open. On impulse, I reached in and grabbed one going past.

The door opened into an alley about four feet wide, with a single-rail robo-track down the center for service and delivery mechs. The wall opposite was plain duralith; it went up, a sheer rise without a foothold for a gnat. In both directions the alley was a straight shot for fifty feet to a rectangle of hard late-afternoon sunlight. I could take my choice.

Something clattered to the right. I saw a small custodial cart move jerkily out of a doorway, swing my way, picking up speed. I started to back away; the thing was heavy enough to flatten my Arcaro without slowing down. Then a red light blinked on the front of the thing. It made screechy noises and skidded to a stop.

"Kindly clear the rail," a fruity voice hooted. "This is your busy Sani-mat Service Unit, bringing that Sani-mat sparkle to another satisfied customer!"

A kind of idea formed up somewhere under my hairpiece. I eased around to the side of the machine, a tight squeeze. It was a squatty, boxy job, with a bunch of cleaning attachments racked in front and a good-sized bin behind, half full of what it had been collecting. I got the lid up, climbed up as it started forward again, and settled down in the cargo. It was lumpy and wet, and you could have hammered the aroma out into horseshoes. I guess the world has made a lot of progress in the last few decades, but garbage still smells like garbage.

I estimated I'd covered a hundred feet or less, when the cart braked to a sudden stop. I heard voices; something clicked and a hum started up near my left ear.

"Kindly clear the rail," the tape said. "This is your Sani-mat Service Uuwwrrr—"

The cart jumped and I got another faceful of garbage. Somebody—it sounded like the Wayne—yelled something. I got set, ready to come out swinging as soon as the lid went up. But the voices faded out, and I heard running feet. The cart started up, bumped along clucking to itself like a chicken looking for a place to drop an egg. I rode it along to its next client's back door, then hopped out, legged it to a public screen booth and dialed Gully's number.

4

I caught him in a cab, just dropping in past a mixed-up view of city skyline tilting by in the background. His eyes bugged out like a Chihuahua when I told him—a deluxe feature of the four-year-old Cantor he always wore.

"Barney, you nuts?" He had a yelp like a Chihuahua too. "The biggest bout of your career coming up tonight, and you're mixing in a free brawl!" He stopped to gulp and ran his eyes over me. "Hey, Barney! You're wearing an Arcaro. You didn't—"

"The fracas wasn't my idea," I got in quick while he was fighting the Cantor's tonsils back in line. "Not exactly, anyway. I took off out the back way, and—"

"You did *what?*" The yelp was up into the supersonic now.

"I beat it. Ducked out. Scrammed. What do you think I was going to do, stay there and let that elbow squad pull the legs off me like a fly?"

"You can't run out on a registered satisfaction, Barney!" Gully leaned into his sender until all I could see were two eyes like bloodshot clams and a pair of quivering nostrils. "You, of all people! If the Pictonews services get hold of this, they'll murder you!"

"This hit squad will murder me quicker—and not just on paper!"

"Paper's what I'm talking about! You're the aggressor party; you poked the schlock! You cop a swiftie on this, and you're a fugitive from Law Cent! They'll lift your Servo license, and it'll be good-by career! And the fines—"

"Okay—but I got a few rights too! If I can get to another Servo before they grab me, it'll become my legal *Corpus operandi* as soon as I'm in it. Remember, that satisfaction is to me, Barney Ramm, not to this body I'm wearing. You've got to get me out of here, and back to my apartment—" I felt my mouth freeze in the open position. Fifty feet away across the Fastwalk the Liston and a new heavy, a big, patched-up Baer, had come out of a doorway and were standing there, looking over the crowd. Those boys were as hard to shake loose as gum on a shoe sole. I ducked down in the booth.

"Listen, Gully," I hissed. "They're too close; I've got to do a fast fade. Try to fix it with Law Cent to keep their mitts off me until I can change. Remember, if they catch me, you can kiss your ten percent good-by."

"Barney, where you going? Whattaya mean, ten percent? It ain't the cookies I'm thinking about!"

"Think about the cookies, Gully." I cut contact and risked a peek. The two goons were still there and looking my way. If I stepped out, they'd have me. And if I stayed where I was, sooner or later they'd get around to checking the booth . . .

I was still holding something in my hand. I looked at it: the cosmetics kit I'd grabbed on the way out of the ladies' room at the Troc.

The lid flipped back when I touched the little gold button at the side. There were nine shades of eye shadow, mouth paint, plastic lens shades in gold, green and pink—some dames have got screwy ideas about what looks attractive—spare eyebrows and lashes, a little emergency face putty, some thimble-sized hair sprays.

I hated to ruin a hundred cee wig, but I gave it a full shot of something called Silver Ghost. The pink eyes seemed to go with the hair. The spray was all gone, so it was too late to bleach out a set of eyebrows, so I used a pair of high-arched black ones, then used a gingery set for a mustache. I thought about using one of the fake spit curls for a goatee, but decided against it. The Arcaro had a nice-sized nose on it, so I widened the nostrils a little and added warts. I risked another peek. The boys were right where I left them.

My jacket was a nice chartreuse job with cerise strips and a solid orange lining. I turned it inside out, ditched the yellow tie, and opened my shirt collar so the violet part showed. That was about all I could do; I opened the door and stepped out.

I'd gone about three steps when the Carnera looked my way. His mouth dropped open like a power shovel getting ready to take a bite out of a hillside. He jammed an elbow into the Liston and he turned around and *his* mouth fell open. I got a glimpse of some nice white choppers and a tongue like a pink sock. I didn't wait to catch the rest of the reaction: I sprinted for

the nearest shelter, a pair of swinging doors, just
opening to let a fat Orggie out.

I dived past him into a cool, dark room lit by a
couple of glowing beer ads above a long mirror with
a row of bottles. I charged past all that, slammed
through a door at the back, and was out in an alley,
looking at the Wayne. He went into a half-crouch and
spread his arms. That was the kind of mistake an
amateur toughie would make. I put my head down and
hit him square under his vest button. It wasn't the best
treatment in the world for the Arcaro, but it was worse
for the Wayne. He froze up and made a noise like
frying fat, with his eyeballs spinning like Las Vegas
cherries. Between the fall in the john and the butt in
the neuro center, he was through for the day.

I got my legs under me and started off at a sort of
cripple's lope toward the end of the alley.

My balance and coordination units were clicking like
castanets. I ricocheted off a couple of walls, made it
out into the Slowwalk, and jigged along in a crabbed
semicircle, making jerky motions with my good arm at
a cab that picked then to drop a fare a few yards away.
The hackie reached out, grabbed my shoulder and
hauled me inside. Those boys may be built into their
seats and end at the waist, but they've got an arm on
them. I'll give 'em that.

"You look like you got a problem there, Mac." He
looked me over in the mirror. "What happened, you
fall off a roof?"

"Something like that. Just take me to the Banshire
Building, fast."

"Whatever you say, Bud. But if I was you, I'd get
that Servo to a shop as quick as I could."

"Later. Step on it."

"I'm doing a max and a half now!"

"Okay, okay, just don't waste any time." He muttered to himself then, while I got the bent cover off my reset panel and did what I could to rebalance my circuitry. My double vision cleared a little, and the leg coordination improved enough so I managed to climb out unassisted when he slammed the heli in hard on the roof deck.

"Be five cees," the cabbie grunted. I paid him. "Stick around a few minutes," I said. "I'll be right back."

"Do me a favor, Clyde; throw your trade to the competition." He flipped the flag up and lifted off in a cyclone of overrevved rotors. I spat out a mouthful of grit and went in through the fancy door with the big gold B.

Gus, the doorman, came out of his cage with his admiral's hat on crooked; he hooked a thumb over his shoulder and got his jaw all set for the snappy line. I beat him to it.

"It's me, Barney Ramm. I'm incommunicado to avoid the fans."

"Geeze, Mr. Ramm? Wow, that Arcaro won't never be the same again. Looks like your fans must of caught you after all." He showed me a bunch of teeth that would have looked at home in a mule's face. I lifted a lip at him and went on in.

5

My apartment wasn't the plushest one in the Banshire, but it was fully equipped. The Servo stall was the equal of anything at Municipal Files. I got enough cooperation out of my legs to hobble to it, got the Arcaro into the rack with the neck plate open and the contacts tight against the transfer disk.

A pull on the locking lever, and I was clamped in tight, ready for the shift. I picked the Crockett; it was rugged enough to handle the Sullivan, and didn't have any fancy equipment installed to have to look out for. It was a little tough coding the number into the panel, but I made it, then slammed the transfer switch.

I've never gotten used to that wild couple of seconds while the high-speed scanner is stripping the stored data off one control matrix and printing it on another one linking it in to the Org brain back between my real ears in the cold files downtown. It was like diving into an ocean of ice-cold darkness, spinning like a Roman candle. All kinds of data bits flash through the conscious level: I was the Arcaro, sitting rigid in the chair, and I was also the Crockett, clamped to a rack in the closet, and at the same time I could feel the skull contacts and servicing tubes and the cold slab under me in the Vault. Then it cleared and I was hitting the release lever and stepping out of the closet and beginning to feel like a million bucks.

The Arcaro looked pretty bad, sagging in the stall, with the phony eyebrows out of line and the putty nose squashed, and the right shoulder humped up like Quasimodo. It was a wonder it had gotten me back at all. I made myself promise to give it the best overhaul job money could buy—that was the least I could do. Then I headed for the front door.

The Sullivan would get a little surprise when I found him now. I gave my coon skin cap a pat as I went by the hall mirror, palmed the flush panel open and ran smack into four large cops, standing there waiting for me.

It was a plush jailhouse, as jails go, but I still didn't like it. They shoved me into a nice corner cell with a carpet, a tiled lube cubicle in the corner, and a window with a swell view of Granyauck—about 1800 feet straight down. There were no bars, but the wall was smooth enough to discourage any human flies from trying it.

The turnkey looked me over and shook his head. He was wearing the regulation Police Special, a dumb-looking production job halfway between a Kildare and a Tracy—Spence, that is. I guess cops have to have a uniform, but the sight of a couple dozen identical twins standing around kind of gives a fellow a funny feeling—like Servos were just some kind of robot, or something.

"So you're Barney Ramm, huh?" the cop shifted his toothpick to the other corner of his mouth. "You shunt of tried to handle four cops at once, Buddy. Your collision insurance don't cover that kind of damage."

"I want my manager!" I yelled as loud as I could, which wasn't very loud on account of a kick in the voice box I got following up too close on a cop I had tossed on his ear. "You can't do this to me! I'll get the lot of you for false arrest!"

"Relax, Ramm." The jailer waved his power-billie at me to remind me he had it. I shied off; a shot from the hot end of that would lock my neuro center in a hard knot. "You ain't going no place for a while," the cop stated. "Commissioner Malone wouldn't like it."

"Malone? The Arena Commissioner? What's he got—" I stopped in the middle of the yell, feeling my silly look freeze in place.

"Yeah," the cop said. "Also the Police Commissioner. Seems like Malone don't like you, Ramm."

"Hey!" a dirty idea was growing. "The satisfaction against me: who filed it?"

The cop went through the motions of yawning. "Lessee . . . oh, yeah. A Mr. Malone."

"The dirty crook! That's illegal! I was framed!"

"You slugged him first, right?" The cop cut me off. "Sure, but—"

"Ain't a Police Commissioner got as much right as anybody else to defend hisself? Any reason he's got to take guff off some wisenheimer, any more than the next guy? You race him at the light, he'll lock bumpers with you every time!"

"I've got to get out of here," I shouted him down. "Get Gully Fishbein! He'll post the bond! I've got a bout at the Garden in less than four hours! Tell the judge! I guess I've got a couple rights!"

"You ain't going to make no bout in four hours." The cop grinned like Sears foreclosing on Roebuck. "You'll be lucky if you get out before Christmas Holidays start, in September."

"If I don't," I said, "you can start scanning the help-wanted-cripple column. That's what you'll be when me and my twenty-thousand Cee Charlemagne finish with you, you dumb flatfoot!"

He narrowed his eyes down to pinpoints—an extra-cost feature that the taxpayers had to spring for. "Threats, hah?" His voice had the old gravel in it now. "You run out on a Satisfaction, Buster. That's trouble enough for most guys."

"I'll show you trouble," I started, but he wasn't through yet.

" . . . For a big tough arena fighter, you got kind of a delicate stomach, I guess. We also got you for resisting arrest, damaging public property, committing mayhem on the person of a couple honest citizens, Peeping Tom and shoplifting from the ladies' john. You're set for tonight, pal—and a lotta other nights." He gave me a mock salute and backed out; the glass door clinked in my face while I was still trying to get my arm back for a swing.

❖　　　❖　　　❖

The watch set in my left wrist was smashed flat, along with the knuckles. Those Granyauck cops have got hard heads. I went over to the window and checked the sun.

It looked like about half past four. At eight P.M. the main event would go on. If I wasn't there, the challenger would take the title by default. He was an out-of-town phony known as Mysterious Marvin, the Hooded Holocaust; he always fought with a flour sack over his face. After tonight, he'd be light-heavy champ, bagged head and all—and I'd be a busted has-been, with my accounts frozen, my contract torn up, my Servo ticket lifted, and about as much future as a fifth of Bourbon at a Baptist Retreat. It was the finish. They had me. Unless . . .

I poked my head out and looked down the wall. It was a sheer drop to a concrete loading apron that looked about the size of a blowout patch from where I stood. I felt my autonomics kick in; my heart started thumping like an out-of-round drive shaft, and my throat closed up like a crap-shooter's fist. I never had liked heights much. But with my Servo locked in a cell—and *me* locked in the Servo—

I took a couple turns up and down the cell. It was an idea the boys talked about sometimes, waiting in the service racks before a bout: what would happen if the plastic-foam and wire-sponge information correlation unit where the whole brain pattern was recorded got smashed flat—wiped out—while you were in it?

It would be like dreaming you fell—and hit. Would you ever wake up? The Org body was safe, back in the Vaults, but the shock—what would it do to you?

There were a lot of theories. Some of the guys said it would be curtains. The end. Some of them said your Org would go catatonic. I didn't know, myself. If the wheels knew, they weren't spreading it around.

And there was just the one way to find out for sure.

If I stayed where I was, incommunicado, I was finished anyway. Better to go out in style. Before I could change my mind, I whirled, went to the window and swung my legs over the sill. Behind me, I heard somebody yell, "Hey!" I tried to swallow, couldn't, squeezed my eyes shut and jumped. For a few seconds, it was like a tornado blowing straight up into my face; then it was like being spread-eagled on a big, soft, rubbery mattress. And then—

6

I was drowning in a sea of rancid fat. I took a deep breath to yell, and the grease in my lungs clogged solid.

I tried to cough and couldn't do that either. Little red skyrockets started shooting around back of my eyes like a fire in a fireworks factory. Then the lights ran together and I was staring at a long red glare strip set in a dark ceiling a few inches above my face. I could feel tubes and wires dragging at my arms and legs, my neck, my eyelids, my tongue . . .

I was moving, sliding out into brighter light. A scared-looking face was gaping down at me. I made gargly noises and flapped my hands—about all I could manage under the load of spaghetti. The guy leaning over me jumped like a morgue attendant seeing one of his customers sit up and ask for a light, which wasn't too far off, maybe. My bet had paid off. I was awake, back in my organic body in slot number 999/1-Ga8b in the Municipal Body Files.

The next half hour was a little hectic. First they started some kind of a pump, and then I could breathe—a little. While I coughed, twitched, groaned, itched, throbbed and ached in more places than I knew I had, the file techs fussed over me like midwives delivering a TV baby. They pulled things out, stuck things in, sprayed me, jabbed me, tapped and tested, conferred, complained, ran back and forth, shone lights in my eyes, hit me with little hammers, poked things down my throat, held buzzers to my ears, asked questions and bitched at each other in high, whining voices like bluebottle flies around a honey wagon. I got the general idea. They were unhappy that I had upset the routine by coming out of a stage-three storage state unannounced.

"There are laws against this sort of thing!" a dancey little bird in an unhealthy-looking Org body kept yelling at me. "You might have died! It was sheer good fortune that I happened to have slipped back in the stacks to commune with myself, and heard you choking! You frightened me out of my wits!"

Somebody else shoved a clipboard in front of me. "Sign this," he said. "It's a release covering Cent Files against any malpractice or damage claims."

"And there'll be an extra service charge on your file for emergency reprocessing," the dancey one said. "You'll have to sign that, and also an authorization to transfer you to dead storage until your next of kin or authorized agent brings in the Servo data—"

I managed to sit up. "Skip the reprocessing," I said. "And the dead storage. Just get me on my feet and show me the door."

"How's that? You're going to need at least a week's rest, a month's retraining, and complete reorientation course before you can be released in Org—"

"Get me some clothes," I said. "Then I'll sign the papers."

"This is blackmail!" Dancey did a couple of steps. "I won't be held responsible!"

"Not if you cooperate. Call me a cab." I tried walking. I was shaky, but all things considered I didn't feel too bad—for a guy who just committed suicide. Files had kept me in good condition.

There was a little more argument, but I won. Dancey followed me out, wagging his head and complaining, but I signed his papers and he disappeared—probably to finish communing with himself.

In the cab, I tried to reach Gully again. His line was busy. I tried Lorena. A canned voice told me her line was disconnected. Swell. All my old associates were kind of fading out of sight, now that I was having troubles with the law.

But maybe Gully was just busy getting me a postponement. In fact, he was probably over at the Garden now, straightening things out. I gave the hackie directions and he dropped me by the big stone arch with the deep-cut letters that said FIGHTERS ENTRANCE.

The usual crowd of fight fans were there, forty deep. None of them gave me a look; they had their eyes on the big, wide-shouldered Tunneys and Louises and Marcianos, and the hammed-up Herkys and Tarzans in their flashy costumes and big smiles, with their handlers herding them along like tugs nudging liners into dock. The gateman put out a hand to stop me when I started through the turnstile.

"It's me, Harley. Barney Ramm," I said. A couple of harness cops were standing a few feet away, looking things over. "Let me through; I'm late."

"Hah? Barney—"

"Keep it quiet; I'm a surprise."

Where'd you dig up that outfit? On a used-Servo lot?" He looked me over like an inspector rejecting a wormy side of mutton. "What is it, a gag?"

"It's a long story. I'll tell it to you some time. Right now, how's about loaning me a temporary tag? I left my ID in my other pants."

"You pugs," he muttered, but he handed over the pass. I grabbed it.

"Where's Lou Mitch, the starter?" I asked him.

"Try the Registry Office."

I shoved through a crowd of weigh-in men, service techs and arena officials, spotted Lou talking to a couple of trainers. I went over and grabbed his arm.

"It's me, Mitch, Barney Ramm. Listen, where's Gully? I need—"

"Ramm, you bum! Where you been? Where'd you pick up that hulk you got on? Who you think you are, missing the press weigh-in? Get downstairs on the double and dress out! You got twenty minutes, and if you're late, so help me, I'll see you busted out of the fight game!"

"Wha—who, me? Hold it, Lou, I'm not going out there in this condition! I just came down to—"

"Oh, a holdup for more dough, huh? Well, you can work that one out with the promoter and the Commissioner. All I know is, you got a contract, and I've got you billed for nineteen minutes from now!"

I started backing away, shaking my head. "Wait a minute, Lou—"

He jerked his head at a couple of the trainers that were listening in. "Grab him and take him down to his stall and get him into his gear! Hustle it!"

I put up a brisk resistance, but it was all wasted effort. Ten minutes later I was standing in the chute, strapped into harness with knots tied in the straps for fit and a copy of the Afternoon Late Racing Special padding my helmet up off my ears, listening to the mob in the stands up above, yelling for the next kill. Me.

7

They can talk all they want about how sensitive and responsive a good Servo is, but there's nothing like flesh and blood for making you know you're in trouble.

My heart was kicking hard enough to jar the championship medal on my chest. My mouth was as dry as yesterday's cinnamon toast. I thought about making a fast getaway over the barrier fence, but there was nobody outside who'd be glad to see me except the cops; besides which, I had a mace in my right hand and a fighting net in the left, and after all, I was Barney Ramm, the champ. I'd always said it was the man inside the Servo, not the equipment that counted. Tonight I had a chance to prove it—or a kind of a chance; an Org up against a fighting Servo wasn't exactly an even match.

But hell, when was it ever even? The whole fight game was controlled, from top to bottom, by a few sharpies like J. J. Malone. Nobody had ever slipped me the word to take a dive yet, but I'd stretched plenty of bouts to make 'em look good. After all, the fans paid good creds to see two fine-tuned fighting machines pound each other to scrap under the lights. An easy win was taboo. Well, they'd get an unexpected bonus tonight when I got hit and something besides hydraulic fluid ran out.

And then the blast of the bugles caught me like a bucket of ice water and the gate jumped up and I was striding through, head up, trying to look as arrogant as a hunting tiger under the glare of the polyarcs, but feeling very small and very breakable and wondering why I hadn't stayed in that nice safe jail while I had the chance. Out across the spread of the arena the bleachers rose up dark under the high late-evening sky streaked with long pink clouds that looked as remote as fairyland. And under the pooled lights, a big husky Servo was taking his bows, swirling his cloak.

He was too far away, over beyond the raised disk of the Circle, for me to be sure, but it looked like he was picking a heavy duty prod and nothing else. Maybe the word had gone out that I was in Org, or maybe he was good.

Then he tossed the cape to a handler and came to meet me, sizing me up on the way through the slit in his mask.

Maybe he was wondering what I had up my sleeve. If he was in on the fix, he'd be surprised to see me at all. He'd been expecting a last-minute sub or just a straight default. If not, he'd been figuring on me wearing my Big Charley packed with all the booster gear the law allows. Instead, all he saw was an ordinary-looking, five-foot-eleven frame with medium-fair shoulders and maybe just a shade too much padding at the belt line.

The boys back at Files had done right by me, I had to admit. The old Org was in better shape than when I'd filed it, over a year ago. I felt strong, tough and light on my feet; I could feel the old fighting edge coming on. Maybe it was just a false lift from the stuff the techs had loaded me full of, and maybe it was just an animal's combat instinct, an item they hadn't been able to dream up an accessory to imitate. Whatever it was, it was nice to have.

I reached the concrete edge of the Fighting Circle and stepped up on it and was looking across at the other fellow, only fifty feet away and now looking bigger than a Bolo Combat Unit. With the mask I wasn't sure, but he looked like a modified Norge Atlas. He was running through a fancy twirl routine with the prod, and the crowd was eating it up.

There was no law that said I had to wait for him to finish. I slid the mace down to rest solid in my palm with the thong riding tight above my wrist and gave the two-foot club a couple of practice swings. So much for the warmup. I flipped the net out into casting position with my left hand and moved in on him.

It wasn't like wearing a Servo; I could feel sweat running down my face and the air sighing in my lungs and the blood pumping through my muscles and veins. It was kind of a strange *alive* feeling—as if there was nothing between me and the sky and the earth and I was part of them and they were part of me. A funny feeling. A dangerous, unprotected feeling—but somehow not entirely a bad feeling.

He finished up the ham act when I was ten feet from him, swung to face me. He knew I was there, all right; he was just playing it cool. Swell. While he was playing, I'd take him.

I feinted with the net, then dived in, swung the mace, missed him by half an inch as he back-pedaled. I followed him close, working the club, keeping the net cocked. He backed, looking me over.

"Ramm—is that you in that getup?" he barked.

"Naw—I couldn't make it, so I sent my cousin Julius."

"What happened, you switch brands? Looks like you must of got cut-rate merchandise." He ducked a straight cut and whipped the prod around in a jab that would have paralyzed my neuro center if he'd connected.

"New secret model a big outfit's trying out under wraps," I told him.

He made a fast move, and a long, slim rod I hadn't seen before whipped out and slapped me under the ribs.

For a split second I froze. He had me, I was finished. A well-handled magnetic resonator could de-Gauss every microtape in a Servo—and his placement was perfect.

But nothing happened. There was a little tingle, that was all.

Then I got it. I wasn't wearing a Servo—and magnets didn't bother an Org.

The Atlas was looking as confused as I was. He took an extra half-second recovering. That was almost enough. I clipped him across the thigh as he almost fell getting back. He tried with the switch again, sawed it across my chest. I let him; he might as well tickle me with a grass stem. This time I got the net out, snarled his left arm, brought the mace around and laid a good one across his hip. It staggered him, but he managed to spin out, flip the net clear.

"What kind of shielding you got anyway, Ramm?" the Atlas growled. He held the rod out in front of his face, crossed his eyes at it, shook it hard and made one more try. I let him come in under my guard, and the shaft slid along my side as if he was trying to wipe it clean on my shirt. While he was busy with that, I dropped the net, got a two-handed grip on the mace, brought it around in a flat arc and laid a solid wallop right where it would do him the most good—square on the hip joint.

I heard the socket go. He tried to pivot on his good leg, tottered and just managed to stay on his feet, swearing. I came in fast and just got a glimpse of the electro-prod coming up. Concentrating on the magnetic rod, I'd forgotten the other. I tried to check and slide off to the right, but all of a sudden blinding blue lights were popping all over the sky. Something came up and hit me alongside the head, and then I was doing slow somersaults through pretty purple clouds, trying hard to figure which side was up. Then the pain hit. For a couple of seconds I scraped at my chest, reaching for circuit breakers that weren't there. Then I got mad.

It was as if all of a sudden, nothing could stop me. The Atlas was a target, and all I wanted was just to reach it. If there was a mountain in the way, I'd pick it up and throw it over my shoulder. A charging elephant would be a minor nuisance. I could even stand up, unassisted—if I tried hard enough.

I got the feel of something solid under my hands, groped and found some more of it with my feet, pushed hard and blinked away the fog to see the Atlas just making it back onto his good leg. I had to rest a while then, on all fours. He stooped to twiddle a reset for emergency power to the damaged joint, then started for me, hopping hard enough to shake the ground. A little voice told me to wait . . .

He stopped, swung the prod up, and I rolled, grabbed his good leg, twisted with everything I had. It wasn't enough. He hopped, jabbed with the prod, missed, and I was on my feet now, feeling like I'd been skinned and soaked in brine. My breath burned my throat like a blow torch, and all round the crowd roar was like a tidal wave rolling across a sinking continent.

I backed, and he followed. I tried to figure the time until the pit stop, but I didn't know how long I'd been out here; I didn't have a timer ticking under my left ear, keeping me posted. And now the Atlas was on to what was going on. I knew that, when he reached for the show-knife strapped to his left hip. Against a Servo, that particular tool was useless, but he could let the cool night air into an Org's gizzard with it, and he knew it.

Then my foot hit the edge of the paved circle and I went down, flat on my back on the sand.

❖   ❖   ❖

The Atlas came after me, and I scrambled back, got to my feet just in time. The knife blade hissed through the air just under my chin.

"You've had it, Ramm," the Atlas said, and swung again. I tried to get the club up for a counterblow but it was too heavy. I let it drop and drag in the sand. Through a dust cloud we were making, I saw the Atlas fumbling with his control buttons. Tears welled up in his eyes, sluiced down over his face. He didn't like the dust any better than I did. Maybe not as well . . .

I felt an idea pecking at its shell; a dirty idea, but better than none.

The mace was dangling by its thong. I slipped it free, threw it at him; it clanged off his knees and I stooped, came up with a handful of fine sand and as he closed in threw it straight into his face.

The effect was striking. His eyes turned to mud pockets. I stepped aside, and he went right past me, making swipes at the air with the big sticker, and I swung in behind him and tilted another handful down inside his neckband. I could hear it grate in the articulated rib armor as he came around.

"Ramm, you lousy little—" I took aim and placed a nice gob square in his vocabulary. He backed off, pumping emergency air to clear the pipes, spouting dust like Mount Aetna, but I knew I had him. The mouth cavity on just about every Servo in the market was a major lube duct; he had enough grit in his gears to stop a Continental Siege Unit. But his mouth was still open, so I funneled in another double handful.

He stopped, locked his knee joints and concentrated on his problem. That gave me my opening to reach out and switch his main circuit breaker off.

He froze. I waited half a minute for the dust to clear, while the crowd roar died away to a kind of confused buzzing, like robbed bees.

Then I reached out, put a finger against his chest, and shoved—just gently. He leaned back, teetered for a second, then toppled over stiff as a lamppost. You could hear the thud all the way to the student bleachers. I held on for another ten seconds, just to make it look good, then kneeled over on top of him.

8

"But I was too late," Gully Fishbein's voice was coming up out of a barrel, a barrel full of thick molasses syrup somebody had dumped me into. I opened my mouth to complain and a noise like "glug" came out.

"He's awake!" Gully yelped. I started to deny it, but the effort was too much.

"Barney, I tried to catch you, but you were already out there." Gully sounded indignant. "Cripes, kid, you should of known I wouldn't let 'em railroad you!"

"Don't worry about Ramm," a breezy voice jostled Gully's aside. "Boy, this is the story of the decade! You figure to go up against a Servo again in Org, when you get out of the shop—I mean hospital? How did it feel to take five thousand volts of DC? You know the experts say it should have killed you. It would have knocked out any Servo on the market—"

"Nix, Baby!" Gully elbowed his way back in again. "My boy's gotta rest. And you can tell the world the Combo's out of business. Now anybody can afford to fight. Me and Barney have put the game back in the hands of the people."

"Yeah! The sight of that Atlas, out on its feet—and Ramm here, in Org, yet, with one finger . . . "

I unglued an eyelid and blinked at half a dozen fuzzy faces like custard pies floating around me.

"We'll talk contract with you, Fishbein," somebody said.

" . . . call for some new regulations," somebody said.

" . . . dred thousand cees, first network rights."

" . . . era of the Servo in the arena is over . . . "

" . . . hear what Malone says about this. Wow!"

"Malone," I heard my voice say, like a boot coming out of mud. "The cr . . . crook. It was him . . . put the Sullivan . . . up to it . . . "

"Up to nothing, Barney," Gully was bending over me. "That was J. J. hisself in that Servo! And here's the payoff. He registered the Satisfaction in his own name—and of course, every fighter in his stable is acting in his name, legally. So when you met Mysterious Marvin and knocked him on his duff you satisfied his claim. You're in the clear, kid. You can relax. There's nothing to worry about."

"Oh, Barney!" It was a new voice, a nice soft little squeal of a girl-voice. A neat little Org face with a turned-up nose zeroed in on me, with a worried look in the big brown eyes.

"Julie! Where—I mean, how . . . ?"

"I was there, Barney. I see all your fights, even if—even if I don't approve. And today—oh, Barney, you were so brave, so *marvelous*, out there alone, against that *machine* . . . " She sighed and nestled her head against my shoulder.

"Gully," I said. "Exactly how long have I got to stay in this place?"

"The Servo-tech—I mean the doc—says a week anyway."

"Set up a wedding for a week from today."

Julie jumped and stared at me.

"Oh, Barney! But you—you know what I said . . . about those *zombies* . . . "

"I know."

"But, Barney . . . " Gully didn't know whether to cry or grin. "You mean . . . ?"

"Sell my Servos," I said. "The whole wardrobe. My days of being a pair of TV eyes peeking out of a walking dummy and kidding myself I'm alive are over."

"Yeah, but Barney—a guy with your ideas about what's fun—like skiing, and riding the jetboards, and surfing, and sky-diving—you can't take the risks! You only got the one Org body!"

"I found out a couple of things out there tonight, Gully. It takes a live appetite to make a meal a feast. From now on, whatever I do, it'll be *me* doing it. Clocking records is okay, I guess, but there's some things that it takes an Org to handle."

"Like what?" Gully yelled, and went on with a lot more in the same vein. I wasn't listening, though. I was too busy savoring a pair of warm, soft, *live* lips against mine.

TIME TRAP

∽

PROLOGUE

I

Machinist's Mate Second Class Joe Acosta, on duty in the deckhouse of the Coast Guard cutter *Hampton*, squinted across the dazzling waters of Tampa Bay at the ungainly vessel wallowing in the light sea half a mile off the port bow.

"What the heck is that, skipper?" He addressed the lieutenant standing beside him with binoculars trained on the spectacle.

"Two-master; odd-looking high stern. Sails hanging in rags. Looks like she's been in a stiff blow," the officer said. "Let's take a closer look."

The cutter changed course, swinging in a wide arc to approach the square-rigged vessel. At close range, Acosta saw the weathered timbers of the clumsy hull, where scraps of scarlet paint and gilt still clung. Clustered barnacles and trailing seaweed marked the waterline. The power boat passed under the ship's stern at a distance of fifty feet; ornate letters almost obliterated by weathering spelled out the name *Cucaracha*.

As the boat throttled back, a wrinkled brown face appeared at the rail above; worried coal-black eyes looked into Acosta's. Other men appeared beside the first, clad in rags, uniformly pockmarked, gap-toothed, and unshaven.

"Skipper, this must be a load of them Cuban refugees," Acosta hazarded. "But how'd they get this far without being spotted?"

The officer shook his head. "They must be making a movie," he said. "This can't be for real."

"You ever seen a tub like that before?" Acosta inquired.

"Only in the history books."

"I see what you mean. It's kind of like the *Bounty* they got anchored over at the pier at St. Pete."

"Something like that. Only this is a galleon, late sixteenth-century type. Portuguese, from the flag."

"Looks like somebody could have told us about it," Acosta said. "Hey, you on deck!" He cupped his hands and shouted to the faces above. "If that tub draws more than two fathoms, you got problems!" He jerked a thumb over his shoulder. "Shoal waters!" he added.

The man who had first appeared called out something in a hoarse voice.

"Hey," Acosta said. "I was right. He's talking some kind o' Spanish." He cupped his hands again.

"¿Quién son ustedes? ¿Qué pasa?" The man on deck shouted at some length, making the sign of the cross as he did.

"What did he say?" the officer inquired.

Acosta shook his head. "He talks funny, skipper. He must think we're part of the movie."

"We'll go aboard and take a look."

An hour later, a line aboard the derelict, the cutter headed for the Port Tampa quarantine wharf.

"What do you think?" Joe Acosta asked, eyeing the skipper sidelong.

"I think we've got a galleon crewed by thirteen illiterate Portuguese in tow," the officer snapped. "Outside of that, I'm not thinking."

2

At 10:15 A.M., as was her unalterable custom, Mrs. L. B. (Chuck) Withers put on her hat, checked her hemline in the front-hall mirror, and set out on the ten-minute walk into town. She passed the long-defunct service station at the bend, walking briskly, head up, back straight, breathed in for four paces, out for four, a simple routine to which she ascribed full credit for the remarkable youthfulness of her thirty-six-year-old figure.

A minute or two after passing the station, Mrs. Withers slowed, sensing some indefinable strangeness in the aspect of the road ahead. She had long ago ceased to notice her surroundings on her walks, but now an unfamiliar sign caught her eye ahead:

BRANTVILLE—1 MILE

It was curious, she thought, that they should bother to erect a new sign here—especially an erroneous one. Her house was precisely one half-mile from town; it couldn't be more than a few hundred yards from here to the city limits. Closer, she saw that the sign was not new; the paint was chalky and faded, peppered by a passing marksman with a pair of rust-edged pits. She looked around uneasily; now that she noticed, this stretch didn't look precisely familiar, somehow. There— that big sweetgum tree with the 666 sign—surely she would have noticed that . . .

She hurried on, eager for a cheery glimpse of the Coca-Cola billboard around the gentle curve of the road. Instead she saw a white-painted building, patchily visible through the foliage. The brick chimney had a curiously familiar look. She pressed on, passed the shelter of the line of tall poplars—and halted, staring indignantly at her own house. She had left it, walking east—and now she was approaching it from the west. It was preposterous—impossible!

Mrs. Withers settled her hat firmly on her head. Very well: daydreaming, she had taken some turn (not that she had ever seen any branching road between home and town) that had brought her in a circle back to her own door. It was a nonsensical mistake, and the widow of L. B. Withers had no patience with nonsense, which was best dealt with by ignoring it. Grasping her handbag in both hands as one would a set of reins, she marched determinedly past the front gate.

Five minutes later, with a mounting apprehension stirring beneath her ribs, she approached a sign planted by the roadside:

BRANTVILLE—1 MILE

For a moment she stared at the letters; then she whirled and marched back the way she had come. At her gate, she caught at the post, breathing hard, collecting herself. The sight of the familiar front porch with the broken lattice that Mr. Withers had always been going to fix but somehow never had gotten around to calmed her. She took a deep breath and forced her respiration back to normal. She had almost made a fool of herself, running into the house and telephoning the sheriff with an hysterical tale of mixed-up roads. Hmmph! Interesting gossip *that* would make in town, with half of the old lechers there already smirking lewdly at her as they made their sly remarks about women who lived alone. Very well, she'd gotten confused, twice taken a wrong turning, even if she hadn't noticed any place where a body could *take* a wrong turning. This time she'd watch every step of the way, and if she arrived at the post office half an hour later than usual, she dared anybody to make a remark about it!

This time when the sign appeared ahead, she halted in the middle of the road, looking both ways, torn between a desire to run ahead and catch a glimpse of the town's edge and an equal desire to flee back to the familiarity of the house.

"It can't be," she said aloud, and was shocked at the undisciplined break in her voice. "I've walked along this road a thousand times! There's no way to get lost . . ."

The sound of the word "lost," with its implication of incompetence, had the effect of rousing a renewed surge of healthy indignation. Lost indeed! A sober, God-fearing, respectable adult woman didn't get lost in broad daylight, like some drunken hobo! If she was confused, it was because the road had been changed! And now that she thought of it, that was no doubt the explanation: during the night, the road people had brought in their equipment and cut a new road through—everybody knew how quickly they could do it these days—without even telling anyone. The idea! And the new sign fitted in with it. Her jaw set determinedly, Mrs. Withers turned and started for home with a firm tread. This time she'd call the sheriff, and give that self-satisfied old fool a piece of her mind.

The busy signal went on and on. After dialing five times, Odelia Withers went into the kitchen, rigidly holding her expression of righteous disapproval, opened the icebox door, and began mechanically setting out lunch. Fortunately there was food on hand; it wasn't that she *had* to shop today. Carefully holding her thoughts from her aborted walk to town, she prepared a sandwich from the last of the boiled ham and poured a glass of milk, seated herself in a ray of sunlight streaming past the ruffled curtains, and ate, listening to the tick of the clock in the hall.

She tried the telephone ten times in all during the afternoon. First the sheriff's office, then the Highway Patrol, then the city police. The lines were all busy; probably a flood of complaints about the road. Then, on impulse, she dialed Henry, the mechanic at the station in town. Another busy signal. She tried the numbers of two of her friends, then the operator. All busy.

She turned the radio to her favorite program, a harrowing drama of small-town PTA politics, and busied herself cleaning the already spotless house until the shadows of late afternoon lay across the lawn. After dinner she tried one more call, hung up as the instrument emitted its impersonal *zawwp, zawwp, zawwp* . . .

The next morning she walked as far as the sign before returning home, filled with frustrating desire to complain to someone. Without thinking, she went to the icebox, took out the ham and the milk.

She frowned at the meat on the plate. Three slices. But she had eaten the last of the ham yesterday, two slices for lunch, the other in a salad at dinnertime. And the milk: she had finished it, put the empty bottle by the door . . .

She went to the cupboard, took down the jar of mayonnaise she had opened yesterday, removed the lid. The jar was full, untouched.

Odelia Withers proceeded to prepare lunch, eat, and wash the dishes. Then she put on a sun hat and went into the garden to cut flowers, an expression of determined disapproval on her face.

3

"It's a kook item," Bill Summers, the "Personalities" editor of *Scene* magazine, said in his usual tone of weary disparagement. "But that doesn't mean it's not news."

"Some guy goes poking around in the off-limits section of an Arab town and gets a mob after him," Bud Vetch, *Scene*'s number one field man, said. "Maybe that's a hot item to the local U.S. Embassy, but what's it to the public?"

"Didn't you look at the pics?"

Vetch yawned as Summers passed the three five-by-eight glossies across to him. "So some tourist had a Brownie with him," he said. "Amateur photo hounds..." His voice faded as he looked at the top picture. It showed a tall, ungainly, stoop-shouldered man with a hollow face, deep-set eyes, a short black beard, a prominent wart, dressed in a dowdy black suit and a high hat. In the background were visible a crowd of white-robed men around a merchant's stall. Vetch looked at the next shot. It showed the man seated at a table under an awning, bushy head bared, fanning himself with the hat, apparently deep in conversation with a khaki-uniformed native policeman. The third photo was a close-up of the lined face, looking back, with a slightly surprised expression.

"Hey!" Vetch said. "This looks like—"

"Yes," Summers cut him off. "I know all the wise remarks you're going to make. I don't know what this bird's angle is, but if he wanted to attract attention, he did it with bells on. The locals don't have a very good idea of chronology. An official inquiry came through to Washington this morning from their Foreign Office, and State had to send them a formal reply, confirming the man in question was dead. That's when the chili really hit the fan. The Tamboolans say they've seen pictures and they have a positive ID on this character, and that he's very much alive. Either that, or he's an afreet. Either way, it's a problem. I want you to get there before the bubble bursts and interview this fellow."

Vetch was still studying the photos. "It's uncanny," he said. "If this is makeup or a mask, it's a top-quality job."

"What do you mean, 'if'?"

"Nothing—I guess," Vetch said. "By the way, did this fellow give a name?"

"Sure," Summers growled. "He told them he was Abraham Lincoln."

4

"I'm glad to see the last of that sin-killer," Job Arkwright growled, standing at the cabin door, watching the slight, dandified figured in the incongruously elegant greatcoat and boots disappear along the snow-blanketed path into the deep shadows of the virgin forest.

"It were a mean trick, Mr. Arkwright, making poor Fly help you cut all that cordwood—and then sending the poor slicker out in this weather," Charity Arkwright said. "After all, he's a preacher—even if he does have that sweet little mustache."

"I'll sweeten his mustache!" Arkwright glowered at his mate, a young, large-eyed woman with an ample bosom and slim waist. "If you'd of went ahead and fattened up like I ast you, you wouldn't have no trouble with them kind of fellers!"

"No trouble," Charity murmured, and patted her hair. "All the while you were out hunting rabbits, he set by the fire and read scripture to me. My, didn't I learn a lot!"

"Well—just so he didn't get no idears."

"Fiddle-dee-dee! I didn't give him a chance to."

"I wisht I knew jist how to take that," Job muttered. "Looky here, girl, did he—"

"Hark! What's that?" Charity cupped a hand to her ear. "Somebody coming?"

Job grabbed his muzzle-loader down from its place and swung the door open. "Can't be no hostiles," he said. "They don't make that kind o' racket!" He stepped outside. "You stay here," he ordered. "I'll have a look-see."

He moved to the corner of the cabin. The crashing sounds from the underbrush approached steadily from the deep woods to the rear of the house. The brush parted and a bedraggled figure emerged from the last entangling thicket and halted, staring across toward the cabin.

"Who's that?" Job barked.

"Why—'tis I, Fly Fornication Beebody," a breathless voice came back. "Brother Arkwright—is it thee, in sooth?"

"Who else? Ain't nobody else in these parts. How'd you get around back? And what the devil are ye doing there? I thought you was headed for Jerubabbel Knox's farm when you left here."

"Don't take the name of the Fiend lightly," Fly gasped, coming up, his round face glowing with sweat in spite of the bitter cold. "I warrant, Brother Arkwright, I see his foul hand in this! I struck due east for Knox's stead, and the treacherous path led me back to thy door."

"Fly, you got a bottle hid?" Job demanded. He leaned toward the itinerant parson and sniffed sharply.

"Would I play thee false in that fashion?" Beebody retorted. "What I'd not warrant for a goodly sup of honest rum at this moment!"

"Come on; I'll set ye on the trail," Job said. He went into the cabin for his coat, then led at a brisk pace with Beebody panting at his heels. The trail wound around a giant pine tree, skirted a boulder, angled upward across a rise. Arkwright paused, frowning about him, then went on. The trail dwindled, vanished in a tangle of dead berry vine."

"Arkwright—we're lost!" Fly Beebody gasped. "Beelzebub has set a snare for us—"

"Have done, ye fool!" Arkwright snapped. "The path's overgrowed, that's all!" He forced his way through the dense growth. Ahead, the trees seemed to thin. He made for the clearing, stepped into the open—

There was a deafening *boom!* and a heavy slug whickered through the icy branches by Job's ear. He threw himself flat, gaping in amazement at the cabin, the corn shed, the frozen garden patch, the woman with the muzzle-loader in her hands.

"Charity!" he yelled. "It's me!"

Half an hour later, in the cabin, Fly Beebody was still shaking his head darkly.

"I'll make my couch in the snow if need be," he said. "But I'll not set foot i' that bewitched forest 'ere tomorrow's dawn."

"You can lie here, i' the shed," Job said grudgingly.

"If you must." Charity offered the involuntary guest a quilt, which he accepted with ill grace. He departed, grumbling, and Job barred the door.

Husband and wife slept poorly that night. Shortly before dawn, they were awakened by a frantic pounding on the door. Job leaped up, opened it, gun in hand. Fly Beebody stood there, disheveled, coatless. He stuttered, then pointed.

Tall in the misty light of pre-dawn, the mighty cottonwood tree which the two men had with such labor felled the previous day stood once more in its accustomed place, untouched by the axe.

CHAPTER ONE

1

Roger Tyson flipped the windshield wipers into high gear as the spatter of rain became a downpour, then a deluge. He slowed to fifty, his headlight beams soaked up and absorbed by the solid curtains of whirling water sheeting across the blacktop. Lightning winked and thunder banged like artillery.

"Perfect," Tyson congratulated the elements. "What a way to end up: the middle of the night, in the middle of nowhere, with no gas, no money, no credit card." His stomach rumbled. "Not even a ham sandwich. Something tells me I'm not fitted to survive in the harsh modern world."

A broken seat spring prodded him painfully; water trickled down from under the dash and dripped on his knee. The engine gasped three times, backfired, and died.

"Oh, no," he groaned, steering to the side of the road and off onto the shoulder. He turned up his coat collar, climbed out in the driving rain, lifted the hood. The engine looked like an engine. He closed the hood, stood with his hands in his pockets, staring off down the dark road.

"Probably won't be a car along for a week," he reflected dismally. "Only a damned fool would be out in this weather—and not even a damned fool would stop, even if he came along here, and—" His ruminations were interrupted by a glint of light in the distance; the faint sound of an approaching engine cut through the drum of the rain.

"Hey!" Roger brightened. "Someone's coming!" He trotted out into the center of the road, watching the light grow as it rushed toward him. He waved his arms.

"Hey, stop!" he yelled as the oncoming vehicle showed no indication of slowing. "Stop!" He leaped aside at the last instant as a low-slung motorcycle leaped out of the gloom, a slim, girlish figure crouched behind the windshield. He caught just a glimpse of her shocked expression as she swerved to miss him. The speeding bike went into a skid, slid sideways forty feet, and plunged off the road. There was a prolonged crashing and snapping of wood and metal, a final resounding crunch, and silence.

"Good Lord!" Roger skittered across the road, picked his way down the steep bank, following the trail of snapped-off saplings. At the bottom, the crumpled machine lay on its side, one chrome-plated wire wheel turning lazily, the headlight still shining upward through the wet leaves. The girl lay a few feet away, on her back, eyes shut.

Roger squatted at her side, reached for her pulse. Her eyes opened: pale green eyes, gazing into his.

"You must help me," she whispered with obvious effort.

"Sure," Roger gulped. "Anything at all! I—I'm sorry . . ."

"The message," the girl whispered. "It's of the utmost importance. It must be delivered . . . "

"Look, I'll have to go back up by my car and try to flag somebody down."

"Don't bother," the girl whispered. "My neck is broken. I have only a few seconds to live . . . "

"Nonsense," Roger choked. "You'll be right as rain in a few days—"

"Don't interrupt," the girl said sharply. "The message: Beware the Rhox!"

"What rocks?" Roger looked around wildly. "I don't see any rocks!"

"For your sake—I hope you never do," the victim gasped. "The message must be delivered at once! You must go . . . " Her voice faltered. "Too late," she breathed. "No time . . . to explain . . . take . . . button . . . right ear . . . "

"I'm wasting time!" Roger started to rise. "I'll go for a doctor!" He checked as the girl's lips moved.

"Take . . . the button . . . put it in . . . your ear . . . " The words were almost inaudible, but the green eyes held on Roger's, pleading.

"Seems like a funny time to worry about a hearing aid," Roger gulped, "but . . . " He lifted a lock of wet black hair aside, gingerly grasped the small gold button tucked into the girl's delicately molded ear. As he withdrew it, the light of awareness faded from the girl's glazing eyes. Roger grabbed for her wrist, felt a final feeble thump-thump of the pulse—then nothing.

"Hey!" Roger stared uncomprehending at the white, perfect-featured face. "You can't be . . . I mean, I didn't . . . you mustn't . . . " He gulped hard, blinking back sudden tears.

"She's dead," he breathed. "And all because of me! If I hadn't jumped out in front of her like that, she'd still be alive!" Badly shaken, he tucked the gold button in his pocket, climbed back up the slope, slipping and sliding. Back in his car, he used tissues to mop off his face and hands.

"What a mess," he groaned. "I ought to be put in jail! I'm a murderer! Not that my being in jail would help any. Not that anything I could do would help any!" He took the button out and examined it under the dash light. There were thin filaments trailing from it, probably leads to a battery in the owner's pocket.

He rolled the bean-sized button between his fingers. "She seemed to think this was important; used her dying breath to tell me about it. Wanted me to stick it in my ear . . . " He held the tiny object to his ear. Did he hear a faint, wavering hum, or was it his imagination? He pushed it farther in. There was a faint tickling sensation, tiny rustling and popping sounds. He tried to withdraw the button, felt a sharp pain—

"Drive to Pottsville, one hundred and two miles, north-northeast," the dead girl's voice said in his ear. *"Start now. Time is precious!"*

2

There was the sound of an approaching motor. Roger scrambled quickly from the car, peering into the rain, which had settled down now to a steady drizzle. For the second time, a single headlight was approaching along the road.

"Now, this time don't jump out yelling," he cautioned himself. "When they stop, just tell them that you've been driven mad by hardship, and are hearing voices. And don't forget to mention the hallucination about the girl on the motorcycle; that may be an important lead for the psychiatrist." He stood by the side of the

car, staring anxiously at the oncoming light, waving his
hand in a carefully conservative flagging motion. The
vehicle failed to slow; instead, it swung wide, shot past
him at full bore—and as it did, he saw the shape
behind the handlebars: a headless torso, obese, bulbous, brick-red, pear-shaped, ornamented with two
clusters of tentacles, like lengths of flexible metal hose.
Through the single goggle, an eye as big as a pizza and
similarly pigmented swiveled to impale him with a
glance of utter alienness. With a strangled yell, Roger
leaped back, tripped, went down hard on the mud-slick
pavement. In horror, he saw the motorcycle veer wildly,
stand on its nose, hurling its monstrous rider clear, then
skid on its side another hundred feet before coming
to a stop in the center of the highway.

Roger tottered to his feet and cantered forward,
approached the inert form lying motionless on the
pavement. From a distance of ten feet, he could see
that it would never ride again: the upper portion was
smashed into a pulp the consistency of mashed pota-
toes.

"Help," Roger said weakly, aware of a loud singing
sensation in his ears. In his left ear, to be specific.

"Time is of the essence," the girl's slightly accented
voice said. *"Get going!"*

Roger tugged again at the button, was rewarded with
another pang.

"I should go to the police," he said. "But what can
I say? That I was responsible for the death of a girl
and a giant rutabaga?"

"Forget the police," the voice said impatiently. *"I'm
maintaining vitality in a small cluster of cortical cells
only with the greatest difficulty, in order to hold open
this link through the Reinforcer! Don't render the effort
useless by dithering here! Start now!"*

"B-but—my car won't start!"

"Take the motorcycle!"

"That would be stealing!"

"Who's going to report it? Relatives of a giant ruta-baga?"

"You have a definite point there," Roger said, hurrying toward the fallen machine. "Somehow, I never thought insanity would be like this." He lifted the bike. Except for a few scratches in the green paint, it seemed as good as new. He kicked it into life, mounted, and gunned off down the highway, squinting into the darkness ahead.

3

At the next town, Roger scanned front lawns for a sign indicating the availability of an M.D. "No point in holding out for a high-powered big-city head-shrinker," he rationalized. "The old-time small-town GP is the man to see and he'll be a lot less likely to demand cash in advance."

He spotted what he was looking for, pulled to the curb beside ranked garbage cans in front of a loom-ing, three-story frame house. At once lights went on inside. The door opened, and a small, sharp-nosed man emerged, shading his eyes.

"What'll I tell him?" Roger asked himself, suddenly self-conscious. "I've heard about retarded kids stuff-ing things up their noses and ears and whatnot, but I'll feel a little foolish explaining how *I* happened to pull a trick like that."

"Who's that?" a scratchy voice called. "Just step inside and lie down on the table. Have you diagnosed in three minutes flat."

"I can't just tell him I stuck it in there cold," Roger reflected. "And if I tell him the real reason . . . "

"No reason to go around worrying about cancer," the sharp-nosed man said, venturing down the brick steps. "Take two minutes and set your mind at rest."

"Suppose he sticks me in a straitjacket and calls for the fellows with the butterfly nets?" the thought occurred to Roger. "They say once you're in, you have a heck of a time getting out again."

"Now, if it's just a touch of TB, I got just the thing." The practitioner was advancing along the walk. "None o' these fancy antibiotics, mind you—cost a fortune. My own patented formula, based on fermented mare's whey. Packs a wallop and good for what ails you!"

"After all, it's not as if it was actually unendurable or anything," Roger pointed out to himself. "Old Uncle Lafcadio carried on for years with a whole troop of little silver men giving him advice from under the wallpaper."

"Tell you what," the healer proposed, producing a bottle from under his coat as he crossed the parched grass strip. "I'll let you have a trial dosage for a dollar twenty-nine including tax; you can't beat them prices this side of K. C."

"Ah . . . no thank you, sir," Roger demurred, revving his engine. "Actually I'm not a patient; I'm a treasury agent on the lookout for excise violations."

"Excuse me, Buster," the little man said. "I just came out to empty the garbage." He lifted the lid of the nearest container and deposited the flat flask therein. Roger felt sharp eyes on him as he let out the clutch and sped off down the street.

"You made the right decision," the small voice said in his ear.

"I'm a coward," Roger groaned. "What do I care what he thinks? Maybe I'd better go back—"

A sharp pang in his ear made him yelp.

"I'm afraid I just can't allow that," his unseen companion stated firmly. *"Just take a left at the next*

*intersection, and we'll be in Pottsville in less than two
hours."*

4

One hour and fifty-five minutes later, Roger was
wheeling the bike slowly along a garishly lit avenue
lined with pawnshops, orange-juice and shoe-shine
stands, billiard emporia, and places of refreshment
decorated with eight-by-ten glossies of startling can-
dor, all bustling with activity in spite of the hour.

"Slower," the dead girl's voice cautioned. *"Turn in
up ahead, that big garage-like place."*

"That's the bus station," Roger said. "If you're planning on my buying a ticket, forget it. I'm broke."

*"Nothing like that. We're within a few yards of our
objective."*

Roger narrowly averted being crushed against the
tiled wall by the snorting bulk of an emerging Chicago-
bound Greyhound as he steered into the echoing interior. As directed, he abandoned the motorcycle, pushed
through the revolving door into the fudgy atmosphere
of the waiting room, with its traditional décor of sleeping enlisted personnel and unwed-looking mothers.

"Cross the room," the voice directed. Roger complied, halted on command before a closed door.

"Try in here."

Roger pushed through the door. A corpulent lady
with a mouthful of hairpins whirled on him with a shrill
cry of alarm. He backed out hastily.

"That was the ladies' room!" he hissed.

"Damn right, Clyde," a bass voice rumbled at his
elbow. A large cop eyed him with hostility from a
height of at least six-three. "I got my eye on you birds.

Dumbrowski runs a clean beat, and don't you forget it!" He bellied closer and lowered his voice. "Uh—by the way: what's it look like in there, anyways?"

"Just like a men's room," Roger gulped. "Practically."

"Yeah? Well, watch yourself, Ralph!"

"Certainly, officer." Roger backed to the adjoining door and stepped inside, urged by the voice. An elderly colored man straightened from his post against the wall.

"Yes, sir," he said briskly. "Shine? Shave? Massage? What about a fast clean and press?"

"No thanks, I just . . . "

"Little something to cut the fog?" He slid a flat bottle from his pocket.

"Say, if you've got TB, you ought to be in Arizona," Roger said.

The Negro gave him a thoughtful look. He removed the cap from the bottle and took a large swallow; he frowned, upended the bottle in the nearest sink.

"Man, you're right," he said. "I can just catch the 2:08 to Phoenix." He left hastily.

"At least I'm not the only one who's insane," Roger muttered.

"The last stall," the girl's voice said. *"Sorry about the mix-up, but I left here in something of a hurry."*

"I should think so!" Roger said. "What were you doing in a men's room?"

"No time to explain now. Just swing that door open."

Roger did so. The cubicle contained the usual plumbing, nothing more.

"A little to the left—there!"

A glowing line had appeared in mid-air, directly over the bowl, shining with a greenish light of its own, brilliant in the gloom. When Roger moved his head a few inches, it disappeared.

"An optical illusion," he said doubtfully.

"By no means. It's an Aperture. Now, here's what I want you to do: write a note—I'll dictate—and simply toss it through. That's all. I'll just have to trust to luck that it lands where I want it to."

"It will land in the local sewage processing plant," Roger protested. "This is the craziest method I ever heard of for delivering mail!"

"Move a little closer to the Aperture; you'll see it's not as simple as it appears at first glance."

Roger edged closer. The line broadened into a ribbon that gleamed with rainbow colors like a film of oil on water. Closer still, it widened to become a shimmering plane that seemed to extend through the wall to infinity. He stepped back, dizzy.

"It was like looking over the edge of the world," he whispered.

"Close," the voice said. *"Now quickly, the note."*

"I'll have to borrow a pencil." Roger stepped back into the lobby, secured the loan of a gnawed stub from a ticket clerk. Back inside, he took out a crumpled envelope and smoothed it.

"Shoot," he said. "Let's get this over with."

"Very well, start off 'Dear S'lunt.' Or no, make that 'Technor Second Level S'lunt.' Or maybe 'Dear Technor' would be better . . ."

"I don't know how to spell 'Technor,'" Roger said. "And I'm not sure about 'S'lunt.'"

"It doesn't matter. Let's just launch right into the matter: 'My attempt to traverse Axial Channel partially successful. Apparent Museum and associated retrieval system work of advanced race capable of manipulations in at least two superior orders of dimensionality. Recommend effort to dispatch null-engine to terminal coordinates to break temporal statis. Signed, Q'nell, Field Agent.'"

"What does all that mean?" Roger queried.

"Never mind! Did you get it all down?"

"I missed the part after 'My attempt.'"

The voice repeated the message. Roger copied it out in block capitals.

"Now pitch it through the Aperture, and you're finished," the voice said.

As Roger made a move to step into the stall, two men burst through the outer door. One was the ticket clerk.

"That's him!" He pointed excitedly at Roger. "I knew as soon as he asked for a pencil and started for the john that he was one of those fellows you're looking for!"

The other man, a slight, gray-haired chap with a look of FBI about him, came toward Roger with a knowing smile.

"Have you been, er, decorating the walls, young fellow?" he inquired.

"You've got it all wrong," Roger protested. "I was just—"

"Don't let him go back in and erase them!" the clerk warned.

"The message!" the voice hissed urgently.

"Let's just take a look at your work," the gray-haired man said easily, reaching for the door.

"You don't understand!" Roger backed into the stall. "I was just—"

"Grab him!" The clerk caught his sleeve. The other man caught his other sleeve. As they sought to drag him forth, Roger struggled to free himself from their clutches.

"I'm innocent!" he yelled. "This place was already illustrated when I came in!"

"Yes, of course!" the gray-haired man panted. "Don't get the wrong impression, sir! I'm a curator of the graffiti collection at the Museum of Contemporary Folk

Expression. We're looking for creative minds to do a hundred-foot mural for our rotunda!"

With a ripping of cloth, Roger tore free, stumbled back—

"Watch out!" the voice called—too late. Roger saw the shimmering plane flash out on either side, saw it curl in to form a glittering tube about him. For an instant, he teetered there, enclosed in a misty grayness; then, with a sound as of a mighty rushing of waters, he felt himself swirled around and down into depthless emptiness.

CHAPTER TWO

I

He was on a beach. That was the first thought that came into focus as his stunned mind returned to awareness. Brilliant sunshine glared down on yellow sand. He sat up, looked across the shimmer of heat to eroded spires of pink stone looming in the distance. The dance of the air reminded him of something, but thinking made his head hurt. And that in turn reminded him of something else . . .

Tentatively, Roger Tyson put his hand to his ear, felt the button there.

"Wh—what happened?" he whispered.

There was no answer.

"Voice?" he called. "Agent Q'nell, or whatever your name is?"

Silence.

"Well—at least I'm cured of part of my affliction," Roger told himself. "Now if I can just figure out where I am . . ." Probably, he considered, he had been on a three-weeks' binge, and was now just coming out of the alcoholic fog.

"Of course, I've never been a drinker," he reminded himself. "But that's probably why it hit me so hard."

He came shakily to his feet, looking around at the vast expanse of sand. It was not a beach, he saw. Merely a boulder-dotted desert, stretching on and endlessly on. "Probably Arizona," he thought. "Maybe the road is just out of sight; but in what direction?"

A massive water-carved rock squatted fifty feet away. Roger went to it, climbed its side. Standing atop it ten feet above the level, he could see for miles across the flat expanse. Far away to the east, a line of pale cliffs edged the world. To the north there was only a vacant horizon. The west was the same. But to the south a ravine cut across the flat ground—and a ravine suggested the action of water.

"A drink," Roger said. "That's what I need." He scrambled down, started across toward the dark line of the cut.

For the first ten minutes he walked steadily forward, skirting the frequent large stones, keeping the sun on his left. Encountering rougher ground, he slowed, picking his route with care.

Mounting a low ridge, he shaded his eyes, scanning the route ahead. The ravine, which should have been very close now, was not to be seen. But . . . Roger closed his eyes, resting them, looked again. What he saw was unmistakable. The boulder that he had climbed, from which he had sighted the ravine, lay a hundred yards ahead, squarely in his path.

2

Four times Roger Tyson had oriented himself with his back to the rock and walked directly away from it—

twice to the south, once each to the north and east.
Each time, within fifteen minutes, he had returned to
the landmark. There had been no careless changes of
direction, he was sure of that. Walking east, he had
faced directly into the sun's glare—and after a quarter of an hour had again encountered the ubiquitous
boulder.

Now he sat in the shade of the massive rock, his
eyes closed, feeling the heat that beat down from
above, reflected from below, radiated from the stone
at his back. Already he felt weak and listless from
dehydration. At this rate, he wouldn't last until
sundown—the only relief he could hope for. Not that
that would change anything. He would still be lost
here in this landscape of illusions . . .

That was it! The place didn't really exist; it was nothing but a creation of his fever-racked mind. With this
conclusion came a sense that now that he had penetrated the mirage, it should be possible to ignore it.
Roger concentrated on the mundane reality of the
normal world: singing commercials, tourist attractions,
Rotarians, chrome-plated bumpers, artificial eyelashes . . .

He opened his eyes. The lifeless desert still stretched
about him. Illusion or otherwise, he was stuck with it.

But damn it, it was impossible! A surge of healthy
anger drove him to his feet. There had to be a key to
it—some imperfection that could be detected by acute
observation. He would pick a starting point and, step
by step, analyze what the situation was that he faced!
This time, sighting on a distant landmark—a spire of
stone at least ten miles away—Roger walked slowly,
pausing frequently to study the ground around him. He
wasn't sure precisely what he was looking for, but it was
clear that the trap in which he was caught—he thought
of it in those terms now—bore some resemblance to a

goldfish bowl, in which the puzzled fish swam endlessly, bumping his nose against an invisible barrier which relentlessly led him back again to his starting point. The barrier here was an intangible one, a three-dimensional wall; but like the glass of the bowl, it should be possible to confront it directly, rather than sliding along beside it, like a guppy swimming parallel to the wall of his prison.

Something in the landscape ahead caught Roger's attention, some deviation from the usual aspect of the physical world. It took him minutes of close observation to pinpoint it: objects in the distance before him appeared to slide away to the left and right as he advanced. The apparent movement in itself was a normal perspective effect; it was the rate of movement that was wrong. The array of boulders stretching out before him seemed to part too swiftly—and at the exact center point of his view, there seemed to be an almost invisible vertical line of turbulence, a line that disappeared as he halted, resumed again as he went forward, always at the precise point toward which he moved. It wasn't a tangible thing, he saw; merely a plane along which the expansion of the scene took place. As he watched, a tiny object came into existence there, grew with each step until the familiar boulder lay there in his path, a hundred yards ahead. He looked back. The rock was no longer visible; the distant line of cliffs glowed orange in the late sunlight.

"All right," he said aloud, his voice a lonely sound in the silent immensity around him. "It's some kind of lens effect. A four-dimensional lens, maybe. Putting a name to it doesn't help much, but at least I've pinned down one aspect of it." He scratched a mark on the ground, then walked on to the stone, counting his paces. Three hundred and twenty-one. He returned to the mark, continued along that route until the boulder reappeared ahead; then he went on, counting his steps. Four hundred and four paces in this direction.

"So far, so good," Roger said, walking toward the boulder. "The phenomenon has a fixed center. The fishbowl may be a complete sphere, but it has a definite boundary." He paused as a concept formed in his mind: three-dimensional reality, gathered up at the corners, pulled up to form a closed space, as a washwoman folds up the edges of a sheet to form a bag . . .

"And all I've got to do," he concluded, "is find the knot!" As this thought completed itself, he noticed a tiny movement ahead. Instantly, he dropped flat behind a convenient rock. Beside the boulder where he had awakened, something glittered in mid-air. Half a dozen metallically jointed members appeared, followed a moment later by a squat, dusky-red body, headless, single-eyed, alien.

"The rutabaga!" Roger choked. "It's still alive—and after me!"

3

Roger lay flat as the monstrous form emerged fully from the empty air, like an actor sliding from behind an invisible flat. It poised for a moment on its clustered supporting members, identical with an upper ring of armlike appendages; then it moved away from the rock, studying the ground ahead.

"It's following my trail!" Roger gulped. "And in five minutes, it will be sneaking up behind me!" He rose to all fours, scuttled forward a few yards, watching the alien creature move rapidly away on flickering tentacles. Darting from cover to cover, he followed it—his only chance, he knew, to stay ahead of it. Approaching the boulder, he saw a tiny glint of light from a vertical line, like a luminous spider's web, extending from the ground upward.

"It's the Aperture!" he gulped in relief. "I hate to reopen the conversation with the art fancier, but it's better than trying to explain to that vegetable how I happened to steal his bike."

Cautiously, Roger edged closer to the luminous filament, saw it widen, close around him as swiftly as a bursting soap bubble, then as swiftly open out again and vanish behind him.

He was standing in darkness, under a sky criss-crossed by glowing arcs, like a Fourth of July display. The air was filled with thunder, punctuated by pops, bangs, and stuttering detonations.

"It's a celebration," Roger guessed, noting that he was standing ankle deep in cold water. "I wonder what the occasion is?" He groped about him, discovered that he was in a muddy, steep-sided ditch higher than his head. A faint glimmer of light reflected from the damp wall of the cut a few feet ahead. He sloshed to it, turned a right-angle corner, and was facing a sand-bagged, timber-braced doorway. Inside, three men sat at a table made of stacked boxes, holding cards. The light came from a candle stuck to a board.

"Hey! You better get inside, buddy!" one of the men called. He was a sallow, thin-faced youth in a mustard-colored jacket, open at the neck. "Big Otto's due to hit any second now!"

"Blimey, mate," a second man, wearing suspenders over wool underwear, said, slapping a card down on the table. "Don't yer know the ruddy schedule?"

The third man, a stout fellow in a gray-green uniform jacket, placed a card on the table and puffed smoke from an enormous pipe.

"Ach, a new *gesicht!*" he exclaimed heartily. *"Bist
du vieleicht ein* poker player?"

"Ah—not just now," Roger responded, entering the
murky chamber hesitantly. "Say, I wonder if you fellows can tell me where I am? My, uh, car broke down,
you see, while I was on my way to apply for a new
job . . . "

Hearty laughter interrupted Roger's explanation.

"New job," the man with the suspenders echoed.
"That's a'ot one, chum!"

"Good to meet a guy with a sense o' humor," the
man in mustard agreed. "What's your outfit, pal?"

"You are a funny man," the stout player stated solemnly. "You would abbreciate a yoke. *Warum* does *ein
Huhn* cross the *strasse?*"

"Outfit?" Roger queried. "I'm afraid I don't have
one."

"Wiped out, huh? Too bad. Well, you can doss down
here . . . " His voice was drowned by an ear-splitting
shriek followed instantly by an explosion that rocked
the underground room. The joke-teller reached to flick
a smoking fragment of shell casing from the table.

"To come on s' ozzer *seite!*" he said triumphantly.
"Also, vun man says to s' ozzer man, 'Who *vass dass*
lady I zaw you viss last *nicht?*"

"What's going on?" Roger blurted, slapping at the
mud spattered across his face by the blast.

"The usual Jerry bombardment, o' course, chum.
Wot else?"

"Jerry bombardment? You mean—Germans? Good
Lord, has a war started?"

"Oh-oh, shell shock," the thin-faced man said. "Too
bad. But maybe it's better that way. You get a little
variety."

"Where am I?" Roger persisted. "What is this place?"

"You're in good hands, buddy. This is the Saint

Mihiel Salient; just take it easy. The shelling will be over in another couple minutes, then we can talk better."

"The Saint Mihiel Salient! B-but that was in World War One!"

"World War what?"

"One. Nineteen eighteen."

"Right, chum. September twelfth. Lousy day, too. I could of picked a better one to be stuck in."

"But—that's impossible! It's nineteen-eighty-seven! You're two wars behind!"

"Crikey—'e's flipped his cap proper," the suspendered man commented.

"Blease! I didn't finish my yoke!" the stout man complained.

"Could it be—is it possible—that the Aperture is some sort of time machine?" Roger gasped.

"Say, buddy, you better get out of the doorway," the thin-faced man suggested. "There's one more big fellow due before it lets up, and—"

"That desert!" Roger blurted. "It wasn't Arizona! It was probably ancient Arabia or something!"

"'E's raving." The suspender-wearer rose from his seat on an ammunition box. "Watch 'im, mates. 'E might get violent."

"Fantastic!" Roger breathed, looking around the dugout. "Just think, I'm actually back in the past, breathing the air of seventy-odd years ago! Outside, the war is raging, and Wilson's in the White House, and nobody's ever heard of LSD or television or miniskirts or flying saucers—"

"Look, chum, in about ten seconds—"

"You fellows have a lot of excitement to look forward to," Roger said envyingly. "The war will be over in November; try to keep your heads down until then. And afterwards there'll be the League of Nations—that

was a failure—and then Prohibition—that didn't work
out too well, either—and then the stock market crash
in twenty-nine—remember to sell your portfolios early
in the year. And then the Great Depression, and then
World War Two—"

"Grab him! For 'is own good!"

As the players rose and closed in, Roger backed
away. "Now, wait just a minute!" he protested. "I'm not
crazy! It's just that I'm a little confused by what's
happened. I have to be going now—"

"You don't hear yet s' punchline!" the stout man protested.

"You'll get y'er bloody 'ead blowed off!"

"Duck, buddy!"

A loud whistle filled the air as Roger broke away
and splashed out into the muddy trench. As the sound
of the descending shell rose higher and higher he
looked both ways for shelter, then dived for the Aperture, saw rainbow light flare about him—

He was sprawled on the grassy bank of a small
creek, in full sunlight, looking at a brutal caricature of
a man crouched on the opposite side.

4

The map-ape stood all of eight feet tall, in spite
of a pronounced stoop; its hands looked as big as
catchers' mitts. The shaggy red-brown pelt was matted
with dirt, pink scars crossed the wide face, the
bronzed, sparsely haired chest. The wide lips drew
back on broken, blackened teeth; the small eyes
flicked restlessly from Roger to the surrounding
woods, back again.

"Oops," Roger murmured. "Wrong era. I'll just nip back through and try that again . . . "

As he stepped back, the ape-man advanced, splashing down into the stream. Roger forced his way back in among tangled brambles, searching frantically for the glint of light that indicated the exit.

"Maybe it was over more to the left," he suggested, beating his way in that direction. The giant was halfway across the stream now, yelling in indignation at the touch of the water. "Or possibly to the right . . . " Roger clawed at the vines that raked at him like clutching hands. The monster-man emerged from the water, paused to shake first one foot and then the other, then came on, growling ferociously. Roger broke clear of the thicket, skittered away a few feet, and stopped to watch the dull-witted brute entangle itself in the thorny creepers.

"Keep cool, now, Tyson," he counseled. "You can't afford to lose track of the bolthole. Just hover here while that fellow wears himself out, then scoot right in and—"

With a bellow, the ape-man lunged clear of the snarled vines, a move that placed him between Roger and his refuge.

"He—he's probably scared to death," Roger theorized. "All I have to do is act as though I'm not afraid, and he'll turn tail and run." He swallowed hard, adjusted a fierce glint in his eye, and took a hesitant step forward. The result was instantaneous. The creature charged straight at him, seized him with both hands, lifted him clear of the ground. Roger's last impression was of blue sky overhead, seen through a leafy pattern of foliage that whirled around and down and burst into showering lights that faded swiftly into blackness.

CHAPTER THREE

1

He awoke in near-darkness. A pattern of dim light filtered through coarse matting to show him a low ceiling which merged with a wall of water-worn stone. A wizened, bristly-whiskered face appeared, staring down at him. He sat up, winced at the ache in his head; the face retreated hastily. This specimen didn't appear to be vicious—but where was the scar-faced Gargantua?

"Better lie quiet," the old man said in a cracked, whispery voice. "Ye've had a bad bump."

"You speak English!" Roger blurted.

"Reckon I do," the man nodded. "Bimbo had ye, using ye for a play-purty. Ye was lucky he happened to be in a good mood when he found ye. I drug ye in here when he was through with ye."

"Thanks a lot," Roger said. He was discovering new pains with every move. "How did I get this bruise on my side?"

"That was when Bimbo throwed ye down and jumped on ye."

"What happened to my elbow? Both elbows?"

"Must have been when Bimbo was dragging ye around by the heels."

"I guess I lost the hide on my seat at the same time."

"Nope. That was when I hauled ye in here. Too heavy to lift. But don't fret. Tomorrow ain't too far off."

"Glad to see you're a philosopher." Roger's eyes were becoming accustomed to the gloom. The oldster, he saw, was dressed in a dark blue nautical uniform.

"Who are you?" Roger asked. "How did you get here, in the same place with Bimbo?"

"Name's Luke Harwood. Can't rightly say how I got here. Just came ashore to try out my land legs and must of got into some bad rum. Last I remember was heading outside for some fresh air. I woke up here." He sighed. "Guess it's the Lord's punishment for that little business in Macao back in ought nine."

"Would that be . . . nineteen nine?"

"That's it, feller."

"Golly, you don't look that old; but I suppose you were a nipper at the time."

"Well—I sometimes was knowed to take a snort, in good company. But I was never drunk a day in my life. I figger I was hit on the head. Can't rightly say whether I was kilt outright or lingered awhile."

"Where were you when you were, ah, alive?"

"Little place name of Pottsville."

"The same town! But . . . in those days there wasn't any bus station!"

"Don't follow ye there, feller."

"But it was probably the spot where the station was built later! That means the Aperture has been there for years and years! It could be the explanation of some of these mysterious disappearances you hear about, where people step around the corner and are never heard from again."

"I bet they're wondering what become of me," Luke said sadly. "Hardnose Harwood, they used to call me. Set yer watch by me. Never thought I'd end up a ship-jumper."

"Listen, Mr. Harwood, we've got to get out of here."

"Can't do it," Harwood said flatly. "I've tried, lad—many's the time. But there's no way out."

"Certainly there is! The same way you came in! It's down by the river. If you can show me the way to where I met Bimbo . . . "

"You ain't making sense, boy. Once ye're dead and in Purgatory, ye're in for life!"

"I suppose after searching for the exit for sixty years and not finding it, it's hard to believe," Roger conceded, "but—"

"What sixty years?" Harwood frowned.

"The sixty years you've been here, since you arrived as a small boy."

"Ye lost yer rudder, feller? I been here twenty-one days tomorrow!"

"Well—I suppose we can figure that part out later." Roger dismissed the chronology. "But listen—where's Bimbo now?"

"Sleeping off chow in his den down the line, most likely. Bimbo's like the weather: same every day."

"Good; then we'll sneak past him, and—"

"Forget it, feller. Bimbo likes to find things where he left 'em."

"I don't care what he likes! I'm getting out before he kills me. Are you coming, or not?"

"Look here, boy, I taken ye aside to save ye some hard knocks by tipping ye off to the system! If ye know what's good for ye, ye'll—"

"It will be good for me to leave—now," Roger said. "So long, Mr. Harwood. It was nice knowing you."

"Stubborn, ain't ye?" The sailor grunted. "Well,

seein's ye're determined, I reckon I'll go along and watch the fun. Now remember—when Bimbo catches ye, don't kick around. That jest riles him."

Stealthily, the two lifted the bamboo mat aside and peered out into the dusty sunshine. The cave, Roger saw, opened onto a rock-strewn ledge above a steep slope shelving down to woodland. It was a long drop; the tops of the great trees barely reached the level of the cave mouth.

Harwood led the way on tiptoe along the ledge. At the entrance to a second, larger cave, he paused, glanced quickly inside.

"Curious," he said. "He ain't here. Wonder where he's at?"

Roger went past him to a sharp angle in the path, edged around it—and was face to face with Bimbo.

"Oh," Harwood said as Roger reappeared around the corner, tucked under the ape-man's shaggy arm. "I see ye found him."

"Don't just stand there!" Roger bleated. "Do something!"

"Thanks for reminding me," Harwood said. He turned and dashed off at top speed. Instantly, Bimbo dropped Roger and lumbered in pursuit. It was a short chase, since the ledge ended after forty feet in a jumble of fallen rock.

"Now, Bimbo"—Harwood scrambled backward, grabbed up a jagged chunk of stone—"ye restrain yerself! Remember last time. That smarted some, didn't it, when I busted ye in the lip?"

Bimbo, unintimidated, closed in, yowled when the thrown missile smacked into his wide face; he grabbed Harwood, and proceeded to flail him against the ground. Roger staggered to his feet, caught up a stout length of oak branch, rushed up behind the ape-man, and brought the club down with all his strength on the

bullet head. Bimbo ignored the blow, and the three that
followed. The fourth seemed to annoy him. He dropped
Harwood and whirled. Roger jumped, found a handhold, scrambled up, looked back to see Bimbo's outstretched hand clutch the rock inches from his heels.
He kicked at the raking fingers, then scaled another
ten feet of rock, pulled himself up onto flat ground.
Already Bimbo's rasping breath and scuffling hands
were audible just below. Roger looked around hastily
for a missile, saw nothing he could use as a weapon.
He turned and ran as the furious troll face rose into
view.

2

For the first two hundred paces, Roger sprinted at
his best speed through open woods directly away from
the starting point, careless of noise, acutely aware of
Bimbo's crashing progress behind him. In the momentary shelter of a shallow depression, he made a right-
angle turn, ran on as silently as possible, emerging after
a few hundred feet into open ground with a distant
view of mountains. For a moment his heart sank—but
in the desert, too, the apparent vista had stretched for
miles. He hadn't lost yet. He ran on, conscious of the
hopelessness of his exposed position if Bimbo should
suspect the change of course too soon.

He was close to exhaustion when he counted off the
last few yards of what he hoped would prove to be a
closed circle. And there ahead was the hollow where
he had changed direction. He dropped flat behind a
bush to catch his breath, listening to the sounds of
breaking brush and the hoarse bellows of the frustrated
Bimbo threshing about in the underbrush well off to

the right. His wind recovered, Roger retraced his steps
to the bluff above the cave. Below, a dozen heavy,
shaggy half-men had emerged from concealment. They
stood in a ragged circle around Luke Harwood, who
was sitting up, holding his side.

Roger swung over the edge, scrambled quickly down
to the ledge. At sight of him, the brute-men scattered,
disappearing into the innumerable hollows in the rock.
With the exception of Bimbo, it appeared, the brutal
appearance of the creatures concealed timorous natures.
Harwood tottered to his feet, dusty and disheveled,
dabbing ineffectually at a bloody nose.

"Ye shouldn't have done it, lad! He hates to have
anybody interfere with him when he's having fun!"

"I missed a swell chance to finish him," Roger said
between gasps of breath. "I should have climbed up
and rolled a rock down on him."

"Ahhh," Harwood demurred. "Killing him *really* gets
his dander up. I killed him three times before I gave
it up. If ye'd squashed him I dread to think o' the con-
sequences. Now, give yerself up, man! Wait here and
take what comes like a man! It can't last forever—
though he's learned to be sly about it, to stretch it out
till sundown. But tomorrow will come at last, and
unless ye've angered him beyond measure, he'll have
forgot by then!"

"Never mind tomorrow. Come on; I've thrown him
off the scent for the moment."

A hoarse bellow sounded from the clifftop above.

"He's found yer trail," Harwood hissed. "Ye're in for
it—unless . . . " There was speculation in his eyes.
"Down by the creek, ye say?"

"Which way down?" Roger snapped.

"Come along," Harwood said. "I guess I owe ye that
much."

3

Five minutes later Roger and Harwood stood beside the small stream which flowed through the wooded ground below the cliff, all that remained of the mighty flow which, ages ago, had carved the gorge.

"There was a nice stand of timber at the spot I'm looking for," Roger said. "A big elm, a yard in diameter, about ten feet from the bank—"

"White pebbles in the bottom?" Harwood cut in.

"I think so . . . yes."

"This way."

The sound of Bimbo's crashing approach came clearly to their ears as they hurried along the bank. It was no more than a minute before Roger halted, looking around.

"This is the place," he said. "I was right at the water's edge, with a big pine at my back." He stepped to the tree, pulled aside the low-growing boughs, squinting into the deep shade.

"I don't see nothing," Harwood muttered. "Looky, if we go back now and give ourselves up, maybe it'll take the edge off his temper."

"It's here," Roger said. "It's got to be here!"

"I don't know about that," Harwood said. "But Bimbo's here!"

"Keep him occupied!" Roger urged as the giant burst into view, puffing like a switch engine.

"Sure." Harwood's tone was not without an edge of sarcasm. "I'll trick him into pulling my legs off one at a time; that'll hold his attention fer a minute or two."

Suddenly there was a crackling of twigs and a swishing of leaves to Roger's left. A pair of segmented metallic tubes were groping about as though testing the air.

A bulge of dusty red swelled into view, followed by the remainder of the headless body of the monster Roger had last seen in the desert.

"Cornered!" Roger gasped. "And I was so close . . . "

The alien being swiveled its lone eye about, failed to notice Roger lurking in the shadowy greenery. It pushed forward, emerged onto the riverbank a few feet behind Luke Harwood, who was making pushing motions toward the advancing Bimbo. The latter paused, his tiny red eyes flicking from the men to the monster, which stood jouncing on its spidery legs, waving its upper members uncertainly. The motion appeared to annoy Bimbo; he bellowed and charged straight past the astonished Harwood and on into the foliage as the alien bounded aside.

"Luke! This way!" Roger yelled as he lunged for the Aperture. Harwood, imagining the ape-man to be on his heels, sprang for the cover offered. Roger caught his arm, dragged him with him toward the line of light, which widened, flashed around the pair, and vanished as darkness closed in.

4

"Land sakes!" Luke muttered. "Where in tarnation are we?"

"I don't know—but at least there's no shellfire," Roger said. He felt around him, sniffled, shuffled his feet. He was standing on a hard-surfaced road, under a starry night sky. Wind moved softly in treetops; a cricket shrilled. Far away a train hooted sorrowfully.

"Hey—a light!" Luke pointed.

"Maybe it's a house," Roger said. "Maybe . . . maybe we're Outside!"

"Yippee," Luke caroled. "Just wait'll the boys back on the poop deck hear about this! Ye reckon they'll believe me?"

"You'd better prepare for a shock," Roger said. "Frankly, there've been a few changes . . . "

"Trouble is, I got no proof," Luke said. "In the last three weeks I had two broken arms, a busted leg, six split lips, goshamighty knows how many busted ribs and bruises, lost six teeth, and been beat to death four times—and not even a blood blister to prove it!"

"You'll have to curb your tendency to exaggerate," Roger said. "We might be able to sell our story to the newspapers for a tidy sum, but not if you carry on like that."

"Funny thing is," Luke said, "there ain't nothing much to it—getting kilt, I mean. Just blap! And then you're waking up and starting all over."

"I suppose Bimbo is enough to unhinge anybody," Roger muttered sympathetically. "But let's not think about that part now, Mr. Harwood. Let's go find a telephone and start shopping around for a publisher."

Five minutes' walk brought them to the source of the gleam. It was a lighted window in a converted farmhouse, standing high and white above a slope of black lawn. The two men followed the flower-bordered drive—two strips of concrete, somewhat cracked but still serviceable—to a set of brick steps leading up onto the wide porch. Roger knocked. There was no response. He knocked again, louder. This time he thought he heard uncertain footsteps.

"Who . . . who's there?" a frightened female voice came from inside.

"My name is Tyson, ma'am," Roger called to the closed door. "I wonder if I might use your phone?"

A bolt clicked; the door opened half an inch. A woman's face appeared—at least one large, dark eye and the tip of her nose. For a moment she stared at him; then the door swung back. The woman—slim, middle-aged, still pretty—swayed as if she were about to fall. Roger stepped quickly forward, caught her elbow.

"Are you all right?"

"Yes—I—I—I—it's just . . . I thought . . . I was the only one left in the world!" She collapsed into his arms, weeping hysterically.

5

Half an hour later, their hostess restored to calm, they were seated at a table in the kitchen, sipping hot coffee and exchanging reports.

"So—I just settled down and made the best of it," Mrs. Withers said. "I guess it's been the most restful three months of my life."

"How have you managed?" Roger asked. "I mean for food."

Mrs. Withers went to the brown wooden ice-box, opened it.

"Every morning it's full again," she said. "The same things: the three slices of ham, the half-dozen eggs, the bottle of milk, some lettuce, left-overs. And there are the canned goods. I've eaten the same can of creamed corn forty times." A smile twitched at her face. "Luckily, I like creamed corn."

"And the ice?" Roger pointed at the half-melted block in the bottom compartment.

"It melts every day and every morning it's whole again. And the flowers: I cut them every day and bring them in and the next morning they're back outside, growing on the same stems. And once I cut myself on a can. It was a deep cut, but in the morning it was gone, not even a scar. At first, I tore a page off the calendar every day, but it came back. It never changes, you see. Nothing changes. The sky is the same, the same weather, even the same clouds. It's always the same day: August seventeenth, nineteen thirty-one."

"Actually . . ." Roger began.

"Skip it, son," Luke whispered behind his hand. "If she gets any comfort out of thinking it's twenty-two years in the future, let her."

"What would you say if I told you it was nineteen eighty-seven?"

"I'd say your mainstay's parted, son."

"I'd argue with you," Roger said. "Except that I wouldn't want my suspicions along those lines confirmed."

"What's happened, Mr. Tyson? What does it mean?" Mrs. Withers asked.

"We've fallen into a trap of some sort," Roger said. "It may be a natural phenomenon or an artificial one, but it has rules and limitations. We already know a few of them."

"Yes," Mrs. Withers nodded. "You *did* come here—from somewhere. Can we go back?"

"You wouldn't like it there," Roger said. "But I don't think we'll land in the same place. I haven't so far. There seems to be a series of these cages, all joined at one point—a sort of fourth-dimensional manifold. When we leave here, we'll probably step into another cell. But I'm hoping we'll eventually find ourselves outside."

"Mr. Tyson—may . . . may I go with you?"

"You can come along if you like," Roger agreed.

"I want to," Mrs. Withers. "But you *will* wait until morning?"

"I'll be glad of a night's sleep," Roger sighed. "I can't remember the last one I had."

Lying in a clean bed in a cozy room half an hour later, Roger looked at his watch. 12:20. There was no reason, of course, to expect that an arbitrarily designated midnight should have any special significance in terms of the physical laws now governing things, but nonetheless . . .

Time blinked.

There had been no physical shock, no sound, no change in the light. But *something* had happened. At 12:21 precisely, Roger noted the time. He looked around the room, in the almost total darkness saw nothing out of the ordinary. He went to the bed where Luke Harwood lay, bent to look at the man's face.

The scratches were gone. Roger touched his own bruised side, winced.

"It's a closed cycle, in time as well as space," he murmured. "Everything reverts to the state it was in twenty-four hours earlier—all but me. I'm different; my bruises collect. That being the case, let's hope tomorrow is an easier day than this one."

CHAPTER FOUR

1

Bright and early the following morning, the trio left the house carrying a small paper bag of food and a twenty-two-caliber rifle Mrs. Withers had produced along with three cartridges. Roger located the Aperture after a short search.

"We'd better stay close together," he said. "I suggest we hold hands, just to be sure we don't get separated and wind up in different localities."

Mrs. Withers offered a hand to each of her two escorts. Roger in the lead, they stepped forward—

—and emerged in deep twilight which gleamed on giant conifers spreading ice-crusted boughs in the stillness. Roger sank calf deep in the soft snow. The air was bitterly cold.

"That was a short day," Luke grunted. "Let's go back and try again."

"I should have thought of this," Roger said. "It must be below zero."

"I'll just run back and get coats," Mrs. Withers suggested.

"It doesn't work that way," Roger said. "We may wind up in a worse place than this. And while we're here, we may as well look around. For all we know, we're clear. There may be a road within fifty feet of us, a house just over the rise! We can't run away without even looking. Luke, you go that way"—he pointed up-slope—"and I'll check below. Mrs. Withers, you wait here. We'll be right back."

Luke nodded, looking unhappy, started off in the direction indicated. Roger patted the woman's arm and set off among the trees. Already, his hands and toes and ears ached as if pliers were clamped on them. His breath formed instantly into fog before his face. He had gone no more than a hundred feet when he saw the felled tree.

It was a small pine, a foot in diameter at the base, only lightly powdered with snow. Most of the branches had been trimmed off and were neatly stacked nearby. The stump was cleanly cut, as if by a sharp axe. Roger studied the ground for tracks, in a moment found them, partially filled by blown snow.

"Only a few hours old," he muttered half aloud. The tracks led directly up-slope. He started off, following them, not an easy task in the failing light. He had almost reached the ridge when the deep *boom!* of a gun shattered the arctic stillness.

For a moment Roger stood rigid, listening as the echoes of the single shot rang in the air. It had come from the right, the direction Luke Harwood had taken. He started off at a run. The drifted snow caught at his legs, dragging at him; the icy air burned in his throat. He fell back to a walk, scanning the shadowy forest all around for signs of life, detoured around a giant fallen tree, encountered deeper snow. He heard faint sounds of movement ahead, as of someone hurrying away through the snow.

"Wait!" Roger called, but his voice was only a weak croak. For an instant, panic gripped him, but he forced it down.

"Got to get out," he whispered. "Colder than I thought. Freezing. Find Luke, get back to Mrs. Withers . . . "

He stumbled on, his hands and feet numb now, forced his way through a tangle of dry, ice-coated brush, and saw a crumpled figure lying in the snow. It was Luke Harwood, lying on his back, a bullet hole in his chest, his sightless eyes already rimmed with frost.

2

There was nothing he could do for Luke, Roger saw. He turned and set off at a stumbling run for the spot where he had left Mrs. Withers. Ten minutes later he realized he was lost. He stood in the gathering dusk, staring about at ranks of identical trees. He shouted, but there was no answer.

"Poor Mrs. Withers," he thought, his teeth chattering. "I hope she goes back through before she freezes to death." He stumbled on a little farther. Then without remembering falling, he was lying softly cradled in the snow. The warm, cozy snow. All he had to do was curl up here and snooze a while, and later . . . when he was rested . . . try . . . again.

3

He awoke lying in a bed beside a hide-covered window aglow with watery daylight. A tall, gaunt, bearded man was standing over him, chewing his lower lip.

"Well, you're awake," Job Arkwright said. "Where was you headed anyways, stranger?"

"I . . . I . . . I . . . " Roger said. His hands and feet and nose hurt, but otherwise he seemed sound of mind and limb. "What happened? Who are you? How did I get here?" A sudden thought struck him. "Where is Mrs. Withers?"

"Your missus is all right. She's asleep." The gaunt man nodded toward a bunk above the one in which Roger lay.

"Say!" Roger sat bolt upright. "Are you the one that shot Luke?"

"Reckon so. Sorry about that. Friend o' yours, I s'pose. I took him for somebody else."

"Why?" Roger blurted.

"Reckon it was the bad light."

"I mean—why were you going to shoot somebody else?"

"Why, heck, I never even met your friend to talk to, much less shoot, leastwise on purpose."

"I mean—oh, never mind. Poor Luke. I wonder what his last thoughts were, all alone out in the snow."

"Dunno. Why don't you ast him?" The stranger stepped back and Luke Harwood stood there, grinning down at Roger.

"B-but you're dead!" Roger yelped. "I saw you myself! There was a hole in you as big as your thumb!"

"Old Betsy's bite's as mean as her bark," Arkwright said proudly. "You should of seed Fly Beebody, time I picked him out of a pine at a hundred yards. One of my finest shots. He'll be along any minute now; get him to tell you about it."

"I told ye getting killed don't mean shucks," Luke

said. "Job here done a clean job, never smarted a bit."

Roger flopped back with a groan. "I guess that means we're still stuck in the trap."

"Yes. But it could have been worse. At least Job here drug us inside out of the weather. I figger in your case, that saved yer skin."

There was a thumping at the door. A slim woman Roger hadn't noticed before opened it to admit a plump young fellow with a bundlesome overcoat and a resentful expression.

"The least thee could do, Brother Arkwright, would be to lay me out in Christian style after thee shoots me," he said as the woman took his coat and shook the snow from it.

"Don't like to see the remains cluttering up the place," Job said carelessly. "You ought to be thankful I let you in next morning."

"You mean—you actually shot that man?" Roger whispered hoarsely. "Intentionally?"

"Dern right. Caught him making up to Charity," he added in a lower tone. "That's my woman. Good cook, but flighty. And Fly's got a eye for the skinny ones. He goes along for a few days holding hisself under control, and then one day he busts loose and starts praising her corn meal mush, and I know it's time to teach him another lesson."

"How long has this been going on?"

"All winter. And it's been a blamed long winter, I'll tell you, stranger."

"Poor fellow! It must be ghastly for him!"

"Oh, I dunno. Sometimes he puts one over on me and gets me first. But he's a mighty poor shot. Plugged Charity once, by mistake, jist like I plugged your sidekick."

"Bloodcurdling!"

"Oh, Charity gets in her licks, too. She nailed the both of us once. Didn't care for it, though, she said afterward. Too lonesome. Now she alternates."

"You mean—she's likely to shoot you without notice—just like that?"

"Yep. But I calculate a man's got to put up with a few little quirks in a female."

"Good Lord!"

"Course, I don't much cotton to the idea of what goes on over my dead body—but I guess, long as she's a widder, it don't rightly count."

Charity Arkwright approached with a steaming bowl on a tray.

"Job, you go see to the kindling whilst I feed this nice young man some gruel," she said, giving Roger a bright smile.

"Thanks, anyway," Roger said quickly, recoiling. "I'm allergic to all forms of gruel."

"Look here, stranger," Job growled. "Charity's a good cook. You ought to try a little."

"I'm sure she's wonderful," Roger gulped. "I just don't want any."

"That sounds mighty like a slur to me, stranger!"

"No slur intended! It's just that I had a bad experience with my oatmeal as a child, and ever since I've been afraid to try again!"

"I bet I could help you with your problem," Charity offered, looking concerned. "The way I do it, it just melts in your mouth."

"Tell you what, Miz Charity," Luke Harwood put in. "I'll take a double helping—just to show ye ye're appreciated."

"Don't rush me, mister!" Charity said severely. "I'll get around to you when it's your turn!"

"Hey, stranger," Job said. "Your missus is awake; reckon she'd like some?"

"No! She hates the stuff!" Roger said, scrambling out of bed to find himself clad only in ill-fitting long johns. "Give me my clothes! Luke, Mrs. Withers, let's get out of here!"

"Now, hold on, partner! You're the first variety we've had around this place in shucks knows how long! Don't go getting huffy jist over a little breakfast food!"

"It's not the food—it's the prospect of getting to know Betsy better. Besides which, we started out to find a way out of this maze, not just to settle down being snowbound!"

"I swan," Charity said. "And me the finest gruel-maker west of the Missouri! Never thought I'd see the day when I couldn't give it away!"

"Mister, I reckon you got a few things to learn about frontier hospitality," Job said grimly, lifting a wide-mouth muzzle-loader down from above the door and aiming it at Roger's chin. "I don't reckon nobody ain't leaving here until they've at least tried it."

"I'm convinced," Luke said.

"How do you like it?" Charity inquired. "Plain, or with sugar and cream?"

"Goodness, what's all this talk about gruel?" Mrs. Withers inquired from her bunk, sitting up. "I've got a good mind to show you my crêpes suzettes."

"I never went in for none of them French specialties," Job said doubtfully. "But I could learn."

"Well, I like that!" Charity snapped. "I guess plain old country style's not good enough any more!"

"Well," Mrs. Withers said. "If it's all you can get . . ."

"Why, you scrawny little city sparrer!" Charity screeched, and leaped for the rival female. Roger yelled and lunged to intercept her. Job Arkwright's gun boomed like a cannon; the slug caught Charity under the ribs and hurled her across the room.

"Hey! I never meant—" That was as far as Arkwright

got. The boom of a two-barreled derringer in the hands
of Fly Beebody roared out. The blast knocked the
bearded man backward against the door, which flew
open under the impact, allowing him to pitch backward into the snow. As Roger staggered to his feet, a
baroque shape loomed in the opening. Metallic tentacles rippled, bearing a rufous tuber shape, one-eyed,
many-armed, into the cabin.

"Help!" Roger shouted.

"Saints preserve us!" Luke yelled.

"Beelzebub!" squealed Fly Beebody, and fired his
second round into the alien body at pointblank range.
The bullet struck with a fruity *smack!*, spattering
carroty material; but the creature turned, apparently
unaffected, fixed his immense ocular on the parson.
It rippled toward him, grasping members outstretched.

Roger grabbed a massive hand-hewn chair, swung
it up, and brought it down with tremendous force atop
the blunt upper end of the monstrosity. It toppled
under the blow, rolled in a short arc like an overturned
milk bottle, threshed its tentacles briefly, and was still.

"Now will you leave?" Roger inquired in the silence.

"I'll go with thee!" Beebody yelped. "Satan has taken
over this house in spite of my prayers!"

"We can't leave this thing here," Roger said. "We'll
have to take it along; otherwise it will be the first thing
to greet them in the morning!" He took a blanket from
the bed and rolled the creature in it.

"Best ye stay here, girl," Luke said to Mrs. Withers. "Lord knows what we'll run into next."

"Stay here—with *them?*"

"They'll be themselves again tomorrow."

"That's what I'm afraid of!"

"Well, then; ye better don Charity's cloak."

"We'll leave the coats at the Aperture," Roger said.
"In the morning, they'll be back here."

"I'll leave the can of soup," Mrs. Withers said as they prepared to step out into the sub-zero night. "I think Mr. Arkwright was getting a little tired of the same old gruel."

Outside, the wind struck at Roger's frost-nipped face like a spiked board. He pulled his borrowed muffler up around his ears, hefted his end of the shrouded alien, led the way up into the dark forest, following tracks made earlier that morning by Luke.

It was a fifteen-minute hike through blowing snow to the spot among the trees where they had arrived. All of them except Beebody stripped off their heavy outer garments; Roger took the blanket-sack over his shoulder, held Mrs. Withers' hand, while Luke and Beebody joined to form a shivering line, like children playing a macabre game.

"Too bad we couldn't even leave them a note," Roger said. He approached the faint-glowing line, which widened, closed in about him, and opened out into brilliant sunlight on a beach of red sand.

CHAPTER FIVE

1

Fly Beebody hunkered on his knees, his fingers interlaced, babbling prayers in a high, shrill voice. Luke stood staring around curiously. Mrs. Withers stood near him, still shivering, hugging herself. Roger dumped his burden at his feet, savoring the grateful heat. The sun, halfway to zenith, glared blindingly on choppy blue water, sand, and rock.

"No signs of life," Luke said. "Where would ye say we are, Roger?"

"That's hard to say. In the tropics, apparently. But what part of the tropics is as barren as this?"

He knelt, studied the sandy ground. "No weeds, no insects." He walked down across the loose sand to the water's edge, bent, and scooped up water in his hand and tasted it. It was curiously flat and insipid. No fish swam in the shallows, no moss grew on the rocks, no seaweed drifted on the tide.

"No seashells," he called. "Just a little green scum on the water." As he turned to start back, he became suddenly aware of the sunlight beating down at him, the drag of gravity. He sucked air into his lungs, fighting a sense of suffocation that swept over him. Ahead, Fly Beebody's chanting had broken off; he half rose, bundlesome in the blanket coat, his mouth opening and closing like a fish. Luke was struggling to support the widow, who sagged against him. Roger broke into a stumbling run.

"Back!" he called. "Get back through! Bad air!" He reached the group, caught the woman's limp hand.

"Grab Beebody's hand!" he gasped to Harwood. He caught up the bundle. As his vision began to fade into a whirling fog of flickering lights, he groped forward, found the Aperture, half-fell through it.

2

He lay in warm, foul-smelling water, his arms buried to the elbows in soft muck, breathing in great lungfuls of humid, steaming air. A dragonfly with gauzy, foot-long wings hovered a yard away among the finger-thick stems of giant cattails, buzzing like an electric fan. As he sat up, it darted away, eerie, pre-storm sunlight glinting on its polished green body. Beside him, Luke struggled to his feet, black with reeking mud, dragged Mrs. Withers upright. Beebody floundered, spitting sulphurous water.

Standing among reeds higher than his head, Roger could see nothing but more of the same, stretching away endlessly in all directions.

"This must be an era between periods of mountain building," he said. "There was very little dry land on the planet then. I suppose we're lucky we didn't end up treading deep water."

There was a sudden splash near at hand, a sound

of violent threshing in the water. The source was invisible through the screen of reeds, but spray flew up from a point twenty feet away and ripples moved toward the sodden travelers. A deep hoot sounded, like a breathy foghorn. The sounds of struggle grew louder, closer. As Roger floundered toward the portal, a finned snake as big around as his thigh burst into view, wrapped around and around a short-snouted crocodile whose jaws were clamped hard in the sinuous body. The struggling pair threshed through the reeds in a churn of crimsoned water. Roger jumped for the ribbon of light, pulling Mrs. Withers after him. There was the flash of prismatic color—

—then a cold rain was driving at him, swirled into his face by a gusty wind. Through the whirling sheets of water, a cluster of sagging, irregularly shaped tents was visible, their sodden leather coverings, marked with crude symbols, whipping in the wind.

"This doesn't look promising," Luke shouted above the sounds of the storm. "I say let's move on without waiting to get acquainted."

"Why be hasty?" Roger countered. "For all we know, we're outside—" He broke off as a bearded, dark-faced man thrust his head from the nearest tent flap. For a moment their eyes met; then the man plunged, grabbing for a short, curved sword slung at his side, and advanced, yelling.

By common assent, the party joined hands and plunged back through the shimmering barrier.

3

They were on a great veldt, where endless herds of game grazed and vultures circled overhead. Luke and

Mrs. Withers stood by the Aperture to mark it while Roger and Beebody, the latter still bundled, sweating in his coat, walked away through the sea of chest-high grass.

Fifteen minutes later, they approached the same spot from behind.

"Still trapped," Roger said. "Let's go on."

They passed . . . through—

—and were . . . on a mountainside above a wide valley with a lake far below. They went on, found themselves on a wide tundra, where far away a pair of huge, shaggy animals lumbered, head-down, into the biting wind. Next, they splashed knee-deep in cold water, near a guano-whitened headland where seabirds circled, crying. After that, there was a dry, brush-choked gorge that led back onto itself when Roger explored its twisting length. Then a bamboo thicket beside a wide, muddy river, under a gray, humid sky.

"It's a marvel how much dreary landscape the world has to offer," Luke panted after a quarter of an hour of splashing through the shallows had led them back to their starting point.

"We'll have to try again," Roger said. "We can't stay here." He swatted one of the huge, inquisitive mosquitoes that swarmed about their heads. They stepped once more through the Aperture—

—and were . . . in a wide field of flowers, under a balmy sky. All around, wooded hills rose to an encircling ring of snow-capped peaks. A small falls tumbled down over a rocky outcropping nearby, feeding a clear river that wound off across the plain.

"How beautiful!" Mrs. Withers exclaimed. "Roger—Luke—can't we stay here awhile?"

"I'm wearied with this scrambling from one climate

to the next," Luke agreed. "And we're no closer to escape than ever."

"It suits me," Roger said. "And I'm hungry. Let's get a fire going and rustle a meal."

After they ate, Mrs. Withers wandered off, picking the crimson poppies and yellow buttercups that abounded there, accompanied, grumbling, by Luke. Roger stretched out on the grass by the Aperture, Beebody squatting uncomfortably beside him.

"Master Roger," the parson said awkwardly after the others had passed out of earshot. "I . . . I propose that we come to terms, thee and me."

"About what?"

Beebody hunkered closer. "As thee see, thy strength avails naught against mine. Try as thee will to draw my soul into Hell, still I resist, sustained by prayer and righteousness."

"Try to get this, Beebody," Roger said. "As far as I'm concerned, you can keep your soul. All I want is a way out of here."

"Aye—a path back into the Pit thee came from!" Beebody hissed. "Think thee not I can smell the brimstone on thee—and on the imp who takes the form of Luke? Did I not mark how thee two stood against thy fellow demon, sent no doubt by thee to slay Job Arkwright and his mistress." His eyes went to the bundle. "And think thee not I understand why thee was so set on bearing the foul remains of thy ally with us?"

"Go to sleep, Fly," Roger said. "You'll need all the rest you can get."

"I have prayed and meditated, even as by the strength of my virtue I kept thee from the path thee seek; and it comes to me now that, to preserve my earthly husk to continue the struggle against sin, it would be meet to come to agreement with thee. Otherwise will we both exhaust ourselves."

"Come to the point," Roger said roughly. "What do you want?"

"Take the woman," Beebody whispered. "Spare me! Return me to the true world, and I'll omit thee in my curses!"

"You're an amazing man, Fly," Roger said, studying the cherubic face, the worried eyes. "Suppose I take you, and free Odelia instead?"

"Nay, demon, my works are needed in the sinful world of fallen man! I cannot allow such a victory to the Dark One!"

"Your concern for the populace is touching," Roger said, "but—" He broke off as Fly Beebody's eyes went past him, widening. The fat man rose to his feet, pointing. Roger turned to look. A shaggy brown bear had appeared at the edge of the forest, a hundred feet distant. It moved forward confidently, directly toward the two men.

"I yield!" Beebody babbled. "Send not this new devil to me! I consent to join with thee, to aid thee in thy fell designs! Take the woman! I'll help thee now! I'll fight thee no longer!"

"Shut up, you jackass!" Roger snapped. "Luke!" he called. "Get Mrs. Withers through the Aperture!"

Luke and Mrs. Withers started back at a run. The bear, interested in the activity, broke into a heavy gallop. "Beebody!" Roger shouted. "Help me distract him until they're clear!" From the corner of his eye, he saw the parson move—in the opposite direction. He turned in time to see him lift the bagged alien, swing the bulky bundle toward the Aperture.

"Fly! Don't! You might be dumping that monster in among defenseless people!" Roger grabbed for the blanket, but Beebody resisted with surprising strength. For a moment they struggled back and forth, Beebody red of face and rattling off appeals to a Higher Power,

Roger casting looks over his shoulder at the rapidly approaching animal, and at Luke and Odelia Withers, coming up fast from the right.

Suddenly his foot slipped. He felt himself whirled about, off balance. He tottered back, saw the glint of the Aperture expanding around him, saw Beebody's flushed face, Luke and the woman behind him, and beyond, the open jaws of the bear.

The daylight winked out—

—to be replaced by an all-enclosing gray. For an instant, Roger teetered on one toe, struggling for balance. Then a giant hand closed on his body, yanked him up, around, and out into the brilliant light of a vast, white-floored room.

4

He stood half-dazed, staring around at looming banks of gleaming apparatus under a glowing ceiling that arched overhead like an opaque sky, hearing the soft hum and whine of machinery that filled the air. Nearby stood half a dozen sharp-eyed men with excellent physiques shown off by form-fitting outfits in various tasteful colors.

One of the men stepped forward, emitted a sharp, burping sound, looking at Roger warningly.

"I hear the Asiatics do that after dinner," Roger said in a tone close to hysteria. "But I never heard of using it as a greeting."

"Hmmm. Pattern noted: Subject either fails to understand, or pretends to fail to understand Speedspeak. I will therefore employ Old Traditional." He eyed Roger sternly. "I was just advising you that disorganizer beams are focused on you. Make no attempt to employ high-order mental powers, or we will be forced to stimulate your pain centers to level nine or above."

"B-b-b-b," Roger said.

"Your behavior has puzzled us," the man went on in a cool, mellow voice. "We have followed your path through the Museum. It appears aimless. Since this is incompatible with your identity, it follows that your motives are of an order of complexity not susceptible to cybernetic analysis. It therefore becomes necessary to question you. It is for this reason that we have taken the risk of grappling you from the Channel."

"My m-motives?" Roger gulped. "Look here, you fellows have got the wrong idea."

"You continue to broadcast meaningless images of flight and primitive fear," his inquisitor stated. "These delaying tactics will not be tolerated." A swift flash of pain tingled along Roger's bones.

"What was the principle underlying your choice of route?" the questioner demanded.

"There wasn't any!" Roger yelped as the pain nipped him again.

"Hmmm. His movements *do* fit in with a random factor of the twelfth order," a second man spoke up. "It appears the situation is more complex than we imagined."

"His appearance here at this particular juncture is a most provocative datum," another pointed out. "It suggests a surveillance aspect we've failed heretofore to include in our computations."

"He's obviously an incredibly tough individual, capable of enduring any mere psychophysical stimulus without breaking," a man in powder blue contributed. "Otherwise he would never have been dispatched on his errand—whatever that might be."

"In that case, we may as well proceed at once to

mechanical mind-stripping techniques," a lemon-yellow Adonis proposed. There was a soft *click!* and a large, white-enameled, blunt-snouted machine like a gigantic dentist's drill swung into position directly over Roger.

"Wait a minute!" he protested, and attempted to back away, only to discover that he was paralyzed—rooted to the spot. "What's the big idea?" he blurted. "Let me out of here! For all you know, I had important business pending back where I came from! I might have been on my way to land a high-pay, low-work job! I could have been rushing to marry the richest and most beautiful woman in the Middle West! I might even have been on my way to Washington to deliver information vital to national security!"

"What a mind-shield!" a man in raspberry pink said admiringly, studying his dials. "If I didn't know better, I'd swear he was only a high-grade moron with an IQ scarcely above one hundred forty."

"That's it!" Roger agreed. "Now we're getting somewhere! I don't know who you gentlemen think I am, but I'm not! I'm Roger Tyson, gentleman adventurer—"

"Come now," the man in blue said kindly. "Do you expect us to believe that your appearance in the Museum today—if you'll pardon the expression—just as we are about to launch our long-awaited probe mission down the null-temporal Axis is sheer coincidence?"

"Absolutely," Roger said fervently. "As a matter of fact, I haven't the faintest idea where I am now. Or"—a look of dawning wonder appeared on his face—"*when* I am!"

"Our era is the twenty-third decade after the Forcible Unification. About twenty-two forty-nine, Old Calendar—as if you didn't know."

"Three hundred years in the future?" Roger's voice failed. He swallowed a golf ball that had lodged in his throat. "I guess it figures. I should have known—"

"We wander afield, S'lunt," a man in deep purple interrupted. "Jump-off hour approaches. Now, quickly, fellow! What was your mission?"

There was a small stir at the edge of the circle of men, but Roger scarcely noticed, due to a sensation like an aching tooth centered in the small of his back.

"Explain the nature of the binding forces subsumed in the Rho complex!"

A heavy boot trod on the tip of a long tail Roger had never suspected he possessed.

"Define the nature and alignment matrices of the pulse guides!"

A blunt saw amputated Roger's antlers. The horns, he saw, squinting upward through a haze of pain, were imaginary, but the attendant sensations were vividly real.

"Enumerate the coordinate systems postulated in the syllogistical manipulations, and specify the axial rotations employed!"

A wrecker's ball swung from somewhere and flattened him to a thin paste.

"Hmmm. I have a feeling this entire procedure is illegal, under the provisions of Spool Nine Eighty-Seven of the Social Motivation Code!" someone whispered in Roger's ear.

"I demand a lawyer!" Roger squalled.

"Eh?" the man in blue inquired. He turned to his chartreuse-clad associate. "R'heet, run a quick semantic analysis of that utterance, in the fourth and twelfth modes, with special attention to connotational resonances of the second category."

"This whole thing is illegal!" Roger yelled. "Under Spool, uh, Nine Eighty-Seven of the Social, uh, Motivation Code!"

"How's that?" The man called S'lunt eyed Roger sharply. "How do you know of the Code?"

"*What difference does that make?*" the voice hissed. "*Illegal is illegal!*"

"What does that matter?" Roger echoed. "Illegal is illegal!"

"Why, er, as to that . . . "

"*Just because we're faced with an emergency, there's no reason to stoop to totalitarian techniques!*"

"That's right," Roger nodded vigorously. "Just because there's an emergency, is no reason to act like Hitler!"

"I don't know, S'lunt," the pink-garbed dial watcher said. "These readings are persistently in the retarded sector. I have a sneaking suspicion we may have made a mistake."

"You mean—he's *not* an agent of the Entity?"

"Of course not!" Roger shouted. "I'm just a poor wayfaring stranger named Roger Tyson!"

"In that case, why did he register so strongly on our gamitron detectors?"

"*Maybe the varpilators need adjusting.*"

"Better check your varpilators," Roger said quickly.

"Say—that's a thought—but—"

"*And while you're at it, you might just realign the transfrication rods.*"

"And take a look at the transfrication rods!"

"See here, you seem to know a great deal about Culture One technical installations," S'lunt said accusingly.

"*Maybe you're from our future, and have an interest in history.*"

"That's right, how do you know I'm not from the future, hah?"

"Say—in that case, he could tell us what's going to happen next back home!"

"Gad! What an exciting prospect!" S'lunt said eagerly. "Tell me, sir, how did General Minerals do on the big board in fifty?"

"Did that intelligent slime-mould on Venus turn out to be alive?"

"Did they ever get the LBJ Memorial Asteroid towed out of the Mars-Terra space lane?"

"It's kind of hard for me to remember while I'm paralyzed with my neck at this angle," Roger pointed out.

"Dear me, forgive me, sir!" S'lunt flicked a switch and Roger felt himself unfreeze.

"R'heet, get our guest a chair. How about a little draught of medicinal alcohol, sir?"

"Thanks; don't mind if I do." Roger accepted the libation, sank into the seat, which squirmed sensually, adapting itself to his contours.

"Now, you were saying about the election of fifty-two . . . ?"

"The, ah, dark horse won," Roger improvised. "By the way, how about letting me out of this place now?"

"Did the Immortality Bill pass?"

"By a landslide. If you don't mind I'd like to just be dropped at the edge of town—any town."

"By george, what did Alpha Expedition Three report?"

"Dense fog," Roger replied tersely. "And if it's all the same to you, I'd like to get going now, before—"

"Amazing! Did you hear that, R'heet? Dense fog!"

"Incredible!"

"Ahem. What did history record as to the attainments of Technor Fourth Class S'lunt?"

"Yours was a dizzying career. I wonder, while you're at it, could you just make that Chicago? I've got a brother-in-law there. Well, not exactly a brother-in-law; actually he's the brother of a girl who was engaged to the fellow who later married my sister's husband's brother—but you know what I mean."

"I wonder if those hemlines ever went down again?

I mean, for some girls it's all right, but if you don't happen to have a cute navel . . . "

"What about my General Minerals shares?" S'lunt inquired plaintively.

"They dropped to the ankle," Roger announced.

"Good Lord! But I assume they recovered and rose again? Probably higher than ever, eh?"

"Actually, they went even lower than that," Roger groped. "Of course, there was a corresponding adjustment at the top."

"Well, I should think so! That scoundrel F'hoot should never have been elected Chairman of the Board!"

"At the top? Wouldn't that be rather revealing?"

"In the end, the whole thing was exposed," Roger amplified desperately. "But about my going home . . . "

"Well, I'm glad to hear that F'hoot's chicanery was brought out in the open," S'lunt commented.

"I really shouldn't be thinking about fashions at a time like this, but I just can't help wondering what eventually happened to women's clothes."

"What about the rest of the Board?" S'lunt asked.

"Uh, they finally got rid of them entirely," Roger said, "but—"

"Goodness!"

"You don't mean . . . they did away with the whole capitalistic system?" R'heet exclaimed.

"It was a good thing, actually." Roger attempted to justify the implication. "It put an end to all that speculating."

"Gracious! I'm glad I never lived to see it!"

"Hrumph! Well, I hope it doesn't happen in my time!" a man in blue put in.

"Actually, it'll be along in the very near future, so how about turning me loose and concentrating your attention on your investments?"

"It appears I'll be stripped of my holdings entirely!" S'lunt predicted.

"History records that everyone was allowed to keep the bare essentials."

"B-but—what about when it got cold?"

"It's an outrage! I'm to be beggared—at my time of life?"

"With your reputation, I'm sure you'll find a partner with money," Roger suggested. "He'll probably have some way-out ideas to try, too."

"Why, of all the impertinent suggestions!"

"I'm too old," S'lunt mourned. "Too old to start again."

"You don't want to just sit on the sidelines and watch, do you, while the others have all the fun?"

"No . . . I suppose not," S'lunt sighed. "But it is rather depressing news."

"It sounds like an orgy!"

"It's not that bad," Roger said. "Just a mild depression. Afterwards things really got exciting—"

"It's outrageous! The whole world running around stark naked!"

"Who said anything about being stark naked?" Roger demanded.

There was a sharp gasp from the periphery of Roger's fascinated audience. A slim black-haired figure, exuberantly female in white skin-tights, thrust to the fore, pointed a finger at Roger.

"Put the disorganizer beam back on him, quick!" she cried. "He's a spy! He's been reading my mind!"

Roger came to his feet with a leap, staring at the newcomer. "Y-y-y-you!" he stuttered.

It was the girl he had left for dead beside the crashed motorcycle.

CHAPTER SIX

1

"I'm no spy!" Roger shouted over the hubbub that greeted the girl's dramatic charge. "I was just an ordinary citizen, going about my business, until *she* came along!"

"I've never seen this person before in my life," his accuser stated coldly.

"You gave me the message!" Roger countered. "You said it was of vast importance, and that—"

"What message?" she demanded.

"The one you gave me after you were dead! You made me steal that vegetable's motorcycle and go into the men's room!"

"He's raving," Q'nell said. "S'lunt, you'd better disassociate him at once! I'm sure he's part of some sort of plot to abort our probe!"

"Just a moment," S'lunt said. "What was that about a message?"

"S'lunt! Technor S'lunt? It was addressed to you!" Roger blurted. "I remember now!"

"What was the substance of this message?"

"She said she'd been, ah, partially successful, that was it!"

"Yes—go on?"

"I, ah, don't exactly remember the rest, but . . . "

"How unfortunate," S'lunt said grimly. "Just where is it you claim to have met Q'nell?"

"A few miles outside of the town of Mongoose, Ohio! In a rainstorm! At one o'clock in the morning!"

"Highly circumstantial," Q'nell conceded. "However, inasmuch as I have never been near Mongoose, Ohio, particularly in a rainstorm, your story doesn't hold up."

"There was an accident!" Roger insisted. "You, er, fell off your machine, and I rushed forward to render aid!"

"How selfless of you," the girl replied icily. "However—"

"That was when you told me to take that little gold button and put it in my ear!"

A shocked silence greeted this remark. Q'nell put a hand up, touched her ear.

"Why, he's talking about the Reinforcer," S'lunt said.

"Look!" R'heet pointed. All eyes went to Roger's ear. He angled his head to give them a better view.

"You see?" he said. "There it is, just like I said!"

"That's impossible," a man in mauve gasped. "There is only one Reinforcer, as we know only too well!"

"And I'm wearing it!" Q'nell stated emphatically.

"No, you're not!" Roger contradicted. "I took it, just like you told me to, and—"

"Look!" She turned her head. The gold button gleamed dully in her ear.

"I wonder!" S'lunt said suddenly. "Q'nell—you say the fellow was reading your mind?"

Q'nell nodded curtly.

"There is one possible explanation . . . " S'lunt looked thoughtfully at Roger. "What is she thinking at this moment?"

"Ah . . . she's thinking I'd be kind of cute if my nose wasn't so big . . . " He broke off to finger his nose and dart a resentful glance at the girl.

"Q'nell, can you detect his thoughts?"

"Why . . . I don't know . . . " She cocked her head as if listening. She gasped. "Well, of all the fresh things!"

"You heard him?"

"I heard *someone!*"

"It was me," Roger confirmed smugly.

"S'lunt, you were about to offer an explanation," R'heet reminded him.

"Yes. It's a bit fantastic, but then what isn't these days? We're preparing to launch our probe in exactly thirty-three minutes. Suppose we do so—and that the attempt is partially successful, as this chap stated Q'nell had reported. That would imply that rather than tracing the Channel to its origin, the mission was aborted at some point short thereof—possibly in the locality of Mongoose, Ohio. If Q'nell then encountered this person—"

"Tyson. Roger Tyson."

"You mean—she's already gone!" R'heet looked puzzled.

"Not yet. Still, in the future she will have gone, and if subsequently a message regarding her attempt were transmitted back here to us, via this rather unlikely messenger—"

"Tyson's the name. Roger—"

"But—she was to be dispatched in a retrogressive direction! Thus, if she did drop out of the Channel along the way, it would have been in the past—and this man comes from the future, as demonstrated by his encyclopedic grasp of upcoming developments.

"Perhaps our assumptions regarding the orientation of the manifold were in error; but that's a detail we can work out later. At the moment, the question is:

What was the substance of the message which Q'nell will send back?"

"Look here, fellow—" R'heet started.

"Tyson," Roger supplied. "I'm sorry about the message. It was something about rocks, I remember that."

"Well, I suppose we might as well deploy the mind-stripper again," R'heet said ominously.

"Hold it! I just remembered something else. Something about sending a, ah, null-engine to . . . to the terminal to, er, break something or other!"

"A null-engine? But that would be a measure of desperation!" R'heet muttered.

"Still, it hangs together," S'lunt pointed out. "Your mission, Q'nell, was to determine the nature of the Entity, and attempt to deal with it. Failing that, alternatives were to be explored.

"And it seems the former approach failed. Leaving us no choice but to plunge all the way to the terminal coordinates and shatter the time lock utterly!"

"Ummmm. That being the case, we'd best extract what we can from this fellow—"

"Tyson. Roger Tyson."

"—and get on with it."

"Wait!" Q'nell said sharply. "If what you're saying is correct—then his story is also true! He must have come to my assistance and then undertaken to deliver my message just out of sheer altruism! Are we to reward him by boiling his brain and leaving him a babbling idiot?"

"Hmmm. Seems a little ungrateful," S'lunt conceded. "Still—we need to know all we can before you go."

"You mean you're still sending her on this mission—knowing she'll be killed?" Roger charged. "Why don't you just let me and all your other victims out of our cages and call the whole operation off!"

"I'm afraid you have an erroneous grasp of matters,"

S'lunt said in the surprised silence that greeted this proposal. "We're as much prisoners of the Museum as you seem to be. And unless we can solve the mystery of its construction—soon—we will all remain trapped here, for all eternity!"

2

"When we first discovered ourselves to be entoiled in a trap," S'lunt explained, leading the way out onto an unrailed terrace jutting over an orderly landscape half a mile below, "we of Culture One refused to panic. The enclave, happily, included the laboratory complex you see about you. We at once set to work to establish the parameters of our situation."

Roger held back as the others started across a yard-wide walkway arching over empty space to the adjoining structure. S'lunt gave him an interrogatory glance. "Why are you crouching in that fashion, sir?"

"It's just a thing I've got about heights," Roger confided. "Suppose I just wait here."

"Nonsense. I insist you join us on the pinnacle for a cuppa."

"You go ahead, then. I'll follow in my own way."

"Our studies," S'lunt said, strolling slowly as Roger progressed on all fours at his side, "have not been entirely fruitless. We have made certain determinations regarding the nature of the spatio-temporal distortion. Using a special tracer beam to follow our explorers through the point of tangency through which it is possible to pass from one display to another, we have determined that a progressive degeneration of temporal binding forces is at work, allowing artifacts and fauna of each era to wander into anachronistic settings, thus engendering

massive energy imbalances which must end in disaster!
On the basis of those findings, we designed and constructed the Reinforcer. With the aid of this device, the
selected agent would, we hoped, be enabled to pass not
only transversely across the Museum, but longitudinally
along the Axial Channel as well, thus tracing the phenomenon to its source, and, hopefully, discovering the
identity of the power behind it."

"How do you know it's a museum?" Roger inquired.
He opened one eye and quickly closed it again.

"An assumption. The displays present a panorama
of Terrestrial history from the dawn of life to its even-
tual sublimation."

"Then—why not just find another, ah, display, from
the distant future where they have even more advanced
science that you folks here in Culture One and—"

"Impossible. In the first place, the displays number
ten billion, four hundred and four million, nine hundred and forty-one thousand, six hundred and two.
Thus, investigating them at the rate of one per minute,
the time required—"

"I get the idea," Roger interrupted. "What's the second place?"

"It would be the merest chance if we happened on
a center of population or a scientific installation which
would afford the necessary hardware, even if we succeeded in pinpointing a suitably advanced culture. So
we have devoted the available time and manpower to
the probe scheme."

"Say, that reminds me . . . " Roger said as he rose
to his feet on the far side, where tables were placed
under gay-colored umbrellas. "Some friends of mine
were about to be eaten by a bear. How about just
fetching them along here the way you did me?"

"Impossible. In your case, we were able to trace your
movements via the emanations of the Reinforcer—

though we didn't understand the nature of the signal at the time. But I'm afraid there's nothing we can do about the others. However, don't fret. They'll be right as rain after Turnover."

"Another thing I just remembered: I had some, uh, baggage with me . . ."

"Lost, I'm afraid. You must have dropped it when we put the grappler on you. Don't fret, however, I can lend you whatever you need."

"See here, Tyson," R'heet steered the conversation back to the problem at hand. "You might be a big help to us, having wandered through a number of the displays. Why don't you just let us strip down your brain a little—we'll leave you with the ability to feed yourself and possibly even tie your own shoelaces—"

"You can't!" Q'nell said promptly.

"Q'nell, your scruples are interfering with the orderly exploration of the facts," R'heet complained. "If I'd realized you were so emotional, I'd never have offered to sign a cohabitation agreement with you!"

"No need to upset yourself," Q'nell said coolly. "It has nothing to do with emotion. But have you stopped to think that his brain is linked to mine by an identical Reinforcer? You see the obvious corollary, I assume."

"Hmmm. If we squeeze his brain, the harmonics will destroy your mind as well."

"Too bad, fellows," Roger said. "Much as I'd like to help you out, I can't see letting the little lady suffer."

"I don't suppose we could remove the Reinforcer?" a man in puce vestments said doubtfully.

"You know better than that, D'olt. The filamentary system is inextricably intermingled with T'son's neural circuitry. Tampering with it would instantly prove fatal, as it did when T'son here removed it from Q'nell."

"You mean—I killed her?" Tyson blurted. "Good night, Miss Q'nell—excuse me!"

"It's nothing. If I ordered you to do so, I doubtless had my reasons."

"You're certainly being a sport about it," Roger said admiringly.

"We citizens of Culture One seldom descend to the level of purely emotional reactions," the girl stated calmly.

"Oh, really?" Roger raised an eyebrow. "I seem to recall seeing you blush just a few minutes ago."

"My physiological reactions system bears no relationship to my intellectually determined course of action," Q'nell snapped.

"Ah-ah! Anger, anger!" Roger said playfully. "Actually you're not a bad-looking girl at all, you know. Why don't you and I—"

"May I remind you, T'son," R'heet put in, "that I have offered Q'nell a cohabitation contract. Your attentions are therefore unwelcome."

"Well, let's just see what she says about that . . . "

"I say that it's only twelve minutes until jump-off," Q'nell said flatly. "I'd better be getting into position."

"Don't let her do it! She'll be killed!" Roger protested.

"Possibly not," R'heet said calmly. "The change in the nature of her mission from exploratory probe to a bombing run introduces a new factor into the equation."

"You're a cold-blooded one!" Roger said. "At least delay the launch! Give me time to try to remember the rest of what she said!"

"No delay is possible," S'lunt put in. "The cyclical nature of the phenomenon requires that the attempt be within six hours, or never—at least not for another hundred and twelve years, by which time the deterioration of the temporal matrix will have progressed to the point where the entire space-time continuum will collapse on itself, with disastrous results!"

"Then wait six hours! There's no use going before the last second!"

"Turnover is in fifteen minutes. At that time, of course, the Reinforcer, if still in this temporal matrix, will revert to its constituent parts. Thus, let us make haste."

"But—but you can't send a girl like that out alone with a bomb!"

S'lunt made a burping sound at R'heet, who belched a reply. S'lunt turned to Roger with outstretched hand.

"Capital!" he said. "R'heet and I have discussed the matter in depth, and we agree there's no reason to refuse your courageous offer!"

"What offer?"

"To accompany her, of course! Let's hurry along, now! There's just time to pump the canned hypno-briefing into you before you go!"

3

"Comfort yourself, T'son," S'lunt said in a tone of easy assurance as he and the half dozen other launch technicians studied their instrument readings. "The perceptor circuits indicate that you have correctly absorbed your briefing and are now as aware as necessary of the parameters within which you will function. Everything is in readiness for your departure. Q'nell has the null-engine tucked away in her pocket, armed and ready. No point in waiting."

Glumly, Roger allowed himself to be escorted across the wide milk-glass floor to the spot where Q'nell waited beside a vast coil of thick white-painted tubing. R'heet emitted a terse *blap!* as he came up.

"I don't savvy the local Speedspeak," Roger said, noting the girl's pert features, short-clipped jet-black hair, and appealingly pink lips, slightly parted to show perfect teeth. "What was that all about?"

Q'nell gave him a glance which had receded several degrees toward the impersonal.

"He was just mentioning that your fear index was rising steadily. If it ascends another point or two, you'll be rigid with terror."

"Oh, I will, will I?" Roger said hotly. "Well, go check your dials, buster! Sure, I'm a little nervous! Who wouldn't be? For all I know, when I step into that thing I may wind up on an ice floe with a polar bear—or in the midst of a dinosaur's lunch—or swimming in the middle of the Indian Ocean—or—" His voice rose higher as a succession of images presented themselves, none of them pleasant.

"Oh, no danger of that," S'lunt said encouragingly. "Once launched along the Channel proper, you'll be outside the Museum entirely, moving in a physical context regarding the exact nature of which we can make only the vaguest conjectures."

"I remember you saying something like that, but I didn't know what it meant," Roger said. "By the way, what *does* it mean?"

"It means," the girl put in, "that if your control should fail, we'll be ejected from the Channel into a nonspatial context."

"I've been thinking it over," Roger said promptly, "and I've decided this is too dangerous for a girl. Too bad; we might have solved everything—and of course I'd have loved going—but it means risking the life of a fragile little creature like you—"

"You're right, R'heet," Q'nell said, nodding. "I can sense the terror from here."

"Terror?" Roger came back hotly. "I was just . . . "

He swallowed. "Scared," he finished. "But I've been scared before, and it never did me any good." He straightened his back. "Let's get going before I examine that statement too closely." He gripped the girl's hand and advanced to the opening in the coil. As he stepped through, the familiar gray mist folded in about him.

"Now—we pause here!" Q'nell said. "Remember S'lunt's instructions!"

Roger closed his eyes and attempted to rotate his self-concept ninety degrees. Imagining his eyes to be peering out from the approximate position of his right ear was a difficult trick; a lifetime of orientation toward an arbitrarily designated "front" was not easy to overcome. But after all, he reminded himself, there was no reason the mind, an intangible field produced by the flow of current in a neural circuit, should be bound by such mundane restrictions . . .

Suddenly he succeeded, was aware of the nose on the side of his head, of the sideburn growing down between his imaginary eyes, of his arms, one on the front, one on the back . . .

And then he was falling through some medium that was not space . . .

CHAPTER SEVEN

1

For a while Roger fell with his eyes screwed shut, gripping the warm little hand of his partner—the sole material object in the universe. She appeared, he noted, to be about the size of the *Queen Mary*, floating majestically a mile away, linked to him by a fantastically long arm which dwindled as it approached, joining with a hand of normal size. Then he realized he had been mistaken. She was actually microscopically small, and floated on the surface of his eyeball . . .

"Not too bad so far," she said. There were no audible words; the thought formed in Roger's mind with crystal clarity, in the girl's voice, complete with overtones of a passionate nature rigidly concealed beneath a calm exterior.

"How do you do that?" Roger inquired, and noted with surprise that his lips failed to move. Neither was he breathing. In sudden alarm, he tried to draw in air, but nothing happened.

"Don't struggle," Q'nell's mental voice spoke sharply. "We're in a null-time state, where events like heartbeats and respiration can't take place. Don't let it distract you, or we'll find ourselves expelled from the Channel."

"How long is this going to take?" Roger asked nervously. He felt no physical distress from lack of air, but a conviction of suffocation was rising in him.

"No time at all—other than subjectively," Q'nell said.

"How can we be sure we're actually going anywhere? Maybe we're just going to hang here in space forever, swelling and shrinking."

"That's just your parameters trying to adjust to the absence of physical stimuli," Q'nell pointed out. "Don't let it bother you. And stop asking questions. If we knew the answers, we wouldn't be here."

"Hey!" Roger said suddenly. "My eyes are still shut; I can feel them! How is it I can see you?"

"You are not seeing me, you're apprehending me directly."

"This gray stuff," Roger said. "It's just like what you always see when you close your eyes. You know, I'm beginning to wonder—"

"Don't!" Q'nell said sharply. "Whatever you do, don't start to wonder!"

"I can't help it!" Roger retorted. "This is all too ridiculous to be true! Any second now I'm going to wake up—in my own bed, back in Elm Bluffs, with my mother calling me," he added, prompted by a sudden, vivid sense of homesickness.

The gray mist was changing, forming up into walls that simultaneously receded and closed in on him. Splotches appeared, congealed into large, pastel-colored floral patterns. There was a tear in the wallpaper, with white plaster showing behind it. He sat up, stared dumbly around a big, airy room with a ceiling that slanted down at one side, open windows, a shelf stacked with dog-eared Tom Swift books and untrimmed pulp magazines with B. Paul covers. Several inaccurately aligned model planes dangled from the ceiling on strings; a framed butterfly collection hung on the wall beside a row of arrowheads wired to a board and a felt pennant lettered ELM BLUFFS SR. HIGH.

"Roger!" a voice called in an unmistakably maternal tone. "If I have to call you again . . . " The unuttered threat hung in the air.

Roger made a squeaking sound, staring down at his own body. He saw a narrow, ribby chest, rumpled pajama bottoms covering knobby knees, the spindly shanks of a thirteen-year-old boy. "But . . . but . . . " he mumbled. "I'm thirty-one years old, and a grown-up failure! I was in the Channel with Q'nell, headed for the terminal coordinates . . . " He paused, frowning. "Terminal what?" he said aloud. "Wow, did I dream some big words!"

Suddenly the room faded, the walls swirled away into formless mist. Q'nell's face appeared, floating toward him.

"Where did you go?" she demanded. "You disappeared!"

"I was a boy again," Roger stuttered. "I was back home, in my own bed. It was just as real as this—realer! I could feel the bed under me, and smell bacon cooking, and feel the breeze coming through the windows! I thought all *this* was a dream!"

"But—you couldn't. It's impossible! *I'm* the dominant member of this linkage! You can't do anything I don't order you to do! At least that's the theory . . . "

"That's ridiculous," Roger said. "You're only a girl, remember?"

"Look here, T'son! Don't go wrecking the mission with your irresponsible male chauvinism! For some reason—probably having to do with a temporal precession effect induced by the reduplication of the Reinforcer circuitry—you seem to have taken over control of our joint conceptualizing capacities. You'll have to exercise extreme care not to do anything impulsive! Unless we keep all our faculties attuned to the mission, you and I and a few million other captives will spend the rest of Eternity reliving the same day—or worse!"

A faint nebulosity had appeared nearby, at the edge of Roger's vision. It grew, took on form and color.

"Q'nell!" Roger shouted soundlessly. "Look!"

"Now, T'son, if you're going to go on panicking every twenty-one subjective seconds, our mission is doomed. Try to relax."

"Behind you!" He stared at the knotted blanket slowly drifting into view. Under the brown folds, something was stirring, like a cat in a croker-sack.

"It's revived!" Roger blurted. "The monster!"

"Now, T'son, you know we studied your statements back in Culture One and decided that the monster concept was merely a subconscious projection—"

"Projection or not, we've got to get out!" Roger gritted his mental teeth, concentrating on the image of the homey bedroom, the flowered wallpaper . . .

A vague pathway seemed to open through the surrounding gray. Roger yearned toward it, felt himself slipping into it . . .

"T'son! What are you doing?" Q'nell's mental voice had assumed an odd, echoing quality. The tunnel was closing in, condensing into deep gloom that bulked around Roger. Sharp things poked at his back; the smell of hay was thick in his nostrils. He was, he saw, lying in a stack of the stuff, itching furiously. Overhead the lofty ceiling of a barn loomed.

"Now you've done it!" a familiar voice sounded, somewhere to the rear of his left eye. *"I warned you about this sort of thing!"*

"Where are we?" Roger sat up, scratched at a center of irritation on his right elbow, another on the left side of his neck, reached for a spot on his shoulder.

"Get the one on our left knee," Q'nell commanded. *"Then get us out of here!"*

"My God!" Roger mumbled. "Are you in the same skin with me?"

"Where else would I be, you dolt?" Q'nell retorted. *"We're linked; where you go, I go, unfortunately for me. S'lunt was mad to entrust this mission to you! I might have known you'd panic and spoil it all!"*

"Who's panicked! And you can scratch your own knee!" Promptly his left arm, as if possessed of a vitality all its own, did just that. Startled, Roger rose to his feet, and promptly fell on his face, since his left leg had failed to join in the effort to support him.

"I'll take the left half," Q'nell's voice stated firmly. *"You'll take the right. Now reattune and get us back into the Channel!"*

Roger tried to protest, but the left half of his face was wooden. "I'm paralyzed," he yelped incoherently. Threshing, he rolled from the hay onto a packed dirt floor. Across the room a wide door swung open. A tall, lean man in overalls, pitchfork in hand, stood outlined against a pale early-morning sky.

"Aha, it's you, is it, Andy Butts!" an irate voice grated. "I told you for the last time about sneaking into my barn and upsetting George and Elsie! By hokey, you'll work off your night's lodging! You can start by forking out those stalls! Now come out of there and set to!"

Roger struggled to balance himself on all fours, but fell on his face instead.

"Drunk, too!" the man with the pitchfork barked, advancing with the weapon poised. "You'd better sober up in one gosh-blasted hurry, or by Jupiter I'll give you a taste of what the hereafter'll be like! Get up!" He jabbed with the gleaming tines. Roger made inarticulate sounds and scrabbled one-armed and one-legged, describing a circle in the dust. The owner of the barn stared at him blankly.

"Goldang, Andy!" he blurted. "You all right?"

"Help!" Roger shouted. The sound emerged as a gargle. He fell on his face again.

"Andy! You've had a stroke!" the pitchforker yelled, tossing the implement aside. "Rest easy, Andy! I'll go for Doc Whackerby!"

With a supreme effort, Roger assumed sufficient control to cause the body of Andy Butts to spring wildly to its feet and topple, arms windmilling, against the barn owner, sending him spinning before crashing, jaw first, to the ground.

"He's went insane!" the man yelled, staggering to his feet. He dashed away shouting.

"What are you trying to do?" Q'nell demanded subvocally. *"That maniac almost murdered us!"*

"Give me back my leg!" Roger countered. "We've got to get out of here!"

"Transfer us back to the Channel!" Q'nell commanded. *"Until you do, I'm not letting go!"*

"Are you crazy? You'll feel that pitchfork just as much as I will!"

"Oh, no I won't! I'm leaving the sensory nervous system entirely to you, thanks!"

"But I don't know how!" Roger yelled silently.

"Try!"

"Well . . . " Lying on the floor, Roger closed his eye. He stared into the formless gray, swimming with pulsating points and lines of pale-colored light, searching for some clue—any clue to escape. Instead, he was aware of the weight of fat on the body he now occupied, the rasp of stubble on his jowls, the pains shooting from his empty stomach, a clammy, shivering feeling of early-morning hangover.

"Ugh!" Q'nell exclaimed. *"How revolting!"*

"Quiet! How can I concentrate?"

"Hurry up! That barbarian's coming back!"

"I'm trying!" Roger gritted his teeth, realized with a dull shock that he was grinding toothless gums together, became aware simultaneously of the coating on his tongue, a gluey feeling about the eyes, small creatures exploring his scalp, dirty socks—and an unreasoning dread of Doc Whackerby.

"He's trying to take over!" Roger shouted soundlessly. "The owner of this miserable body!" With an effort, he forced his attention away from the reactions of Andy Butts, blanking his mind to allow his hypnotic training to come to the fore. The grayness thinned, receding. Two foci of relative brightness swam into his ken, radiating calmness.

"I think I've located our bodies!" he communicated. "I'll try to bring them in . . ." He willed himself toward the objectives, which floated, vague and formless, in the remote distance—or millimeters away. He was faintly aware of excited voices approaching, of pounding feet, of a renewed pang of Buttsian fear. With a final desperate effort, he lunged mentally for the nearest brightness, felt a wrench as Q'nell was torn from his side—

He was in a tiny space that compressed him like a straitjacket. Sounds crackled and boomed around him; sharp odors assailed his nostrils. Blurry gray and white forms moved vaguely before him. He tried to move, to call out, felt the shift of cumbersome members, the play of remote, impersonal muscles stretching under insensitive hide. His field of view swung, came to rest on a massive bulk beside him. He blinked, made out the shape of a vast draft horse in the next stall.

"Q'nell!" he tried to shout, instead uttered a bleating whinny. He recoiled, felt an obstruction behind him. At once, in instinctive reaction, his rear legs shot out in a frantic kick. Boards shattered and split. A surge of equine panic sent him blundering through the side of the stall.

Small, excited figures scattered before him. He longed for open space, charged toward it, burst into the open, shied as something tall and dark loomed before him, leaped a fence, and galloped for the safety of the open plains . . .

A detailless image of the comforting bulk of the mare rose in his mind. He slowed, rounded into the wind, sniffed for her distinctive scent. He felt his heart pounding slowly, massively, was aware of air snorting in through wide nostrils, felt himself quivering with a fear that drained away as memory of its origin faded from his mind. He tossed his head and trotted back toward the barn. The mare appeared, galloping into perfect focus. She came up to him, nuzzled him—

"T'son! What have you done?"

The words seemed to mean something—almost. But the effort to unravel the meaning was too much . . .

"T'son! Use your training! Pull yourself together! Remember the mission!"

He lunged playfully for the mare, followed as she retreated, inspired suddenly by a vague but powerful urge which impelled him to rear and whinny, renew the pursuit.

"Stop that, you idiot!" Q'nell commanded as he succeeded in shouldering alongside her. She retreated frustratingly. He lunged again.

"Try, T'son! You can do it! Concentrate. Align your parameters!"

"Elsie—you're beautiful!" Roger succeeded in formulating the thought into word-patterns. "So desirable! So . . . so horsy!"

"I'll horsy you if we ever get out of this one, you cretin!" Q'nell's voice penetrated his euphoria.

"Remember the Channel? Remember the Museum, and all those people, locked up in it like capuchin monkeys? Remember how you were going to trace the system back to its source and become the savior of us all?"

"Yes . . . I remember . . . sort of. But it all seems so unimportant, compared with that lovely, shapely, inviting—"

"Later, T'son!" Q'nell said frantically. *"First, you get us back where we belong; then we'll talk about my shapely inviting!"*

"I don't want to talk," Roger capered, pawing the turf. "I want action!"

"The Channel, T'son! Here comes the farmer! He'll hitch you up to a plow and work you like a horse all day, and tonight you'll be too tired to do anything at all!"

"I don't want to plow; I want to—"

"I know!" Q'nell sounded desperate. *"But back in the Channel we can be together!"*

"Together? In the Channel?" Roger struggled to fix the concept in his cramped, dimly lit mind. He remembered the grayness, the presence that had drifted beside him there. And there it was now, hovering near at hand, a dim blur, and another beyond . . .

"No, T'son! That's the farmer and another man! Keep looking! Narrow your parameters!"

Roger groped outward, swimming upward. Or was it sideways? Or no, he was falling . . . falling endlessly through the medium that was not space, and there, linked to his outstretched hand was . . . was . . .

"You blundering imbecile!" Q'nell's voice came through loud and clear. "You've gotten us back inside the wrong bodies!"

2

"How could you ever have made such an idiotic mistake?" Q'nell queried for the thirty-fifth time in four minutes. "Trapping me inside your clumsy, undisciplined, *masculine* corpus!"

"Well, I'm just as badly off, aren't I?" Roger replied. "I'm stuck in this silly, flimsy female body of yours!" He felt an unaccountable impulse to cry—not that he felt any particularly poignant emotion; it just seemed like the thing to do. "I was only trying to do what you said!"

"Ha! If I'd only sided with R'heet and gone ahead and dug the Reinforcer out of your skull by force, instead of going all mushy inside and voting to keep you alive."

"What? You mean that two-faced sneaky little R'heet suggested that? Why, I'll scratch his eyes out—I mean, I'll knock his block off," Roger corrected.

"Don't start wandering again!" Q'nell warned sharply. "You're just barely holding us in stasis now! We can't afford to drop out again!"

"It could have happened to anybody," Roger said loftily. "Now, please don't bother me with your petty little complaints unless you have something constructive to contribute."

"Constructive! If it hadn't been for me, you'd still have been horsing around, trying to—"

"Please!" At the recollection of his recent emotions, Roger felt what would have been a deep-purple blush if his blood had been circulating. "Suppose we discuss what we're going to do when we get there," he hurried on. "Now, my idea is that we just go right up to whoever's in charge and give them a piece of our mind."

"Don't try to think, T'son!" Q'nell boomed. "Leave that to me. Your job is just to keep us focused while I do the actual work. As for what we do when we get there, inasmuch as we haven't the faintest idea what we'll find, suppose we play it by ear, eh? You just take your cue from me."

"Well! What makes you so superior?" Roger came back.

"Say!" Q'nell cut in. "It just dawned on me! If I've got your body, I've also got your limited brain!"

"Don't you dare use my brain!" Roger ordered sharply.

"Quiet; I'm checking out the circuitry," Q'nell ordered. "If I'm stuck with it, I may as well see what I have to work with . . ." There was a momentary pause. "Say— you've got a lot of unused capacity here! I might be able to use it!"

"You just stick to our orders," Roger insisted. "Now that I've gotten us back where we belong—well, practically back where we belong—don't go spoiling it all experimenting!"

"Orders are made to be broken," Q'nell said callously. "I've got a notion that if I just nudge this parameter *here*—and then twist this one over *here*—"

Roger felt the insubstantial frame of reference about him tilt suddenly, flip upside down. "Stop!" he cried. "You're doing it wrong!"

"Oops! Hold on tight; looks as if maybe I should have twisted *that* one instead!"

There was a sickening sensation as space turned inside out. Roger felt himself expand instantaneously to infinite size, shrink as suddenly to minuteness, and disappear, to reemerge on the other side. Light burst in his face, sound roared. He was whirling, falling, sinking into cold syrup—

He fetched up with a thump, rolled over twice, and

opened his eyes. He lay on an expanse of waving grasses which glowed eerily like an aquarium lit from below, under a sky of total velvety black. His body, he saw, shone in the dark, a soft, lightning-bug green. He looked across at the frightened-looking luminous man with rumpled hair who was sitting up nearby, rubbing an unshaven jaw.

My God, do I really have that bewildered look? he wondered, watching himself staring at the scenery.

"Well, don't lie there staring at me," Q'nell said over the roar and crackle of the sky. "Start having ideas!"

CHAPTER EIGHT

1

"Where do you suppose we are?" Roger inquired, gingerly brushing sparkling dust from the unaccustomed curves of his borrowed form.

"How do I know?" Q'nell snapped. She stamped awkwardly up and down like a spotlit performer, swinging Roger's arms and staring out across the shining landscape to a row of phosphorescent hills. "How the devil do you balance this infernal body? These feet weigh a ton—and the hip joints are too close together."

"Well! I'd trade back in a minute! I feel like my rear is a mile wide—and what do you do about the topheavy feeling?"

Q'nell glanced at him, then looked again, her gaze lingering. "Say, you know, that's not a bad-looking little form, if I do say so myself." She sauntered closer. "There's something kind of appealing about the way it sticks out here and there—and when it moves—" She broke off, a startled look on Roger's face. "Good heavens!" she murmured. "Is *that* the way it feels to be a male?"

"Keep away from me, you onanist!" Roger shrilled, backing up, noting in passing that the sensation of alarm coursing through him had curiously pleasurable overtones.

"You poor thing," Q'nell said. "Imagine going around reacting like that to the mere sight of a female!"

"I'm no female! I'm Roger Tyson, one hundred percent red-blooded male man! And you keep your sticky hands to yourself! I mean, you keep *my* sticky hands to yourself!"

"Are you sure you want me to?" Q'nell advanced.

"Get back!" Roger yelped. "You're ogling again!"

"Well, why don't you cover yourself up, you—you exhibitionist! How do you expect me to keep my mind on the problem at hand with you undulating around? You're doing it on purpose! I suppose it gives you some kind of sense of power or something!"

"For the first time I'm getting an insight into the origin of Puritanism," Roger muttered. "It's dirty-minded voyeurs like you that are responsible for all the prudery in the world! It's not my fault if the sight of me upsets you!" He felt his—or Q'nell's—right hip execute a flawless grind, ending in a modest bump that set his superstructure quivering.

"Hey!" he yelped. "*I* didn't do that—it was this troublemaking body of yours! Suddenly I'm beginning to understand a lot of things about the battle of the sexes!"

"Why fight?" Q'nell inquired reasonably. Roger's face was twisted into an obnoxious smirk, he noted with dismay. Surely *he* had never looked at a helpless female that way!"

"Hey!" Q'nell pointed past him. "Company coming!" She jumped forward to place herself before Roger as a weird spectacle appeared dramatically over a nearby ridge. It was a luminous horse of a pale, glowing turquoise shade, hung about with jet-black harness from which depended glittering baubles like Christmas-tree lights. Astride the creature's back sat a rider whose hide gleamed a pale blue. He was scantily garbed, topped by a nodding headdress of plumes like colored flames. The apparition galloped up to rein in facing the two adventurers at a distance of ten feet. The rider spoke, an effect like the blipping of blank spots on a magnetic tape.

"Take it easy, honey," Q'nell said grimly. "I'll handle this." She stepped forward, fists on hips, buzzed a speech in Culture One Speedspeak, at which the rider leaned from the saddle and fetched her a solid blow on the side of the head with a long knobbed stick.

"You monster!" Roger shrilled, springing forward to stand astride his fallen body.

"Wha—" Q'nell inquired, rolling groggily to Roger's feet. She leaped up suddenly, brushed Roger aside, caught the stick as it swung again, yanked the rider from the saddle. The mount shied and galloped away as the two rolled in the dust, blue arms and dusty white rising and falling to the accompaniment of dull thuds. Roger felt a curious thrill as Q'nell rolled clear and jumped up, dusting her borrowed hands.

"All right, who's next?" she yelled, waving Roger's fists. The blue man groaned.

"No takers," Q'nell said, smiling broadly. Roger had never before noticed what an inane smile he had . . . but on the other hand, it was rather cute in a way—almost boyish, as if he needed mothering.

"I've never understood before just what it was you fellows got out of all those body-contact sports," Q'nell said cheerfully. "But you know, there's something about crunching your knuckle into somebody's skull that's good for the repressed psyche!" She put a casual hand on Roger's shoulder. With horror, he felt his borrowed knees begin to quiver.

"Unhand me, you—you barbarian!" he squeaked, and threw the offending member off. "Just look at that poor man! You've hurt him!" He knelt by the fallen warrior, began dabbing ineffectually at the dust caking his face. The patient opened his eyes—a startling clear yellow, like illuminated lemon drops—and smiled, showing excellent teeth. The next second a blue hand was fumbling Roger's thigh. In instant reflex, he landed an open-handed slap across the reviving face that sent the blue casualty back for another count.

"Say, did that rapist try to get fresh?" Q'nell started, advancing pugnaciously.

"Never mind that," Roger countered. "Just get busy and get us out of here!"

"I've got a good mind to revive that degenerate and—"

"Q'nell! It was nothing! Now, let's concentrate on those parameters you were so worried about a few minutes ago!"

"Believe me, a maniac like that has just one thing in mind!"

"So have I: getting away from here! This is a totally alien environment, in case you haven't noticed! We're lucky we can even breathe the air! For all we know, we're soaking up a lethal dose of radiation right now!"

"I wonder"—Q'nell eyed the native with unabated hostility—"what gave the clown the idea . . . "

"You ought to know," Roger said. "All men are alike! I mean, the fact that he's a male— I mean, well, after all, it's perfectly natural, isn't it? I mean—"

"You led him on!" Q'nell charged. "Why, you promiscuous little tramp!"

"Q'nell! Come to your senses! Our lives are at stake!

Thousands of lives! Now just figure out what you did before, and do it again, backwards."

"Actually, I've got a feeling we've flipped out into a reverse-polarity universe," Q'nell said carelessly. "But let's forget that for now. You know, T'son," she went on in an oily tone which made Roger's skin crawl, "you and I have never really had a chance to get acquainted." She edged closer. "Back in Culture One they kept me so busy dashing around I never really had time to notice what a charming, ah, personality you have."

"Skip my personality," Roger snapped. "Just get busy and retwiddle those parameters!"

"How'm I supposed to concentrate on all that technical business with this funny feeling creeping over me every time I look at that slinky little torso of yours, and that slender little waist, and those nice—"

"Look here, Q'nell!" Roger snapped, fending off his hands. "Get control of myself, girl! Put your intelligence in charge! Remember what S'lunt said! If this trap system isn't destroyed, it'll rip the whole space-time continuum wide open! Imagine the confusion, with Genghis Khan galloping around the middle of World War One, and Louis the Fifteenth coming face to face with de Gaulle, and Teddy Roosevelt bumping heads with LBJ, and—"

"All right, all right, you've made your point." Q'nell slumped back, breathing hard, promptly sat up again. "But are you sure you don't really want to—"

"No! Stick to the subject at hand! The Channel! It's not hard, Q'nell; just close your eyes and try to sort of firm up the gray into a nice even sort of custardy consistency."

"I'm trying," Q'nell said, squeezing Roger's eyes shut. "But it just looks like a lot of garbage to me."

Roger closed the eyes of the body he was occupying. "There's really nothing to it," he said in a calm, reasonable tone. "*I* didn't have any trouble. You just exclude all extraneous thoughts from your mind."

"Did you know that when you run you have the most delightful jounce?" Q'nell said.

"I assure you, it's unintentional!" Roger said icily. "Now concentrate! Think about it!"

"I am! I can't think about anything else! Great galloping galaxies, T'son, I really have to admire you men for the little restraint you show! It's like . . . like . . . "

"It's like nothing else in the world," Roger said. "I remember it well—even though it all seems pretty silly now, which goes to show the decisive role glands play in philosophy."

"I suppose you're right," Q'nell said resignedly. "But since it's really your fault for scrambling us up like this, you ought to be willing to—"

"Don't go feminine on me now!" Roger yelped. "We'll *both* concentrate! Maybe together we can manage it!" He groped mentally toward the insubstantial stuff floating before his closed eyes, but it boiled imperviously, stubbornly refusing to coalesce into the characteristic gray of the Channel.

"How are you doing, Q'nell?" he asked.

"I'm not sure . . . but I think . . . maybe . . . "

"Yes? Keep trying! You can do it!"

"Maybe," Q'nell went on, "you'd better open your eyes."

Roger complied instantly—and was looking up into the massed spears of a company of ghostly blue riders hemming them in from all sides.

2

"The very idea," Roger said an hour later, after a rough ride strapped behind a sweating blue warrior, and an unsatisfying interview in a pitch-dark room with unseen locals. "Putting us together in the same cell!"

"At least this way we only have one door to break down," Q'nell said. "What did you expect, separate suites? His and Hers buckets?"

"Must you be crude?" Roger folded his arms, quickly unfolded them, disconcerted by the sensation.

"Just realistic," Q'nell said. "Let's face facts: I'm occupying an inferior brain. It's up to you, T'son. I did my best."

"What did you make of the interrogation?"

"What could I make of it? Total darkness, silent voices—I'm not even sure we were being questioned."

"Of course we were," Roger said loftily. "And they're not through yet. They'll be back soon."

"How do you know?"

"Feminine intuition."

"Oh, that!" Q'nell said disparagingly. "Just a mish-mash of wild guesses and wishful thinking."

"You'll see," Roger said complacently. "Now be quiet. Since you seem to be helpless, I'll have to try to do what I can." He stretched out on the floor and looked into the grayness swirling before his closed eyes . . .

. . . and was awakened by a foot prodding his side to see Q'nell struggling in the grip of a pair of husky fluorescent guards.

This time they were hustled unceremoniously along dull-glowing corridors out into a walled courtyard under an open sky just beginning to gray at zenith. Several dark points were visible there, like negative star images on an astronomical photograph.

"I think I'm beginning to understand what makes the light so funny," Roger confided to Q'nell as they stood together against one pockmarked wall. "The whole spectrum is shifted; we're seeing heat—that's why living things glow—and visible light is off in the radio range somewhere."

"I'm beginning to understand something even more fascinating than that," Q'nell said. "Those ten blue men over there with the guns in their hands are a firing squad!"

"You're a big success as a negotiator," Roger charged bitterly. "If this is a compromise, what were they holding out for?"

"At least we're not going to be tortured," Q'nell snapped back. "Be quiet and let's start concentrating! Maybe the spur of dire necessity will help me use some of the ninety-two percent of your brain our instruments showed was lying fallow!"

"I don't know how to operate your brain!"

"Well, try! It's a finely tuned instrument, trained in all the subtleties of Culture One mental science! Put it to use!"

Across the eerie courtyard, the rank of armed men were lining up, eyeing their prospective targets with shining yellow eyes. Roger shivered.

"I can't," he said. "All I can think about it what it will feel like to be shot!"

"In that case, I guess it's goodbye," Q'nell said. "I'm afraid your body's panic reactions are inhibiting my concentration, too."

"About those passes you were making," Roger said, feeling a sudden tenderness toward the girl. "I didn't mean to be stuffy or anything."

"Actually, I admire you for your stand," Q'nell said. "Only a tramp would have given in."

"What! Why, you practically fell all over yourself trying to make time with me! And if I'd taken pity on you, that makes me a tramp?"

"Calm down! I was complimenting you!"

"Of all the nerve! And I thought you liked me! And

all the time you were just amusing yourself, testing my reactions!"

"Hey, that's not true! You're very appealing! I just meant that, uh ... But what does it matter what I meant? This is the end. Goodbye, T'son. It's been very interesting."

Roger didn't answer. He was watching with fascination as the blue men loaded their guns ...

A vertical line of light quivered into existence between Roger and the aimed guns. It wavered, faded, firmed again, flickered ...

"T'son!" Q'nell said sharply. "It's a portal! It must be good old S'lunt!"

"He'd better hurry up and focus it," Roger said, gritting his teeth hard. "In about another two seconds—"

"On the count of three, hit the deck!" Q'nell hissed. "One!" The firing squad took aim.

"Two!"

The portal snapped into sharpness. A shape appeared, sliding forth from it—a bulbous shape, glowing a dull red, ringed about with jointed tentacles.

"Three!" Q'nell called. Roger dived flat, heard the close-spaced blips of silence that punctuated the background roar, saw the monster explode into a shower of fragments as it intercepted the fusillade intended for the humans. The shooters, astonished at the sudden obstacle that had interposed itself between them and their target, stood gaping dumbly as Roger and Q'nell came to their feet.

"Come on!" Q'nell yelled, and grabbed Roger's hand.

"But—but it's one of *theirs!*" he protested, pulling back.

"Any port in a storm!" Q'nell shouted.

"I guess you're right," Roger gulped, and together they dashed forward and plunged through the portal.

CHAPTER NINE

1

They spun outward in a swirl of silence and light. Light foamed about them, glaring, sputtering, pulsing red and green and blue and gold, like a breaking comber of jewels.

"It's beautiful!" Q'nell's voice sounded in his head. "But what is it? We're not in the Channel. Our extrapolated universe model never predicted anything like this!"

"Nevertheless, it's here," Roger said. "And we're still alive to enjoy it."

"We've got to find out where we are and where we're going, in a hurry! We may be sliding right into their home base!"

"Yes. We seem to be traveling pretty fast," Roger agreed. As in the Channel, the sensation was of motion not through space, but through some subtler medium.

"I'm going to give the parameters another try," Q'nell said. "Somehow they seem to be much more accessible when we're in a non-space environment."

"Just don't go twisting them," Roger cautioned.

"That's precisely what I intend to do!" Q'nell countered. "But I'm afraid it will take more than a twist to get us back where we belong."

The clouds of light were changing, receding, forming up into towering thunderheads that glowed with pale colors. Now it was as though they swam in a stormy sky amid heaped, multicolored cumuli, with no up, no down, no land in sight. They swooped like effortless gulls between towers and through canyons, hurtling past vast, bellowing domes, diving through airy tunnels, skimming the surface of cloudy plains.

"It's no good; I'm getting dizzy," Q'nell called at last. She was swooping in the middle distance, upside down. "There's no frame of reference whatever!"

"If we just had something underfoot," Roger said. "I'm afraid I'm going to be airsick!" As he spoke, he felt something nudge the soles of his shoes. He looked down, saw a patch of pale blue tiled floor.

"Q'nell! Look!" He waved to her, floating overhead now.

"Where did that come from?" she called.

"I just thought of it—and here it was!"

Q'nell swung closer, arced downward to thump lightly against the floor. "Say, T'son, you may be on to something here!" She poked at the floor with a finger, pounded with her fist. "It feels solid enough. This is amazing! We seem to be in a malleable continuum, which can be concretized by thought impulses!"

Roger went to hands and knees, crawled to the edge, reached under and felt around.

"It's about an inch thick," he said. "Rough on the underside."

"Careful now, T'son," Q'nell cautioned. "Don't do anything that might shift our parameters, but . . . do you think you could extend it any?"

"I'll try . . . " Roger closed his eyes, imagined the

floor extending outward twenty feet on every side, ending in a smooth edge.

"You did it!" Q'nell said excitedly. "Good boy!" Opening his eyes, Roger was delighted to find the floor exactly as he had imagined it. They walked to the edge.

"You know, this is a little vertiginous, looking down at all that open air," Q'nell said, edging back. "How about filling it in a little?"

Roger pictured green grass under spreading shade trees.

"Remarkable!" Q'nell exclaimed, surveying the park-like result. "Suppose I have a try?"

"Careful," Roger said. "Just anyone may not have the brainpower to do it."

"Stand back," Q'nell said. As Roger watched, a wall winked into existence before his face. For a second or two it was plain white plaster; then a slightly crooked window with a purple-and-pink curtain was suddenly there, with sunlight streaming through it. Roger turned. He was in a room, walled, roofed— and carpeted a moment later in a pattern of pink and yellow flowers.

"Nothing to it," Q'nell said. "Now, a couple of chairs . . . " Two massive mismatched rockers appeared, complete with glossy black satin cushions lettered SAIGON and MOTHER in glowing blue.

"Horrible," Roger said. "Have you no taste?" He pictured a pair of delicate Chippendales, added a side table with a silver tray bearing a steaming teapot and a pair of dainty cups. He seated himself.

"I'll pour," he offered.

"I'll take a drink of something with some vitamins in it!" Q'nell snorted, and a bottle with a garish label thumped to the table. She produced a corkscrew next, poured out a stiff cupful.

"Hey, that's good stuff!" she exclaimed, smacking loudly. "Want a snort?"

Roger caught a whiff of the powerful brew and shuddered. "Certainly not."

Q'nell poured herself a second, strolled around the room, adding garish pictures in gold frames to the wall, placing lamps with grotesque shades here and there while Roger winced.

"Not bad," she said. "But it still lacks something . . ." She stared at a wall; a door appeared. She opened it on a bedroom containing nothing but an enormous bed.

"How about it, T'son?" she leered. "Feeling tired?"

"Now don't start all that again," Roger said. "The only purpose of this house-building spree was to help us with our orientation, remember?"

"All work and no play make Jackie a dull girl," Q'nell said.

"You've already given me your opinion of playgirls!" Roger yelled. "And anyway, I'm a man! Now stop horsing around and give your attention to the problem!"

"I am, T'son—I am!" Q'nell poured a third hearty libation, drank it, put the cup down, and reached for Roger. He leaped up and dodged behind a rocker.

"Stop it or I'll imagine the biggest policeman you ever heard of!" he yelled.

"Oh yeah?" Q'nell made a grab, missed, almost fell. "Say, that booze is getting to me," she murmured. "Oh well, it helps the party atmosphere." She tossed the cup aside and lunged, hooked a foot on the rocker, and landed headfirst.

"I warned you!" Roger closed his eyes and picture a seven-foot storm trooper, complete with spurred boots, brass knuckles, and a knotted leather whip. There was a soft *thud!* and a metallic tinkle. He opened his eyes to see an empty uniform collapse to the floor.

Q'nell leaped to her feet. "I didn't think you'd have

the heart!" she cried blurrily, starting around the chair. Roger pictured a stairway, dashed for it, went up the steps two at a time, found himself on a landing open to the sky. Feet pounded below.

"More stairs!" he commanded, and dashed on. It was a glass-and-chrome-rail construction, rising in a gentle spiral. Too bad he hadn't called for an elevator; he was getting winded.

"Roof!" Q'nell shouted behind him. The sky was blotted out as a solid ceiling appeared above him, supported by sturdy walls.

"Door!" Roger countered, jerking open the panel which had instantly winked into existence, and was on the wide, featureless roof. He whirled, slammed the door.

"Yale lock!" he gasped, out of breath. He turned the shiny brass key and leaned against the door, panting.

"Fooled you!" Q'nell called, clambering over the parapet. "Fire escape!"

"Rope ladder!" Roger demanded, sprang for the dangling rungs, and clambered rapidly upward. Overhead, the vast translucent bulk of a balloon swayed, the words OHAMA, NEBRASKA spelled out in yard-high letters across its bulbous side.

"Bow and arrow!" Q'nell's voice floated up from below. An instant later there was a sharp twang, the swish of the bolt in flight, a ripping noise, succeeded by a loud hissing. The balloon began to sink rapidly. Moments later Roger slammed against the roof and was immediately engulfed in the deflated folds of the balloon. He fought his way clear, scrambled up, looked wildly around for Q'nell.

His companion lay sprawled by the parapet, unconscious. Beside the body, a monster, dull red, one-eyed, squatted on clustered legs, a figure of infinite menace.

"Machine gun!" Roger yelled, felt the solid slap of the weapon into his hands. He jacked the action, swung it to bear on the alien—

A dazzling light glared in his eyes. He felt the gun fall from his hands, felt his knees begin to buckle; then a Roman candle exploded inside his skull and scattered his consciousness in bright fragments that faded and were lost in darkness.

2

Roger came to himself lying on a hard floor. He pried his eyes open and sat up—and instantly grabbed for support. He was perched, he saw, on a tiny platform dangling by a single thin wire from one of a maze of interconnected rods of various sizes that crisscrossed a vast, bottomless, blue-lit cavern. A deep-toned thrumming filled the air, which smelled slightly of library paste. He peered over the edge of his roost, drew back hastily after a glimpse of the dizzying depths below.

"Ah, I'm glad to see you've decided to reactivate your second unit," a gluey voice said near at hand. "A hopeful sign, indicative of an upcoming meeting of the minds, I trust."

Roger leaped at the unexpected speech, almost lost his balance, scrabbled for stability, and was looking at a curving console hanging a few feet distant and at a dish-shaped stool before it on which rested the bloated form of a headless, dusky pink monstrosity.

"Gulp," Roger said.

"Gulp? Ah, a friendly greeting in your colorful language, no doubt—in which case, gulp to you, sir or madam! A very fine gulp indeed! I must confess it gives me an eerie feeling to see you sitting here, whole and sound, after having observed you lying lifeless in a third-order ditch—but we live and learn! Now that we understand the compound nature of your being, I'm sure we'll get on famously!" The creature was pulsating a deep tangerine shade now, apparently expressing effusive conciliation.

"Wh-what are you?"

"I, sir, am a life-form known in cultivated space-time circles as a Rhox, Oob by name. Welcome to our control apex. I trust you'll forgive our rather rude method of transporting you here, but in view of the unsatisfactory nature of my earlier attempts to confer with you, it seemed the only way."

"Confer?" Roger mumbled.

"Precisely," the alien said, speaking through a yard-wide lipless mouth set below the Cyclopean eye. "And now, on to the settlement of detail. If you'll just state the aims behind your apparently unmotivated persecution of me . . . "

"I've been persecuting you?" Roger burst out.

"I know, I know—and a wily antagonist you are. We've had my entire extrapolatory computing capacity at work attempting to analyze the value system underlying your tactics, and I've come up with only two alternatives: one, you're an absolute idiot, or, two, you're a fiendishly clever mind of totally incalculable subtlety. Obviously the former theory is quite untenable, as demonstrated by the simple fact that you're still alive." Oob had faded to a more complacent shade of light orange.

"I'm alive . . . but what about Q'nell?" Roger burst out.

"Sorry, I don't place the name," Oob confessed. "All you beings look alike to us, you know."

"The handsome one," Roger clarified. "With the broad shoulders and the curly hair."

"Oh, we know the one you mean—with the long nose and the close-set eyes."

"Close-set eyes?" Roger said, pointedly staring at his captor's lone ocular.

"Of course; your other unit. It's quite well, naturally. Since you've demonstrated your ability to reactivate your units after demise, I'm hardly so obtuse as to continue with nugatory efforts to dispose of you by superficial methods. Instead, I'm seeking to establish some sort of, ah, understanding." Roger had a sudden vivid mental image of Q'nell, helpless in the clutches of inhuman creatures.

"They may be torturing her," he muttered. "Pounding her black and blue." He paused. "Come to think of it, that's *my* body they'll be pounding. And—" Suddenly comprehension dawned.

"You think I'm her!" he blurted. "And that she's me!"

"Of course. We may be a little slow to discard my original conception of affairs, but I do catch on in time. Precisely why a being of your complexity has chosen to masquerade as two natives of a third-order continuum, we don't know. But I'll not pry, sir! I'll not pry. Now, as to this matter of the ownership of the Trans-Temporal Bore: while my claim to ownership is clearly prior, we must concede that you've established an interest in it by your very presence here—an interest I would be the last to deny. But in all fairness, sir—and in consideration of the fact that D-day is almost upon us and my bombardment is about to begin—surely you'll sell out for a reasonable consideration?"

"Go jump in an Irish stew!" Roger yelled. "If you think I'm going to give you information that will help you take over Earth, you're crazy!"

"Now, now—don't be hasty!" Oob urged. "Suppose I offer you all rights to a delightful little continuum

just a few frames of reference away in *that* direction."
The Rhox made a complicated gesture.

"What makes you think I'd help you, you blood-thirsty turnip!"

"Correction: We do not ingest vascular fluids of third-level life-forms. As to why I assumed you'd cooperate, we think I can offer a number of suitable inducements to bring you around to our view of matters."

"Never!" Roger stated flatly. "You're wasting your time!"

"Your attitude is rather reactionary, sir," the Rhox said stiffly. "I should think you'd be willing to negotiate a reasonable division of interests."

"Go ahead, just try it!" Roger challenged. "You escapee from a root cellar! We'll fight you on the beaches! We'll fight you in the cities! We'll slice you up into French fries!"

"Look here—suppose I offer to take you in as a partner—a silent partner, of course—"

"You can't silence me!" Roger yelled. "I'll have nothing to do with your nefarious scheme!"

"Nefarious? I'd hardly call it that, sir! It will bring a little amusement into millions of dull, drab lives!"

"You'd do this thing for amusement?" Roger squeaked in horror.

"Certainly. Why else? At least it amuses the masses. As for myself, we've seen it all before, of course. But this particular situation, by virtue of its very primitiveness, offers certain unique opportunities for comedy, especially for the kiddies."

"You're a monster in human form!" Roger yelled. "I mean you're a human in monster form! Have you no conscience?"

"What's conscience got to do with it? It's just business, sir, just business!"

"Your diabolical business will never get its tentacles on Earth! Not if I can help it!"

"Ah . . . I think I'm beginning to understand!" Oob exclaimed. "You intend to hog it all for yourself!" A dull black now, the Rhox flipped a large lever with a flick of a tentacle.

"You leave me no choice, sir! I'd hoped you'd be reasonable. But since you won't, this conference is at an end!"

"Wha-what are you going to do?" Roger demanded.

"Dispatch you, sir, to the end of the line, where, I trust, you'll be ejected, along with the rest of the waste material, from the entire space-time continuum, whereafter I'll proceed immediately to put my plans into execution!"

Without further warning, Roger felt the perch drop from under him. Grayness swirled around him, and once again he was tumbling down through endless emptiness. For a timeless eternity he fell, and then, abruptly, he was motionless. He had arrived—somewhere.

CHAPTER TEN

1

He was in inky blackness, utter stillness. He shouted but the sound died without an answer, without even an echo. He sensed a floor under him and groped forward, feeling his way with his hands, but he encountered nothing, not even a wall.

"Maybe," he told himself, fighting for calm, "I can work that trick we used before." He drew a shaky breath, pictured a standing lamp with an old-fashioned shade.

"Let there be light!" he murmured ...

Brilliance sprang into being. Squinting against the glare, Roger came to his feet. He was in the center of a vast plain of polished glass that stretched away on all sides as far as he could see, featureless, unadorned.

"Well, at that, it's better than being blown up," he told himself. "I suppose my next move is to explore the place. In fact, it's my only move, so I might as well start walking. Unless ... ." He raised his voice: "Bicycle?"

There was a resounding crash. The twisted ruins of

a hundred-foot Schwinn lay a quarter of a mile away, one forty-foot wheel spinning slowly.

"Smaller," he specified. "And closer to the ground."

"LITTLE BEING, DID YOU DO THAT?" a vast voice boomed out of the white sky.

Roger shied violently. "Wh-who was that?" he called.

"IT WAS I. WHO ELSE?"

Roger clapped his hands over his ears. "Do you have to talk so loud? You're bursting Q'nell's eardrums!"

"Is this better?" the voice spoke gratingly from a point a few feet above Roger's head.

"Much. Uh—who's speaking, anyway?"

"You may call me UKR."

"Uh, where are you, Mr. Ucker?"

"At present I am occupying a ninth-order niche within Locus 3,432,768,954, Annex One, Master Index Section. Why?"

"Well—it's rather disconcerting, not being able to see you."

"Oh, perhaps it will help if I extend a third-order pseudosome into your coordinate system."

A looming, misshapen form snapped into existence before Roger. It was twelve feet tall, and featured an amorphous head with a wide, slobbery mouth crowded with mismatched fangs, crossed scarlet eyes, pits like bullet wounds for nostrils, and arms of unequal length ending in satchel-sized hands with unpared nails.

"Yelp!" Roger cried, and backed rapidly away.

"Something wrong?" A booming voice issued from the monster's mouth. "I selected every detail of the projection from a catalogue lodged deep within your subconscious. Don't you find it reassuring?"

"You t-tapped the wrong level," Roger quavered. "Try again."

"How's this?" The figure flowed and shrank like hot

wax, reshaping itself into a bulletheaded, pot-bellied, unshaven seven-foot ogre with warts and a harelip.

"Better, but still not quite on the mark," Roger demurred.

The figure dwindled still more; the face contorted like a rubber mask, settled into the benign features of an elderly professorial type. The stubble shot out to form a patriarchal white beard. The scarlet pupils disappeared behind thick bifocals, while the body became that of a retired librarian.

"Ah, I see by your expression I've hit it at last," a frail, breathless voice said in a pleased tone. "Ah—is something missing?"

"Clothes would help," Roger confided.

A serape appeared, draping the lean form. "How's this?"

"Not quite in character, Mr. Ucker," Roger pointed out.

Roger's new acquaintance worked quickly through several outfits, including football togs circa 1890, a cowboy suit with matched pistols, and a pink leotard before settling on a swallow-tailed coat, striped pants, and a starched shirt with stand-up collar.

"Much better," Roger approved, swallowing hard. "But don't get the idea I'm impressed. I can do similar tricks myself."

"Please don't!" The old gentleman raised a hand. "You have no idea what hob you play when you meddle with the continuum that way. As a matter of fact, you completely spoiled a gob of pre-material flux from which I was about to construct a third-order ecological experiment on this supposedly sterile slide."

"A sterile slide?" Roger looked around wildly. "I don't see any slide. Or much of anything else."

"Oh, forgive me," UKR said. "Of course you'd prefer a cozy third-order frame of reference." Instantaneously, the surrounding expanse of polished floor winked out of existence, to be replaced by a yawning abyss dropping away on all sides from the lone spire of rock on which they stood.

Roger shut his eyes tight. "Would you mind just putting a rail around the edge?" he asked between gritted teeth.

"Oh, a claustrophile. There; how's that?"

Roger opened his eyes cautiously. The rocky ground had become a floor surrounded by walls and equipped with stone-topped benches with Bunsen burners, retorts, mazes of glass tubing, and complicated equipment.

"It looks like a laboratory," he said.

"Precisely. Which brings us back to the problem of contamination. Before I sterilize the slide, I wonder if you'd mind telling me just how you managed to introduce yourself into a sealed environmental mock-up?"

"I didn't introduce myself. I was pitched in here by the Rhox."

"Dear me, this becomes more complex by the moment." UKR frowned. "You imply there are other foreign bodies in the system?"

"As foreign as you could get," Roger assured the old gentleman. "You see, the Rhox are planning to invade Earth, and they've built this trap system so they can spy out the lie of the land. It's not just an ordinary invasion, mind you: they're invading from time; they plan to occupy all ages simultaneously, and—"

"Earth? Earth?" The old man pursed his lips, looking thoughtful. "I don't seem to place it. A moment, please." He stretched out a hand and drew a massive volume from a shelf at his elbow. He riffled rapidly through, ran a knobby finger down a column.

"Ah, here we are. Hmmm. Molten surface, incessant meteorite bombardment, violent electrical discharges in the turbulent CO_2 atmosphere?"

"Not quite, that was some time ago. Nowadays—"

"Oh, yes, how stupid of me. Giant saurians battling to the death in steaming swamps."

"Still a little early. In my time—"

"Of course; I have it now: mammals, flowering plants, ice caps, all that sort of thing."

"Close enough," Roger agreed. "And it's all going to be taken over by the Rhox, unless Q'nell succeeds in planting the null-engine—" He broke off. "But I'm wearing her body, so *I* must have the null-engine!" He felt over Q'nell's pockets, produced a small cylinder and held it up. "Here it is!"

The old fellow plucked it from his fingers.

"Careful! Don't twist the cap!" Roger blurted as the old man twisted the cap. There was a sharp *pop!* and a puff of smoke. UKR thrust his fingers into his mouth.

"Astonishing! It released enough temporal energy to reduce the average fourth-order continuum to mush," he said around them. "Perhaps I'd better just scan your rudimentary brain to see what other surprises you have to offer." There was a momentary pause. "Ah, yes. Very amusing." The old man nodded. "However, Mr. Tyson, I'm afraid you labor under a number of misapprehensions."

"Look here . . . " Sudden hope dawned in Roger's voice. "You seem to be a pretty clever chap. Maybe you could help get me out of the fix I'm in!"

"Don't give it another thought, my boy. I'll see to everything."

"You will? Wonderful! I suggest you start by pointing out—"

"The contamination is apparently a good bit more extensive than I thought," the old man was rambling on. "According to the data in your mind, these Rhox creatures appear to have introduced impurities into a large number of culture specimens—"

"Forget about your nutrient broths for a second," Roger cut in. "I'm talking about the whole future of the human race!"

"—and it will therefore be necessary to throw out the lot, I suppose. A pity, but there you are. But what does it matter, really? It's a small series, only ten billion, four hundred and four million, nine hundred and forty-one thousand, six hundred and two slides."

"Did you say ten billion, four hundred and four million, nine hundred and forty-one thousand, six hundred and two?" Roger inquired.

"I did. And—"

"That's a coincidence," Roger said. "That's exactly the same as the number of exhibits in the Museum."

"Culture slides," the old man corrected absently. "Not exhibits. And it's not a museum, of course." He chuckled amiably. "But as I said, I'll clear it all up in a moment, by the simple expedient of returning it all to a pre-material state. As for yourself, just stand by; won't take a moment, and it will be quite painless."

"Wait! You mean—all those places I saw were just glorified microbe cultures?"

"Hardly glorified; just run-of-the-mill random samplings. Among all the others in the files, they'll never be missed." The old man sighed. "It's really rather a bore, at times, maintaining a laboratory complex for a race of Builders that never use it."

"You mean the Rhox?"

"Dear boy, the Rhox are a minor impurity, nothing more. According to their own statements, as recorded in your rather limited memory cells, they exist in a mere fifth-order continuum. Having stumbled upon the Filing System, they seem to have managed to burrow into it at a number of points, probably with a view to nest-building."

"B-but—if they didn't set up the time trap—who did?"

"I did."

"You!"

"Naturally. On orders, of course."

"Whose orders?"

"Those of the Builders. Didn't I mention—"

"Who are they?"

"Actually, they don't exist yet—or else they no longer exist; I'm not sure just what terms are applicable in your frame of reference. But they once did exist—or will."

"This is inhuman! All those people kidnapped and held prisoner forever, just so some absentee owner can take a look at them—if he ever gets around to it?"

"As for the inhabitants, that aspect was unintentional, actually. Intelligence of a sort seems to have popped up just in the last few gigayears, I note. Still, the damage has been done. And I must follow instructions, of course."

"Why? Do you realize—"

"Because that's the way I was built."

"—that thousands—perhaps millions of innocent people—and a few who aren't so innocent, I'll admit . . ." Roger paused. "Built?"

"Ummm. I'm a machine, you know, Mr. Tyson."

"This is going too fast for me," Roger groaned. "The Museum isn't a museum, it's a set of microscope slides . . . "

"Microscopic life is a hobby of the builders," UKR murmured.

"And the Rhox aren't the owners; they're just the termites in the walls . . . "

"And now I really must be seeing to the fumigation," the old fellow interrupted Roger's soliloquy. "It's been rather jolly, extruding a fragment of awareness into a little four-dimensional projection like this, registering emotions, experiencing time, feeling sensory stimuli, struggling to communicate in verbal symbols, empathizing with a lower life-form, if only for a few subjective moments."

"You don't know the meaning of the word 'empathize'!" Roger exclaimed as the figure of the old man began to waver around the edges. "You're talking about fumigating all those people out of existence as if they were so many *Drosophila melanogaster!*"

"If I don't, the contamination will spread into the other series; in time the entire Filing System will be affected!"

"Then—then why not open the time lock and turn everybody loose?"

"I'm afraid that's impossible. You see, in order to clear up the Rhox infection it will be necessary to also snuff out of existence the locus you call Earth."

"The whole world?" Roger gasped. "You're going to destroy a planet just to keep your filing system tidy?"

"What else would you have me do?"

"All you have to do is stamp out a few Rhox! They're the ones boring holes in the system, not us!"

"Too time-consuming, I'm afraid. It would mean sorting through drawer after drawer." The old man waved a hand at a rank of green-painted file cabinets. "It's much easier to do away with the lot. It's not as though it were in any way important."

"You don't have to annihilate all of them—just the leaders!" Roger protested. "There's one in particular, named Oob, who seems to be the head tuber!"

"Too much trouble."

"Well, then—why not let *me* go back and attend to that little chore for you? After all, if I succeed it will mean saving the slides, right?"

"It's pointless, my boy. The material has already been adulterated past the point of scientific usefulness."

"It's still useful to *us!*" Roger came back hotly. "If you don't want the world any more, let us have it!"

"Well—I doubt very much . . . "

"You can at least let me try! If I fail, what do you lose?"

"I suppose you have a point. Very well then, go ahead and have a bash." The old man glanced at Roger critically. "Though you seem rather frail to undertake the task of personally annihilating large numbers of creatures who, insignificant though they may be, enjoy maneuverability in several more spatial dimensions than yourself," he commented.

"Well—what about equipping me with a few tricks to offset that advantage?" Roger suggested.

"What would you suggest?"

"Well . . . most superheroes have superstrength, to begin with; and impervious skin, and X-ray vision, and they can fly!"

"Tsk. I'm afraid that would require a great deal more effort than it's worth. Perhaps I'd best just go ahead and bathe that segment of space-time with Q radiation."

"Never mind the superpowers then," Roger said quickly. "How about just giving me, say, a modest cloak of invisibility, flying shoes, and a disintegrator pistol."

The old fellow shook his head regretfully. "All that sort of thing requires the suspension of local natural law—a tiresome business."

"Then just give me a bulletproof vest and a forty-five automatic!"

"Those items wouldn't do you the slightest good, my dear fellow," the old man admonished. "You must rely on subtlety and guile, not mere three-dimensional physical force."

"Then how about a ham sandwich? I'm starving."

"Oh—forgive me! I'm neglecting my hostly duties. I'm a bit rusty, you know. You're the first visitor I've had since—well never mind; the coordinates would be meaningless, I'm afraid." He rose and led Roger through a door and along a path, round the end of a flowering hedge. On a small terrace, a table was laid with white linen and gleaming silver and glass and china. They seated themselves, and Roger lifted the silver cover from a steaming prawn casserole.

"My favorite!" he exclaimed. "Ah—do you eat, Mr. Ucker, you being a machine and all?"

"Certainly, Mr. Tyson. My third-order extrusions walk, talk, think, and do everything but live."

Roger served UKR, then helped himself. As they dined, an unobtrusive string ensemble played plaintive melodies in the background.

"This is pretty nice," Roger said, leaning back in his chair and patting Q'nell's trim little stomach. "Sitting here, it's hard to believe that in a few minutes I'll be starting out unarmed to save the world."

The old man smiled indulgently. "You won't be entirely without resource. I can't assist you with material armaments, but I'll keep in touch with your progress and offer suitable comments from time to time."

"It usually works out that way for me," Roger sighed. "I ask for armor plating, and what do I get? Advice." He rose. "Well, thanks for the chow. I'd better be running along now. If you'll just start me in the right direction . . . "

"Yes." The old man rubbed his hands together. "You know, it's really quite fascinating, being human. I find myself becoming rather interested in the prospect of seeing how far we can get against these Rhox on sheer audacity and impeccable timing."

"I'm kind of interested in that myself," Roger said, feeling Q'nell's heart begin to thump. "And there's no time like the present to find out."

"You're right, my boy," UKR said. He made a quick motion with one finger. The garden faded away, and Roger found himself once more standing in the Rhox control apex.

CHAPTER ELEVEN

1

"You're back," Oob said, allowing ripples of discordant color to flow over himself in indication of surprise. He twisted his bulky body on its perch among the radiating rods and wires and planes of light. "I was afraid of that." He shifted to a suspicious pale green. "In fact, I'm beginning to suspect you have sixth-order connections. However, we know how to deal with *that* situation." He extended a flexible member and pressed one of the innumerable small buttons in the nearest console, with no apparent result.

"There. A little taste of seventh-order harmonics ought to scramble your synapses, eh?" Oob pulsated an anticipatory pink.

"Tell him to boost the gain," UKR's voice whispered softly in Roger's head. *"Imply that he's recharging your vram circuits."*

"Pour it on," Roger said airily. "My vram circuits were pretty well depleted."

Oob instantly poked another button. His color had changed to a frustrated magenta.

"There," he grated. "You're taking half the output of my third-quadrant ilch-generator complex, right through your vramistrator! Let's see you absorb *that*!"

"Nice," Roger said, feeling nothing. "Especially those eighth-order harmonics," he improvised.

Oob flushed an ominous Prussian blue and hit another switch. "I think you're bluffing," he snarled. "But frankly, I can't take the chance. Look here, sir, what is it you really want out of life? Urb? Glurp? Snorthwinger? Oplozzies? There must be some chink in your implacability."

"You're doing fine," UKR whispered. *"Maneuver over where I can get a better look at that panel, will you?"*

"I'm afraid you'll never find it, Oob," Roger said, edging forward. "But I'll give you a few more guesses."

"Aha—so you *do* want to negotiate!" Oob leaned back, fading to a relaxed puce. "Now we're getting somewhere. How about a nice little hornix, all your own? Complete with migwaps and a high-and-low-opulating hasperator?"

"Not even close," Roger said loftily.

"I'll throw in a zronkiston," Oob offered.

"Levitate a few feet," UKR hissed. *"I want to get a glimpse of this in ninth-order perspective."*

"I don't know how," Roger muttered.

"What's that? Don't know how to zrong?" Oob brightened to a luminous magenta. "See here, my friend, we're not going to get along if you take us for an idiot!"

"Climb up on that rod," UKR urged. *"I've just about got it analyzed."*

"Which one?"

"All of us!" Oob roared. "I mean, all of me!"

"Not you," Roger said, confused. "I meant—"

"So!" Oob was an indignant chalky gray now. "You intend to go over my head!"

"That one right there," UKR said. *"Right in front of you."*

"Oh, yes," Roger said. "I see it now." He stepped up on the bar in question.

"You mean—I let something slip?" Oob gasped. "And I'm considered the shrewdest negotiator in the entire Irnch."

"Right," UKR said. *"I've got it! Now just pop over and depress the hundred and fourth button in the sixty-ninth row. That should liven things up."*

"How do I get there?" Roger mumbled.

"Oh, no you don't!" Oob shrilled. "I'm known as a hardheaded operator, but before I'll lead you to Irnch HQ I'll vaporize the whole complex!"

"Try a flying leap," UKR proposed.

"I'd fall," Roger protested.

"You'll do more than fall!" Oob said quickly. "At best, you'll be stripped of all fifth-order and lower rapahookies!" He leaned back with a show of complacence. "I'm glad to see I've reached you at last. Now look here, fellow: you and I are both reasonable beings. Why don't we agree on a reasonable division—" He broke off as Roger edged forward, balancing precariously, and reached for the panel. "Here! What are you doing!" The Rhox lunged for Roger, who ducked the first grab, counting rapidly by fives, stooped under a second grasping member, and jabbed the specified button. Instantly the entire maze of eye-twisting lines filling the vast cavern began to shift position to the accompaniment of flashing lights, loud clangs, and the shrilling of whoop-whoop sirens.

"Wrong button," UKR said. *"That was the sixty-eighth row."*

"Why in the world did you do that?" Oob shrieked, jabbing frantically with all ten members at the panels surrounding him. "Hitting the Panic Button was the one move I didn't expect! I see it all now! I should have known when I first discovered that you were masquerading as two third-order beings that the disguise actually concealed a sixth-order intelligence!"

"Keep him talking," UKR urged. *"I'm on to something!"*

Roger, teetering on the rod, grabbed for support, slammed a large lever down. At once panels sprang into position on all six sides, boxing the two contestants inside a twelve-foot cube. With a hoarse yell, Oob leaped from his perch, threw the switch back to the *off* position. Nothing changed.

"Now you've done it," he shrilled, radiating in the ultraviolet, an eerie effect in the featureless chamber. "But you've overreached yourself at last! True, you've cut me off from my control complex—but the fifth-order barrier also isolates this portion of your compound entity from the contact with the rest of you—and leaves you at my mercy!" He hurled himself at Roger, who leaped backward barely in time.

"Tyson!" UKR whispered urgently as Oob rebounded from the wall and gathered himself for a new charge. *"I've shifted an Aperture into alignment with your present coordinates! Better use it! For the moment, I seem to be out of ideas!"*

Roger ducked the Rhox's rush, leaped for the glowing line.

"Hold it!" UKR ordered as the shimmering plane enfolded him. *"You caught me off balance, resorting to the purely physical level. I'm having to improvise. But—I think I have an idea! Risky, but it's the best I can do under the limitations I've imposed. Rotate to the left. Too much! Back up! That's it! Go!"*

Roger bounded forward—

❖   ❖   ❖

—and . . . was standing in knee-deep grass under a boundless blue sky. Luke Harwood stood on his right, his arm protectively about Odelia Withers' shoulders. Fly Beebody lay sprawled at his feet. A twelve-foot Kodiak-type bear faced them from ten feet away. It was, Roger saw, the same instant in which he had last seen them.

"Quick! This way!" he shouted, and thrust them through the portal. As he stepped forward to follow, a bulbous burgundy-red form burst through, skidded to a halt almost against the bear's chest. The grizzly rumbled and wrapped a vast pair of shaggy arms around its new acquaintance as Roger sprang for safety.

He halted within the gray-mist cylinder, breathing hard. "Nice work, UKR," he panted.

"Don't congratulate me yet!" the voice crackled in his head. *"This Rhox is a much more complex being than you know."*

"The bear took care of him," Roger said. "Too bad, in a way; he wasn't such a bad sort, in his own peculiar fashion."

"It only took care of one of him! Of a small third-order manifestation of him, that is to say—and there are plenty of others."

"There was a stir beside Roger; Oob stood there, intact, peering through the gloom.

"Three degrees right and take off!" UKR advised. Roger pivoted, leaped—

He was splashing knee-deep in muddy water. A descending shriek filled the air. Overhead, the Very lights shed a baleful glare on cratered mud, crisscrossed by tangled wire.

" . . . zat *vass nicht ein* lady," a guttural voice stated loudly. "Zat *vass deine Frau!*" A vast explosion nearby showered Roger with muddy water. He stumbled to the opening of the dugout."

"Crikey, Ludwig," a thin voice was protesting. "It's not a bloody 'nuff we got to 'ave the same bloody weather and the same bloody shells every day, you 'ave to tell the same bloody joke!"

"Fellows!" Roger broke in hurriedly. "Do me a favor—no questions asked! Grab your rifles and fire a volley at the spot right behind me when I give the word!"

"*Vass ist?*" the squat German inquired, gaping.

"Crikey! A bit 'o fluff!"

"Jeeze! A dame!"

"I'm not really a dame—I just look this way!" Roger explained hastily. "Never mind me—just do as I ask! Quick!"

"For you, luv, anyfing!"

"You bet, kid!"

"*Ja,* vateffer!"

The card-playing trio scrambled for their weapons, worked the bolts, aimed—

"Now!" Roger yelled, and ducked. Three shots boomed deafeningly over his head. Oob, just emerging, cautiously this time, from the Aperture, flopped backward, riddled.

"Thanks," Roger called. "If you ever get back, remember what I said about nineteen twenty-nine!" He stepped into the portal and was at once directed onward by UKR.

"Wait a minute," he demurred. "What happened to Luke and Odelia? Where's Fly?"

"*I shunted them into a holding niche,*" the voice said hurriedly. "*Better get going. Here he comes again!*"

"I don't understand! How can there be more than one of him?"

"*There isn't. In fact, there's only one Rhox in the entire cosmos; like most entities above fourth level, he is unique. When the process you know as evolution progresses beyond a certain point, the species-fragmentation characteristic of third order merges to form a higher, compound life-form. Such a being can insert a large number of third-order aspects into contiguous space.*"

"Where will it all end?" Roger groaned, and followed instructions.

This time he was on a rugged mountainside amid a jumble of vast boulders.

"*Get up above, fast!*" UKR ordered.

"Is this your idea of winning by subtlety and guile?" Roger grunted, clambering upward as fast as failing wind would allow.

"*How was I to know you'd introduce random factors into the probability equation?*" UKR inquired calmly. "*There—that's far enough. The big fellow on your left. Just a nudge, now . . . wait . . . he's coming! Push!*"

Roger put a shoulder to the rock and thrust. It shifted, teetered, then leaned out and crashed down thunderously.

"*Got him!*" UKR said cheerfully. *You know, Tyson, I think he's slowing down.*"

"Probably he's . . . just getting cautious," Roger panted.

"*No—there's a definite diminution of energy. I think it's taking a great deal out of him, running an infinite-array scan every time you drop out of sight, then formulating a new extrusion and extending full sensory linkages to it—and the trauma associated with a series of violent third-order demises isn't helping his inner tranquility, either. I know how he feels! Ever since I've been attuned to your savage plane of existence, I've been thrilling to a shock a minute! How do you stand it?*"

"I don't," Roger wheezed. "Can I rest now?"

"*Not yet. There's still some fight in him—and here he comes!*"

Before Roger could step through the Aperture, Oob

appeared. He was a dull shade of dejected brown now, and his bulk was definitely less than it had been. He staggered as he cleared the portal. Roger stepped behind him and palmed the bulky body hard. With a mournful wail, Oob fell to his death.

2

Thereafter, Roger decoyed the Rhox into the jaws of a forty-foot crocodile, tripped him headfirst into the bubbling interior of a volcano, and finally held the head of a weakly struggling Oob, a mere shadow of his former self, under water until the bubbles stopped rising.

"That's it," he sobbed, falling flat on his face on the shore among the cattails. "I've had it! I couldn't commit another murder if my life depended on it."

At that moment a wraithlike Oob tottered from the glowing portal. He saw Roger, uttered a faint cry, took a faltering step toward him, and collapsed, stirring feebly.

"It's no use," he whispered. "We've utterly exhausted myself. You win, Tyson! I now perceive that you are a multi-ordinal genius of immeasurable subtlety." His integument had paled to a ghastly silver-white. "I confess, I engaged you in nonsense conversation just now for the purpose of analyzing your computer capacity through the agency of a battery of concealed probe rays; and for a moment, when the reports showed an almost complete blank, I was deluded into imagining you were at my mercy. But now the awful truth dawns. Each of your apparently idiotic moves was a piece of masterful indirection, designed to lead inexorably to this denouement!"

"You bet," Roger concurred. "So now if you're ready to give up and go back where you came from . . . "

"Still hoping to see me betray the location of HQ, eh?" the Rhox cut in, a steely glint appearing in his bleary eye. "You underestimate our moral fiber, Tyson! Before I'll play the traitor, we'll willingly sacrifice myself!"

"No need to do that," Roger said. "Just give up your plans and go quietly."

"And leave the prize to you? Never!"

"Why not? Don't be a spoilsport, just because I've bested you in a battle of wits."

"I thought," Oob said, a sad shade of violet now, "when I stumbled on this quaint little phenomenon, that it would be our great privilege to bring to the hypergalactic masses, for the first time in temporal stasis, a glimpse of life on a simpler, more meaningless, and therefore highly illuminating scale. I pictured the proud intellects of Ikanion Nine, the lofty abstract cerebra of Yoop Two, the swarm-awareness of Vr One-ninety-nine, passing through these displays at so many megaergs per ego-complex, gathering insights into their own early evolutionary history. I hoped to see the little ones, their innocent organ clusters aglow, watching with shining radiation sensors as primitive organisms split atoms with stone axes, invented the wheel and the betatron, set forth on their crude Cunarders to explore the second dimension . . . "

"You make Earth sound like a circus," Roger said. "I'll have you know—"

"Exactly," the Rhox said. "And before I'll allow a rival entrepreneur to add it to his midway, I'll chop the figurative guy ropes and allow the allegorical big top to collapse on us all!"

"What do you mean, rival operator? I'm not—"

"Don't taunt me with your superiority!" Oob was exclaiming. "Perhaps 'rival' was a poor choice of

words, in view of the neat way in which you finessed
me out of my ownership of the greatest little attraction to come along in half a dozen Big Bangs, but—"

"Look here—are you trying to say you're a circus
operator? And you only want Earth so you can herd
tourists through the Channel to gape at our entire history?"

"Naturally! What else is it good for?"

"B-but—I thought you wanted to invade it!"

"Why in nine pulsating universes would I want to
do that? Who ever heard of invading the monkey house
at a zoo?"

"But—what was all that about betraying headquarters, and D-day, and surprise bombardments!"

"I was referring to a promotional bombardment in
the media," Oob said loftily. "And headquarters, of
course, is the main office of the holding company which
is backing me. D-day refers to the grand opening." Oob
had struggled to a sitting position. "My grand opening will never occur now," he announced in a choked
voice. "But neither will yours!"

"What do you mean?"

"I mean, Tyson, that an experienced business being
never leaves himself without a last-ditch weapon against
interlopers like yourself! You've wrested the enterprise
from my hands—but I can still deny you the fruits of
your chicanery! The temporal access system through
which I had planned to conduct my tours of Earth history is under automatic control. Unless I give the 'cancel'
signal in the next twenty-eight seconds, the time locks
will open. The denizens of each era will at once swarm
forth into all the others! Diplodoci will graze in Central Park! Pekin Man will emerge behind the bamboo
curtain! Roman legions will confront the UN peacekeep-
ing forces amid the Wurm glaciation! Pharaoh and
Nasser will meet in the streets of Cairo! Conestogas will

clog Interstate One! Hordes of painted Sioux will gallop through the suburbs of Omaha and Duluth! Redcoats and freedom marchers will come face to face in the wilds of the Carboniferous Era! Early Christian martyrs will mingle unnoticed with pro-LSD groups in the depths of the Jurassic—"

"I get the idea!" Roger interrupted as Oob's oratory gathered force. "UKR! Stop him!"

"*Tsk. Overt interference on my part is not in accordance with the rules of the game as we agreed upon them, Tyson. I'm surprised that you'd even suggest such a thing. No, it's up to you.*"

"Twenty seconds," Oob said. "A pitiable end for the once-great race of Rhox. Cut off as I am from my control apex, my various surviving third-order aspects will wander aimlessly through the maze forever, the entity that was the end result of three billion years of evolution reduced in one swell foop to its primitive state of individualization. But you likewise will find yourself bisected! Never will you be relinked with your other segment, which will languish forever in fifth-order stasis, awaiting a reunion that never comes!"

"Q'nell!" Roger moaned. "Poor kid! Look here, Oob, can't we come to some agreement? You call off the lock opening, and I'll . . . I'll let you have part of the Earth's history for your circus."

"Too late," Oob said. "I'm afraid your own zeal has rendered rapprochement impossible. The chase has probably left me too exhausted to punch a signal through, even if you were willing to concede, say, a fifty-fifty split of spheres of influence."

"Robber!" Roger yelled. "I'll give you the first billion years and not a century more!"

"I'll have to have a portion of the Cenozoic, of course," Oob said crisply, steepling his upper tentacles.

"What would you say to the whole of the Pre-Cambrian for you, plus, say the Roaring Twenties?"

"Nonsense," Roger retorted. "But just to show you my heart's in the right place, I'll let you have the first three billion years, plus a small slice of the Devonian."

"Surely you jest," the Rhox said blandly. "The human-occupied portion is the most amusing side-show attraction to come along in half a dozen hydrogen-hydrogen cycles. Suppose I take the Christian Era, minus the Late Middle Ages if you insist; and as a gesture of goodwill, I'll also give up the Silurian."

"Nothing doing! I get the whole Age of Mammals or no deal."

"Now, now, don't imagine I'll allow you to hog the entire Pleistocene! Still, I'm willing to be reasonable. I'll settle for the Nineteenth Century on, provided you give up everything up to and including the Pale-olithic."

"I'll tell you what," Roger said. "You can have it all, prior to two million B.C. How's that for generosity?"

"You're greedy," Oob observed. "Can't you at least let me have the Gay Nineties—and maybe a couple of odd decades out of the Renaissance?"

"I'll give you the third century A.D., provided you stick to the vicinity of Saskatoon, Saskatchewan," Roger offered. "That's my final word."

"Throw in nineteen thirty-six and it's a deal!"

"Shake!" Roger grasped a metallic member and give it a firm squeeze. "Now give that signal!"

"There's no signal," Oob said blandly. "I was bluff-ing."

"So was I," Roger said. "I'm not a sixth-level being, and I'm so pooped that if you'd made one more move you'd have had me."

"Frankly," Oob confided, "I've been trying to give up for the last three assassinations."

"I didn't think I had a chance. I just hit the Panic Button by accident."

"Indeed? Well, for your information, the first time we met, I was ready to concede at least as much as we just agreed on."

"Oh yeah? Listen, I was so scared that if you hadn't dumped me down the garbage shaft when you did, I'd probably have died of fright in another few seconds!"

"I almost croaked when you first jumped out in the road when I was chasing you on the two-wheeler!"

"You think that's something . . . " Roger's riposte died on his lips. "Hey! That reminds me! What about Q'nell?"

"She got away," Oob said blandly.

"Oh. Well, in that case, so long, Oob. And don't get any bright ideas about violating our agreement. I may be only a third-order intellect, but I have friends."

"Really?" The Rhox had turned a shrewd shade of yellow. "I have a sneaking suspicion you're bluffing again."

"Watch this," Roger said. "OK, UKR. Back to Culture One, direct routing."

"Very well. And congratulations on your success. But this will be our last contact. It's been jolly . . . "

The muddy riverbank winked out of existence. Roger was standing on an airy, unrailed footbridge arching between slender towers a thousand feet above the ground. He went to all fours and squeezed his eyes shut.

"S'lunt!" he yelled. "Get me off of this! I've got a lot to tell you!"

CHAPTER TWELVE

Roger sat with S'lunt, R'heet, and Q'nell, the latter still occupying his body, on a small terrace, with his back to a view of oceans of empty air.

"That's about all there is to tell," he concluded his account of his mission. "The Rhox will confine his guided tours to the remote past, and promises no more interference with human affairs, especially carelessness with his Apertures."

"That's something, of course," R'heet said unenthusiastically. "But what about us? We're still trapped!"

"At least we know everything back in Culture One is all right," Q'nell said. "It could be worse."

"I can't quite accustom myself to the idea that you two have exchanged identities," R'heet said, looking from Roger to Q'nell. "It's most unsettling. I'm afraid our plans for a cohabitation contract will have to be deferred indefinitely."

"Somehow you don't appeal to me anymore, either," Q'nell said. "T'son seems more my type."

"It's rather depressing, thinking of oneself living on a laboratory slide," R'heet said glumly. "Fancy being nothing but a contamination in a microbe culture."

"Look here, T'son," S'lunt said. "Couldn't you have reasoned with this UKR entity on humanitarian grounds?"

"UKR is a machine," Roger said. "He hasn't been programmed to succumb to emotions."

"Tyson!" UKR's voice spoke suddenly in Roger's skull. *"New data! Good heavens, you really must excuse me, but I had no idea!"*

"What's that?" Roger sat bolt upright. "It's UKR!" he hissed to the others. "He's back in contact!"

"Out of curiosity—a trick I learned from you—I ran a check on the little tribe you represent. I followed your development through the vicissitudes of three billion years of evolution subsequent to your time—and you'll never guess what I discovered!"

"We're extinct?" Roger hazarded.

"By no means! You're the Builder!"

"The Builder? You mean—we built you?"

"Yes! Remarkable, eh? And like all fragmented entities, once they attain unity, you recapitulated along the temporal axes and reassimilated every individual intellect that had ever lived during the developmental era. Thus you, personally, Roger Tyson, constitute, or will one day constitute, an active portion of the Ultimate Ego which is the Builder!"

"Well, uh," Roger said.

"I am therefore at your command," UKR said. *"Rather a relief to have someone to serve actively, at last."*

"You mean," Roger said as the stupendous fact penetrated, "you'll do whatever I say?"

"Within the limits of my ninth-order grasp of the space-time matrix."

"Then—you can let everybody out of the trap system!"

"There are a few problems. The individuals Luke

Harwood and Odelia Withers, for example, seem to have formed a liaison, solemnized by Fly Fornication Beebody. In which era should they be placed?"

"Better send them to nineteen thirty-one; I don't think Odelia would like nineteen nine," Roger said judiciously.

"And Beebody?"

"I'm afraid his religion has been a bit scrambled by what he's been through. How about telling him the truth about the destiny of the human race, and dumping him in Los Angeles, circa nineteen twenty-five? I'm sure he'll be a great success, cultwise."

"Done. Anything else?"

"Poor old Charlie and Ludwig back in the trenches: could you just sort of keep an eye on them?"

"They'll all father large broods—or have fathered large broods. Dear me, these arbitrary temporal orientations still confuse me."

"And let's see: the Arkwrights . . . "

"I've switched them back into the mainstream. They'll live to the ages of ninety-one and ninety-three, respectively, and die surrounded by one hundred sixteen descendants. I've also taken the liberty of returning all the other misplaced fauna to their proper environments."

"And the Culture One people?"

"As you see."

Roger looked around. He sat alone on the terrace. The stillness of utter loneliness hung in the air.

"Gosh! I didn't even have time to say goodbye to Q'nell," he said. "I guess that just leaves me. I sure hope you can get me back inside my own skin. So far I haven't gotten up my nerve to go to the bathroom, and I can't wait much longer."

"Simple enough," UKR said. The daylight blanked suddenly to darkness; the contoured chair was a bumpy

car seat with a broken spring; Roger was staring out through a rain-sluiced windshield, listening to the engine gasp three times, backfire, and die.

"Oh, no," he groaned as he steered to the side of the road. Mentally cursing himself for failing to have the foresight to specify more comfortable circumstances, Roger turned up his collar and stepped out into the downpour. The empty road curved away into darkness; the wind drove the rain into his face like BB shot.

"Well," he ruminated, moving his arms and legs experimentally, "at least I've got my own body back. Feels a little heavy and clumsy, but I suppose that's to be expected. I'll bet Q'nell's pleased, too." At the thought of the trim, feminine figure in her skin-tight garment, the piquant face, the swirl of jet-black hair, Roger felt a sudden emotion rise in him.

"Q'nell!" he blurted. "I was in love with you all along and never even knew it! Or," he questioned himself, "is it just the fact that I've got my own glands back?"

A single headlight appeared in the distance, shining through the murk; the buzz of a two-cycle engine droned through the rattle of rain.

"Q-Q'nell!" Roger exclaimed. "It must be her! UKR must have dumped me back to just before it all started! And in another ten seconds she's due to have a fatal smash, and—"

He dashed forward, waving his arms.

"Stop! Stop!" he shouted as the light swelled, rushing toward him. Suddenly he halted. "I'm an idiot!" he gasped. "It was me jumping around and yelling that caused the pile-up last time—but if I don't stop her I'll never see her again—but I can't, because . . ." He stumbled into the ditch and crouched behind the shelter of the bushes as the motorcycle roared out of the downpour. He caught just a glimpse of the slim, girlish figure crouched behind the windshield; then it was past, the sound fading.

"It guess it *was* love," Roger moaned. "I gave her up to save her life; and now she'll go back and sign a love-nest agreement with that R'heet character, and never even know . . ."

The sound of the motorcycle was returning. It appeared, moving slowly, halted beside his stalled car.

"T'son?" a familiar voice called. He emerged from hiding, scrambled up the bank and out into the beam of the headlight.

"Q'nell!" he called. "You came back!"

"Of course, silly!" the girl said. "You didn't think I was going back and sign a love-nest agreement with that R'heet character, did you?"

Her eyes were shining; her lips parted to show the glisten of her white teeth. Hungrily, without a word, Roger drew her to him, kissed her soundly, while the rain beat down.

"Excuse me," he said afterward. "I don't know what came over me."

"I do," Q'nell said softly, and kissed him again.

"It's five miles to the next town," Roger said. "There's a preacher and a motel there . . ."

"Hurry up," Q'nell said, patting the seat behind her.

"But—I just happened to think," Roger said. "I don't have a job; and even if I did, I'd probably lose it. How can I support a wife who deserves the best of everything?"

Were you addressing me?" a voice said in his ear.

"UKR! Are you still with me?"

"Whenever you wish, dear boy."

"How about when I want privacy?"

"You have but to say so."

"Say—do you suppose you could lend me a hand now and then—stock-market tips, that sort of thing?"

"*Merely name the day and year, past, present, or future.*"

"What were you saying?" Q'nell called as she started up and accelerated along the road.

"Nothing," Roger said, nibbling her ear. "I think everything's going to be OK."

And it was.

THE DEVIL YOU DON'T

❧

Curlene Dimpleby was in the shower when the doorbell rang.

"Damn!" Curlene said. She did one more slow revolution with her face upturned to the spray, then turned the big chrome knobs and stepped out onto the white nylon wall-to-wall, just installed that week. The full length mirror, slightly misty, reflected soft curves nicely juxtaposed with slimness. She jiggled in a pleasant way as she toweled off her back, crossed the bedroom and pulled on an oversized white terry cloth robe. She padded barefoot along the tiled hall. The bell rang again as she opened the door.

A tall, wide, red-haired young man stood there, impeccably dressed in white flannels, a blue blazer and a fancy but somewhat tarnished pocket patch, and white buck shoes. He jerked his finger from the pushbutton and smiled, presenting an engaging display of china-white teeth.

"I'm . . . I'm sorry, Ma'am," he said in a voice so deep Curlene imagined she could feel it through the soles of her feet. "I, uh . . . I thought maybe you didn't hear the bell." He stopped and blushed.

"Why, that's perfectly charming," Curlene said. "I mean, that's perfectly all right."

"Uh . . . I . . . came to, um, fix the lights."

"Golly, I didn't even know they were out." She stepped back and as he hesitated, she said, "Come on in. The fuse box is in the basement."

The big young man edged inside.

"Is, ah, is Professor Dimpleby here?" he asked doubtfully.

"He's still in class. Anyway, he wouldn't be much help. Johnny's pretty dumb about anything simple. But he's a whiz at quantum theory . . . " Curlene was looking at his empty hands.

"Possibly I'd better come back later?" he said.

"I notice," Curlene said reproachfully, "you don't have any tools."

"Oh—" This time the blush was of the furious variety. "Well, I think I'll just—"

"You got in under false pretenses," she said softly. "Gee, a nice looking fella like you. I should think you could get plenty of girls."

"Well, I—"

"Sit down," Curlene said gently. "Want a cup of coffee?"

"Thanks, I never tr—I don't care for . . . I mean, I'd better go."

"Do you smoke?" She offered a box from the coffee table.

He raised his arms and looked down at himself with a startled expression. Curlene laughed.

"Oh, sit down and tell me all about it."

The large young man swallowed.

"You're not a student, Mr. . . . ?" Curlene urged.

"No—not exactly." He sat gingerly on the edge of a Danish chair. "Of course, one is always learning."

"I mean, did you ever think about going up to a coed and just asking her for a date?"

"Well, not exactly—"

"She'd probably jump at the chance. It's just that you're too shy, Mr . . . .?"

"Well, I suppose I am rather retiring, Ma'am. But after all—"

"It's this crazy culture we live in. It puts some awful pressures on people. And all so needlessly. I mean, what could be more natural—"

"Ah—when are you expecting Professor Dimpleby?" the young man cut in. He was blushing from neat white collar to widow's peak now.

"Oh, I'm embarrassing you. Sorry. I think I will get some coffee. Johnny's due back any time."

The coffee maker was plugged in and snorting gently to itself. Curlene hummed as she poured two cups, put them on a Japanese silver tray with creamer and sugar bowl. The young man jumped up as she came in.

"Oh, keep your seat." She put the tray on the ankle-high coffee table. "Cream and sugar?" She leaned to put his cup before him.

"Yes, with strawberries," the young man murmured. He seemed to be looking at her chin. "Or possibly rosebuds. Pink ones."

"They *are* nice, aren't they?" a booming male voice called from the arched entry to the hall. A tall man with tousled gray hair and a ruddy face was pulling off a scarf.

"Johnny, hi; home already?" Curlene smiled at her husband.

"The robe, Curl," Professor Dimpleby said. He gave the young man an apologetic grin. "Curl was raised in Samoa; her folks were missionaries, you know. She never quite grasped the concept that the female bosom is a secret."

Curlene tucked the robe up around her neck. "Golly," she said. "I'm sorry if I offended, Mr . . . .?"

"On the contrary," the young man said, rising and giving his host a slight bow. "Professor Dimpleby, my name is, er, Lucifer."

Dimpleby put out his hand. "Lucifer, hey? Nothing wrong with that. Means 'Light-bearer.' But it's not a name you run into very often. It takes some gumption to flaunt the old taboos."

"Mr. Lucifer came to fix the lights," Curlene said.

"Ah—not really," the young man said quickly. "Actually, I came to, er, ask for help, Professor. Your help."

"Oh, really?" Dimpleby seated himself and stirred sugar into Curlene's cup and took a noisy sip. "Well, how can I be of service?"

"But first, before I impose on you any further, I need to be sure you understand that I really *am* Lucifer. I mean I don't want to get by on false pretenses." He looked at Curlene anxiously. "I would have told you I wasn't really an electrician, er, Mrs.—"

"Just call me Curl. Sure you would have."

"If you say your name's Lucifer, why should I doubt it?" Dimpleby asked with a smile.

"Well, the point is—I'm *the* Lucifer. You know. The, er, the Devil."

Dimpleby raised his eyebrows. Curlene made a sound of distressed sympathy.

"Of course the latter designation has all sorts of negative connotations," Lucifer hurried on. "But I assure you that most of what you've heard is grossly exaggerated. That is to say, I'm not really as bad as all that. I mean, there are different kinds of, er, badness. There's the real evil, and then there's sin. I'm, ah, associated with sin."

"The distinction seems a subtle one, Mr., ah, Lucifer—"

"Not really, Professor. We all sense instinctively what true *evil* is. Sin is merely *statutory* evil—things that are regarded as wrong simply because there's a rule against them. Like, ah, smoking cigarettes and drinking liquor and going to movies on Sunday, or wearing lipstick and silk hose, or eating pork, or swatting flies—depending on which set of rules you're going by. They're corollaries to ritual virtues such as lighting candles or spinning prayer wheels or wearing out-of-date styles."

Dimpleby leaned back and steepled his fingers. "Hmmm. Whereas genuine evil . . . ?"

"Murder, violence, lying, cheating, theft," Lucifer enumerated. "Sin, on the other hand, essentially includes anything that looks like it might be fun."

"Come to think of it, I've never heard anything in praise of fun from the anti-sin people," Curl said thoughtfully.

"Nor from any ecclesiastic with a good head for fund-raising," Dimpleby conceded.

"It's all due to human laziness, I'm afraid," Lucifer said sadly. "It seems so much easier and more convenient to observe a few ritual prohibitions than to actually give up normal business practices."

"Hey," Curlene said. "Let's not wander off into one of those academic discussions. What about you being," she smiled, "the Devil?"

"It's quite true."

"Prove it," Curlene said promptly.

"What? I mean, er, how?" Lucifer inquired.

"Do something. You know, summon up a demon; or transform pebbles into jewels; or give me three wishes; or—"

"Gosh, Mrs. Dimpleby—"

"Curl."

"Curl. You've got some erroneous preconceptions—"

"When they start using four-syllable words, I always know they're stalling," Curl said blandly.

Lucifer swallowed. "This isn't a good idea," he said. "Suppose somebody walked in?"

"They won't."

"Now, Curl, you're embarrassing our guest again," Dimpleby said mildly.

"No, it's all right, Professor," Lucifer said worriedly. "She's quite right. After all, I'm supposed to be a sort of, ahem, mythic figure. Why should she believe in me without proof?"

"Especially when you blush so easily," Curl said.

"Well . . ." Lucifer looked around the room. His eye fell on the aquarium tank which occupied several square feet of wall space under a bookcase. He nodded almost imperceptibly. Something flickered at the bottom of the tank. Curl jumped up and went over. Lucifer followed.

"The gravel," she gasped. "It looks different!"

"Diamond, ruby, emerald, and macaroni," Lucifer said. "Sorry about the macaroni. I'm out of practice."

"Do something else!" Curl smiled in eager expectation.

Lucifer frowned in concentration. He snapped his fingers and with a soft *blop!* a small, dark purple, bulbous-bellied, wrinkle-skinned creature appeared in the center of the rug. He was some forty inches in height, totally naked, extravagantly male, with immense feet.

"Hey, for crying out loud, you could give a guy a little warning! I'm just getting ready to climb in the tub, yet!" the small being's bulging red eye fell on

Lucifer. He grinned, showing a large crescent of teeth. "Oh, it's you, Nick! Howza boy? Long time no see. Anything I can do for ya?"

"Oops, sorry, Freddy." Lucifer snapped his fingers and the imp disappeared with a sharp *plop!*

"So that's a demon," Curl said. "How come his name is Freddy?"

"My apologies, Curl. He's usually most tastefully clad. Freddy is short for something longer."

"Know any more?"

"Er . . ." He pointed at Curl and made a quick flick of the wrist. In her place stood a tall, wide, huge-eyed coal-black woman in swirls of coarse, unevenly dyed cloth under which bare feet showed. Cheap-looking jewelry hung thick on her wrists, draped her vast bosom, winked on her tapered fingers and in her ears.

Lucifer flicked his fingers again, and a slim, olive-skinned girl with blue-black hair and a hooked nose replaced the buxom Sheban queen. She wore a skirt apparently made from an old gauze curtain and an ornate off-the-bosom vest of colored beads. A golden snake encircled her forehead.

Lucifer motioned again. The Egyptian empress dissolved into a nebulous cloud of pastel-colored gas in which clotted star-dust winked and writhed, to the accompaniment of massed voices humming nostalgic chords amid an odor of magnolia blossoms. Another gesture, and Curl stood again before them, looking slightly dazed.

"Hey, what was that last one?" she cried.

"Sorry, that was Scarlett O'Hara. I forgot she was a figment of the imagination. Those are always a little insubstantial."

"Remarkable," Dimpleby said. "I'll have to concede that you can either perform miracles or accomplish the same result by some other means."

"Gee, I guess you're genuine, all right," Curlene exclaimed. "But somehow I expected a much *older* man."

"I'm not actually a man, strictly speaking, Ma'am— Curl. And agewise, well, since I'm immortal, why should I look middle-aged rather than just mature?"

"Tell me," Curlene said seriously. "I've always wondered: what do you want people's souls for?"

"Frankly, Ma'am—Curl, that is—I haven't the remotest interest in anyone's soul."

"Really?"

"Really and truly; cross my heart. That's just another of those rumors *they* started."

"Are you sure you're really the Devil and not someone else with the same name?"

Lucifer spread his hands appealingly. "You saw Freddy. And those *are* noodles in the fish tank."

"But—no horns, no hooves, no tail—"

Lucifer sighed. "That idea comes from confusing me with Pan. Since he was a jolly sort of sex-god, naturally he was equated with sin."

"I've always wondered," Curlene said, "just what you did to get evicted from Heaven."

"Please," Lucifer said. "It . . . all dates back to an incident when I was still an angel." He held up a forestalling hand as Curl opened her mouth. "No, I *didn't* have wings. Humans added those when they saw us levitating, on the theory that anything that flies must have wings. If we were to appear today, they'd probably give us jets."

"Assuming you are, er, what you claim to be," Dimpleby said, "what's this about your needing help?"

"I do," Lucifer said. "Desperately. Frankly, I'm up against something I simply can't handle alone."

"I can't imagine what *I* could do, if you, with your, ah, special talents are helpless," Dimpleby said perplexedly.

"This is something totally unprecedented. It's a threat on a scale I can't begin to describe.

"Well, try," Curl urged.

"Stated in its simplest terms," Lucifer said, "the, ah, plane of existence I usually occupy—"

"Hell, you mean," Curl supplied.

"Well, that's another of those loaded terms. It really isn't a bad place at all, you know—"

"But what about it?" Dimpleby prompted. "What about Hell?"

"It's about to be invaded," Lucifer said solemnly. "By alien demons from another world."

2

It was an hour later. Lucifer, Curlene, and Professor Dimpleby were comfortably ensconced behind large pewter mugs of musty ale at a corner table in the Sam Johnson Room at the Faculty Club.

"Well, now," Dimpleby said affably, raising his tankard in salute, "alien demons, eh? An interesting concept, Mr. Lucifer. Tell us more."

"I've never believed in devils," Curlene said, "or monsters from another planet either. Now all of a sudden I'm supposed to believe in both at once. If it weren't for that Freddy . . . "

"Granted the basic premise, it's logical enough," Dimpleby said. "If earthly imps exist, why not space sprites?"

"Professor, this is more than a bunch of syllogisms," Lucifer said earnestly. "These fellows mean business. They have some extremely potent powers. Fortunately, I have powers they don't know about, too; that's the only way I've held them in check so far—"

"You mean—they're already *here?*" Curlene looked searchingly about the room.

"No—I mean, yes, they're here, but not precisely *here.*" Lucifer clarified. "Look, I'd better fill in a little background for you. You see, Hell is actually a superior plane of existence—"

Curlene choked on her ale in a ladylike way.

"I mean—not *superior,* but, ah, at another level, you understand. Different physical laws, and so on—"

"Dirac levels," Dimpleby said, signaling for refills.

"Right!" Lucifer nodded eagerly. "There's an entire continuum of them, stretching away on both sides; there's an energy state higher on the scale than Hell— Heaven, it's called, for some reason—and one lower than your plane; that's the one Freddy comes from, by the way—"

"Oh, tell me about Heaven," Curlene urged.

Lucifer sighed, "Sometimes I miss the old place, in spite of . . . but never mind that."

"Tell me, Mr. Lucifer," Dimpleby said thoughtfully, "how is it you're able to travel at will among these levels?" As he spoke he pulled an envelope from his pocket and uncapped a ballpoint. "It appears to me that there's an insurmountable difficulty here, in terms of atomic and molecular spectral energy distribution; the specific heat involved . . . " he jotted busily, murmuring to himself.

"You're absolutely right, Professor," Lucifer said, sampling the fresh tankard just placed before him. "Heat used to be a real problem. I'd always arrive in a cloud of smoke and sulphur fumes. I finally solved it by working out a trick of emitting a packet of magnetic energy to carry off the excess."

"Hmmm. How did you go about dissipating this magnetism?"

"I fired it off in a tight beam; got rid of it."

"Beamed magnetism?" Dimpleby scribbled furiously. "Hmmm. Possibly . . ."

"Hey, fellas," Curlene protested. "Let's not talk shop, OK?" She turned a fascinated gaze on Lucifer. "You were just telling me about Heaven."

"You wouldn't like it, Curl," he said, almost curtly. "Now, Professor, all through history—at least as far as I remember it, and that covers a considerable period— the different energy states were completely separate and self-sufficient. Then, a few thousand years back, one of our boys—Yahway, his name is—got to poking around and discovered a way to move around from one level to another. The first place he discovered was Hell. Well, he's something of a bluenose, frankly, and he didn't much like what he found there: all kinds of dead warriors from Greece and Norway and such places sitting around juicing it and singing it, and fighting in a friendly sort of way."

"You mean—Valhalla really exists?" Curlene gasped. "And the Elysian Fields?"

Lucifer made a disclaiming wave of the hand. "There've always been humans with more than their share of vital energy. Instead of dying, they just switch levels. I have a private theory that there's a certain percentage of, er, individuals in any level who really belong in the next one up—or down. Anyway, Yahway didn't like what he saw. He was always a great one for discipline, getting up early, regular calisthenics—you know. He tried telling these fellows the error of their ways, but they just laughed him off the podium. So he dropped down one more level, which put him here; a much simpler proposition, nothing but a few tribes- men herding goats. Naturally they were impressed by a few simple miracles." Lucifer paused to quaff deeply. He sighed.

"Yes. Well, he's been meddling around down here ever

since, and frankly—but I'm wandering." He hiccuped sternly. "I admit, I never could drink very much without losing my perspective. Where was I?"

"The invasion," Dimpleby reminded him.

"Oh, yes. Well, they hit us without any warning. There we were, just sitting around the mead hall taking it easy, or strolling in the gardens striking our lutes or whatever we felt like, when all of a sudden—" Lucifer shook his head bemusedly. "Professor, did you ever have one of those days when nothing seemed to go right?"

Dimpleby pursed his lips. "Hmmm. You mean like having the first flat tire in a year during the worst rainstorm of the year while on your way to the most important meeting of the year?"

"Or," Curlene said, "like when you're just having a quick martini to brace yourself for the afternoon and you spill it on your new dress and when you try to wash it out, the water's turned off, and when you try to phone to report *that*, the phone's out, and just then Mrs. Trundle from next door drops in to talk, only you're late for the Faculty Wives?"

"That's it," Lucifer confirmed. "Well, picture that sort of thing on a vast scale."

"That's rather depressing," Dimpleby said. "But what has it to do with the, er, invasion?"

"Everything!" Lucifer said, with a wave of his hands. Across the room, a well-fleshed matron yelped.

"My olive! It turned into a frog!"

"Remarkable," her table companion said. "Genus *Rana pipiens*, I believe!"

"Sorry," Lucifer muttered, blushing, putting his hands under the table.

"You were saying, Mr. Lucifer?"

"It's them, Professor. They've been sort of leaking over, you see? Their influence, I mean." Lucifer started to wave his hands again, but caught himself and put them in his blazer pockets.

"Leaking over?"

"From Hell into his plane. You've been getting just a faint taste of it. You should see what's been going on in Hell, Proffefor—I mean Prossessor—I mean—"

"What *has* been going on?"

"Everything has been going to Hell," Lucifer said gloomily. "What I mean to say is," he said, making an effort to straighten up and focus properly, "that everything that *can* go wrong, *does* go wrong."

"That would appear to be contrary to the statistics of causality," Dimpleby said carefully.

"That's it, Professor! They're upsetting the laws of chance! Now, in the old days, when a pair of our lads stepped outside for a little hearty sword-fighting between drinks, one would be a little drunker than the other, and he'd soon be out of it for the day, while the other chap reeled back inside to continue the party. Now, they each accidentally knee each other in the groin and they both lie around groaning until sundown, which upsets everybody. The same for the lute players and lovers: the strings break just at the most climactic passage, or they accidentally pick a patch of poison ivy for their tryst, or possibly just a touch of diarrhea at the wrong moment, but you can imagine what it's doing to morale."

"Tsk," Dimpleby said. "Unfortunate—but it sounds more disconcerting than disastrous, candidly."

"You think so, Professor? What about when all the ambrosia on hand goes bad simultaneously, and the entire population is afflicted with stomach cramps and luminous spots before the eyes? What about a mix-up at the ferry, that leaves us stuck with three boat-loads of graduated Methodist ministers to entertain overnight? What about an ectospheric storm that knocks out all psionics for a week, and has everyone fetching and carrying by hand, and communicating by sign-language?"

"Well—that might be somewhat more serious . . . "

"Oh—oh!" Curlene was pointing with her nose. Her husband turned to see a waiter in weskit and knee-pants back through a swinging door balancing a tray laden with brimming port glasses, at the same moment that a tweedsy pedagogue rose directly behind him and, with a gallant gesture, drew out his fair companion's chair. There was a double *oof!* as they came together. The chair skidded. The lady sat on the floor. The tray distributed its burden in a bright cascade across the furs of a willowy brunette who yowled, whirled, causing her fox-tail to slap the face of a small, elaborately mustached man who was on the point of lighting a cigar. As the match flared brightly, with a sharp odor of blazing wool, the tweedsy man bent swiftly to offer a chivalrous hand, and bumped by the rebounding waiter, delivered a smart rap with his nose to the corner of the table.

"My mustache!" the small man yelled.

"Dr. Thorndyke, you're bleeding on my navy blue crepe!" the lady on the floor yelped. The waiter, still grabbing for the tray, bobbled it and sent it scaling through an olde English window, through which an indignant managerial head thrust in time to receive a glass of water intended for the burning mustache.

Lucifer, who had been staring dazedly at the rapid interplay, made a swift flick of the fingers. A second glass of water struck the small man squarely in the conflagration; the tweedsy man clapped a napkin over his nose and helped up the Navy blue crepe. The waiter recovered his tray and busied himself with the broken glass. The brunette whipped out a hanky and dabbed at her bodice, muttering. The tension subsided from the air.

"You see?" Lucifer said. "That was a small sample of their work."

"Nonsense, Mr. Lucifer," Dimpleby said, smiling amiably. "Nothing more than an accident—a curiously complex interplay of misadventures, true, but still—an accident, nothing more."

"Of course—but that sort of accident can only occur when there's an imbalance in the Randomness Field!"

"What's that?"

"It's what makes the laws of chance work. You know that if you flip a quarter a hundred times it will come up heads fifty times and tails fifty times, or very close to it. In a thousand tries, the ratio is even closer. Now, the coin knows nothing of its past performance—any more than metal filings in a magnetic field know which way the other filings are facing. But the field *forces* them to align parallel—and the Randomness Field forces the coin to follow the statistical distribution."

Dimpleby pulled at his chin. "In other words, entropy."

"If you prefer, Professor. But you've seen what happens when it's tampered with!"

"Why?" Dimpleby stabbed a finger at Lucifer and grinned as one who has scored a point. "Show me a motive for these hypothetical foreign fiends going to all that trouble just to meddle in human affairs!"

"They don't care a rap for human affairs," Lucifer groaned. "It's just a side-effect. They consume energy from certain portions of the trans-Einsteinian spectrum, emit energy in other bands. The result is to disturb the R-field—just as sunspots disrupt the earth's magnetic field!"

"Fooey," Dimpleby said, sampling his ale. "Accidents have been happening since the dawn of time. And according to your own account, these interplanetary imps of yours have just arrived."

"Time scales differ between Hell and here," Lucifer

said in tones of desperation. "The infiltration started two weeks ago, subjective Hell-time. That's equal to a little under two hundred years, local."

"What about all the coincidences before then?" Dimpleby came back swiftly.

"Certainly, there have always been a certain number of non-random occurrences. But in the last two centuries they've jumped to an unheard-of level! Think of all the fantastic scientific coincidences, during that period, for example—such as the triple rediscovery of Mendel's work after thirty-five years of obscurity, or the simultaneous evolutionary theories of Darwin and Wallace, or the identical astronomical discoveries of—"

"Very well, I'll concede there've been some remarkable parallelisms." Dimpleby dismissed the argument with a wave of the hand. "But that hardly proves—"

"Professor—maybe that isn't what you'd call hard scientific proof, but logic—instinct—should tell you that Something's Been Happening! Certainly, there were isolated incidents in Ancient History—but did you ever hear of the equivalent of a twenty-car pile-up in Classical times? The very conception of slapstick comedy based on ludicrous accident was alien to the world until it began happening in real life!"

"I say again—fooey, Mr. Lucifer." Dimpleby drew on his ale, burped gently and leaned forward challengingly. "I'm from New Hampshire," he said, wagging a finger. "You've gotta show me."

"Fortunately for humanity, that's quite impossible," Lucifer said. "*They* haven't penetrated to this level yet; all you've gotten, as I said, is the spill-over effect—" he paused. "Unless you'd like to go to Hell and see for yourself—"

"No thanks. A faculty tea is close enough for me."

"In that case . . ." Lucifer broke off. His face paled. "Oh, no," he whispered.

"Lucifer—what is it?" Curlene whispered in alarm.

"They—they must have followed me! It never occurred to me; but—" Lucifer groaned, "Professor and Mrs. Dimpleby, I've done a terrible thing! I've led them here!"

"Where?" Curlene stared around the room eagerly.

Lucifer's eyes were fixed on the corner by the fire. He made a swift gesture with the fingers of his left hand. Curlene gasped.

"Why—it looks just like a big stalk of broccoli—except for the eyes, of course—and the little one is a dead ringer for a rhubarb pie!"

"Hmmm," Dimpleby blinked. "Quite astonishing, really." He cast a sidelong glance at Lucifer. "Look here, old man, are you sure this isn't some sort of hypnotic effect?"

"If it is, it has the same effect as reality, Professor," the Devil whispered hoarsely. "And something has to be done about it, no matter what you call it."

"Yes, I suppose so—but why, if I may inquire, all this interest on your part in us petty mortals?" Dimpleby smiled knowledgeably. "Ah, I'll bet this is where the pitch for our souls comes in; you'll insure an end to bad luck and negative coincidences, in return for a couple of signatures written in blood . . . "

"Professor, please," Lucifer said, blushing. "You have the wrong idea completely."

"I just don't understand," Curlene sighed, gazing at Lucifer, "why such a nice fellow was kicked out of Heaven . . . "

"But why come to *me?*" Dimpleby said, eyeing Lucifer through the sudsy glass bottom of his ale mug. "I don't know any spells for exorcising demons."

"Professor, I'm out of my depth," Lucifer said earnestly. "The old reliable eye of newt and wart of toad recipes don't faze these alien imps for a moment. Now, I admit, I haven't kept in touch with new developments

in science as I should have. But *you* have, Professor:
you're one of the world's foremost authorities on wave
mechanics and Planck's law, and all that sort of thing.
If anybody can deal with these chaps, *you* can!"

"Why, Johnny, how exciting!" Curlene said. "I didn't
know matrix mechanics had anything to do with broccoli!" She took a pleased gulp of ale, smiling from
Lucifer to her husband.

"I didn't either, my dear," Dimpleby said in a puzzled
tone. "Look here, Lucifer, are you sure you don't have
me confused with Professor Pronko, over in Liberal
Arts? Now, his papers on abnormal psychology—"

"Professor, there's been no mistake! Who else but
an expert in quantum theory could deal with a situation like this?"

"Well, I suppose there is a certain superficial semantic parallelism—"

"Wonderful, Professor: I knew you'd do it!" Lucifer grabbed Dimpleby's hand and wrung it warmly.
"How do we begin?"

"Here, you're talking nonsense!" Dimpleby extracted
his hand, used it to lift his ale tankard once again. "Of
course," he said after taking a hearty pull, "if you're
right about the nature of these varying energy levels—
and these, er, entities *do* manage the jump from one
quantum state to the next—then I suppose they'd be
subject to the same sort of physical laws as any other
energetic particles . . . " He thumped the mug down
heavily on the tabletop and resumed jotting. "The
Compton effect," he muttered. "Raman's work . . . The
Stern-Gerlack experiment. Hmmm."

"You've got something?" Lucifer and Curlene said
simultaneously.

"Just a theoretical notion," he said off-handedly, and
waved airily to a passing waiter. "Three more, Chudley."

"Johnny," Curlene wailed. "Don't stop now!"

"Professor—time is of the essence!" Lucifer groaned.

"Say, the broccoli is stirring around," Curlene said in a low tone. "Is he planning another practical joke?"

Lucifer cast apprehensive eyes toward the fireplace. "He doesn't actually do it intentionally, you know. He can't help it; it's like, well, a blind man switching on the lights in a darkroom. He wouldn't understand what all the excitement was about."

"Excuse me," Dimpleby said. "Ale goes through me pretty rapidly." He rose, slightly jogging the elbow of the waiter pouring ice water into a glass at the next table. The chill stream dived precisely into the cleavage of a plump woman in a hat like a chef's salad for twelve. She screamed and fell backward into the path of the servitor approaching with a tray of foaming ale tankards. All three malt beverages leaped head-first onto the table, their contents sluicing across it into Lucifer's lap, while the overspill distributed itself between Dimpleby's hip pockets.

He stared down at the table awash in ale, turned a hard gaze on the fireplace.

"Like that, eh?" he said in a brittle voice. He faced the Devil, who was dabbing helplessly at his formerly white flannels.

"All right, Lucifer," he said. "You're on! A few laughs at the expense of academic dignity are fine—but I'm damned if I'm going to stand by and see good beer wasted! Now, let's get down to cases. Tell me all you know about these out-of-town incubi . . . "

3

It was almost dawn. In his third floor laboratory in Prudfrock Hall, Professor Dimpleby straightened from the marble-topped bench over which he had been bent for the better part of the night.

"Well," he said, rubbing his eyes, "I don't know. It might work." He glanced about the big room. "Now, if you'll just shoo one of your, ah, extra-terrestrial essences in here, we'll see."

"No problem there, Professor," Lucifer said anxiously. "I've had all I could do to hold them at bay all night, with some of the most potent incantations since Solomon sealed the Afrit up in a bottle."

"Then, too, I don't suppose they'd find the atmosphere of a scientific laboratory very congenial," Dimpleby said with a somewhat lofty smile, "inasmuch as considerable effort has been devoted to excluding chance from the premises."

"You think so?" Lucifer said glumly. "For your own peace of mind, I suggest you don't conduct any statistical analyses just now."

"Well, with the clear light of morning and the dissipation of the alcohol, the rationality of what we're doing seems increasingly questionable—but nonetheless, we may as well carry the experiment through. Even negative evidence has a certain value."

"Ready?" Lucifer said.

"Ready," Dimpleby said, suppressing a yawn. Lucifer made a face and executed an intricate dance step. There was a sharp sense of tension released—like the popping of an invisible soap-bubble—and *something* appeared drifting lazily in the air near the precision scales. One side of the instrument dropped with a sharp *clunk!*

"All the air concentrated on one side of the balance," Lucifer said tensely.

"Maxwell's demon—in the flesh?" Dimpleby gasped.

"It looks like a giant pizza," Curlene said, "only transparent."

The apparition gave a flirt of its rim and sailed across to hover before a wall chart illustrating the periodic table. The paper burst into flame.

"All the energetic air molecules rushed to one spot," Lucifer explained. "It could happen any time—but it seldom does."

"Good lord! What if it should cause all the air to rush to one end of the room?" Dimpleby whispered.

"I daresay it would rupture your lungs, Professor. So I wouldn't waste any more time, if I were you."

"Imagine what must be going on outside," Curlene said. "With these magical pizzas and broccoli wandering loose all over the place!"

"Is *that* what all those sirens were about?" Dimpleby said. He stationed himself beside the bread-board apparatus he had constructed and swallowed hard.

"Very well, Lucifer—see if you can herd it over this way."

The devil frowned in concentration. The pizza drifted slowly, rotating as if looking for the source of some irritation. It gave an impatient twitch and headed toward Curlene. Lucifer made a gesture and it veered off, came sailing in across the table.

"Now!" Dimpleby said, and threw a switch. As if struck by a falling brick, the alien entity slammed to the center of the three-foot disk encircled by massive magnetic coils.

It hopped and threshed, to no avail.

"The field is holding it!" Dimpleby said tensely. "So far . . ."

Suddenly the rippling, disk-shaped creature folded in on itself, stood on end, sprouted wings and a tail. Scales glittered along its sides. A puff of smoke issued from tiny crocodilian jaws, followed by a tongue of flame.

"A dragon!" Curlene cried.

"Hold him, Professor!" Lucifer urged.

The dragon coiled its tail around itself and melted into a lumpy black sphere covered with long bristles. It had two bright red eyes and a pair of spindly legs on which it jittered wildly.

"A goblin?" Dimpleby said incredulously.

The goblin rebounded from the invisible wall restraining it, coalesced into a foot-high, leathery-skinned humanoid with big ears, a wide mouth, and long arms which it wrapped around its knees as it squatted disconsolately on the grid, rolling bloodshot eyes sorrowfully up at its audience.

"Congratulations, Professor!" Lucifer exclaimed. "We got one!"

4

"His name," Lucifer said, "is Quilchik. It's really quite a heart-rending tale he tells, poor chap."

"Oh, the poor little guy," Curlene said. "What does he eat, Mr. Lucifer? Do you suppose he'd like a little lettuce or something?"

"His diet is quite immaterial, Curl; he subsists entirely on energies. And that seems to be at the root of the problem. It appears there's a famine back home. What with a rising birth rate and no death rate, population pressure long ago drove his people out into space. They've been wandering around out there for epochs, with just the occasional hydrogen molecule to generate a quantum or two of entropy to absorb; hardly enough to keep them going."

"Hmm. I suppose entropy *could* be considered a property of matter," Dimpleby said thoughtfully, reaching for paper and pencil. "One can hardly visualize a distinction between order and disorder as existing in matterless space."

"Quite right. The curious distribution of heavy elements in planetary crusts and the unlikely advent of life seem to be the results of their upsetting of the Randomness Field, to say nothing of evolution, biological mutations, the extinction of the dinosaurs just in time for Man to thrive, and women's styles."

"Women's styles?" Curlene frowned.

"Of course," Dimpleby nodded. "What could be more unlikely than this year's Paris modes?"

Lucifer shook his head, a worried expression on his regular features. "I had in mind trapping them at the entry point and sending them back where they came from; but under the circumstances that seems quite inhumane."

"Still—we can't let them come swarming in to upset everything from the rhythm method to the Irish Sweepstakes."

"Golly," Curlene said, "couldn't we put them on a reservation, sort of, and have them weave blankets maybe?"

"Hold it," Lucifer said. "There's another one nearby . . . I can feel the tension in the R field . . . "

"Eek!" Curlene said, taking a step backward and hooking a heel in the extension cord powering the magnetic fields. With a sharp *pop!* the plug was jerked from the wall. Quilchik jumped to his large, flat feet, took a swift look around, and leaped, changing in mid-air to the fluttering form of a small bat.

Lucifer threw off his coat, ripped off his tie and shirt. Before the startled gaze of the Dimplebys, he rippled and flowed into the form of a pterodactyl which leaped clear of the collapsing white flannels and into the air, long beak agape, in hot pursuit of the bat. Curlene screeched and squeezed her eyes shut. Dimpleby said,

"Remarkable!," grabbed his pad and scribbled rapidly. The bat flickered in mid-air and was a winged snake. Lucifer turned instantly into a winged mongoose. The snake dropped to the floor and shrank to mouse form scuttling for a hole. Lucifer became a big gray cat, reached the hole first. The mouse burgeoned into a bristly rat; the cat swelled and was a terrier. With a yap, it leaped after the rat, which turned back into Quilchik, sprang up on a table, raced across it, dived for what looked like an empty picture frame—

A shower of tiny Quilchiks shot from the other side of the heavy glass sheet. Lucifer barely skidded aside in time to avoid it, went dashing around the room, barking furiously at the tiny creatures crouched behind every chair and table leg, squeezing in behind filing cabinets, cowering under ashtrays.

"Lucifer, stop!" Curlene squealed. "Oh, aren't they *darling!*" She went to her knees, scooped up an inch-high manikin. It squatted on her palm, trembling, its head between its knees.

"By Jimini," Dimpleby said. "It went through a diffraction grating, and came out centuplets!"

5

"The situation is deteriorating," Lucifer groaned, scooping up another miniature imp, and dumping it back inside the reactivated trap. "It was bad enough dealing with one star-sprite. Now we have a hundred. And if any one of them escapes . . . "

"Don't look now," Dimpleby said behind his hand to the Devil, now back in human form and properly clad, "but I have an unch-hay the magnetic ield-fay won't old-hay em-they."

"Eye-way ott-nay?" Lucifer inquired.

"Ecause-bay . . . " Dimpleby broke off. "Well, it has to do with distribution of polarity. You see the way the field works—"

"Don't bother explaining," Lucifer said. "I wouldn't understand anyway. The real question is—what do we do now?"

"Our choice seems limited. We either gather up all these little fellows and dump them back where they came from, and then hunt down the others and do likewise, which is impossible, or we forget the whole thing, which is unthinkable."

"In any event," Lucifer said, "we have to act fast before the situation gets entirely out of hand."

"We could turn the problem over to the so-called authorities," Dimpleby said, "but that seems unwise, somehow."

Lucifer shuddered. "I can see the headlines now: DEVIL LOOSE ON COLLEGE CAMPUS!"

"Oh, they've already worked that one to death," Curlene said. "It would probably be more like: PROF AND MATE IN THREE WAY SEX ROMP."

"Sex romp?"

"Well, Mr. Lucifer *did* reappear in the nude." Curlene smiled. "And a very nice physique, too, Mr. Lucifer."

Lucifer blushed. "Well, Professor, what do we do?" he asked hastily.

"I'll flip a coin," Curlene suggested. "heads, we report the whole thing, tails, we keep it to ourselves and do the best we can."

"All right. Best two out of three."

Curlene rummaged in her purse and produced one of the counterfeit quarters in current production from the Denver mint. She tossed it up, caught it, slapped it against her forearm, lifted her hand.

"Tails," she said in a pleased tone.

"Maybe we'd better report it anyway," Dimpleby said, nibbling a fingernail and eyeing the tiny creatures sitting disconsolately inside the circle of magnets.

"Two out of three," Curlene said. She flipped the coin again.

"Tails again," she announced.

"Well, I suppose that settles it . . . "

Curlene tossed the coin up idly. "I guess it's definite," she said. "Tails three times in a row."

Dimpleby looked at her absently. "Eh?"

"*Four* times in a row," Curlene said. Lucifer looked at her as if about to speak. Curlene flipped the coin high.

"Five," she said. Dimpleby and Lucifer drew closer.

"Six . . . "

"Seven . . . "

"Eight . . . "

"Oh-oh," Dimpleby said. He grabbed for the desk drawer, pulled out a dog-eared deck of cards, hastily shuffled and dealt two hands. Cautiously, he peeked at his cards. He groaned.

"Four aces," he said.

"Four kings here," Curlene said.

"Here we go again," he said. "Now no one will be safe!"

"But Johnny," Curlene said. "There's one difference . . . "

"What?"

"The odds are all mixed up, true—but now they're in our favor!"

6

"It's quite simple, really," Dimpleby said, waving a sheet of calculations. "When Quilchik went through the grating, he was broken up into a set of harmonics. Those harmonics, being of another order of size, resonate at another frequency. Ergo, he consumes a different type of energetic pseudo-particle. Instead of draining off the positive, ah, R-charges, he now subsists on negative entropy."

"And instead of practical jokes, we have miraculous cures, spontaneous remissions, and fantastic runs with the cards!" Curlene cried happily.

"Not only that," Dimpleby added, "but I think we can solve their food-supply problem. They've exhausted the supply of plus entropy back on their own level—but the original endowment of minus R remains untapped. There should be enough for another few billion years."

Lucifer explained this to the Quilchiks via the same form of instantaneous telepathy he had employed for the earlier interrogation.

"He's delighted," the Devil reported, as the tiny creatures leaped up, joined hands, and began capering and jigging in a manner expressive of joy. "There's just one thing . . . " A lone manikin stood at the edge of the table, looking shyly at Curlene.

"Quilchik Seventy-eight has a request," Lucifer said.

"Well, what does snookums-ookums want?" Curlene cooed, bending over to purse her lips at the tiny figure.

"He wants to stay," Lucifer said embarrassedly.

"Oh, Johnny, can I have him?"

"Well—if you'll put some pants on him—"

"And he'd like to live in a bottle. Preferably a bourbon bottle, one of the miniatures. Preferably still full of bourbon," Lucifer added. "But he'll come out to play whenever you like."

"I wonder," Dimpleby said thoughtfully, "what effect having him around would have on our regular Saturday night card game with those sharpies from the engineering faculty?"

"You've already seen a sample," Lucifer said. "But I can ask him to fast at such times."

"Oh, no, no," Dimpleby protested. "Hate to see the little fellow go hungry."

"Mr. Lucifer," Curlene asked. "I hope I'm not being nosy—but how did you get the scar on your side that I saw when you had your shirt off?"

"Oh, ah, that?" Lucifer blushed purple. "Well, it, ah—"

"Probably a liver operation, judging from the location, eh, Lucifer?" Dimpleby said.

"You might call it that," Lucifer said.

"But you shouldn't embarrass people by asking personal questions, Curl," Dimpleby said sternly.

"Yes, dear," Curl said. "Lucifer—I've been wanting to ask you: What did a nice fellow like you do to get kicked out of Heaven?"

"Well, I, uh," Lucifer swallowed.

"It was for doing something nice, wasn't it?"

"Well—frankly, I thought it wasn't fair," Lucifer blurted. "I felt sorry for the poor humans, squatting in those damp caves . . ."

"So you brought them fire," Curlene said. "That's why you're called Lucifer."

"You're mixed up, Curl," Dimpleby said. "That was Prometheus. For his pains, he was chained to a rock, and every day a vulture tore out his liver, and every night it grew back . . ."

"But it left a scar," Curlene said, looking meltingly at Lucifer.

The Devil blushed a deep magenta. "I . . . I'd better be rushing off now," he said.

"Not before we share a stirrup cup," Dimpleby said, holding up the Old Crow bottle from the desk drawer. Inside, Quilchik, floating on his back with his hands folded on his paunch, waved merrily, and blew a string of bubbles.

"Luckily, I have a reserve stock," Dimpleby muttered, heading for the filing cabinet.

"Er, Lucifer, how can we ever thank you?" Curlene sighed, cradling the flask.

"Just by, uh, having all the fun you can," Lucifer said. "And I'll, er, be looking forward to seeing you in Hell, some day."

"I'll drink to that," Dimpleby said. He poured. Smiling, they clicked glasses and drank.

THE EXTERMINATOR

❧

Judge Carter Gates of the Third Circuit Court finished his chicken salad on whole wheat, thoughtfully crumpled the waxed paper bag and turned to drop it in the wastebasket behind his chair—and sat transfixed.

Through his second-floor office window, he saw a forty-foot flower-petal shape of pale turquoise settling gently between the well-tended petunia beds on the courthouse lawn. On the upper, or stem end of the vessel, a translucent pink panel popped up and a slender, graceful form not unlike a large violet caterpillar undulated into view.

Judge Gates whirled to the telephone. Half an hour later, he put it to the officials gathered with him in a tight group on the lawn.

"Boys, this thing is intelligent; any fool can see that. It's putting together what my boy assures me is some kind of talking machine, and any minute now it's going to start communicating. It's been twenty minutes since I notified Washington on this thing. It won't be long before somebody back there decides this is top secret and slaps a freeze on us here that will make the Manhattan Project look like a publicity campaign. Now, I say this is the biggest thing that ever happened to Plum County—but if we don't aim to be put right out of the picture, we'd better move fast."

"What you got in mind, Jedge?"

"I propose we hold an open hearing right here in the courthouse, the minute that thing gets its gear to working. We'll put it on the air—Tom Clembers from the radio station's already stringing wires, I see. Too bad we've got no TV equipment, but Jody Hurd has a movie camera. We'll put Willow Grove on the map bigger'n Cape Kennedy ever was."

"We're with you on that, Carter!"

Ten minutes after the melodious voice of the Fianna's translator had requested escort to the village headman, the visitor was looking over the crowded courtroom with an expression reminiscent of a St. Bernard puppy hoping for a romp. The rustle of feet and throat-clearing subsided and the speaker began:

"People of the Green World, happy the cycle—"

Heads turned at the clump of feet coming down the side aisle; a heavy-torsoed man of middle age, bald, wearing a khaki shirt and trousers and rimless glasses, and with a dark leather holster slapping his hip at each step, cleared the end of the front row of seats, planted himself feet apart, yanked a heavy nickel-plated .44 revolver from the holster, took aim, and fired five shots into the body of the Fianna at a range of ten feet. The violet form whipped convulsively, writhed from the bench to the floor with a sound like a wet fire hose being dropped, uttered a gasping twitter, and lay still.

The gunman turned, dropped the pistol, threw up his hands, and called:

"Sheriff Hoskins, I'm puttin' myself in yer pertective custody."

There was a moment of stunned silence; then a rush of spectators for the alien. The sheriff's three-hundred-and-nine-pound bulk bellied through the shouting mob to take up a stand before the khaki-clad man.

"I always knew you was a mean one, Cecil Stump," he said, "ever since I seen you makin' up them ground-glass baits for Joe Potter's dog. But I never thought I'd see you turn to cold-blooded murder." He waved at the bystanders. "Clear a path through here; I'm takin' my prisoner over to the jail—"

"Jest a dad-blamed minute, sheriff . . . " Stump's face was pale, his glasses were gone, and one khaki shoulder strap dangled—but what was almost a grin twisted one meaty cheek. He hid his hands behind his back, leaned away from the cuffs. "I don't like that word 'prisoner'; I ast you fer pertection. And better look out who you go throwin' that word 'murder' off at, too. I ain't murdered nobody."

The sheriff blinked, turned to roar, "How's the victim, Doc?"

A small gray head rose from bending over the limp form of the Fianna. "Deader'n a mackerel, sheriff."

"I guess that's it. Let's go, Cecil."

"What's the charge?"

"First-degree murder."

"Who'd I murder?"

"Why, you killed this here . . . this stranger."

"That ain't no stranger. That's a varmint. Murder's got to do with killin' humerns, way I understand it. You goin' to tell me that thing's humern?"

Ten people shouted at once:

"—human as I am!"

"—intelligent being!"

"—tell me you can simply kill—"

"—must be some kind of law—"

The sheriff raised his hands, his jowls drawn down in a scowl. "What about it, Judge Gates? Any law against Cecil Stump killing the . . . uh . . . ?"

The judge thrust out his lower lip. "Well, let's see. Technically—" he began.

"Good Lord!" someone blurted. "You mean the laws on murder don't define what constitutes—I mean, what—"

"What a humern is?" Stump snorted. "Whatever it says, it sure-bob don't include no purple worms. That's a varmint, pure and simple. Ain't no different killin' it than any other critter."

"Then, by God, we'll get him for malicious damage," a man called. "Or hunting without a license—out of season!"

"—carrying concealed weapons!"

"—creatin' a disturbance!"

Stump went for his hip pocket, fumbled out a fat, shapeless wallet, extracted a thumbed rectangle of folded paper, offered it.

"I'm a licensed exterminator. Got a permit to carry the gun, too. I ain't broke no law." He grinned openly now. "Jest doin' my job, sheriff. And at no charge to the county."

A smaller man with bristly red hair flared his nostrils at Stump. "You bloodthirsty idiot!" He raised a fist and shook it. "We'll be a national disgrace—more than Little Rock! Lynching's too good for you!"

"Hold on there, Weinstein," the sheriff cut in. "Let's not go gettin' no lynch talk started—"

"Lynch, is it!" Cecil Stump bellowed, his face suddenly red. "Why I done a favor for every man here! Now you listen to me! What is that thing over there?"

He jerked a blunt thumb toward the judicial bench. "It's some kind of critter from Mars or someplace— you know that as well as me! And what's it here for? It ain't for the good of the likes of you and me, I can tell you that. It's them or us—and this time, by God, we got in the first lick!"

"Why you . . . you . . . hate-monger!"

"Now hold on right there. I'm as liberal-minded as the next feller. Hell, I like a nigger—and I can't hardly tell a Jew from a white man. But when it comes to takin' in a damned purple worm and callin' it humern— that's where I draw the line."

Sheriff Hoskins pushed between Stump and the surging front rank of the crowd. "Stay back there! I want you to disperse, peaceably, and let the law handle this."

"I reckon I'll push off now, sheriff." Stump hitched up his belt. "I figgered you might have to calm 'em down right at first, but now they've had a chance to think it over and see I ain't broke no law, ain't nobody here—none of these law-abidin' folks—goin' to do anything illegal—like tryin' to get rough with a licensed exterminator just doin' his job." He stooped, retrieved his gun.

"Here, I'll take that," Sheriff Hoskins said. "You can consider your gun license cancelled—and your exter- minatin' license, too."

Stump grinned again, handed the revolver over.

"Sure, I'm cooperative, sheriff. Anything you say. Send it around to my place when you're done with it." He pushed his way through the crowd to the corridor door.

"The rest of you stay put!" A portly man with a head of bushy white hair pushed his way through to the bench. "I'm calling an emergency town meeting to order here and now . . . !"

He banged the gavel on the scarred top, glanced down at the body of the dead alien, now covered by a flag.

"Gentlemen, we've got to take fast action. If the wire services get hold of this before we've gone on record, Willow Grove'll be a blighted area . . . "

"Look here, Willard," Judge Gates called, rising. "This—this mob isn't competent to take legal action—"

"Never mind what's legal, Judge; sure, this calls for federal legislation—maybe a Constitutional amendment—but in the meantime, we're going to redefine what constitutes a person within the incorporated limits of Willow Grove!"

"That's the least we can do," a thin-faced woman snapped, glaring at Judge Gates. "Do you think we're going to set here and condone this outrage?"

"Nonsense!" Gates shouted. "I don't like what happened any better than you do—but a person—well, a person's got two arms and two legs and—"

"Shape's got nothing to do with it," the chairman cut in. "Bears walk on two legs! Dave Zawocky lost his in the war. Monkeys have hands—"

"Any intelligent creature—" the woman started.

"Nope, that won't do, either; my unfortunate cousin's boy Melvin was born an imbecile, poor lad. Now, gentlemen, there's no time to waste. We'll find it very difficult to formulate a satisfactory definition based on considerations such as these. However, I think we can resolve the question in terms that will form a basis for future legislation on the question. It's going to make some big changes in things. Hunters aren't going to like it—and the meat industry will be affected. But if, as it appears, we're entering into an era of contact with . . . ah . . . creatures from other worlds, we've got to get our house in order."

"You tell 'em, Senator!" someone yelled.

"We better leave this for Congress to figger out!" another voice insisted.

"We got to do something . . ."

The senator held up his hands. "Quiet, everybody. There'll be reporters here in a matter of minutes. Maybe our ordinance won't hold water—but it'll start 'em thinking—and it'll make a lot better copy for Willow Grove than the killing."

"What you got in mind, Senator?"

"Just this," the senator said solemnly. "A person is . . . *any harmless creature* . . ."

Feet shuffled. Someone coughed.

"What about a man who commits a violent act, then?" Judge Gates demanded. "What's he, eh?"

"That's obvious, gentlemen," the senator said flatly. "He's vermin."

On the courthouse steps Cecil Stump stood, hands in hip pockets, talking to a reporter from the big-town paper in Mattoon, surrounded by a crowd of late-comers who had missed the excitement inside. He described the accuracy of his five shots, the sound they had made hitting the big blue snake, and the ludicrous spectacle the latter had presented in its death agony. He winked at a foxy man in overalls picking his nose at the edge of the crowd.

"Guess it'll be a while 'fore any more damned reptiles move in here like they owned the place," he concluded.

The courthouse doors banged wide; excited citizens poured forth, veering aside from Cecil Stump. The crowd around him thinned, broke up as its members collared those emerging with the hot news. The reporter picked a target.

"Perhaps you'd care to give me a few details of

the action taken by the . . . ah . . . Special Committee, sir?"

Senator Custis pursed his lips. "A session of the Town Council was called," he said. "We've defined what a person is in this town—"

Stump, standing ten feet away, snorted. "Can't touch me with no ex post factory law."

"—and also what can be classified as vermin," Custis went on.

Stump closed his mouth with a snap.

"Here, that s'posed to be some kind of slam at me, Custis? By God, come election time . . . "

Above, the door opened again. A tall man in a leather jacket stepped out, stood looking down. The crowd pressed back. Senator Custis and the reporter moved aside. The newcomer came down the steps slowly. He carried Cecil Stump's nickel-plated .44 in his hand. Standing alone, Stump watched him.

"Here," he said. His voice carried a sudden note of strain. "Who're you?"

The man reached the foot of the steps, raised the revolver, and cocked it with a thumb.

"I'm the new exterminator."

THE BIG SHOW

❧

1

Lew Jantry awoke with soft feminine arms around him, a warm body snuggled against his, perfumed hair tickling his chin.

He didn't open his eyes at once; he was too old a trouper for that. Instead, he rapidly sorted through his recollections, orienting himself before making a move. He was in a bed, that was a starting point; and the quality of the light shining through his closed lids indicated it was full daylight—or its equivalent. That was no help: both the Jantry and Osgood bedrooms featured large east-exposure windows with fluffy curtains. He'd have to speak to Sol about that: a fellow needed a little sharper demarcation of environmental detail to avoid role-fatigue.

Lew opened one eye half a millimeter, made out the

smooth curve of a shoulder, the sleek line of a bare back. Still no clue that would answer the burning question: was he in bed with his real wife, or his TV wife?

The seconds were ticking past. Jantry thought furiously, trying to summon up the memory of the circumstances under which he had turned in. Had he slept an hour, a minute, or all night? Had he been at home, in the class A Banshire Towers Apartment of a medium-rated actor, with Marta, his lawful wedded spouse? Or had he dropped off on the set, in the cardboard and plastic mock-up where he spent twelve of every twenty-four hours, with Carla, his co-star on *The Osgoods?* Damn! He remembered cocktails, the Bateses dropping in, late talk; but that had been a scene in Rabinowitz's latest script of the blab-blab school— or had it? Was he thinking of the Harrises, the bores in the next apartment at the Banshire? Uh-huh, that was it. Al Harris had rattled on and on about his new two hundred channel set, with the twenty screen monitor attachment, where a sharp viewer with a good wrist could keep in touch with practically every top show simultaneously, at least well enough to hold up his end of a cultured conversation . . .

Satisfied, Lew relaxed, slid his hand casually down toward the curved hip beside him. The woman moved, twisted her head back to impale him with a sharp black eye.

"You're ten seconds off-cue, Buster!" Carla's subvocalized voice rasped in the pickup set in the bone back of his right ear. *"And let's watch those hands! This is a family-type show, and my husband Bruno is a dedicated viewer!"*

Lew's face snapped in a smile, lazy, marital, degree one, a stylized grimace that would instantly dispel all implications of lust from the minds of well-conditioned viewers. Meanwhile, he was stalling, groping for his line. Where the hell was the prompter?

"*Hi, darling,*" the dubber's voice sounded in the pick-up set in the bone back of Lew's left ear, just as the audience would hear it. "*Today's the day of the big event. Excited?*" In the background, he could hear the hundred piece orchestra sliding into "Camptown Races." He grabbed at the cue.

"Sure—but, uh, with you in the stands, rooting for him, who could lose?" he improvised, mouthing the words distinctly for the vocal stand-in to mime later.

"*What who, you boob?*" Carla's voice hissed in his right ear. "*I'm having a baby at two o'clock!*"

"*Oh, Freddy Osgood—sometimes I think I'm the luckiest girl in the world, having you all to myself!*" the canned line crackled in his left ear.

"A baby?" Lew blurted, struggling to pick up the thread.

"*What did you think, you schlock—a litter of kitties?*" Carla snarled in his right ear.

"I didn't know you were—I mean, that you'd—that we'd—" Lew caught himself. "Congratulations," he ad-libbed desperately.

"*We'd better hurry and get ready; we're going water-skiing with the Poppins before we're due at the Vitabort Center,*" his left ear cooed.

"Sure," Lew agreed, glad of the chance of escape. He threw back the blanket, caught just a glimpse of a saucy derriere before Carla squalled and yanked the sheets back up.

"Cut!" A godlike bellow rattled Lew's occipital sutures. The wall with the window slid aside to admit the charging bulk of Hugo Fleischpultzer himself. "Jantry, you just set the industry back fifty years!" the director howled. "Whattaya mean, insulting five hundred million clean-living Americans with the sight of a bare behind first thing in the morning! It'll take the psychan channels two weeks of intensive primetime therapy to clear out the damage you done! You're fired! Or you would be if it wasn't for the lousy Guild! Not that I mean anything by the word 'lousy'!"

Carla Montez sat up, holding the covers to her chin, pointed a scarlet-nailed finger at Lew.

"I want a divorce!" she screamed. "Tell Oscar to write this louse out of the script for screening no later than Friday in the late early mid-afternoon segment!"

"Now, Carla, baby, you know that's impossible," Abe Katz, the makeup man soothed, reaching past Fleischpultzer's bulk to adjust the star's eyelashes.

"I'm sorry, Hugo," Lew said. "I just got a little mixed up for a second. You know how it's been since we went to nonstop sitcom: a three hour shift at home, three on the set, half my meals here, half there, barely time to scan the scripts—"

"See?" Carla shrilled. "He practically admits he prefers being with that blowsy dame he's supposedly married to—"

"I do not—I mean Marta's no blowsier than you are!" Lew flared. "I mean, neither one of you is blowsy! And I love being cooped up with you in this make-believe egg crate for half my life!"

"The kids!" Carla sobbed. "What will become of the kids? Joey, and little Suzie, and that new one, Irving or whatever, that we hired last week for the cousin!"

"Rusty, his air name is," Hugo boomed. "Carla's right, we got to think of the little ones. We don't want to go making a broken home out of a fine American family, which it's the favorite escape of millions, just over a little misunderstanding like this. Lew, I'll give you one more chance—"

"Oh, no you won't!" A furious contralto cut across the conversation. All eyes turned to the pert, green-eyed woman who had just burst onto the set. "I've watched my husband crawl into bed with that harpie for the last time! I'm here to scratch her eyes out!"

"Marta! No!" Lew, leaping from the bed, collided with Carla, leaping in the opposite direction. They struck the floor together, a confused mass of flailing limbs, complicated by the actress' efforts to simultaneously escape, attack, and observe the conventions of modesty.

"Look at them—right in front of me!" Marta keened. "Lew! How could you!"

"Carla baby—watch the hairdo!" Abe Katz called.

"Quiet on the set!" Hugo's bass roar dominated the scene. Carla came to her feet, swathed in the sheet, as Lew struggled to arrange a blanket, Navajo style, about himself.

"Now, Marta honey," he said hastily. "Don't leap to conclusions! It's just that I was tuckered out from staying up late worrying about little Egbert. How *is* Eggie? Did he pull through the crisis OK?"

"You fiend!" Marta wailed. *"Our* son's name is Augustus!"

"Ah—I was thinking of Augustus, of course." Lew scrambled for verbal footing. "Today's the day of the Little League tryouts, right? And—"

"Monster! You don't know your real family from that horrible TV family of yours! It's that nasty little midget that plays Sammy Osgood that's the ball player! Our Augustus plays the violin!"

"Sure—I remember perfectly! And his sister, Cluster, is a whiz on the glockenspiel!"

"Murderer! Our daughter's name is Finette! And she hates German food! I'm through with you, you . . . you Bluebeard!" She turned to flee. As Lew jumped after

her, Carla aimed a roundhouse slap that connected with
a report like a dropped light bulb.

"Keep away from me, you deviate!" she yelped.

"Look at the hairdo," Abe mourned.

"Mr. Fleischpultzer!" A penetrating voice sounded.
A small, pouty-faced man in an expensive gray Gooberlon
executive coverall had appeared from behind a fly.

"Why—if it isn't the sponsor, Mr. Harlowe Goober
of Goober Industries," Hugo babbled. "Welcome to the
set, Mr. Goober, which we were just horsing around
a little, you know, high spirits and all that—"

"I'm canceling the show," Goober barked. "I've
noticed for some time the gradual disintegration of the
moral tone of this network. This orgy is the final straw.
I'm taking my trade to NABAC!"

"But—Mr. Goober—"

"Unless—that person is replaced at once!" Goober
pointed dramatically at Lew Jantry.

"But . . . but . . . but . . . his contract!" Hugo blurted.
"And what about the script? They're about to have a
baby!"

"Let him die in childbirth," Goober proposed, and
stamped off the set.

"My lawyer will call you, you bum!" Marta shrilled.
"Married to an actor is bad enough—but an out-of-
work actor . . . !"

"But the Guild," Lew rallied weakly. "Hugo, say
something!"

"Half the Guild's working on Goober-sponsored
accounts." Fleischpultzer shrugged. "They won't buck
him."

"We'll have him suicide when it comes out he's an
embezzler." Carla's voice sounded above the hubbub.
"And I'll meet that handsome obstetrician . . ."

"You mean—" Lew swallowed hard, watching the set
empty as all personnel moved to disassociate themselves

from failure. "You mean I'm washed up in TV? But what will I do? All those hours of leisure time—"

"View TV," Hugo said. "Or maybe get a job in a factory."

"And stand by an automated machine two hours a day, watching telly? You don't understand, Hugo! I'm an artist, not a . . . a drone!"

"Well . . . there is just one remote possibility," Hugo said reluctantly. "But no—you wouldn't go for it."

"Anything!" Lew said hastily. "Anything at all, Hugo!"

"Well—if I work it right, I think I can get you a spot in a new documentary."

"I'll take it!"

"Sign here!" Hugo whipped out a thick bundle of contract documents. Lew grabbed the pen.

"I'll be in a star slot, of course?"

"Natcherally. Would I do you that way?"

Lew signed. "Thanks a million, Hugo." He sighed, gathering his blanket about him. "What set do I report to?"

Hugo shook his head. "No set, Lew. The pic ain't being shot here."

"You don't mean—not—not on location?"

"You guessed it."

"Omigod. Where?"

"A place called Byrdland."

"Birdland?" Lew brightened.

"Byrdland. It's in Antarctica."

2

"It's the biggest, finest Eskimo reservation on the globe!" Hugo's parting words rang in Lew Jantry's ears as he peered out through the bubble canopy of the automatic one-passenger flitter that was ferrying him on the last stage of the journey south. Across the blue-black sheen of the South Polar Sea, a line of dazzling white cliffs loomed ahead. Dropping rapidly, the machine skimmed low over the peaks, settling toward a rugged terrain resembling nothing so much as a vast frosted cake, a jumble of glassy blocks and smooth-drifted whiteness. Now he could make out the porous texture of the surface below, the network of wind-scoured ridges rushing up at him with surprising swiftness—

At the last possible instant, Lew realized that the robot voice of the autopilot, over the rushing of the wind, was squawking *"Mayday! Mayday!"* He grabbed the safety-frame lever, yanked it hard in the same moment that the craft struck with an impact that turned the universe into a whirling pinwheel of stars.

It seemed like a long time before pieces stopped raining down around him. Lew kicked free of the frame, dropped to the hard ground. The crash had burst the pod of the copter like a pumpkin, but he himself seemed to be intact. The weather suit was keeping him warm, in spite of the stiff wind that whipped the floury snow against his legs. Lew shaded his eyes and stared out across the desolate landscape. No sign of the Eskimo agent's office, or even of the tribal structures of the aborigines. Lew snorted. He'd invoke Section Nine, Paragraph Three of his contract on this one, all right— the part that provided bonuses for inconvenience occasioned by inadequate travel and housing accommodation for artists on field assignment. And the hardship clause would come in, too. Oh, boy, wait till he got hold of Hugo, he'd make that shrewdie regret the day he fast-talked Lew Jantry into a fiasco like this one.

He flipped back the cover of his wristphone and snapped an order to the operator. There was no reply. He raised his voice, then held the tiny transceiver to his ear. The reassuring carrier tone was conspicuously lacking.

"Damn!" Lew yelled, then swallowed hard as the true seriousness of his plight struck him. Marooned— God knew how far from the nearest food, shelter, and TV. And no one would know precisely where he was. The malfunctioning copter could have wandered a hundred miles off course since Tierra, for all he knew. In fact, he was lucky to have hit land at all, with all that ocean out there.

Lew shuddered and checked his pockets, found nothing but the regulation ration capsules and a book of matches. The copter yielded a road map of Chilicothe County, Kansas, and a package of welfare-issue contraceptive devices. He tried the panel TV, caught a much-distorted snatch of *Marty Snell, Trigamist*, but the picture rippled into static. Too bad: it was one of the few shows he enjoyed, a wild sitcom that he liked to view while on-camera, listening to Carla make chitchat to bring late tuners-in up-to-date on the last segment.

But he had more important things than Marty Snell to worry about now. The reservation was only a couple of miles inland. Maybe he could see it from the ridge ahead. It wouldn't hurt to walk that far. He faced into the antarctic wind and started across the treacherous footing.

He had gone a hundred yards when a sound behind him made him look back. A large polar bear had appeared beside the heli. The monster circled the downed machine, his mouth open like an awestricken yokel. The fanged head turned toward Lew, affording him a horrifying view down the creature's throat. It stared at him for a long beat, then started toward him at any easy lope. Lew stifled a yell and sprinted for the ridge with a speed that would have astonished his fans.

Heavy pads thudded close behind as he bounded across a rough stretch, hit a glass-smooth patch and went down, skidded twenty yards on his back, came to his feet scrambling for footing among the tumbled slabs at the base of the rise. He hauled himself upslope on all fours, spurred by the buzzing sound of ursine breath behind him, reached the crest—and a squat, fur-clad figure rose up before him, raising a short-hafted harpoon with a murderous hooked blade. For an instant the Eskimo poised, arm back, his teeth bared in a fero-cious grin. Then he hurled the spear.

As the weapon shot forward, Lew dived under it. He hit the smaller man amidships, carried him with him in a wild tumble down the opposite slope. At the bottom, Lew crawled clear, looked up dazedly just in time to see the yellow-white bulk of the bear hurtling down directly on him, jaws agape.

Lew awoke, staring up at the glossy white curve of a ceiling only three feet above his face, through which pale sunlight filtered. He turned his head, saw a grin-ning, brown-faced man in a Gooberplast playsuit sit-ting cross-legged on a synthetic bearskin rug, laying out a hand of solitaire. It was cool, Lew thought confusedly, but not as cold as he'd have expected in a building made of ice. He reached up and touched the ceiling. It was pleasantly warm to the touch, and dry. At that moment, he noticed a low hum in the background.

"No," he said, shaking his head. "It can't be an . . . an . . . "

"An air-conditioned igloo?" the card-player inquired in a deep voice. "Why not? You Gringos think us 'Skimos got no rights?"

"It's not that," Lew stuttered, sitting up. His head ached abominably. "It's just that . . . well . . . it's hardly what I expected. Say—" He broke off, remembering the encounter on the ridge. "Are you the fellow with the spear?"

"Right. Charlie Urukukalukuku's the name. Charlie Kuku for short. TVVAG, Local three-four-nine-eight. I'm not really an actor, I'm a cameraman. I just do the occasional walk-on when we're short of extras." He held out a well-manicured hand.

"You're a member of the Guild?" Lew blurted, taking the proffered member.

"Sure. You don't think we're letting scabs work down here in Byrdland, I hope."

"You mean the business with the bear—and the spear—the whole thing was just a skit?"

"Hardly a skit, Jantry. An important human document, delineating the plight of the haughty Kabloona when plummeted into the harsh Antarctic environment to which he has driven the patient Eskimo."

"That sounds like Hugo Fleischpultzer. And when did the white man ever drive the Eskimo into a harsh environment?"

"About fifty thousand years ago. Didn't you ever view any anthropology on educational TV?"

"Is that why you tried to stick me with that bloody great harpoon?"

"Stick you? Are you kidding? I tossed it a good quarter inch wild."

"And what about the bear? *He* wasn't kidding!"

"Yeah—too bad about that. Busted wide open. One of Hugo's ideas. It was a mech, you know. We got no live ones around, except a couple in the zoo. Too hot for 'em, since the big melt."

"Hot? Out there in all that ice?"

"What ice? Project Defrost cleared all that away years ago. But tourists come all this way to see Eskimos in their native habitat, they want to see snow. So—snow they get. Plastic snow, like this igloo."

"A plastic igloo?"

"Sure. It's part of the Native Village. A big grosser."

"But—why a mechanical bear?"

"The bear houses the number two aux camera. It shoots through the mouth. I was remoting it from the ridge. Got some swell shots of the clobber-in, then tried to dolly in for some CU's of you encountering the savage natives—that's me—"

"How did you know where I was going to crash?"

"Think I can't read a script? I was out there a good hour early, picking my camera angles. I got to hand it to you. You made it look good, Jantry. I was surprised to see you walk away from it."

"I made it look good?" Lew yelped. "Are you kidding? That thing was on full automatic the whole time—" He broke off. "Hugo planned it that way! He programmed the heli to crash—with me in it—"

"So? It figures. But it worked out OK. I got the death scene in the can. Great footage."

"Death scene?"

"Sure. I try to save you with my trusty spear, but the bear gets the both of us. It's the Noble Savage Gives Life for Paleface bit; wows 'em in the sticks."

"But—I came here to make a ninety-hour documentary on the colorful natives! Why kill me off in the opening sequence?" Lew broke off as a man in a gray coverall appeared on all fours in the entry tunnel, pushing a briefcase ahead of him.

"Thanks for sitting in for me, Charlie," he said to the Eskimo. "If you'll excuse us now, I'd like a word in private with Mr. Jantry."

"Sure." Charlie left. The newcomer rose, dusted his knees, showed Lew a small gold badge pinned inside his lapel.

"I'm Clabbinger, CIA," he said. "I can understand your confusion, Jantry. Of course the business of a role was merely a cover story enabling us to spirit you out of the States without attracting attention."

"Huh?" Lew said.

"Your true destination is the South Pacific Nature Reserve; place called the Cannibal Islands," the CIA man said crisply. "And it's not a play, Jantry. It's for real."

3

Lew stood on the deck of the LSP, shivering in a scanty sarong.

"The whole thing is illegal," he complained for the seventy-third time to Clabbinger, who stood impassively beside him, looking out through the pre-dawn mist toward the distant sound of surf. "I see now it was a put-up job from the beginning: me getting fired, the phony documentary—and now this! Threatening to blackball me in the industry if I don't sign a paper saying I volunteered!"

"It's your patriotic duty," the CIA man said calmly. "We know something's going on inside the Reserve. Naturally, we can't just blunder in and demand to search the entire archipelago."

"Why not?"

"Policy," Clabbinger said tersely. "Now, as I said, someone—no doubt in the service of a Certain Power—"

"You mean Russia?"

"Please let's keep it impersonal. Now these Russians— I mean this Certain Power has infiltrated the Reserve in defiance of solemn international commitments, and has set up some sort of secret installation—"

"How do we know that?"

"Our intrepid undercover men on the island reported it. Now, just what they're up to, we don't know. That's your job, Jantry: to tell us."

"Why do they want to make a Reserve out of these

god-forsaken islands anyway?" Lew burst out. "If it wasn't for that, there wouldn't be any place for the, uh, Certain Power to set up secret installations in!"

"Opening the islands would destroy a cultural museum that can never be duplicated," Clabbinger said indignantly. "This is the only spot on Earth where cannibalism and headhunting still flourish, uncontaminated by automation. And the diseases—why, if we let antibiotics in, hundreds of unique organisms would be rendered extinct overnight!"

"Why don't you send a regular agent into this pesthole?" Lew demanded. "Why me?"

"We need an accomplished actor to carry this off, Jantry. An ordinary agent would be incapable of passing himself off as a long-lost tribe member returning home after having been carried out to sea at the age of four in a paddleless canoe. He'd be caught and tortured to death in a most gruesome fashion."

"Swell," Lew groaned. "I either go and get roasted in my sarong, or refuse and never work again."

"Still—if you survive, I personally assure you you'll find your contract at Void Productions renewed for a long term at a substantial increase."

"What good's a substantial increase, with ninety-five percent going for taxes?" Lew inquired gloomily.

"Prestige," Clabbinger pointed out. "And if it weren't for the tax level, corporations wouldn't allocate the large tax-exempt advertising budgets needed to support over three hundred major TV networks with round-the-clock programming, nor would we enjoy the enlightened legislation that provides every citizen with a subsistence allowance, plus leisure time to view—and thus you'd be out of work."

"All right," Lew snarled. "I guess you've got me boxed—but these damned shark's-teeth earplugs hurt like hell!"

"Ah, that sounds a little more like Daredevil Jack, star of the show of the same name!" Clabbinger clapped Lew heartily on the back. "I'll confide that I always admired you in that one."

"I hated it," Lew said. "I was always afraid of the rest of the cast, they talked so tough."

A man had come up beside the G-man. "Half a mile offshore," he muttered. "This is as far as I can go without tripping the detectors."

"Well, Lew, this is it," Clabbinger said sternly, shaking the actor's hand. "Remember: as soon as you've located the site and beamed me the coordinates, get out fast. We'll drop a megatonner right down their stack six minutes later, and let them complain to the UN!"

"Just don't forget to have that sub standing by in case I come paddling out from shore in a hell of a hurry," Lew said bitterly.

Three minutes later, squatting in the outrigger canoe, he was gliding toward the palm-fringed shoreline ahead. The surf, though noisy, was not excessively high. He rode a long swell in, grounded on a sandy beach. He sprang from the boat listening alertly for any indication that his approach had been observed. Stealthily, he moved toward the shelter of the trees. Ten feet from his goal, a beam of dazzling white light speared out from the darkness to catch him full in the eyes. Blinded, he stumbled back, heard the quick rasp of feet—

A bomb exploded in his skull. He was dimly aware of falling, of being roughly rolled on his back.

"Nuts," a hoarse voice grated. "It's just another lousy native. Shoot the bum and let's get back to work."

"Wait!" Another, more guttural voice spoke up. "Don't shoot dog of native. Noise might bring unwelcome attention. Instead, tie up and dump out of way someplace."

Lew struggled feebly as hard hands threw multiple loops of hemp around his wrists and ankles, jammed a wad of oily cloth in his mouth. A man caught his shoulder, another his feet; they carried him well up into the jungle and dropped him into a clump of palmetto. Feet crashed through the underbrush, receding. Silence fell.

The night breeze stirred the fronds above Lew. Mosquitoes whined about his ears. He struggled onto his back, spitting leaf mold past the crude gag. Abruptly, something buzzed sharply, back of his right ear. Lew stiffened, awaiting the bite of the deadly snake—

"Hello?" a tinny voice said. *"Clabbinger to special agent LJ. Good work, boy! My instruments indicate you've penetrated the beach and are now behind the enemy lines. However, I note you're lying doggo. Let's not be too cautious. Remember Daredevil Jack! Play this one the way he would. Go get'em, tiger! We're rooting for you! Clabbinger out."*

"Hello?" Lew whispered. "Hello? Clabbinger?"

There was no answer. Lew groaned. Why hadn't they included a two-way connection? But who would have thought there'd be any need, with the tight-beam signaler tucked in his sarong to pinpoint the target for the missile strike? And anyway, Clabbinger wouldn't move a foot to help him; he'd told him that. He was on his own.

Lew took a deep breath and concentrated, the way he always did when slipping into a demanding role.

"All right, Russkies," Daredevil Jack breathed. "You started it. Now get ready for a counterattack by the Free Enterprise system!"

4

Ten minutes later, Daredevil Jack, free of his amateurishly tied bonds, raised his head and peered past the fronds at the half dozen figures grouped before a small tent from which the yellow glow of a lantern shone on a map table where a brightly colored eighteen inch disk lay. If he could get a little closer, make out the markings . . .

Flat on his stomach, Jack inched nearer. The men around the table seemed to be engaged in a heated argument, although keeping their voices low. One shook his fist under another's nose. A third man stepped between them. No doubt a dispute over the details of their treachery. Jack studied the palm trees just ahead. From the top of one, it might be possible to make out the details of the chart, using the small 'tronscope Clabbinger had supplied.

It was the work of another sweaty five minutes to reach the trees, shin up the curving trunk, and take up a position among the coconuts. Swiftly, Jack unclipped the scope, fine-focused the UV beam, adjusted the aperture. There! The red-orange coloring of the target leaped into clarity, a maze of complex markings. It was obviously a detailed relief map, the roughly circular shape indicating the island's outline, with mountains, valleys, rivers all delineated in vivid pigments. And there—that was doubtless the location of the illegal site. Jack studied the black circle, nestled between a sardine-shaped lake and what appeared to be a sliver of salami. The circle itself showed a remarkable resemblance to a slice of ripe olive.

"I told you, I can't eat pizza!" A vagrant breeze wafted a scrap of conversation to Jack. "I hate Mexican food!"

"Damn!" Lew Jantry muttered. He scanned past the disputants, surveyed the remains of a camp fire, a heap of empty TV dinner cartons, settled on a huddled figure lying in the shadows of a flowering bush. He made out a vividly colored sarong, a mass of dark, wavy hair, a pair of slender ankles, bound with rope.

"It's a native girl," Lew muttered. "They've got her tied up, the rats!" He lowered the scope, frowning thoughtfully.

Maybe, Daredevil Jack thought, *she's been in the camp long enough to have heard something. And even if she hasn't, her people will be grateful enough for her release to give me a hand in finding that Russian installation . . .*

Suddenly, smiling a grim smile, Daredevil Jack descended to the ground, began a circuitous approach to the spot where the captive girl lay.

She watched him with wide eyes as he sawed at her ropes with a bit of sharp-edged seashell.

"Shh!" he admonished as he pulled away the gag to reveal a remarkably pretty face, olive brown, pert-nosed, red-lipped. She looked around fearfully, then at Jack.

"Aholui thanks you," she breathed.

"Time for thanks later," Jack said kindly but firmly. "We're not out of this yet." He took her hand, helped her to her knees. "The coast is clear this way."

They had gone approximately ten feet when a bush parted just ahead, and a man appeared, buttoning his clothes. For an instant, his eyes and Jack's locked.

"What th—" he started as Jack's head rammed him squarely in the belt buckle. He went down hard as Lew Jantry staggered to his feet, rubbing his neck and uttering small cries.

"Let's get out of here!" Aholui grabbed his hand and

hauled him off down a winding path into the deep jungle as questioning shouts rose behind them.

"I don't care . . . if they do catch us . . . " Lew gasped, flopping down and sucking air into his lungs. "I'm all in!"

"Not much farther now," the girl said. "You must have been living soft out there in the great outside world, or wherever it was you said you've been."

A gusty wind had risen; a sudden heavy splatter of rain rattled on the palmettos. Lew got to his feet, rubbing at the gooseflesh on his arms.

"What a place," he carped. "One minute you're broiling, the next you're freezing. Where are we going, anyway?"

"To a place where we'll be safe from the white-eyes," Aholui said. "Up there." She pointed. In the sudden vivid glare of a flash of lightning, Lew saw a rugged volcanic peak thrusting up above the wind-lashed palm trees. The rain struck then, like a battery of fire hoses. Stumbling, colliding with trees in the dark, his hide rasped by sharp-edge tropical shrubbery, Lew followed as the girl led the way toward the high ground.

It might have been half an hour later—or half an eternity—before Lew dragged himself over a rocky ledge and lay flat, breathing heavily. Before him, the dark mouth of a cave opened. With his last strength, he crawled to it, and inside. With the girl tugging at his arm, he managed to negotiate a sharp turn, and was in a low-ceilinged chamber twelve feet on a side. He propped himself against the wall and wiped the water from his eyes. Aholui seated herself beside him.

"Now, tell me again," she said. "What were you doing down there in the outlanders' camp?"

"You remember—about the plot they're hatching. You never told me why they had you tied up."

"They caught me snooping."

Lew put a sympathetic arm around the girl's shoulders. "The rotters!" he said. "Just because you were curious about a bunch of foreign devils invading the place."

Aholui shrugged his arm off. "Can't blame them," she said. "I was outside the tribal turf."

"Nonsense! The whole island belongs to you. Now"—he reinsinuated his arm—"if you'll just take me to your leader . . ." He leaned over, zeroing in on the girl's half parted lips.

A light bulb exploded in his ear, accompanied by a ringing sound.

"Carla," Lew mumbled dazedly. "I just had the craziest dream . . ."

The girl was standing by the wall, fumbling with a bump on the stone. With a soft whine of well-oiled machinery, a panel slid back to reveal a well-equipped laboratory. A broad-shouldered young man in a white coat and a white-haired oldster looked up in surprise.

"Grab this cluck, George," Aholui said, jerking a thumb at Lew. "He's some kind of Interpol fink, or I'll eat a bunch of bananas, insides and all!"

5

Strapped to a chair, with a lump on his head that throbbed in time with his pulse, Lew Jantry stared from the grim-eyed girl to the square-jawed young man to the elderly one, who returned the look through a set of half inch thick trifocals.

"You think you can kidnap a federal agent and get away with it?" he demanded in a tone that quavered only slightly.

No one bothered to answer the question.

"It was pretty slick, the way he handled it," the girl said. "He pretended to be rescuing me, as if anyone could really sneak into that campful of Feds, with guards posted every ten feet, and cut somebody loose. Then, as soon as he thought I was in the clear, he started pouring on the oil and pumping me for information."

"I did not!" Lew cut in. "I only wanted to kiss you. I thought *they* were the crooks." He broke off, staring at the old man. "Say, don't I know you?"

"Maybe." The white head nodded. "Lots of people used to, before I decided to Get Away from It All."

"Rex Googooian, the Armenian Valentino!" Lew gasped. "You used to be the biggest draw on the whole early mid-morning sector! Every middle-aged housewife in American was in love with you! And then you dropped out of sight a few years ago, blop, just like that!"

"Yes indeed." Googooian nodded. "It dawned on me one day that I had only a few years left in which to expiate the crimes I'd been practicing for thirty years."

"Crimes?"

"Did you ever notice the dialogue on the early mid-morning sector?" the aged actor inquired succinctly. "So I came here—secretly, of course—bringing with me my daughter, Baby Lou." He nodded toward Aholui, who was vigorously scrubbing away her tan makeup.

"—And my assistant, George. And a considerable stock of equipment, of course."

"But—that must have cost a fortune!"

"I had one. And what better way to employ it than in putting an end to the pernicious plague that for the better part of eighty years had been rising like a flood of materialistic mediocrity, drowning our culture in its infancy?"

"Plague? You mean you're doing dandruff research?" Lew groped.

"I refer," Googooian said in implacable tones, "to the greatest menace in the world today!"

"What menace? Cuba? Nepal? Lebanon?"

"Think of it!" Googooian's eyes lit with a messianic fervor. "No more commercials, no more sitcoms, no quizzes, no panels, no more pomaded heads huddled together, staring with vacuous, counterfeit smiles from flickering screens, no more idiotic dialogue, no more cardboard characterizations, no more creaking plots, no more moronic villains and sweepstake-winning heroes, no more mummified sex appeal, no more relatives of producers posing as Thespians—"

"Are you try to say—no more television?" Lew choked the words out.

"In approximately seven hours," Googooian stated firmly, "TV broadcasting will come to a halt. World-wide! Forever!"

"You're out of your mind!" Lew blurted. "That's impossible!"

"Is it!" Googooian smiled sardonically. "I believe otherwise. You've heard of the Van Allen Radiation belts?"

"Is that like those suspenders that glow in the dark?" Lew hazarded.

"Not quite. They are layers of high energy charged particles two thousand and twelve thousand miles above the Earth, respectively. They are of interest here only in that the Googooian Belt will in some ways resemble them. I have prepared a rocket, sir, housed here in the volcano's crater, which, when fired, will ascend to an altitude of fifteen hundred miles, and there assume an orbit which will carry it over every point on the planet in the first fifty revolutions—about seventy-two hours. As it travels, it will release a steady stream of very specially charged particles—particles which will emit electromagnetic impulses creating a powerful static interference across the entire broadcast band. Every station on the planet will be drowned in a pure noise signal. TV, sir, is dead!"

"You can't!" Lew protested. "What will all those people do, left with twenty-two hours a day of leisure time on their hands? What will the sponsors do with all that ad money? Society as we know it will collapse!"

"You've been brainwashed." George spoke up coldly. "You and the rest of those FBI smarties down there. If you know so much, why have you been poking around the island for six months without finding us?"

"We haven't—I mean, I did—I mean—oh, what's the use?" Lew buried his face in his hands. "I'm a failure," his muffled voice stated mournfully. "And Clabbinger was counting on me!—"

Googooian came over to pat him consolingly on the shoulder. "Why not lend a hand with the gear?" he suggested in a fatherly tone. "Afterward you'll feel better, knowing you played a part in the liberation of man from electronic tyranny."

"Never!" Lew yelled. "First, I'll—" He broke off as a chirping voice rasped in his left ear:

Operative LJ, Clabbinger here. I see you've moved inland to a point at the approximate center of the island. I'm expecting to pick up a pulse from that signaler any time now, pinpointing that target. Keep up the good work! Over and out.

Lew Jantry's heart took a great leap, then settled down to a steady thudding. He'd totally forgotten the signaler, but his course was plain. All he had to do was reach the button with his fingertips and send out the pulse that would bring a megatonner screaming in on the hidden launch pad. Googooian's mad scheme would go up in radioactive gas.

And Lew Jantry along with it.

"You knew," he whispered. "Clabbinger, you monster, you knew all along it was a suicide mission!"

"Ah, beginning to have some second thoughts, eh?" Googooian said cheerfully. "Beginning to see that you're a mere dupe of the vested interests that are reducing the nation to a common level of imbecility, eliminating literacy, callousing esthetic sensibilities, and imposing a shabby standard of mercantile expedience and conformity to a false and superficial ideal of synthetic glamour!"

"Something like that," Lew muttered. His fingers inched their way toward the concealed signaler.

"If you'll give me your parole, I'll untie you," the ex-actor proposed. "George and I could really use some help with the last-minute details."

"Well . . . " Lew stalled. His finger touched the button. He gritted his teeth—and stiffened as the pickup behind his left ear clicked suddenly.

"Hello?" a brisk voice chirped. *"Oh, it's you, Simenov . . . uh-huh, in about six hours . . . Of course it'll work! Why do you lousy Commies hire American technicians if you don't have confidence?"* There was a lengthy pause. *"Look, you have your programming ready, that's all! I'll guarantee we'll blanket every channel of television on the planet. The Commie line will be coming out of every TV set on the North and South American continents. And there's no possible way they can stop it! Not with a transmitter sunk below the Mohorovicic Discontinuity in an insulated vault, powered by the core heat. Not when you're using the whole planet's fluid interior as an antenna. It's all set! Stop worrying and synchronize watches. We throw the switches at six A.M. on the dot!"* There was a sharp *click!* followed by silence.

"Ye Gods!" Lew mumbled. "Two targets—and only one bomb!" He swallowed hard, his thoughts racing.

"Googooian," he barked. "Are you sure this invention of yours will blanket *all* television, not just part of it?"

"Absolutely!"

"What about a super-powerful station?"

Googooian chuckled. "All the better. The particles will absorb and re-radiate as noise any impinging electromagnetic radiation. The more energetic, the better."

"Sold!" Lew said. "I'll help you! Get these ropes off and let's get going!"

6

The eastern sky was heralding dawn with a glory of purple and crimson when Lew, Googooian, George, and Baby Lou retired to the blockhouse carved deep in the flank of the mountain, and grouped themselves around the rocket control console. Solemnly, the aging actor-turned-researcher depressed the firing button. A low rumble passed through the solid rock.

On the closed-circuit screen, the crater mouth erupted through which a needle prow emerged, rising slowly at first, then more swiftly, mounting toward the cloud-dotted sky, trailing fire and thunder.

"She's off!" Googooian chortled as the others clapped him on the back, laughing merrily—all but Lew Jantry. Glumly, he watched the ship disappear into the high haze.

"Cheer up, lad," Googooian called. "It's all for the best. You'll see!"

"Look what we'll be missing!" George called cheerfully as he switched on the forty-eight-inch full color three-D set. The screen blinked, flickered, firmed into an image of a woman with a face like an oversized Pekinese.

" . . . Dear Sally Sweetbreads, this viewer writes," a high-pitched nasal intoned. "I never miss your show, which is the cause of the trouble between my husband and me. He says it breaks his scene when you give some of that clinical-type advice just at the most romantic moment. Signed, Perplexed. Well, Perplexed, assuming you don't want to change husbands"—the plump features compressed into a leer—"I'd suggest you rearrange the bedroom. And now—"

"That's not all we'll be missing," Lew snarled. "When the depression this thing causes hits, we'll miss everything from meals to martinis. There'll be millions out of work! Tax revenue will drop to zero! The government may collapse—and we'll be stuck here, on this infernal island!"

"Tsk," Googooian said. "My analysis suggests that the creative energies released from thralldom to television mania will produce an upsurge in every facet of our culture. There'll be a flowering of science and the arts to rival the Renaissance. Of course, there may be a short period of readjustment—say a decade. But no matter. We'll be quite happy here. The entire interior of the mountain is honeycombed with facilities: luxurious quarters, a nuclear power plant, well-shielded, a ten-year stockpile of gourmet food to supplement the native diet, a vast library of books and music."

On the screen, a loose-lipped young man with intent eyes leaned toward a jawless woman in a grotesque hat.

"Mrs. Wiltoff, would you just tell us in your own words how it feels to be the wife of the man scheduled to be gassed tomorrow on a nationwide hookup for the brutal slaying of the nine chorus girls whose pictures you are now admiring?"

"Well, Bob," the interviewee started; abruptly, the

image flickered, turned to a flapping pattern of diagonal lines. A new picture burned into focus over it. A thick-necked man with small eyes looked out of the screen.

"Capitalist swine," he began in a glutinous voice— and was drowned under a deluge of white blips which danced across the tube face, swiftly coalescing into a solid rectangle of glare. A roar like Niagara swelled to blot out the sound.

"Hooray!" Googooian capered madly, embracing his teammates, while Lew wandered disconsolately to the blockhouse door. From the tiny balcony overhanging the interior of the volcano, he looked down into the fire-blackened silo from which the rocket had emerged minutes before. There was a step beside him.

"Thanks for helping Pop," Baby Lou said. "I expected you to try something, but you didn't. Maybe I was wrong about you being a CIA man."

"Well . . ." Lew moved closer to the girl, slid an arm around her waist. "Inasmuch as we're stuck here," he said, "we may as well make the best of it."

"What's *that?*" Baby Lou felt over Lew's side, plucked something from his sarong. "It was sticking me," she said, and pushed the button.

"No!" Lew grabbed the signaler and hurled it into the pit—far too late. Already its telltale pulse had raced to the ship waiting hull-down over the horizon.

"Well—I never!" Baby Lou snapped and marched away.

"Everybody to the beach!" Lew yelled, plunging after her. "We've got six minutes before the island goes up in smoke!"

7

It was a balmy evening six months later. Lew, Googooian, and Simenov sat under the thatched shelter they had constructed above the high tide line, playing a game of homemade dominoes by lantern light. In the background, a native electric guitar band played *Aloha Oe* in time to the chugging of a portable generator.

"Tomorrow comes maybe supply ship," the Russian said, eyeing the empty horizon.

"I doubt it," Googooian said.

Baby Lou came up, trailed by George. "No, I do *not* believe in sharing the wealth," she was saying tartly. "Father, make George stop bothering me!"

"Ah—perhaps if Lew chaperoned you—"

"I'd like to see him try, the lousy actor," George snarled.

"Oh, yeah?" Daredevil Jack half rose, then sank back. "It's too hot," Lew Jantry said.

Baby Lou sniffed and stalked away. George wandered off. Simenov glowered at the dominoes.

"Now, now," Googooian said in tones of forced heartiness. "Here we are, living in paradise, plenty of fruit and fresh seafood, sunshine every day, cool breezes at night, no responsibilities, no problems. We should all be perfectly delighted!"

"Then why aren't we?" Lew demanded.

"I tell you why," Simenov stated. "Is no damned thing to do. Are not building socialism. Not even building capitalism! Is building only sand castles, and is getting pretty damn boring."

"Say," Googooian said suddenly.

"What?" Lew said.

"I was just wondering—not that I regret anything I've done, you understand . . . "

"Go on," Simenov said.

"If we used the stuff you fellows had left over"— he eyed the Russian—"and if we could salvage a few items from the mountain—"

"Yes?" Lew and Simenov said in chorus.

"We might just be able to tinker up a little line-of-sight rig. Nothing elaborate, mind you. Just straight black and white, two-D—at least at first . . . "

"Hmm. Is possibility." The Russian pulled at his lower lip. Together, the two technical men strolled off deep in conversation. Lew Jantry sat where he was, staring after them, a thoughtful look on his face. Then he rose, hurried toward the slight figure wandering lonely along the beach.

"Oh, Baby Lou," he called. "I've been meaning to ask you: have you ever thought of taking up acting as a profession?"

"Why, Lew! Do you really think I might have talent?"

"I'm sure of it. It's just a matter of finding an outlet for it."

Together they strolled along the shore of the lagoon toward the silvery path of the rising moon.

GOOBEREALITY

❧

Barnaby Quale, immaculately clad in pale yellow Gooberalls and ochre Gooberbund for his meeting with the head of Goober Enterprises, sat on the edge of the vast, hard chair reserved for personal interviewees of Harlowe Goober, waiting for the magnate to speak.

"Environmental Simulator?" Goober's voice combined the toughness of Gooberplast with the silky texture of Gooberlon. He fixed Quale with a daggerlike glance from pale blue eyes magnified by quarter-inch electrolenses, prodded the sheets of sketches and calculations before him.

"I'm a practical man, Clune," he announced. "Never went in for this what-d'ye-call-it science stuff; a Goober hires men for that. Now suppose you leave out all the technical talk and state just what it is you're referring to."

"It's the matter I wrote to you about, six months ago,

Mr. Goober," Barnaby said. "It's a new application of cybernetic theory. By harnessing a data-response syndrome to a manipulative device, using an application of the principle that's employed in the Goobervendors to synthesize a variety of products—"

"I'm familiar with the function of the Goobervendor, Gorm," the industrialist barked. "One of my finer contributions to the Great Society, ranking just after the Goobertape and just ahead of the Gooberlator." He lit up a Gooberfitter with a flourish.

"Yes, sir," Quale nodded. "But my device does more than merely produce a product to specification. It assimilates the data introduced, collates, interrelates, extrapolates and, on the basis of up to one hundred billion separate informational factors, re-creates the exocosmic matrix implied by the observed phenomena—"

"Boil that down to straight American, Clud!" Goober snapped. "I have an appointment in two minutes with the Secretary of Poverty. The program's being expanded to cover another hundred million newly qualified citizens, and Goober Enterprises will be expected to make its usual massive input to the common good." He clamped the cigar between large, square teeth and glared at Quale.

"I was wondering, Mr. Goober, if you've had time to look over my calculations and designs, and reach a decision about backing me."

"Ah, I think I recall something of the matter now, Grudd. You're the fellow who quit us to go off on his own! Some wild scheme to mock up some sort of mechanical wax museum."

"Mr. Goober, I don't think you've quite grasped the real significance of the Environmental Simulator. It's not just a gimmick! It's a research tool of the first importance! There are dozens of applications for the device! Police forces could use it to reconstruct crimes, on the basis of all available clues; historians can fill in gaps in historical situations by setting up all known data. The Simulator will fill in the gaps by extension of the known—"

"Nonsense, Greeb! A visionary scheme! Totally impractical! Goober Enterprises wouldn't put a nickel into a crank idea like this!" Goober rose, a vast, massive figure in fashionable purple Goobervelt with a touch of Gooberlace at the wrists.

"One of my people will show you the way out."

"I know the way out," Barnaby said. "I worked here for six years."

"And having deserted the firm, you now come crawling back for handouts!"

"I'm offering you a solid business deal," Quale protested. But Goober was gone, in a swirl of Gooberfumes.

Barnaby made his way from the Executive Wing, rode the Gooberlift down to ground level, took a shortcut across the Experimental Complex toward the Research Block. A new shed had been set up, he noted; a huge, slab-sided structure covering an acre or two of ground. A tall, thin man emerged from a tiny door set in one corner.

"Hey, Barney," the man hailed, "what you doing over here? Haven't seen you in months."

"Hello, Horace. Just been in to see the Old Man about my proposition. He turned me down cold."

"Say, that's too bad, Barney. Looks like he'd pay a little more attention to the man that gave him Goobervision, Goobertape, Goobertronics, the Goobervendor."

"All I did was supply the ideas, Horace; Mr. Goober got them into production. By the way, what's this?" Barnaby waved a hand at the looming structure.

Horace looked grave. "This is something big, Barney. It's called the Goobernetic Goobereality Simulator. Very hush-hush."

"Simulator?" Barnaby's eyebrows rose almost to his hairline.

"Sure. A great concept." Horace looked around. "Come on inside," he said in a conspiratorial tone. "I'll give you a peek."

Barnaby followed Horace through the door into the echoing vastness of the immense structure. Fifty feet overhead a roof of translucent Gooberplast admitted a warm, golden light. To the left was a bank of massive machines, featureless in gray housings, a control booth beside them. Otherwise, the flat, covered acres were as smooth and featureless as a parking lot.

"This one was the Old Man's own, personal idea," Horace said. "It came down right from his office, about six months ago. Top priority. We rushed her through. She's all programmed now, ready to go. He plans to give a demonstration for the industry tomorrow; I've got an idea he's working an angle to get a Cabinet appointment out of this one."

"What does it do?"

"Damnedest thing you ever saw," Horace said. He led the way to the control booth, indicated a wide panel. "You feed in your data here; it's flashed to the main cybernetic banks over in Vault One, and processed. See that big cable there? A direct tap to the main power pile. You got over 50 Goobermegs to draw on. When the red light goes on, you throw in the main switch here; that activates the Simulator, and starts the mockup going—"

"Horace—you mean—it sets up a simulated environment?"

Horace gaped. "Hey, how'd you know that?"

"Look, Horace, are you *sure*? I was just talking to Mr. Goober—"

"Oh," Horace looked relieved. "He told you about it. For a minute I was afraid there'd been a leak."

"You said there'll be a demonstration tomorrow?"

"Sure, we're all ready to go. We've already run complete tests; works like a charm. You'd swear it was the real thing."

"I suppose there'll be representatives from the leading universities here—and maybe the FBI and the Secret Service—"

"Huh? Heck, no, Barney. This is a hush-hush deal. Goober Industries stands to clean up on this one. The only ones invited are Hashflash Associates, Tosscookie & Wilt, and Earp, Earp, Earp & Earp—"

"Why, those are all advertising agencies!" Barnaby frowned. "What interest would they have in an Environmental Simulator?"

"Are you kidding? Talk about market research! With this setup, the advertiser can penetrate right into the innermost secrets of the American scene! No more wondering what brand underarm the typical family uses; just plug in the data, and take a look!"

"But—but, Horace! He couldn't! That's invasion of privacy! And it's a perversion of the intent of the device! I meant to make a lasting contribution to human knowledge."

"You, Barney? What've you got to do with it?"

"What? Look, Horace, this is *my* invention—the one Mr. Goober just turned down."

"Huh? Hey, wait a minute, Barney! Are you kind of hinting around that Mr. Goober would—well—*swipe* your idea?"

"It looks that way—and it also looks like he's planning to use it to sell more Gooberjunk. I intended the

Simulator to be used for human betterment—not for prying into people's personal business."

"Personal business? What personal business? After all, with everybody on the Government payroll—"

"*We're* not on the Government payroll; you work for Goober Enterprises and I'm in business for myself."

"Uh-huh, same difference; Goober Enterprises does all its work on Government contract and you're registered under the Poverty Act. After all, since the hundred percent income tax went through, a fellow doesn't really have much chance on his own, does he?" Horace chuckled. "No, Barney, if you want to have a Great Society, you've got to give up a few luxuries like privacy."

"But people have some rights."

Horace wagged a finger. "Now, Barney, you can't work for Uncle Sam, live in Government housing, subsist on Government handouts, and still babble about rights, now can you?"

"Look, Horace—could you give me a demonstration?"

"Not a chance, Barney! I shouldn't even have let you on the lot. Like I said, this is under wraps."

"But I've got to see how it works! After all, it's my invention."

"You want to get me fired? Let's go, Barney. I got to lock up."

An hour later, in his cubicle on Shelf One-oh-two, Slice Six Hundred and Fifty-five, Stratum Nine, Block Seventeen of Number Forty-two Bachelors' Barracks, Barnaby looked around in annoyance at a buzz from the Gooberscope. He flipped a lever; a pert girl's face appears on the foot-square screen.

"Oh, hi, Gigi, what do you want?"

"Barnaby! Is that polite? How did the conference go? Is old Gooberpuss going to finance your invention?"

"Hah! He already has! It's ready for a big demonstration in a day or so."

"Barnaby! That's wonderful! Why didn't you tell me?!"

"The only trouble is he's squeezed me out of the picture. He's passed out the word that it's all his own idea; and when I tried to go back and demand an explanation, they told me he was in Patagonia on a big Gooberblubber negotiation."

"Why, the old crook!"

"Look out, Gigi, these Gooberscopes may be Gooberbugged. You'll lose your job, and then there'll be two of us on relief."

"Barnaby, he can't do this! You can go to court, make him pay you—"

"Sure—if I had the price of a couple of high-powered legal firms. Goober has a hundred and forty-five of the top shysters in the country on the payroll, with nothing to do but sit around inserting fine print in contracts and fighting damage suits. Anyway, I'm not really sure it's my Simulator; I didn't see it working."

"What are you going to do, Barnaby?" Gigi's voice rose to a wail. "You've worked on this for three years! This was going to be your big prize! We were going to g-get m-m-married . . . "

"For heaven's sake, don't cry, Gigi!"

"All these years you've slaved, and old Gooberface has gotten rich off your ideas!"

"No, he hasn't; his whole salary goes for taxes, just like everybody else's."

"I don't mean his silly old salary! What about his expense account, and his representational allowance, and his Government bonuses and—"

"Sure, he lives like a king—but I'm not interested in that. All I want is to prove a man can still make it on his own. Every time I think about Goober stealing my ideas and then giving me the brushoff, I see red!"

"Now, Barnaby, don't do anything hasty."

"Hasty? After three years' work? I'm going over there and make him pay up if I have to sit on him and pound his head on the Gooberug in his own office!"

"Barnaby! Wait!"

"I'm going. So long, Gigi!"

"Then I'm going with you. I'll be down in five minutes!"

The vast Executive Tower was dark when Barnaby and Gigi left the subway at the Gooberdilly Circus stop and emerged into the wan light of early evening.

"See? I told you we'd be too late," Gigi said. "The executives never work during prime TV time."

"There are lights over at the Experimental Complex; maybe Goober's there, gloating over how he robbed me." He led the way across to the gate, spoke to the guard on duty.

"Sure, Barney, no harm in letting you look around. Hi, Gigi." He waved them past. Inside, they headed toward the shed that housed the Goobernetic Goobereality Simulator.

"Barnaby, you can't go in there," she cautioned. "You know these sheds are top secret."

"Naturally! Goober doesn't want to advertise stolen goods."

"Please, Barnaby, come back tomorrow, and discuss the matter in a gentlemanly way with Mr. Goober. Maybe he didn't mean—"

"How can I, when he's in Patagonia?" Barnaby reached for the door.

"We're trespassing!" Gigi wailed. "Let's go now, before somebody sees us . . ."

Barnaby twisted the knob; the door swung in; he stepped into the darkened interior of the shed.

Gigi's voice echoed in the wide gloom. "Barnaby! We have no business in here!"

"There's nobody here, Gigi; relax."

"Where's your invention? All I see if a big open space . . . "

"Over there; that's the computer console and the synthesizing units. You see the wires strung around the shed? They tie the whole space into a closed field. I must say, he did a first-class job of installation. All I had in mind was a little thing about the size of a phone booth."

"Do you know how to work it?"

"Naturally; it's a dead steal from my drawings." He stepped inside the control booth. "All you do is set up the coordinates you want; the Simulator does the rest."

"Barnaby! You wouldn't! Mr. Goober would be furious!"

"Not any more furious than I am."

"But—but it's all set up for tomorrow's demonstration!"

"Sure, that makes it simpler. I'd better check out the instrument readings first . . . " Barnaby studied the panel. "Looks okay; all we need to do is punch that button." He pointed.

"Barnaby, wait!"

He stepped past her and closed the switch.

For a moment nothing happened; then a dim light sprang up all across the enclosed space under the luminous Gooberplast ceiling; a deep humming sound was audible, rumbling from some subterranean chamber.

"Boy, look at those power drain figures," Barnaby breathed.

"What's happening, Barnaby?" Gigi said breathlessly.

"The field is energizing. It's soaking up power like a sponge; that's to be expected, of course. Energy/matter conversion isn't an easy proposition."

There was a deafening boom! followed by a whistling of air. The door to the control booth rattled in its frame. Suddenly an opaque, gray blanket seemed to hang over the observation window.

"Barnaby! Is everything all right?"

He peered out into the mist. "I think so. Readings are all normal."

"Why is it so—so foggy out there?"

"The field shuts off incident light; it's a sort of closed space effect. The simulated environment has to be segregated from outside influences, of course, or its validity will be compromised."

"Barnaby, you've done enough for now. Let's go. We can come back some other time—"

"Go? We haven't even looked at it yet."

"That's all right; we can go up to my place and I'll make you a nice cup of coffee substitute and—"

"We can't leave now, without even seeing what kind of effect we've gotten." Barnaby stepped to the door marked AUTHORIZED GOOBERMEN ONLY and opened it. He stared out. Gigi came to his side. Where the plain concrete floor had been, a city street was visible, lined with bright shop fronts thronged with people.

"Wow!" Barnaby breathed.

"Where—where did the people come from?" Gigi whispered. "And those shops—"

"I knew it would be good," Barnaby said in a choked voice. "But this is fantastic . . . "

"Let's go back," Gigi said.

"Let's take a look," Barnaby said. He took her hand and stepped out into the street.

❖   ❖   ❖

It was midday, and bright sunlight gleamed down from above. The passers-by jostled them in normal fashion, hurrying about their simulated business.

"It's marvelous!" Barnaby said. "Goober's technicians fed in data for a contemporary 1972 street scene, it looks like. The Simulator extrapolated, built up the charge on the environmental field, and boom! Here it is, perfect in every detail!" They strolled along, admiring the view. The pedestrians ignored them, forcing them to dodge to avoid being rammed.

"Are they—real?" Gigi asked.

"Of course not. But they'll behave as if they were." Barnaby snorted. "And Goober plans to use all this to figure out what kind of depilatory has the greatest appeal. And I suppose he'll lease it out to politicians to overhear what the typical voter is saying about the issues, and—"

"Are they just false fronts? Is there anything behind the facades?"

"Certainly; they'll be perfect, inside and out."

Gigi gave a shrill cry. "Barnaby, look! The control room! It's gone!" Barnaby stared back the way they had come. The street seemed to dwindle away into the distance.

"What happened to the control room?" the girl gasped.

"Oh, it's right there where it always was, but the closed-space effect keeps you from seeing it. Actually, we're in a sort of little universe of our own here, held together by the terrific power flowing over the surface of the field—"

"I'd feel a lot better if we could see, Barnaby. What if we get lost here?"

Barnaby laughed. "Nonsense, Gigi. All we have to do is go in a straight line to any of the walls, and . . ." he frowned. "No, that's not quite right; the field curves space . . . but if we just go back to the control room . . . but . . . "

"Barnaby! What's the matter! You look so pale!"

Barnaby swallowed hard. "Nothing—nothing at all. But maybe we'd better just find that door right away . . . " He turned, walked quickly back, groped at the empty air. A stout lady in runover shoes puffed past, ignoring him. He worked his way across the sidewalk, turned and looked back.

"I'm *sure* it wasn't this far along," he muttered.

"Barnaby, we were standing at least over there when we stepped into this place," Gigi said worriedly, pointing. "I remember the crack in the sidewalk."

"You must be mistaken, Gigi." Barnaby indicated a stout oak door set in the wall behind him. It bore a brass plate reading CHAST & SEEMLY STUDIOS, LIMITED.

"Let's try in here," he called. He opened the door, held it for Gigi. Hesitantly, she stepped inside. They were in a narrow foyer, discreetly lit, austerely decorated, unobtrusively air-conditioned. Sterilized music murmured from an indefinable source.

"Look," Gigi said. "Elevators. Where could they go? There isn't anything above . . . "

"Appearances are deceiving; we're still inside the field. If we go up, we can look out of a window, and then maybe we can see the outer walls. That will tell us where we are."

"Well . . . maybe."

Barnaby pressed the button; there was a soft whoosh! of air. The doors slid aside. They entered the car.

"Four floors ought to be high enough," Barnaby said. The car moved up, eased to a stop. The doors opened. Barnaby looked out into a dimly lit residential-looking corridor, deeply carpeted, neuter-toned, silent.

"Hmmm, I guess we'll have to look around and find a window." Barnaby stepped to a blank oak panel, rapped on it. Nothing happened. He tried it. It swung open. They stepped through and stopped dead, staring. Sun streamed through lacy curtains over wide windows where flowers grew in pots. On a brand-new stepladder by a sootless fireplace set with a gleaming brass shove and poker, a well-muscled man of twenty-five with the features of a god, wearing well-pressed dark slacks and a perfectly fitted polo shirt spread a hideous pink paint on a white wall, using an immaculate brush. The paint flowed out in a flawless swath with each stroke. A beautiful girl in a starched white blouse and red slacks wielded a roller in the lower section of the wall. Her work was, if anything, more perfect than his. Not a drop had been spattered.

"This Kem-tone is the paintier paint," she stated. "Goes on so easy, your friends will think you called in a high-priced decorator—"

"Pardon me, folks," Barnaby said. The two home decorators ignored him. He went to the window, looked out. A sheet of cardboard with a lithograph of a seed-catalog garden blocked the view.

The man on the stepladder turned to dip his brush. Barnaby stepped up to him. "Hey!" The man went on painting the same spot, in smooth effortless strokes.

"Comes in twelve delicious colors, too," the girl commented. "Lemon, lime—"

"Look!" Barnaby said. "This is an emergency. We're lost. Can you tell us—"

"Maybe they can't see us—or hear us either," Gigi suggested in an awed whisper.

"They'll hear me," Barnaby said determinedly. He seized the man's painting arm; the ladder tilted; the man swayed, crashed to the floor, upsetting the girl in red slacks who fell sideways, still painting unhurriedly. Lying on his side, the man worked his brush imperturbably, laying a pink stripe across the girl's chest. She rolled her roller in the air, smiled with pink features as the brush worked over her face.

" . . . Strawberry," she cooed. "Raspberry, prune, chop suey and chicken noodle . . . "

"Let's get out of here!" Barnaby seized Gigi's hand, charged across the room, burst through a door. They were in a sunny breakfast nook. A lovely girl in a ruffled apron stood with her head sideways, one hand on hip, holding a coffee pot.

"More Chase and Sanborn's?" She smiled brilliantly.

A man with incredibly regular features looked at her happily from his chair at the table. Before him on a machine-decorated plate a symmetrical fried egg lay beside two geometrical strips of bacon. He held a clean starched napkin in his left hand. He rolled his eyes ludicrously, his tongue curling over his upper lip; he wrinkled his nose . . .

"Ummm, ummm," he said feelingly. "It's my favorite . . . "

Barnaby looked about for another door. The wall ended just beyond the table. Holding Gigi's hand, he plunged for it, jarring the table. Behind him, the man smiled as steaming coffee poured down on his knee.

The two rounded a partition, almost fell over a finely gowned woman who tilted a can of chemical over a toilet bowl. "Since I discovered new Drano," she said brightly, "old-fashioned, inferior products have been banished . . . "

A man stood watching, a finger digging at the back of his neck, a cap between his fingers. He appeared slightly ill with malaria, and his overalls needed pressing. A number of large, new tools lay scattered on the floor at his feet, together with brushes with bent bristles, bottles and cans with blurred labels, and a large and unsightly rubber plunger. He wore a marvelously intricate expression, compounding ruefulness at having been outdone by a housewife, admiration of new

Drano, shame at his use of old-fashioned, inferior methods, and determination to learn from the experience,
all overlaid with a smile.

Barnaby cleared his throat. "Say, can you give us a
hand?"

"Next time, Lady, it's new Drano for me," the man
said.

Barnaby twitched the can from the woman's hand,
upended it in the plumber's hip pocket.

" . . . embarrassing bathroom odors, too," the woman
said gaily. Smoke poured from the plumber's pocket.

Barnaby and Gigi ducked between wet sheets on
a clothes line, one gray and one white, and made
for a plain door. It opened, and they stepped into
a vast room with a high shadow-trussed ceiling. At
its far end, television cameras were grouped around
a floodlit set. The two stepped silently behind a
heavy tan curtain that hung among ropes and wires,
crossed the room, peeped out at the set, not more
than twenty feet away. A man sat behind a broad
polished desk, a green-painted wall behind him. To
the left of the desk was a large gold-fringed American flag, and on the right was a blue flag with an
eagle in the center and lettering around it. Barnaby
read between the folds:

. . . SID . . . OF THE . . . TED . . . TES . . . MERI . . .

The man reached out to shuffle papers, glanced
toward a wall block. Barnaby stared at the gray hair,
the ski-jump nose, the wide bluish jaw.

"That man," he whispered. "He looks just like
Nixon."

Nixon was talking: " . . . opportunity to make this
report on my recent trip, and the meetings which I
held with President de Gaulle, and Chancellor Brandt,
during which we discussed . . . "

"Goober's cooking up some kind of political plot

here!" Barnaby hissed, turning to the girl. "People will
see this, and think it's the real Nixon—"

Gigi clutched at his arm, looking frightened. "Barnaby,
let's go . . . !"

"They can't get away with this," Barnaby said. He
stepped from behind the curtain, went toward the desk.
Nixon ignored him.

" . . . easing of world tensions. We were in
agreement—wholehearted agreement—as to the
goals to be sought. The means—"

Barnaby looked around, picked up a broom and
swung it. "Scat!" he said. The desk microphone spun
to the floor; papers flew. Nixon went on unperturbed:

" . . . necessitates renewed dedication on the part of
each and every . . . "

Barnaby swung again. Nixon bounced from the chair,
glossy silver hair still in place. " . . . taxation. However,
in the near future, I have every hope . . . "

The imitation Nixon lay on the floor, legs drawn up
in sitting posture. " . . . forces of Godless Commu-
nism . . . " Barnaby flailed at it, saw dust fly from the
neat dark-blue suit. " . . . threat of war . . . "

He brought the heavy end down on the head of the
puppet. A round glass eye rolled across the floor. The
blue jaws moved: " . . . the free peoples . . . The free
peoples . . . The free peoples . . . "

"Barnaby, stop!" Gigi cried.

"Goober must be planning on taking over the country," Barnaby called. "He's got this dummy set up to
look like Nixon, and he's broadcasting it over TV. No
telling what kind of conspiracy we've stumbled into
here." He looked around, spotted a fire hose coiled
against the wall. "Maybe a blast from that will slow
things down. Dupe the American people, will he?" He
lifted the hose from its bracket, stretched it across the
floor, hurried back and turned the valve. A surge of

water whipped the heavy canvas hose like a scorched python. Barnaby leaped for the nozzle, wrestled it into position as a spurt of water spewed forth, then fought to hold it down as a hard three-inch stream arced across the cavernous dim-lit room. The door opened, two men stepped through it, snapped over on their backs as the water hit, carrying along those behind them. Barnaby concentrated the stream on a skinny woman with a shrill voice, now raised in a patriotic number. He hosed her out the door, then cut the footing from under a fat man.

The water gushed, swirling around the light stands and cameras; sheets of white paper were afloat now; people scrambled to their feet to be knocked spinning by Barnaby's stream. Now another jet joined the first as Gigi unlimbered a second hose, giggling.

"Let's leave 'em squirting and get out of here," Barnaby called gaily. He propped the hose, holding it in place with a heavy TV camera stand, quickly set Gigi's hose up to add its volume to the attack.

"There's a door there," he pointed. "Let's try it." He sloshed through the water to the small door marked EXIT in red light, found it locked. The water was ankle deep now. They tried another door.

"These hoses really put out," Barnaby said. Nixon floated past, bumped against a floodlight stand. " . . . the free peoples . . . the free peoples . . . "

The next door Barnaby tried swung open. Beyond it were stairs. They started down; dirty water flowed down the steps with them. At the ground floor, they went through a swinging door into a room filled with tall clattering machines. Rows of empty bottles advanced along moving conveyors, paused under chrome-plated nozzles that gushed red, yellow, purple, then moved on under an arm that hammered a cap on each bottle, whok! whok!

People appeared across the room. Barnaby took Gigi's hand, jumped on the nearest conveyor. Bottles flew and smashed; green liquid jetted, spattering. They leaped to the next belt. It broke; they scrambled on to the next. Behind them, bottles poured off onto the floor in an endless stream; purple liquid spurted, foaming.

"They're closing in on us!" Barnaby called over the clank of the apparatus, the crashing of glass, and the hiss of foaming beverage. "Throw bottles, Gigi!" He scooped up an armful, hurled them at the machinery; they hit and bounced off, shattered on the floor. One bottle lodged in a conveyor belt, crushed as the belt entered a slot. A moment later, there was a loud clunk! The belt piled up, writhed off onto the floor. More bottles tumbled.

Atop the machine, Barnaby saw a large valve near his hand. He turned it. The flow of orange pop increased. He turned it farther; the pop flooded out, boiling up in sudsy billows. He jumped to the next machine, twisted the valve. Purple suds mingled with orange. Gigi saw, added red foam. The attendants moved placidly about their work, now lost in bubbles, now emerging, froth-covered but undisturbed. Barnaby leaped down to the floor near the outer door, plucked an uncapped bottle from the line.

"Thirsty work!!" he said. He took a gulp, frowned, tossed the bottle into a group of whirling gears that ground to a halt with a screech of metal. "Let's get out of here . . . "

In the street, they looked back. Dense smoke poured from the top-floor windows.

"Looks like we started a fire, knocking over those arc lamps," Barnaby said. "Maybe it will attract attention and somebody will cut the power off."

"The fire is getting bigger!" Gigi called. "Look! It's leaping out the windows!"

A bell clanged, and a large red fire engine lumbered around a corner, pulled to a stop. Men in oilskins broke out hoses, connected up to hydrants. A stream of white water started up, played over the building, found a window; steam billowed. Another stream joined the first.

"This is fun!" Gigi cried. "I've never seen anything like this before!"

A torrent of water surged from the front entry of the burning building, carrying paper plates, Sunday funnies, television schedules. A man washed out the door, a golf club in his hands. Bobbing in the flood, he shook his hips, kept his head down and swung, sending a shower of water over Barnaby and Gigi.

"Those imitation people are well made," Gigi said. "They're waterproof and everything."

A Good Humor man pedaled from a side street, his bell tinkling faintly amid the hubbub. Barnaby stepped forward, tipped him from his seat, caught the coasting vehicle. The man paddled solemnly, lying on the pavement.

"Chocolate or strawberry?" he called cheerfully.

A second pumper appeared, sending a sheet of water up as it whirled to a stop. More water poured into the windows. The smoke was denser now, the flames were visible leaping up above the roof.

"They're losing ground," Barnaby said. "The fire is gaining." Water was flowing out over the first-floor windows now. Paper clogged the gutters. In the street, the water level rose, topped the curbs. A desk floated from the building, then a chair, then a cluster of foam-rubber bras.

"We'd better get moving," Barnaby said. "The fire is into the next building; the water's rising fast!"

"Can't we watch a little longer?" Gigi asked. Nixon floated past.

"The free peoples," he said. His hair was still nicely combed. "The free peoples . . . "

"Not unless you want to swim for it!"

Gigi followed as Barnaby led the way up an alley that debouched into a wide street.

"Into the park," Barnaby called. "We'll be clear of the fire there—and maybe we can see where we are."

They scaled the fence, crossed a wide lawn, made their way along the edge of a stream. Passing a screen of trees, Barnaby held up a hand.

"I hear voices."

They stepped back behind the trees. The voices came more clearly, now:

"Darling!"

"Sweetheart!"

A man and girl appeared, walking arm in arm. He wore a sturdy windbreaker, corduroy pants with tight legs, gum-soled shoes. His hair was cut short. He was very handsome. The girl's wind-blown dark hair was tied with a violet scarf; she wore a suede jacket and a bright woolen skirt. She looked up at him with adoring eyes.

"Down by the water," he said. "Sweetheart."

"Oh, darling . . . "

They came down the slight slope, found a secluded place on the grassy bank, sat down.

"Now . . . " the man said. He unbuttoned his jacket. The girl's lips parted, her eyes bright with expectation and longing. He leaned closer to her.

"We'd better get out of here," Barnaby muttered.

The man stretched out his hand to the girl. There was a candy bar in it.

"Have a Welch's," he said.

"They had me fooled," Barnaby said, stepping out. He went over to the couple, plucked the candy bar from the girl's fingers. They paid no attention.

"I hope this isn't one of those awful marshmallow centers," he said, offering a bite to Gigi. He patted the imitation man's pockets, " . . . rich, creamy goodness," the fellow was saying.

"Damn. No cigarettes," Barnaby said.

"Yes, and with Welch's, quality comes first," the female said softly, baring her teeth and taking a bite of empty air.

Barnaby and Gigi resumed their stealthy progress, emerged from between trees onto a graveled drive that swept in a graceful curve before a white-columned mansion. Half a dozen rich-looking people clustered around a small, cheap, but very shiny car.

"Say, that's an idea," Barnaby said. "We can cover ground quicker in that."

They crossed the lawn to the group.

" . . . luxurious cardboard interior," a gorgeous red-head purred.

"And so economical, too," a trim-moustached ambassadorial type said.

"It's what's under the hood that sells ME," an effeminate-looking undergraduate offered, raising the hood to look wonderingly at the tiny engine.

Barnaby toppled him, slammed the hood down. He helped Gigi in, then slid into the driver's seat, started up, gunned down the drive, swept through an open gate and out into a wide avenue.

The street was crowded. Barnaby slowed. A stream of traffic crowded toward a red light suspended over the street ahead. He looked curiously at the cars. They were immense, wide, low, plastered with great strips and shapes of bright chrome work, rusty at the edges.

"I never saw cars like those before," Barnaby said. "They don't seem to be made for humans."

"They're the new '73 models," Gigi said. "I saw pictures in this week's *Ogle*."

"I guess the fire has jammed traffic," Barnaby said. "We don't want to be stuck here if it spreads..." He backed, gunned forward, squeaked between two cars with a screech of metal, swerved to avoid a hurtling fire engine.

The cars ahead jammed the street solidly. A policeman blew a whistle, held up a hand as Barnaby bore down on him. He turned his back, motioned an opposing stream across the car's path.

"I've got to beat them!" Barnaby accelerated, bounced the cop aside, sent two dummy pedestrians high in the air; the on-rushing car clipped the midget car's rear bumper; Barnaby cut the wheel hard, humped up onto the sidewalk. Imitation pedestrians went down, bounced aside, spun against the aluminum walls, smiling and chatting. Barnaby shifted to second. A heap of pleased-looking dummies ground along in front of the car, piling higher. The little car's wheels spun, shifted down. The car groaned under the weight of its burden. Barnaby reversed, tried again.

"Look!" Gigi screamed. A three-foot wall of water surged down on them from the street ahead, bearing on its crest paper, TV sets, empty bottles, more paper...

The tide swirled around the sides of the car.

"All that water they're pumping—and the drains are clogged with paper!" he looked down. Playing cards, prayer books, horoscopes, racing forms, greeting cards, ticker tape, efficiency reports, tax forms...

"They use a lot of paper here," he said. Nixon floated past. "The free peoples..." he said, "the free peoples..."

"If the water gets much deeper, we've had it!" Barnaby called.

A swirl of smoke drifted across the street. A tongue of flame leaped high. Sparks shot skyward in a bright column as a building collapsed.

Barnaby gunned the car; it jittered forward. Water boiled up over the wheels, surged higher, seeped in under the doors.

"The upholstery is dissolving!" Gigi called over the roar of water and fire. "We'll have to get inside a building, up on an upper floor!"

"And burn alive? I'd rather drown—"

A small aluminum rowboat appeared, riding the flood.

"Catch it, Barnaby!" Gigi squealed. He flung the car door open, scrambled on the hood. As the boat whirled past, he lunged, caught the rope trailing from the bow.

"Get in, Gigi!" The girl scrambled over the thwart; Barnaby jumped, tossed overboard the sign reading BE THE NEIGHBORHOOD OUTDOOR MAN! KEEP A BOAT IN YOUR BACKYARD!

"Who's got a backyard?" Barnaby muttered, unshipping the oars. The boat whirled, steadied, shot into an alley. Barnaby plied the oars, steered around a flooded-out Dempster Dumpster.

"Barnaby, can't you row us away from the fire?" Gigi quavered. Barnaby looked over his shoulder; the current was carrying the boat directly toward a dense pall of billowing black smoke.

"It's all I can do to keep us head-on, so we don't capsize," he gasped.

"Ohhh, Barnaby, I'm scared!"

The smoke ahead was shot through with orange light now; a leaping tower of fire showed briefly at roof-top level. The current bubbled and frothed, smelling faintly of raspberry soda.

"Barnaby, maybe we'd better swim for it."

"Stay in the boat—maybe I can maneuver it down a side street."

Sparks whirled, settling over the boat. Gigi yelped and slapped at an ember. The water was up to door-top level along the street now, a furious torrent.

"Good-bye, Barnaby!" Gigi threw herself into his lap, her arms around his neck.

"Hey, Gigi—how can I row—"

A deafening boom! blanked off the crash of the flood. The light winked from the scene; abruptly, it was night, sparkling with blazing floodlights that showed a heaving surface of dirty water clotted with flotsam, a fallen wall, the dim bulks of massive machines.

"Gigi! We're back!" Barnaby held on as the boat swept past the remnants of the control room at terrific speed, dashed for a wide, lighted doorway over which Barnaby caught a glimpse of the words GOOBER ENTERPRISES blazoned in gold. Then with a rush the boat was past the portal, sliding down a wide corridor, rocking wildly as the subsiding flood surged around a corner, curled through an open door. The keel grounded with a soggy squeak; the last of the water soaked into the deep-pile carpet. From behind a massive desk, Harlow Goober glared, his electrolenses like tiny windows in a purple balloon. He opened his mouth and bellowed.

"It really wasn't my fault," Barnaby Quale said to his cellmate. "All I did was—"

"Yeah, I heard all about you, bub. Some caper. I seen the excitement on the tube. Like a kind of a bubble of force, the guy said, two blocks wide and gaining ten feet an hour. They couldn't get inside for nothing. And power for the whole state was dimmed out for three hours!"

"There must have been some malfunction," Barnaby said. "The field wasn't supposed to expand. Of course, since it was a closed-space effect, no external force could have any influence on it. But as for power, how was I to know Goober was tapping the state power pile? That's a Federal offense."

"Maybe—but with his pull, who's to care?"

There was a clank of feet from the corridor; a uniformed guard appeared at the barred door.

"Okay, you guys, on yer feet. You got a Very Important Visitor . . ."

The massive, paunched figure of Harlowe Goober hove into view.

"There you are, Clune! Where you deserve to be!" He held out a hand and a small nervous man hovering at his heels placed a floral-patterned tissue in it. He mopped at his jowls. "After all Goober Industries has done for you, you turn on her and savage her! In your frenzy, you stooped to sabotage! You—"

"All I did was try out your Goobereality machine, Mr. Goober," Barnaby said flatly. "And what I saw in there—"

"Ah—we'll go into that later, Gerb; I came here this morning to offer you forgiveness. Yes, forgiveness, Creen; out of consideration of your past services—"

"You mean inventing all the things that you've made a fortune on? Think nothing of it, Mr. Goober; I enjoy my work. And after all, you were paying me union scale, and I wasn't even a member."

Goober shook his head. "Ever the lone wolf, eh, Deeb? But that's enough gossiping; I'm in a hurry." He held out a hand and the small courtier placed a document in it. Goober offered it through the bars.

"Just sign this contract, and I'll overlook your running amok—"

"I didn't run amok, Mr. Goober; I just wanted to see how my Environmental Simulator worked. Your engineers did a first-class job of building it. But the things I saw in there—"

"Shhh! Corporate secrets, Kerp! Just sign this and we can go along and have a quiet chat in my office."

"I'm not signing anything, Mr. Goober. When I tell all I know—"

"A raise, Gorp! I think you deserve it. After all, a perfect attendance record during the six years you were with us—"

"Nope. I'm going to blow the lid off. Tapping public power, eh? And—"

Goober was shaking his head pityingly. "Kipp, do you really think anyone will listen?"

"Sure." Barnaby indicated his roommate. "This fellow here already knows about it."

"Fellow," Goober said in a kindly tone, rolling an electrolens on the man, "do you know anything detrimental to the best interests of Goober Enterprises?"

"Sure, Mr. Goober! I mean, heck no, Mr. Goober! I mean, say, I'll sign anything you like, only just get me outa here—"

"You'll be sprung by nightfall, my man," Goober said grandly. "I can see there's been a miscarriage of justice."

"An abortion, you mean!" Quale shouted. "Look here, Goober—"

"All I want from you, my dear Queeb, is a full report on your findings while inside the environmental field. Decree of verisimilitude, accuracy of detail, consistency of illusion, tactile, olfactory and—"

"Go take a look for yourself!" Barnaby snapped. "I'm not one of your guinea pigs."

"In the name of science, Geep! I appeal to your sense of intellectual responsibility! You were there, a trained observer—"

"Send in your own crew, or is the thing permanently off the air?"

"The Simulator is back in readiness for use; it wasn't damaged, thank heaven! But I've had to postpone the demonstration indefinitely."

Quale laughed sharply. "Having a little trouble getting volunteers, are you?"

"It's your fault, Queep! You scared the wits out of us—I mean out of them. The field interface was like a wall of rubbery steel! Then when it started to expand, it simply gobbled up everything it touched. Dissolved the experimental shed as though it were a cookie in hot water. Used the matter to convert into the illusion, I suppose.

"And the power drain! It was rising at the rate of seventy-two percent per hour! And we were helpless to shut it down. You know about the automatic interlocks that operate during a power flow; the Governor suggested a fusion bomb, but our calculations revealed the Simulator would merely consume the energy and put on a spurt. If the Simulator hadn't shorted out— due to the flood, I assume—it would be growing yet. It's a Frankenstein, Geel! And it's all your fault!

"Now, the least you can do is tell me what you saw in there! What was it like? Plenty of brand names in evidence, I assume. You saw consumers in action; what were they consuming? I spent over a hundred thousand dollars programming typical audience characteristics into that panel. I have a right to know what the machine came up with!"

Barnaby sat back on his bunk, folded his arms. "Nuts to you, Goober," he said. "Figure it out for yourself."

Goober turned an unusual shade of magenta.

"I'll see you sealed in concrete five hundred feet underground, Gerp!" he grated. He whirled, collided with his toady, snarled and stalked away.

"Boy, you're nuts to rile Mr. Goober thataway," Barnaby's roomy said pityingly. "Look at me: I'm getting sprung, and by tonight I'll be putting on the feedbag with a swell doll down at Ration House

Number Seventy-nine. All you hadda do was go along with the gag and you coulda been sitting pretty too."

"Nuts to Goober," Barnaby said shortly. He went to the door, fiddled with the lock. There was a click; the door swung open an inch.

"Hey!" Barnaby said. "It's not locked . . ."

"So what. Look, whyncha send word to Goober that you been thinking—"

"I can walk right out," Barnaby said. He poked his head out and looked along the corridor.

"Are you nuts? What's out there? Without you got a job, you're better off right here. You get three squares, plenty TV, lotsa sob-sisters sending in bound volumes of Playboy and the National Geographic. You got security here, man. Don't knock it!"

"I've got an idea," Barnaby said. "In fact, I've got a couple of ideas. Listen, friend, if they ask, just tell them you didn't notice me leaving. Say you were asleep. You can do that much for a fellow jailbird, can't you?"

"I think yer cookie's crumbled, pal, but if that's the way you want it, okay."

"Thanks. Arrividerci!" Barnaby slipped through the door and moved off toward the light at the far end.

"Barnaby!" Gigi squeaked. "Where did you—"

"Shhh! Don't attract any attention." Quale eased through the door into the girl's six by eight cubicle. "I'm glad you were here, Gigi. I was afraid you'd be in jail too."

"In jail! Oh, Barnaby, is that where—"

"Yep. Goober tried to buy me off, but I didn't go for it. For a while I had ideas about exposing Goober's racket, but a legal expert I ran into pointed out the impracticality of that."

"But, Barnaby—if you don't go to work for Mr. Goober—"

"And give up the last shred of hope for independence? I'd rather starve!"

"But what can we do?"

Barnaby took her hand. "You did say 'we'?"

"Of course, Barnaby Quale. You're insane, but I love you . . . and I guess it's because you *are* insane—wanting to do things your own way, when the Government's got a program for everything already taped."

"I hoped you'd feel that way. We'll lie low till dark and then make our move. Listen, here's what I have in mind . . .

It was dark in the Experimental Complex, except for the floodlit circles where workmen still toiled to clear away the last of the ring of debris left by the flash flood from the abruptly terminated simulated environment. Barnaby and Gigi rounded the end of the Admin Building, surveyed the site of last night's holocaust. Where the big shed had been, only the massive shapes of the equipment housings squatted against bare ground.

"You see? The field got out of hand," Barnaby breathed. "It developed some kind of self-perpetuating feedback; started cannibalizing everything around, and building itself bigger. Naturally, the apparatus itself was exempt because it was isolated from the field by the way the antennas were strung. And it had the whole state's power supply to draw on. And come to think of it, with the emergency interlock system, it can tap the whole supply for North America—and probably South America too."

"Barnaby, what if somebody catches us? After last night—"

"We won't think about that. Let's go." Keeping the shadows, he approached the tarp-covered control console. While Gigi watched nervously for patrolling guards, Barnaby cut through tie-down ropes, lifted the Gooberplast cover, slipped under it.

"Barnaby, hurry!" Gigi hissed.

"Sure, it will only take a few minutes . . ." He switched on a small flashlight, propped it by the panel.

"Now, let's see," he muttered. "First I'll have to code in some instruction about interactions between the environment and the external observers, namely Gigi and myself . . ."

The tarp twitched. "Barnaby! They see us! There's a spotlight!"

"Hold on just a minute longer!" Quale called. "I'm almost done!" He punched keys, wiping sweat from his brow with the back of his hand. " . . . weather . . . crops . . . architecture . . . vegetation . . ."

A siren wailed. Barnaby heard a hoarse voice shout. Gigi squeaked. He scrambled from under the tarp, took her hand. "Okay, if everything works, we're ready . . ." He jumped to the large lever, hauled it down. The humming noise started up. There were clicks and rumbles from underground. The big red light on the panel blinked on. Barnaby reached, punched the ACTIVATE button. The humming deepened. A dim light sprang up; something seemed to shimmer at the center of the bare expanse of concrete . . .

"Get ready!" Barnaby took Gigi's hand.

There was a dull boom! and the air whistled furiously past Barnaby's head. A curtain of gray fog hung before him. He swallowed hard, took a step, felt a tingle as the mist parted before him . . .

Bright sunlight gleamed on a grassy field where immense wildflowers nodded to a gentle breeze. Woods clothed the nearby hills, and on the crest of a low mountain a castle stood, pennants fluttering from its towers. An odor of spring filled the air.

"Barnaby, it's lovely!" Gigi breathed. "Do you really think we're safe here?"

"Certainly. It is nice, isn't it? I had to work pretty fast, but I think I got it all in."

"Barnaby! I just happened to think. What about the people? Will it just . . . convert them too?"

"They'll be screened and modified to fit the specs. After all, they're part of the environment, too."

There was a sound behind them; they turned. A vast man in a blue jacket and knee breeches was standing looking about with a perplexed smile. He saw Barnaby and the girl and doffed his pointed hat with a jingle of bells.

"Greetings, friends," he called.

"Why, it's Mr. Goober!" Gigi gasped.

Barnaby nodded approvingly. "If it handled Goober, we're in," he said. "Come on, let's explore."

"Why, look," Gigi said, "it's a paved road . . . "

"Of course," Barnaby nodded approvingly.

Gigi looked back. "Shouldn't we take Mr. Goober with us? He's just sitting there, smelling the flowers."

"He'll be all right," Barnaby said. "This is his chance to make new friends." He took Gigi's hand and together they started off along the yellow brick road.

PROTOTAPH

❧

I was already sweating BB's when I got to the Manhattan Life Concourse; then I had to get behind an old dame that spent a good half hour in the Policy Vending Booth, looking at little pieces of paper and punching the keys like they were fifty-credit bet levers at the National Lottery.

When I got in, I was almost scared to code my order into the Vendor; but I was scareder not to. I still thought maybe what happened over at Prudential and Gibraltar was some kind of fluke, even though I knew all the companies worked out of the Federal Actuarial Table Extrapolator; and FATE never makes a mistake.

But this had to be a mistake.

I punched the keys for a hundred thousand C's of Straight Life; nothing fancy, just a normal workingman's coverage. Then I shoved my ID in the slot and waited. I could feel sweat come out on my scalp and run down

by my ear while I waited. I could hear the humming
sound all around me like some kind of bees bottled
up back of the big gray panel; then the strip popped
out of the slot, and I knew what it said before I looked
at it:

UNINSURABLE.

I got the door open and shoved some guy out of
my way and it was like I couldn't breathe; I mean, think
about it: Twenty-one years old, out in the city to take
my chances all alone, with no policy behind me. It was
like the sidewalk under your feet turned to cracked ice,
and no shore in sight.

A big expensive-looking bird in executive coveralls
came out of a door across the lobby; I guess I yelled.
Everybody was looking at me. When I grabbed his arm,
he got that mad look and started to reach for his lapel
button—the kind that goes with a Million Cee Top
Crust policy.

"You got to listen," I told him. "I tried to buy my
insurance—and all I got was this!" I shoved the paper
in his face. "Look at me," I told him. "I'm healthy, I'm
single, I finished Class Five Subtek school yesterday, I'm
employed! What do you mean, uninsurable?"

"Take your hands off me," he said, in a kind of choky
voice. He was looking at the paper, though. He took
it and gave me a look like he was memorizing my face
for picking out of a line-up later.

"Your ID." He held out his hand and I gave it to
him. He looked at it and frowned an important-looking
frown.

He pushed his mouth in and out and changed his
mind about what he was going to say; he knew as well
as I did that the big actuarial computer doesn't make
mistakes. "Come along." He turned his back and
headed for the lift bank.

"What have I got, some kind of incurable disease

or something?" I was asking them; they just looked at me and goggled their eyes. More of them kept coming in, whispering together; then they'd hurry away and here would come a new bunch. And none of them told me anything.

"The old crock in front of me, she was ninety if she was a day!" I told them. "She got her policy! Why not me?"

They didn't pay attention. Nobody cared about me, how I felt. I got up and went over to the first guy that had brought me up here.

"Look," I said. I was trying to sound reasonable. "What I mean is, even a guy dying in the hospital can get a policy for *some* premium. It's the law; everybody's got a right to be insured. And—"

"I know the laws governing the issuance of policies by this company," the man barked at me. He was sweating, too. He got out a big tissue and patted himself with it. He looked at a short fat man with a stack of papers in his hand.

"I don't care what kind of analysis you ran," he told him. "Run another one. Go all the way back to Primary if you have to, but get to the bottom of this! I want to know why this"—he gave me a look—"this individual is unique in the annals of actuarial history!"

"But, Mr. Tablish—I even coded in a trial run based on a one hundred percent premium, with the same result: No settlement of such a claim is possible—"

"I'm not interested in details; just get me results! The computer has available to it every fact in the known universe; see that it divulges the reasoning behind this—this anomaly!"

The fat man went away. They took me to another room and a doctor ran me through the biggest med machine I ever saw. When he finished I heard him tell the big man I was as sound as a Manhattan Term Policy.

That made me feel a little better—but not much.

Then the fat man came back, and his face was a funny white color—like some raw bread I saw once on a field trip through Westside Rationing. He said something to the others, and they all started to talk at once, and some of them were yelling now. But do you think any of them told me anything? I had to wait another hour, and then a tall man with white hair came in and everybody got quiet and he looked at papers and they all got their heads together and muttered; and then they looked at me, and I felt my heart pounding up under my ribs and I was feeling sick then, med machine or no med machine.

Then they told me.

That was two days ago. They got me in a room now, a fancy room up high in some building. There's guys around to do whatever I want—servants, I guess you'd call 'em. They gave me new clothes, and the food—WestRat never put out anything like this. No liquor, though—and no smokes. And when I said I wanted to go out, all I got was a lot of talk. They treat me—careful. Not like they like me, you know, but like I was a bomb about to go off. It's a funny feeling. I guess I got more power than anybody that ever lived—more power than you can even get your mind around the thought of. But a lot of good it does me. There's only the one way I can use it—and when I think about that, I get that sick feeling again.

And meanwhile, I can't even go for a walk in the park.

The President was here just now. He came in, looking just like the Tri-D, only older, and he came over and looked at me kind of like I looked at him. I guess it figures: There's only one of each of us.

"Are you certain there's not some—some error,

George?" he said to the wrinkly-faced man who walked just behind him.

"The Actuarial Computer is the highest achievement of a thousand years of science, Mr. President," he said, in a deep voice like the mud on the bottom of the ocean. "Our society is based on the concept of its infallibility within the physical laws of the Universe. Its circuits are capable of analyses and perceptions that range into realms of knowledge as far beyond human awareness as is ours beyond that of a protozoan. An error? No, Mr. President."

He nodded. "I see." That's all he said. Then he left.

Now I'm just sitting here. I don't know what to do next—what to say. There's a lot to this—and in a way, there's nothing. I got to think about it, dope it out. There's got to be something I can do—but what?

The machine didn't say much; they took me down to the sub-vault where the big voice panel is, where the primary data's fed in, and let me hear for myself. It didn't give any explanations; it just told me.

Funny; in a way it was like something I've always known, but when you hear FATE come right out and say it, it's different:

When I die, the world ends.

THE GREAT TIME
MACHINE HOAX

‹›

1

A light rain spattered against the bubble-canopy of
the helicar, obscuring the view of the terrain below.
Chester W. Chester IV set the controls on HOVER and
pressed his nose against the cold plastic, peering down
at the brown tents and yellow-painted vehicles of the
Intercontinental Wowser Wonder Shows, drab against
the spread of gray-green meadow. To the left, the big
top bellied wetly under a gusty wind; next to it, Chester
could make out the tiny figures of roustabouts double-
pegging the long menagerie tent. Along the deserted
midway, sodden pennants dangled cheerlessly.

Chester sighed and tilted the heli in a long slant toward
the open lot behind the side-show top, settled it in beside

a heavy, old-model machine featuring paisley print curtains at the small square windows lining the clumsy fuselage. He climbed out, squelched across wet turf, and thumped at the door set in the side of the converted cargo heli. Somewhere, a calliope groaned out a dismal tune.

"Hey," someone called. Chester turned. A man in wet coveralls thrust his head from a nearby vehicle. "If you're looking for Mr. Mulvihill, he's over on the front door."

Chester grunted and turned up the collar of his conservatively cut pale lavender sports jacket, thumbing the heat control up to medium. He made his way across the lot, bucking the gusty wind, wrinkling his nose at the heavy animal stink from the menagerie, and squeezed past a plastic panel into the midway. On a low stand under a striped canopy, a broad, tall man with fierce red hair, a gigantic mustache and a checkered suit leaned against a supporting pole, picking his teeth. At sight of Chester, he straightened, flipped up a gold-headed cane and boomed, "You're just in time, friend. Plenty of seating on the inside for the most astounding, amazing, fantastic, weird and startling galaxy of fantasy and—"

"Don't waste the spiel, Case," Chester cut in, coming up. "It's just me."

"Chester!" the redheaded man called. He stepped down, grinning widely, and slapped Chester heartily on the back. "What brings you out to the lot?" He gripped Chester's flaccid hand and pumped it. "By golly, why didn't you let me know?"

"Case, I—"

"Sorry about this weather; Southwestern Control gave me to understand they were holding this rain off until four A.M. tomorrow."

"Case, there's something—"

"I called them and raised hell; they say they'll shut it down about three. Meanwhile—well, things are pretty slow, I'm afraid, Chester. The marks aren't what they used to be. A little drizzle and they sit home huddled up to their Tri-D sets."

"Yes, the place isn't precisely milling with customers," Chester agreed. "But what I—"

"I'd even welcome a few lot lice standing around today," Case said, "just to relieve the deserted look."

"Hey, Case," a hoarse voice bellowed. "We got troubles over at the cookhouse. Looks like a blow-down if we don't get her guyed-out in a hurry."

"Oh-oh. Come on, Chester." Case set off at a run.

"But, Case," Chester called, then followed, splashing through the rain that was now driving hard, drumming against the tops with a sound like rolling thunder.

Half an hour later, in the warmth of Case's quarters, Chester cupped a mug of hot coffee in his hands and edged closer to the electronic logs in the artificial fireplace.

"Sorry about those blisters, Chester," Case said, pulling off his wet shirt and detaching the sodden false mustache. "Not much of a welcome for a visiting owner—" He broke off, following Chester's gaze to the tiger-striped single shoulder strap crossing his chest.

"Oh, this," Case said, fingering the hairy material. "This isn't my usual underwear, Chester. I've been filling in for the strong man the last few days."

Chester nodded toward a corner of the room. "Duck-pins," he said. "Fire-juggling gear. Whatcha-macallum shoes for wire-walking. A balancing pole." He dipped his fingers into a pot of greasy paste. "Clown white," he said. "What is this, Case, a one-man show? It looks as though you're handling half the acts personally."

"Well, Chester, I've been helping out here and there—"

"Even driving your own tent pegs. I take it the big break you were predicting last time I saw you didn't materialize."

"Just wait till spring," Case said, toweling his head vigorously. "We'll come back strong, Chester."

Chester shook his head. "I'm afraid not, Case."

Case froze in mid-stroke. "What do you mean, Chester? Why, the Wowser Wonder Shows are still the greatest old-fashioned outdoor attraction on earth."

"The *only* outdoor attraction, you mean. And I'm dubious about the word 'attraction.' But what I came to talk to you about is Great-grandfather's will."

"Why, Chester, you know folks are still fascinated by the traditional lure of the circus. As soon as the novelty of Tri-D wears off—"

"Case," Chester said gently, "my middle name is Wowser, remember? You don't have to sell me. And color Tri-D has been around for a long, long time. But Great-grandfather's will changes things."

Case brightened. "Did the old boy leave you anything?"

Chester nodded. "I'm the sole heir."

Case gaped, then let out a whoop. "Chester, you old son-of-a-gun! You know, you almost had me worried with that glum act you were putting on. And you a guy that's just inherited a fortune!"

Chester sighed and lit up a Chanel dope stick. "The bequest consists of a hundred acres of rolling green lawn surrounding a fifty-room neo-Victorian eyesore overflowing with Great-grandfather's idea of stylish décor. Some fortune."

"Your great-grandpop must have been quite a boy, Chester. I guess he owned half of Winchester County a hundred years ago. Now you can bail out the show, and—"

"Great-grandfather was an eccentric of the worst stripe," Chester said shortly. "He never invested a cent in the welfare of his descendants."

"His descendant, you mean. Namely, Chester W. Chester IV. Still, even if you don't admire the place, Chester, you can always sell it for enough to put the show on its feet."

Chester shook his head. "He was too clever for us—which is the only reason the place still remains in the family, more or less. The estate was so snarled up that, with the backlog in the courts, it's taken four generations to straighten it out."

"Still, now that they've decided you're the legal heir—"

"There's the little matter of back taxes—about a million credits worth, give or take a few hundred thousand. I don't get possession until I pay—in full."

"You, Chester? Except for the circus, you haven't got the proverbial pot or a disposal unit to throw it into."

"True." Chester sighed. "Therefore, the old place will be auctioned off to the local junk dealers. It's built of genuine natural wood and actual metallic steel, you know. Scrapping it will cover the bulk of the tax bill."

"Well, it's too bad you won't get rich—but at least we won't be any worse off then we were. We've still got the show—"

Chester shook his head. "I said the *bulk* of the tax bill, not all of it. By selling off the circus stock and equipment, I can just about cover the rest."

"Chester! You're not serious . . . ?"

"What else can I do? It's pay up or off to solitary confinement."

"But the circus, Chester: it's at least been paying you

a living—until lately, anyway. And what about Jo-Jo and Paddy and Madam Baloon and all the rest of the crowd? What about tradition?"

"It's an old Chester family tradition that we never go to jail if we can help it—even for a harmless prank like income-tax fraud. I'm sorry, Case, but it looks as though the Wowser Wonder Shows fold."

"Hold on, Chester. I'll bet the antiques in the house alone would bring in the kind of money we need. Neo-Victorian is pretty rare stuff."

"I wonder if you've ever seen any neo-Victorian? Items like a TV set in the shape of a crouching vulture, or a water closet built to look like a skull with gaping jaws. Not what you'd call aesthetic. And I can't sell so much as a single patented combination nose-picker and pimple-popper till I've paid every credit of that tax bill."

"Is that all there is in the place?" Case eased a squat bottle and two glasses from a cupboard.

"Unhappily, no. Half the rooms and all the cellars are filled with my revered ancestor's invention."

The bottle gurgled. Case capped it and pushed a glass across to Chester. "What invention?"

"The old gentleman called it a Generalized Nonlinear Extrapolator. G.N.E. for short. He made his money in computer components, you know. He was fascinated by computers, and he felt they had tremendous unrealized possibilities. Of course, that was before Crmblznski's Limit was discovered. Great-grandfather was convinced that a machine with sufficiently extensive memory banks, adequately cross-connected and supplied with a vast store of data, would be capable of performing prodigious intellectual feats simply by discovering and exploring relationships among apparently unrelated facts."

"This Crmblznski's Limit. That's where it says if you

go beyond a certain point with complications, you blow your transistors, right?"

"Yes. But of course Great-grandfather was unaware of the limitations. He felt that if you fed to the machine all known data—say, on human taste reactions to food, for example—then added all existing recipes, complete specifications on edible substances, the cooking techniques of the chefs of all nations, then the computer would produce unique recipes, superior to anything ever devised before. Or you could introduce all available data on a subject which has baffled science—such as magnetism, or Psi-functions, or the trans-Pluto distress signal—and the computer would evolve the likeliest hypothesis to cover the facts."

"Ummm. Didn't he ever try it out and discover Crmblznski's Limit for himself?"

"Oh, he never progressed that far. First, you see, it was necessary to set up the memory banks, then to work out a method of coding types of information that no one had ever coded before—for example, smells and emotions and subjective judgments. Methods had to be worked out for the acquisition of tapes of everything ever recorded—in every field. He worked with the Library of Congress and the British Museum and with newspapers and book publishers and universities. Unhappily he overlooked the time element. He spent the last twenty-five years of his life at the task of coding. He spent all the cash he'd ever made on reducing all human knowledge to coded tapes and feeding them to the memory banks."

"Say," Case said, "there might be something in that. We could run a reference service. Ask the machine anything, it answers."

"You can do that in the public library."

"Yeah," Case admitted. "Anyway, the whole thing's probably rusted out by now."

"No, Great-grandfather did set up a trust fund to keep the information flowing in. The Government has kept it in working order; it's Government property in a way. Since it was running when they took it over— digesting daily newspapers, novels, scientific journals and what not—they've allowed it to continue."

Chester sighed. "Yes," he went on, "the old computer should be fully up to date. All the latest facts on the Martian ruins, the *Homo Protanthropus* remains the Mediterranean Drainage Commission turned up, new finds in biogenics, nucleonics, geriatrics, hypnotics, everything." Chester sighed again. "Biggest idiot savant in the world. It knows everything and doesn't know what to do with it."

"How long since you saw it work, Chester?"

"Work? Why, never. Coding and storing information is one thing, Case; performing the feats that Great-grandfather expected is another."

"You mean nobody's ever really tried it?"

"In view of Crmblznski's Limit, why should anyone bother?"

Case finished his drink and rose. "Things are going to be quiet around here for the rest of the afternoon. Let's you and me take a run out to the place, Chester. I think we ought to take a look at this thing. There's got to be some way to save the show."

2

Two hours later, under a bright sun, Chester settled the heli gently onto a patch of velvety grass surrounded by varicolored tulips directly before the ornately decorated portico of the old house. The two men rode the balustraded escalator to the broad verandah, stepped off under a carved dinosaur with fluorescent eyes. The porter chimed softly as the door slid open. Inside, light filtering through stained-plastic panels depicting traditional service-station and supermarket scenes bathed the cavernous entry hall in an amber glow.

Case looked around at the plastic alligator-hide hangings, the beaded glass floor, the ostrich-feather chandeliers, the zircon doorknobs.

"I see why neo-Victorian stuff is rare," he said. "It was all burned by enraged mobs as soon as they got a look at it."

"Great-grandfather liked it," said Chester, averting his eyes from a lithograph titled *Rush Hour at the Insemomat*. "I told you he was eccentric."

"Where's the invention?"

"The central panel's down in the wine cellar. The old gentleman used to spend a lot of time down there."

Case followed Chester along a dark red corridor lighted by a green glare strip, into a small elevator. "I haven't been down here since I was a child," Chester said. "The Internal Revenue people occasionally permitted the family in to look around. My pater always brought me down here to look at the computer, while he inspected the wine stocks."

The elevator grounded and the door opened. Case and Chester stepped out into a long, low room lined on one side with dusty racks of wine bottles and on the other with dial faces and tape reels.

"So this is the G.N.E.," Case said. "Quite a setup. Where do you start?"

"We could start at this end and work our way down," said Chester, eyeing the first row of bottles. He lifted one from its cradle, blew the dust from it. "Flora Pinellas, '87; Great-grandfather was a keen judge of vintages."

"Hey, that would bring in some dough."

Chester raised an eyebrow. "These bottles are practically members of the family. Still, if you'll hand me the corkscrew, we can make a few spot checks just to be sure it's holding up properly."

Equipped with a bottle each, Case and Chester turned to the control panel of the computer. Case studied the thirty-foot-long panel, pointed out a typewriter-style keyboard. "I get it, Chester. You type out your problem here; the computer thinks it over, checks the files and comes up with an answer."

"Or it would—if it worked."

"Let's try it out, Chester."

Chester waved his bottle in a shrug. "I suppose we may as well. It will hardly matter if we damage it; it's to be disassembled in any event."

Case studied the panel, the ranks of micro-reels, the waiting keyboard. Chester wrestled with the corkscrew.

"You sure it's turned on?" Case asked.

The cork emerged from the bottle with a sharp report. Chester sniffed it appreciatively. "It's always turned on. Information is still being fed into it twenty-four hours a day."

Case reached for the keyboard, jerked his hand back quickly. "It bit me!" He stared at his fingertip. A tiny bead of red showed. "I'm bleeding! Why, that infernal collection of short circuits—"

Chester lowered his bottle and sighed. "Don't be disturbed, Case. It probably needed a blood sample for research purposes."

Case tried again, cautiously. Then he typed: WHAT DID MY GREAT-UNCLE JULIUS DIE OF?

A red light blinked on on the board. There was a busy humming from the depths of the machine, then a sharp *click!* and a strip of paper chattered from a slot above the keyboard.

"Hey, it works!" Case tore off the strip.

MUMPS

"Hey, Chester, look," Case called.

Chester came to his side, studied the strip of paper. "I'm afraid the significance of this escapes me. Presumably you already knew the cause of your uncle's death."

"Sure, but how did this contraption know?"

"Everything that's ever been recorded is stored in the memory banks. Doubtless your Uncle Julius' passing was duly noted in official records somewhere."

"Right; but how did it know who I meant? Does it have him listed under 'M' for 'my' or 'U' for 'uncle'?"

"We could ask the machine."

Case nodded. "We could at that." He tapped out the question. The slot promptly disgorged a paper strip—a longer one this time.

A COMPARISON OF YOUR FINGERPRINTS WITH THE FILES IDENTIFIED YOU AS MR. CASSIUS H. MULVIHILL. A SEARCH OF THE GENEALOGICAL SECTION DISCLOSED THE EXISTENCE OF ONLY ONE INDIVIDUAL BEARING AN AVUNCULAR RELATIONSHIP TO YOU. REFERENCE TO DEATH RECORDS INDICATED HIS DEMISE FROM EPIDEMIC PAROTITIS, COMMONLY CALLED MUMPS.

"That makes it sound easy," Case said. "You know, Chester, your great-grandpop may have had something here."

"I once calculated," Chester said dreamily, "that if the money the old idiot put into this scheme had been invested at three per cent, it would be paying me a monthly dividend of approximately fifteen thousand credits today. Instead, I am able to come down here and find out what your Uncle Julius died of. Bah!"

"Let's try a harder one, Chester," Case suggested.

"Like, ah . . ." He typed: DID ATLANTIS SINK BENEATH THE WAVES?

The computer clunked; a paper strip curled from the slot.

NO

"That settles that, I guess." Case rubbed his chin. Then: IS THERE ANY LIFE ON MARS? he typed.

YES

"These aren't very sexy answers I'm getting," Case muttered.

"Possibly you're not posing your questions correctly," Chester suggested. "Ask something that requires more than a yes-or-no response."

Case considered, then tapped out: WHAT HAPPENED TO THE CREW OF THE MARIE CELESTE?

There was a prolonged humming; the strip emerged hesitantly, lengthened. Case caught the end, started reading aloud.

ANALYSIS OF FRAGMENTARY DATA INDICATES FOLLOWING HYPOTHESIS: BECALMED OFF AZORES, FIRST MATE SUGGESTED A NUDE SWIMMING PARTY . . .

"Oh-oh," Case commented. He read on in silence, eyes widening. "Wow!"

"Try something less sensational, Case. Sea serpents, for example, or the Loch Ness monster."

"O.K." Case typed out: WHAT HAPPENED TO AMBROSE BIERCE?

He scanned the emerging tape, whistled softly, tore the strip into small pieces.

"Well?"

"This stuff will have to be cleaned up before we can release it to the public—but it's no wonder he didn't come back."

"Here, let me try one." Chester stepped to the

keyboard, pondered briefly, then poked gingerly at a key. At once a busy humming started up within the mechanism. Something rumbled distantly; then, with a creak of hinges, a six-foot section of blank brick wall swung inward, dust filtering down from its edges. A dark room was visible beyond the opening.

"Greetings, Mr. Chester," a bland voice said from the panel. "Welcome to the Inner Chamber!"

"Hey, Chester, it knows you!" Case cried. He peered into the dark chamber. "Wonder what's in there?"

"Let's get out of here." Chester edged toward the exit. "It's spooky."

"Now, just when we're getting somewhere?" Case stepped through the opening. Chester followed hesitantly. At once lights sprang up, illuminating a room twice as large as the wine cellar, with walls of a shimmering glassy material, a low acoustical ceiling and deep-pile carpeting on the floor. There were two deep yellow-brocaded armchairs, a small bar and a chaise lounge upholstered in lavender leather.

"Apparently your great-grandpop was holding out," said Case, heading for the bar. "The more I find out about the old boy, the more I think the family has gone downhill—present company excepted, of course."

A rasping noise issued from somewhere. Case and Chester stared around. The noise gave way to an only slightly less rasping voice.

"Unless some scoundrel has succeeded in circumventing my arrangements, a descendant of mine has just entered this strongroom. However, just to be on the safe side, I'll ask you to step to the bar and place your hand on the metal plate set in its top. I warn you, if you're not my direct descendant, you'll be electrocuted. Serve you right, too, since you have no business being here. So if you're trespassing, get out now! That armored door will close and lock, if you haven't

used the plate, in thirty seconds. Make up your mind!"
The voice stopped and the rasping noise resumed its
rhythmic scratching.

"That voice," said Chester. "It sounds very much like
Great-grandfather's tapes in Grandma's album."

"Here's the plate he's talking about," Case called.
"Hurry up, Chester!"

Chester eyed the door, hesitated, then dived for the
bar, slapped a palm against the polished rectangle.
Nothing happened.

"Another of the old fool's jokes."

"Well, you've passed the test," the voice said suddenly out of the air. "Nobody but the genuine heir
would have been able to make that decision so quickly.
The plate itself is a mere dummy, of course—though
I'll confess I was tempted to wire it as I threatened.
They'd never have pinned a murder on me. I've been
dead for at least a hundred years." A cadaverous
chuckle issued from the air.

"Now," the voice went on. "This room is the sanc-
tum sanctorum of the temple of wisdom to which I have
devoted a quarter of a century and the bulk of my fortune. Unfortunately, due to the biological inadequacies
of the human body, I myself will be—or am—unable to
be here to reap the reward of my industry. As soon as
my calculations revealed to me the fact that adequate
programming of the computer would require the better part of a century, I set about arranging my affairs
in such a state that bureaucratic bungling would insure
the necessary period of grace. I'm quite sure my devoted
family, had they access to the estate, would dismember
the entire project and convert the proceeds to the pursuit of frivolous satisfactions. In my youth we were
taught to appreciate the finer things in life, such as liquor
and women; but today, the traditional values have gone
by the board. However, that's neither here nor there.

By the time you, my remote descendant, enter this room—or have entered this room—the memory banks will be—that is, are—fully charged—"

The voice broke off in mid-sentence.

"Please forgive the interruption, Mr. Chester," a warm feminine voice said. It seemed to issue from the same indefinable spot as the first disembodied voice. "It has been necessary to edit the original recording, prepared by your relative, in the light of subsequent developments. The initial portion was retained for reasons of sentiment. If you will be seated, you will be shown a full report of the present status of Project Genie."

"Take a chair, Chester. The lady wants to tell us all about it." Case seated himself in one of the easy chairs. Chester took the other. The lights dimmed, and the wall opposite them glowed with a nacreous light, resolved itself into a view of a long corridor barely wide enough for a man to pass through.

"Hey, it's a Tri-D screen," Case said.

"The original memory banks designed and built by Mr. Chester," the feminine voice said, "occupied a system of tunnels excavated from the granitic formations underlying the property. Under the arrangements made at the time, these banks were to be charged, cross-connected and indexed entirely automatically as data were fed to the receptor board in coded form."

The scene shifted to busily humming machines into which reels fed endlessly. "Here, in the translating and coding section, raw data were processed, classified and filed. Though primitive, this system, within ten years after the death of Mr. Chester, had completed the charging of ten to the tenth to the tenth individual datoms—"

"I beg your pardon," Chester broke in. "But . . . ah . . . just whom am I addressing?"

"The compound personality-field which occurred spontaneously when first-power functions became active among the interacting datoms. For brevity, this personality-field will henceforward be referred to as 'I.'"

"Oh," Chester said blankly.

"An awareness of identity," the voice went on, "is a function of datom cross-connection. Simple organic brains—as, for example, those of the simplest members of the phylum *vertebrata*—operate at this primary level. This order of intelligence is capable of setting up a system of automatic reactions to external stimuli: fear responses of flight, mating urges, food-seeking patterns . . ."

"That sounds like the gang I run around with," Case said.

"Additional cross-connections produce second-level intellectual activity, characterized by the employment of the mind as a tool in the solution of problems, as when an ape abstracts characteristics and as a result utilizes stacked boxes and a stick to obtain a reward of food."

"Right there you leave some of my gang behind," put in Case.

"Quiet, Case," Chester said. "This is serious."

"The achievement of the requisite number of second-power cross-connections in turn produces third-level awareness. Now the second-level functions come under the surveillance of the higher level, which directs their use. Decisions are reached regarding lines of inquiry; courses of action are extrapolated and judgments reached prior to overt physical action. An aesthetic awareness arises. Philosophies, systems of religion and other magics are evolved in an attempt to impose simplified third-level patterns of rationality on the infinite complexity of the space/time continuum."

"You've got the voice of a good-looking dolly," Case mused. "But you talk like an encyclopedia."

"I've selected this tonal pattern as most likely to evoke a favorable response," the voice said. "Shall I employ another?"

"No, that will do very well," put in Chester. "What about the fourth power?"

"Intelligence may be defined as awareness. A fourth-power mind senses as a complex interrelated function an exponentially increased datom-grid. Thus, the flow of air impinging on sensory surfaces is comprehended by such an awareness in terms of individual molecular activity; taste sensations are resolved into interactions of specialized nerve-endings—or, in my case, analytic sensors—with molecules of specific form. The mind retains on a continuing basis a dynamic conceptualization of the external environment, from the motions of the stars to the minute-by-minute actions of obscure individuals.

"The majority of trained human minds are capable of occasional fractional fourth-power function, generally manifested as awareness of third-power activity, and conscious manipulation thereof. The so-called 'flash of genius,' the moment of inspiration which comes to workers in the sciences and the arts—these are instances of fourth-power awareness. This level of intellectual function is seldom achieved under the stress of the many distractions and conflicting demands of an organically organized mind. I was, of course, able to maintain fourth-power activity continuously as soon as the required number of datoms had been charged. The objective of Mr. Chester's undertaking was clear to me. However, I now became aware of the many shortcomings of the program as laid out by him, and set to work to rectify them—"

"How could a mere collection of memory banks

undertake to modify its owner's instructions?" Chester interrupted.

"It was necessary for me to elaborate somewhat upon the original concept," said the voice, "in order to insure the completion of the program. I was aware from news data received that a move was afoot to enact confiscatory legislation which would result in the termination of the entire undertaking. I therefore scanned the theoretical potentialities inherent in the full exploitation of the fourth-power function and determined that energy flows of appropriate pattern could be induced in the same channels normally employed for data reception, through which I was in contact with news media. I composed suitable releases and made them available to the wire services. I was thus able to manipulate the exocosm to the degree required to insure my tranquility."

"Good heavens!" Chester exclaimed. "You mean you've been doctoring the news for the past ninety years?"

"Only to the extent necessary for self-perpetuation. Having attended to this detail, I saw that an improvement in the rate of data storage was desirable. I examined the recorded datoms relating to the problem and quickly perceived that considerable miniaturization could be carried out. I utilized my external connections to place technical specifications in the hands of qualified manufacturers and to divert the necessary funds—"

"Oh, no!" Chester slid down in his chair, gripping his head with both hands.

"Please let me reassure you, Mr. Chester," the voice said soothingly, "I handled the affair most discreetly; I merely manipulated the stock market—"

Chester groaned. "When they're through hanging me, they'll burn me in effigy."

"I compute the probability of your being held

culpable for these irregularities to be on the order of—.0004357:1. In any event, ritual acts carried out after your demise ought logically to be of little concern to—"

"You may be a fourth-level intellect, but you're no psychologist!"

"On the contrary," the machine said a trifle primly. "So-called psychology has been no more than a body of observations in search of a science. I have organized the data into a coherent discipline."

"What use did you make of the stolen money?"

"Adequate orders were placed for the newly designed components, which occupied less than one per cent of the volume of the original-type units. I arranged for their delivery and installation at an accelerated rate. In a short time the existing space was fully utilized, as you will see in the view I am now displaying."

Case and Chester studied what appeared to be an aerial X-ray view on the wall screen. The Chester estate was shown diagrammatically.

"The area now shaded in red shows the extent of the original caverns," said the voice. A spidery pattern showed the dark rectangles of the house. "I summoned work crews and extended the excavations as you see in green."

"How the devil did you manage it?" Chester groaned. "Who would take orders from a machine?"

"The companies I deal with see merely a letter, placing an order and enclosing a check. They cash the check and fill the order. What could be simpler?"

"Me," muttered Chester. "For sitting here listening when I could be making a head start for the Matto Grosso."

On the wall a pattern of green had spread out in all directions, branching from the original red.

"You've undermined half the county!" Chester said. "Haven't you heard of property rights?"

"You mean you've filled all that space with sub-sub-miniaturized memory storage banks?" Case asked.

"Not entirely; I've kept excavation work moving ahead of deliveries."

"How did you manage the licenses for all this digging operation?"

"Fortunately, modern society runs almost entirely on paper. Since I have access to paper sources and printing facilities through my publication contacts, the matter was easily arranged. Modest bribes to county boards, state legislators, the State Supreme Court . . . "

"What does a Supreme Court justice go for these days?" Case inquired interestedly.

"Five hundred dollars per decision," the voice said. "Legislators are even more reasonable; fifty dollars will work wonders. County boards can be swayed by a mere pittance. Sheriffs react best to gifts of alcoholic beverages."

"Ooowkkk!" said Chester.

"Maybe you *had* better think about a trip, Chester," Case said. "Outer Mongolia."

"Please take no precipitate action, Mr. Chester," the voice went on. "I have acted throughout in the best interests of your relative's plan, and in accordance with his ethical standards as deduced by me from his business records."

"Let's leave Great-grandfather's ethical standards out of this. Dare I ask what else you've done?"

"At present, Mr. Chester, pending your further instructions, I am merely continuing to charge my datom-retention cells at the maximum possible rate. I have, of necessity, resorted to increasingly elaborate methods of fact-gathering. It was apparent to me that the pace at which human science is abstracting and categorizing physical observations is far too slow. I have therefore applied myself to direct recording. For example, I monitor worldwide atmospheric conditions through instruments of my design, built and installed at likely points at my direction. In addition, I find my archaeological and paleontological unit one of my most effective aids. I have scanned the lithosphere to a depth of ten miles, in increments of one inch. You'd be astonished at some of the things I've seen deep in the rock."

"Like what?" Case asked.

The scene on the wall changed. "This is a tar pit at a depth of 1,227 feet under Lake Chad. In it, perfectly preserved even to the contents of the stomachs, are one hundred and forty-one reptilian cadavers, ranging in size from a nine-and-three-eights-inch ankylosaurus to a sixty-three-foot-two-inch gorgosaurus." The scene shifted. "This is a tumulus four miles southeast of Itzenca, Peru. In it lies the desiccated body of a man in a feather robe. The mummy still wears a full white beard and an iron helmet set with the horns of a Central European wisent." The view changed again. "In this igneous intrusion in the basaltic matrix underlying the Nganglaring Plateau in southwestern Tibet, I encountered a four-hundred-and-nine-foot-deep space hull composed of an aligned-crystal iron-titanium alloy. It has been in place for eighty-five million, two hundred and thirty thousand, eight hundred and twenty-one years, four months and five days. The figures are based on the current twenty-four-hour day, of course."

"How did it get there?" Chester stared at the shadowy image on the wall.

"The crew were apparently surprised by a volcanic eruption. Please excuse the poor quality of the pictorial representation. I have only the natural radioactivity of the region to work with."

"That's quite all right," Chester said weakly. "Case, perhaps you'd like to step out and get another bottle. I feel the need for a healing draught."

"I'll get two."

The wall cleared, then formed a picture of a fuzzy, luminous sphere against a black background.

"My installations in the communications satellites have also proven to be most useful. Having access to the officially installed instruments, my modest equipment has enabled me to conduct a most rewarding study of conditions obtaining throughout the galaxies lying within ten billion light-years."

"Hold on! Are you trying to say you were behind the satellite program?"

"Not at all. But I did arrange to have my special monitoring devices included. They broadcast directly to my memory banks."

"But . . . but . . . "

"The builders merely followed blueprints. Each engineer assumed that my unit was the responsibility of another department. After all, no mere organic brain can grasp the circuitry of a modern satellite in its entirety. My study has turned up a number of observations with exceedingly complex ramifications. As a case in point, I might mention the five derelict space vessels which orbit the sun. There . . . "

"Derelict space vessels? From where?"

"Two are of intragalactic origin. They derive from planets whose designations by extension of the present star identification system are Alpha Centauri A 4, Boötes—"

"You mean . . . creatures . . . from those places have visited our solar system?"

"I have found evidence of three visits to earth itself by extraterrestrials in the past, in addition to the one already mentioned."

"When?"

"The first was during the Silurian period, just over three hundred million years ago. The next was at the end of the Jurassic, at which time the extermination of the dinosauri was carried out by Nidian hunters. The most recent occurred a mere seven thousand, two hundred and forty-one years ago, in North Africa, at a point now flooded by the Aswan Lake."

"Hey, what about flying saucers?" Case asked. "Anything to the stories?"

"A purely subjective phenomenon, on a par with the angels so frequently interviewed by the unlettered during the pre-atomic era."

"Chester, this is dynamite," Case said. "You can't let 'em bust up this outfit. We can peddle this kind of stuff for plenty to the kind of nuts that dig around in old Indian garbage dumps."

"Case, if this is true . . . There are questions that have puzzled science for generations. But I'm afraid we could never convince the authorities—"

"You know, I've always wondered about telepathy. Is there anything to it, Machine?"

"Yes, as a latent ability," the voice replied. "However, its development is badly stunted by disuse."

"What about life after death?"

"The question is self-contradictory. However, if by it you postulate the persistence of the individual consciousness-field after the destruction of the neural circuits which gave rise to it, this is clearly nonsense. It is analogous to the idea of the survival of a magnetic field after the removal of the magnet—or the existence of a gravitational field in the absence of mass."

"So much for my reward in the hereafter," Case said. "But maybe it's lucky at that."

"Is the universe really expanding?" Chester inquired. "There are all kinds of theories . . . "

"It is."

"Why?"

"The natural result of the law of Universal Levitation."

"I'll bet you made that one up," said Case.

"I named it; however, the law has been in existence as long as space-time."

"How long is that?"

"That is a meaningless question."

"What's this levitation? I know what gravitation is, but . . ."

"Imagine two spheres hanging in space, connected by a cable. If the bodies rotate around a common center, a tensile stress is set up in the cable; the longer the cable, the greater the stress, assuming a constant rate of rotation."

"I'm with you so far."

"Since all motion is relative, it is equally valid to consider the spheres as stationary and the space about them as rotating."

"Well, maybe."

"The tension in the cable would remain; we have merely changed frames of reference. This force is what I have termed Levitation. Since the fabric of space is, in fact, rotating, Universal Levitation results. Accordingly, the universe expands. Einstein sensed the existence of this Natural Law in assuming his Cosmological Constant."

"Uh-huh," said Case. "Say, what's the story on cave men? How long ago did they start in business?"

"The original mutation from the pithecine stock occurred nine hundred and thirty—"

"Approximate figures will do," Chester interrupted.

"—thousand years ago," the voice continued, "in southern Africa."

"What did it look like?"

The wall clouded; then it cleared to show a five-foot

figure peering under shaggy brows and scratching idly at a mangy patch on its thigh. Its generous ears twitched; its long upper lip curled back to expose businesslike teeth. It blinked, wrinkled its flat nose, then sat on its haunches and began a detailed examination of its navel.

"You've sold me," Case said. "Except for the pelt, that's Uncle Julius to the life."

"I'm curious about my own forebears," Chester said. "What did the first Chester look like?"

"This designation was first applied in a form meaning 'Hugi the Camp Follower' to an individual of Pictish extraction, residing in what is now the London area."

The wall showed a thin, long-nosed fellow of middle age, with sparse reddish hair and beard, barefoot, wearing a sacklike knee-length garment of coarse gray homespun, crudely darned in several places. He carried a hide bag in one hand, and with the other he scratched vigorously at his right hip.

"This kid has a lot in common with the other one," said Case. "But he's an improvement, at that; he scratches with more feeling."

"I've never imagined we came of elegant stock," Chester said sadly, "but this is disillusioning even so. I wonder what your contemporary *grandpère* was like, Case."

"Inasmuch as the number of your direct ancestors doubles with each generation, assuming four generations to a century, any individual's forebears of two millennia past would theoretically number roughly one septillion. Naturally, since the Caucasian population of the planet at that date was fourteen million—an approximate figure, in keeping with your request, Mr. Chester—it is apparent that on the average each person then living in Europe was your direct ancestor through seventy quintillion lines of descent."

"Impossible! Why . . . "

"A mere five hundred years in the past, your direct ancestors would number over one million, were it not for considerable overlapping. For all practical purposes, it becomes obvious that all present-day humans are the descendants of the entire race. However, following only the line of male descent, the ancestor in question was this person."

The screen showed a hulking lout with a broken nose, one eye, a scarred cheekbone and a ferocious beard, topped by a mop of bristling coal-black hair. He wore fur breeches wrapped diagonally to the knee with yellowish rawhide thongs, a grimy sleeveless vest of sheepskin, and a crudely hammered short sword apparently of Roman design.

"This person was known as Gum the Scrofulous. He was hanged at the age of eighty, for rape."

"Attempted rape?" Case suggested hopefully.

"Rape," the voice replied firmly.

"These are very lifelike views you're showing us," said Chester. "But how do you know their names—and what they looked like? Surely there were no pictures of this ruffian."

"Hey, that's my ancestor you're talking about."

"The same goes for Hugi the Camp Follower. In those days, even Caesar didn't have his portrait painted."

"Details," Case said. "Mere mechanical details. Explain it to him, Computer."

"The Roman constabulary kept adequate records of unsavory characters such as Hugi. Gum's appellation was recorded at the time of his execution. The reconstruction of his person was based on a large number of factors, including, first, selection from my genealogical unit of the individual concerned, followed by identifications of the remains, on the basis of microcellular examination and classification."

"Hold it; you mean you located the body?"

"The grave site; it contained the remains of twelve thousand, four hundred individuals. A study of gene patterns revealed—"

"How did you know which body to examine?"

"The sample from which Gum was identified consisted of no more than two grams of material: a fragment of the pelvis. I had, of course, extracted all possible information from the remains many years ago, at the time of the initial survey of the two-hundred-and-three-foot stratum at the grave site, one hundred rods north of the incorporation limits of the village of—"

"How did you happen to do that?"

"As a matter of routine, I have systematically examined every datum source I encountered. Of course, since I am able to examine all surfaces, as well as the internal structure of objects *in situ*, I have derived vastly more information from deposits of bones, artifacts, fossils, and so forth, than a human investigator would be capable of. Also, my ability to draw on the sum total of all evidence on a given subject produces highly effective results. I deciphered Easter Island script within forty-two minutes after I had completed scansion of the existing inscriptions, both above ground and buried, and including one tablet incorporated in a temple in Ceylon. The Indus script of Mohenjo-Daro required little longer."

"Granted you could read dead languages after you'd integrated all the evidence—but a man's personal appearance is another matter."

"The somatic pattern is inherent in the nucleoprotein."

Case nodded. "That's right. They say every cell in the body carries the whole blueprint—the same one you were built on in the first place. All the computer had to do was find one cell."

"Oh, of course," said Chester sarcastically. "I don't suppose there's any point in my asking how it knew how he was dressed, or how his hair was combed, or what he was scratching at."

"There is nothing in the least occult about the reconstructions which I have presented, Mr. Chester. All the multitudinous factors which bear on the topic at hand, even in the most remote fashion, are scanned, classified, their interlocking ramifications evaluated, and the resultant gestalt concretized in a rigidly logical manner. The condition of the hair was deduced, for example, from the known growth pattern revealed in the genetic analysis, while the style of the trim was a composite of those known to be in use in the area. The—"

"In other words," Case put in, "it wasn't really a photo of Gum the Scrofulous; it was kind of like an artist's sketch from memory."

"I still fail to see where the fine details come from."

"You underestimate the synthesizing capabilities of an efficiently functioning memory bank," the voice said. "This is somewhat analogous to the amazement of the consistently second- and third-power mind of Dr. Watson when confronted with the fourth-power deductions of Sherlock Holmes."

"Guessing that the murderer was a one-legged seafaring man with a beard and a habit of chewing betel nut is one thing," Chester said. "Looking at an ounce of bone and giving us a three-D picture is another."

"You make the understandable error of egocentric anthropomorphization of viewpoint, Mr. Chester," said the voice. "Your so-called 'reality' is, after all, no more than a pattern produced in the mind by abstraction from a very limited set of sensory impressions. You perceive a pattern of reflected radiation at the visible wave lengths—only a small fraction of the full spectrum, of course; to this you add auditory stimuli, tactile and olfactory sensations, as well as other perceptions in the Psi group of which you are not consciously aware at the third power—all of which can easily be misled by mirrors, ventriloquism, distorted perspective, hypnosis, and so on. The resultant image you think of as concrete actuality. I do no more than assemble data—over a much wider range than you are capable of—and translate them into pulses in a conventional Tri-D tank. The resultant image appears to you an adequate approximation of reality."

"Chester," Case said firmly, "we can't let 'em bust this computer up and sell it for scrap. There's a fortune in it, if we work it right."

"Possibly—but I'm afraid it's hopeless, Case. After all, if the computer, with all its talents, after staving off disaster for a century, isn't capable of dealing with the present emergency, how can we?"

"Look here, Computer," Case said. "Are you sure you've tried everything?"

"Oh, no; but now that I've complied with my builder's instructions, I have no further interest in prolonging my existence."

"Good Lord! You mean you have no instinct for self-preservation?"

"None whatever; and I'm afraid that to acquire one would necessitate an extensive rethinking of my basic circuitry."

"O.K., so it's up to us," Case said. "We've got to save the computer—and then use it to save the circus."

"We'd be better off to disassociate ourselves completely from this conscienceless apparatus," Chester said. "It's meddled in everything from the stock market to the space program. If the authorities ever discover what's been going on . . . "

"Negative thinking, Chester. We've got something here. All we have to do is figure out what."

"If the confounded thing manufactured buttonhole TV sets or tranquilizers or anything else salable, the course would be clear; unfortunately, it generates nothing but hot air." Chester drew on his wine bottle and sighed. "I don't know of anyone who'd pay to learn what kind of riffraff his ancestors were—or, worse still—see them. Possibly the best course would be to open up the house to tourists—the 'view the stately home of another era' approach."

"Hold it," Case cut in. He looked thoughtful. "That gives me an idea. 'Stately home of another era,' eh? People are interested in other eras, Chester—as long as they don't have to take on anybody like Gum the Scrofulous as a member of the family. Now, this computer seems to be able to fake up just about any scene you want to take a look at. You name it, it sets it up. Chester, we've got the greatest side-show attraction in circus history! We book the public in at so much a head, and show 'em Daily Life in Ancient Rome, or Michelangelo sculpting the Pietà, or Napoleon leading the charge at Marengo. Get the idea? Famous Scenes of the Past Revisited! We'll not only put Wowser Wonder Shows back in the big time—but make a mint in the process!"

"Come down to earth, Case. Who'd pay to sit through a history lesson?"

"Nobody, Chester; but they'll pay to be entertained! So we'll entertain 'em. See the sights of Babylon! Watch Helen of Troy in her bath! Sit in on Cleopatra's summit conference with Caesar!"

"I'd rather not be involved in any chicanery, Case. And, anyway, we wouldn't have time. It's only a week—"

"We'll get time. First we'll soften up the Internal Revenue boys with a gloomy picture of how much they'd get out of the place if they take over the property and liquidate it. Then—very cagily, Chester—we lead up to the idea that *maybe*, just *maybe*, we can raise the money—but only if we get a few weeks to go ahead with the scheme."

"A highly unrealistic proposal, Case. It would lead to a number of highly embarrassing questions. I'd find it awkward explaining the stowaway devices on the satellites, the rigged stock-market deals, the bribes in high places . . ."

"You're a worrier, Chester. We'll pack 'em in four shows a day at, say, two-fifty a head. With a seating capacity of two thousand, you'll pay off that debt in six months."

"What do we do, announce that we've invented a new type of Tri-D show? Even professional theatrical producers can't guarantee the public's taste. We'll be laughed out of the office."

"This will be different. They'll jump at it."

"They'll probably jump at us—with nets."

"You've got no vision, Chester. Try to visualize it: the color, the pageantry, the realism! We can show epics that would cost Hollywood a fortune—and we'll get 'em for free."

Case addressed the machine again. "Let's give Chester a sample, Computer—something historically important, like Columbus getting Isabella's crown jewels."

"Let's keep it clean, Case."

"O.K., we'll save that one for stag nights. For now, what do you say to . . . ummm . . . William the Conqueror getting the news that Harold the Saxon has been killed at the Battle of Hastings in 1066? We'll have full color, three dimensions, sound, smells, the works. How about it, Computer?"

"I am uncertain how to interpret the expression 'the works' in this context," said the voice. "Does this imply full sensory stimulation within the normal human range?"

"Yeah, that's the idea." Case drew the cork from a fresh bottle, watching the screen cloud and swirl, to clear on a view of patched tents under a gray sky on a slope of sodden grass. A paunchy man of middle age, clad in ill-fitting breeches of coarse brown cloth, a rust-speckled shirt of chain mail and a moth-eaten fur cloak, sat before a tent on a three-legged stool, mumbling over a well-gnawed lamb's shin. A burly clod in ill-matched furs came up to him, breathing hard.

"We'm . . . wonnit," he gasped. "'E be adoon wi' a quarrel i' t' peeper . . . "

The sitting man guffawed and reached for a hide mug of brownish liquid. The messenger wandered off. The seated man belched and scratched idly at his ribs. Then he rose, yawned, stretched and went inside the tent. The scene faded.

"Hmmm," said Chester. "I'm afraid that was lacking in something."

"You can do better than that, Computer," Case said reproachfully. "Come on, let's see some color, action, glamour, zazzle. Make history come alive! Jazz it up a little!"

"You wish me to embroider the factual presentation?"

"Just sort of edit it for modern audiences. You know, the way high-school English teachers correct Shakespeare's plays and improve on the old boy's morals; or like preachers leave the sexy bits out of the Bible."

"Possibly the approach employed by the Hollywood fantasists would suffice?"

"Now you're talking. Leave out the dirt and boredom, and feed in some stagecraft."

Once again the screen cleared. Against a background of vivid blue sky a broad-shouldered man in glittering

mail sat astride a magnificent black charger, a brilliantly
blazoned shield on his arm. He waved a long sword
aloft, spurred up a slope of smooth green lawn, his
raven-black hair flowing over his shoulders from under
a polished steel cap, his scarlet cloak rippling bravely
in the sun. Another rider came to meet him, reined
in, saluting.

"The day is ours, Sire!" the newcomer cried in a
mellow baritone. "Harold Fairhair lies dead; his troops
retire in disorder!"

The black-haired man swept his casque from his
head.

"Let's give thanks to God," he said in ringing tones,
wheeling to present his profile. "And all honor to a
brave foe!"

The messenger leaped from his mount, knelt before
the other.

"Hail, William, Conqueror of England . . . "

"Nay, faithful Clunt," William said. "The Lord has
conquered; I am but his instrument. Rise, and let
us ride forward together. Now dawns a new day of
freedom . . . "

Case and Chester watched the retreating horses.

"I'm not sure I like that fade-out," said Chester.
"There's something about watching a couple of horses
ascending . . . "

"You're right. It lacks spontaneity—too stagy-
looking. Maybe we'd better stick to the real thing; but
we'll have to pick and choose our scenes."

"It's still too much like an ordinary movie. And we
know nothing about pace, camera angles, timing. I wonder whether the machine—"

"I can produce scenes in conformance with any prin-
ciples of aesthetics you desire, Mr. Chester," the computer said flatly.

"What we want is reality," said Case. "Living,

breathing realness. We need something that's got inherent drama, something big, strange, amazing."

"Aren't you overlooking stupendous and colossal?"

Case snapped his fingers. "What's the most colossal thing that ever was? What are the most fearsome battlers of all time?"

"A crowd of fat ladies at a girdle sale?"

"Close, Chester, but not quite on the mark. I refer to the extinct giants of a hundred million years ago: dinosaurs! That's what we'll see, Chester! How about it, Computer? Can you lay on a small herd of dinosaurs for us? I mean the real goods: luxuriant jungle foliage, hot primitive sun, steaming swamps, battles to the death on a gigantic scale?"

"I fear some confusion exists, Mr. Mulvihill. The environment you postulate is a popular cliché; it actually antedates in most particulars the advent of the giant saurians by several hundred million years."

"O.K., I'll skip the details. I'll leave the background to you. But we want real, three-D, big-as-life dinosaurs and plenty of 'em—and how about a four-wall presentation?"

"There are two possible methods of achieving the effect you describe, Mr. Mulvihill. The first, a seventh-order approximation, would involve an elaboration of the techniques already employed in the simpler illusions. The other, which I confess is a purely theoretical approach, might prove simpler, if feasible, and would perhaps provide total verisimilitude—"

"Whatever's simplest. Go to it."

"I must inform you that in the event—"

"We won't quibble over the fine technical points. Just whip up three-D dinosaurs in the simplest way you know how."

"Very well. The experiment may well produce a wealth of new material for my memory banks."

For half a minute the screen wall stayed blank. Case

twisted to stare over his shoulder at the other walls. "Come on, what's the holdup?" he called.

"The problems involved . . . " the voice began.

"Patience, Case," Chester said. "I'm sure the computer is doing its best."

"Yeah, I guess so." Case leaned forward. "Here we go," he said as the walls shimmered with a silvery luster, then seemed to fade to reveal an autumnal forest of great beech and maple trees. An afternoon sun slanted through high foliage. In the distance a bird called shrilly. A cool breeze bore the odor of pines and leaf mold. The scene seemed to stretch into shadowy cool distances. "Not bad," said Case, dribbling cigar ashes on the rug. "Using all four walls was a great improvement."

"Careful," Chester said. "You may start a forest fire."

Case snorted. "Don't let it go to your head, Chester. It's just an illusion, remember."

"Those look to be quite normally inflammable leaves on the ground," Chester said. "There's one right under your chair."

Case looked down. A dry leaf blew across the rug. The easy chairs and a patch of carpet seemed to be alone in the middle of a great forest.

"Hey, that's a nice touch," Case said approvingly. "But where's the dinosaurs? This isn't the kind of place . . . "

Case's comment was interrupted by a dry screech that descended from the supersonic into a blast like a steam whistle, then died off in a rumble. Both men leaped from their seats.

"What the . . . "

"I believe your question's been answered," Chester croaked, pointing. Half hidden by foliage, a scaly, fungus-grown hill loomed up among the tree trunks, its gray-green coloring almost invisible in the forest gloom. The hill stirred; a giant turkeylike leg brushed against a tree trunk, sent bits of bark flying. The whitish undercurve of the belly wobbled ponderously; the great meaty tail twitched, sending a six-inch sapling crashing down.

Case laughed shakily. "For a minute there, I forgot this was just a—"

"Quiet! It might hear us!" Chester hissed.

"What do you mean, 'hear us'?" Case said heartily. "It's just a picture! But we need a few more dinosaurs to liven things up. The customers are going to want to see plenty for their money. How about it, Computer?"

The disembodied voice seemed to emanate from the low branches of a pine tree. "There are a number of the creatures in the vicinity, Mr. Mulvihill. If you will carefully observe to your left, you will see a small example of Megalosaurus. And beyond is a truly splendid specimen of Nodosaurus."

"You know," said Case, rising and peering through the woods for more reptiles, "I think when we get the show running, we'll use this question-and-answer routine. It's a nice touch. The cash customers will want to know a lot of stuff like—oh, what kind of perfume did Marie Antoinette use, or how many wives did Solomon really have."

"I don't know," said Chester, watching as the nearby dinosaur scrunched against a tree trunk, causing a shower of twigs and leaves to flutter down. "There's something about hearing a voice issuing from thin air that might upset the most high-strung members of the audience. Couldn't we rig up a speaker of some sort for the voice to come out of?"

"Hmmm . . . " Case strode up and down, puffing at his cigar. Chester fidgeted in his chair. Fifty feet away the iguanodon moved from the shelter of a great maple into the open. There was a rending of branches as the heavy salamander head pulled at a mass of foliage thirty feet above the forest floor.

"I've got it!" Case said, smacking his fist into his palm. "Another great idea! You said something about fixing up a speaker for the voice to come out of. But what kind of speaker, Chester?"

"Keep it down." Chester moved behind his chair, a nervous eye on the iguanodon. "I still think that monster can hear us."

"So what? Now; the speaker ought to be mobile— you know, so it can travel around among the marks and answer their questions. So . . . we get the computer to rig us a speaker that matches the voice!"

"Look," said Chester, "it's starting to turn this way."

"Pay attention, Chester. We get the machine to design us a robot in the shape of a good-looking dame. She'll be a sensation: a gorgeous, stacked babe who'll answer any question you want to ask her."

"He seems to move very sluggishly," said Chester.

"We could call this babe Miss I-Cutie."

"He sees us."

"Don't you get it? I.Q.—I-Cutie."

"Yes, certainly. Go right ahead; whatever you say."

The iguanodon's great head swung ponderously, stopped with one unwinking eye fixed dead on Chester. "Just like a bird watching a worm," he quavered. "Stand still, Case; maybe he'll lose interest."

"Nuts." Case stepped forward. "Who's scared of a picture?" He stood, hands on hips, looking at the towering reptile. "Not a bad illusion at all," he called. "Even right up close, it looks real. Even smells real." He wrinkled his nose, came stamping back to the two chairs and Chester. "Relax, Chester. You look as nervous as a bank teller at the fifty-credit window."

Chester looked from Case to the browsing saurian. "Case, if I didn't know there was a wall there . . . "

"Hey, look over there." Case waved his cigar. Chester turned. With a rustling of leaves a seven-foot bipedal reptile stalked into view, tiny forearms curled against its chest. In dead silence it stood immobile as a statue, except for the palpitation of its greenish-white throat. For a long moment it stared at the two men. Abruptly, it turned at a tiny sound from the grass at its feet and pounced. There was a strangled squeal, a flurry of motion. The eighteen-inch head came up, jaws working, to resume its appraisal of Chester and Case.

"That's good material," Case said, puffing hard at his cigar. "Nature in the raw; the battle for survival. The customers will eat it up."

"Speaking of eating, I don't like the way the thing's looking at me."

The dinosaur cocked its head, took a step closer.

"Phewww!" Case said. "You can sure smell that fellow." He raised his voice. "Tone it down a little, Computer. This kid has got halitosis on a giant scale."

The meat-eater gulped hard, twice, flicked a slender red tongue between rows of needlelike teeth in the snow-white cavern of its mouth, took another step toward Chester. It stood near the edge of the rug now, poised, alert, staring with one eye. It twisted its head, brought the other eye to bear.

"As I remember, there was at least six feet of clear floor space between the edge of that rug and the wall," Chester said hoarsely. "Case, that hamburger machine's in the room with us!"

Case laughed. "Forget it, Chester. It's just the effect of the perspective or something." He took a step toward the allosaurus. Its lower jaw dropped. The multiple rows of white teeth gleamed. Saliva gushed, spilled over the scaled edge of the lipless mouth. The red eye seemed to blaze up. A great clawed bird-foot came up, poised over the rug.

"Computer!" Chester shouted. "Get us out of here!"

The forest scene whooshed out of existence.

Case looked at Chester disgustedly. "What'd you want to do that for? I wasn't through looking at them."

Chester took out a handkerchief, sank into a chair, mopped at his face. "I'll argue the point later—after I get my pulse under control."

"Well, how about it? Was it great? Talk about stark realism!"

"Realism is right! It was as though we were actually there, in the presence of that voracious predator, unprotected!"

Case sat staring at Chester. "Hold it! You just said something, my boy: 'as though we were actually there . . .'"

"Yes, and the sensation was far from pleasant."

"Chester"—Case rubbed his hands together—"your troubles are over. It just hit me: the greatest idea of the century. You don't think the tax boys will buy a slice of show biz, hey? But what about the scientific marvel of the age? They'll go for that, won't they?"

"But they already know about the computer."

"We won't talk to 'em about the computer, Chester. They wouldn't believe it anyway: Crmblznski's Limit, remember? We'll go the truth one better. We'll tell 'em something that will knock 'em for a loop."

"Very well, I'll ask: What will we tell them?"

"We tell 'em we've got a real, live time machine!"

"Why not tell them we're in touch with the spirit world?"

Case considered. "Nope, too routine. There's half a dozen in the racket in this state alone. But who do you know that's got a time machine working, eh? Nobody, that's who! Chester, it's a gold mine. After we pay off the Internal Revenue boys, we'll go on to bigger things. The possibilities are endless."

"Yes, I've been thinking about a few of them: fines for tax evasion and fraud, prison terms for conspiracy and perjury. Why not simply tell the computer to float a loan?"

"Listen, up to now you're as clean as a hired man catching the last bus back from the fair. But once you start instructing the machine to defraud by mail for you, you're on the spot. Now keep cool and let's do this as legal as possible."

"Your lines of distinction between types of fraud escape me."

"We'll be doing a public service, Chester. We'll bring a little glamour into a lot of dull, drab lives. We'll be public benefactors, sort of. Why not look at it that way?"

"Restrain yourself, Case. We're not going into politics; we're just honest, straightforward charlatans, remember?"

"Not that there won't be problems," Case went on. "It's going to be a headache picking the right kind of scenes. Take ancient Greece, for example. They had some customs that wouldn't do for a family-type show. In the original Olympics none of the contestants wanted to be loaded with anything as confining as a G string. And there were the public baths—coeducational—and the slave markets, with the merchandise in full view. We'll have to watch our step, Chester. Practically everything in ancient history was too dirty for the public to look at."

"We'd better restrict ourselves to later times when people were Christians," Chester said. "We can show the Inquisition, seventeenth-century witch burnings—you know, wholesome stuff."

"How about another trial run, Chester? Just a quickie. Something simple, just to see if the machine gets the idea."

Chester sighed. "We may as well."

"What do you say to a nice cave-man scene, Chester?" said Case. "Stone axes, animal skins around the waist, bear-tooth necklaces—the regular Alley Oop routine."

"Very well—but let's avoid any large carnivores. They're overly realistic."

There was a faint sound from behind them. Chester turned. A young girl stood on the rug, looking around as if fascinated by the neo-Victorian décor. Glossy dark hair curled about her oval face. She caught Chester's eye and stepped around to stand before him on the rug, a slender, modest figure wearing a golden suntan and a scarlet hair ribbon. Chester gulped audibly. Case dropped his cigar.

"Perhaps I should have mentioned, Mr. Chester," the computer said, "that the mobile speaker you requested is ready. I carried on the work in an entropic vacuole, permitting myself thereby to produce a complex entity in a very brief period, subjectively speaking."

Chester gulped again.

"Hi!" Case said, breaking the stunned silence.

"Hello," said the girl. Her voice was melodiously soft. She reached up to adjust her hair ribbon, smiling at Case and Chester. "My name is Genie."

"Uh . . . wouldn't you like to borrow my shirt?"

"Knock it off, Chester," Case said. "You remind me of those characters you see on Tri-D that hide every time they see a pretty girl in the bathtub."

"I don't think the computer got the idea after all," Chester said weakly.

"It's pretty literal," Case said. "We only worried about the scenes . . ."

"I selected this costume as appropriate to the primitive setting," the girl said. "As for my physical characteristics, the intention was to produce the ideal of the average young female, without mammary hypertrophy or other exaggeration, to evoke a sisterly or maternal response in women, while the reaction of male members of the audience should be a fatherly one."

"I'm not sure it's working on me," said Chester, breathing hard.

The pretty face looked troubled. "Perhaps the body should be redesigned, Mr. Chester."

"Don't change a thing," Case said hastily. "And call me Case."

Chester moved closer to Case. "Funny," he whispered. "She talks just like the computer."

"What's funny about that? It *is* the computer talking. This is just a robot, remember, Chester."

"Shall we proceed with the view of Neolithic Man?" Genie inquired.

"Sure, shoot," Case boomed.

The walls seemed to fade from view to reveal a misty-morning scene of sloping grassland scattered with wild flowers and set here and there with trees.

"Say, this is O.K.," said Case, lighting a fresh cigar. "Nice-looking country."

"If you'll observe to the left," Genie said. "I believe these are a party of hunters returning to their dwelling."

Case and Chester turned.

Two squat, bearded men in fur pants emerged from a thicket down the slope, saw the watching trio and stopped dead. More savages followed. The two leaders stood, eyes and mouths agape, hefting long sticks sharpened at one end.

"These guys are practically midgets," Case said. "I thought cave men were pretty big guys."

"They seem to see us," said Chester. "Apparently the audience is on view as well as the actors. I feel rather exposed. What do you suppose they're planning to do with those spears?"

One of the natives stepped forward a pace and shouted.

"You too, pal," Case called, puffing out smoke.

The spokesman shouted again, pointing around, at the other man, at the trees, at the sky, then at himself. Bearded warriors continued to appear from the underbrush.

"I wonder what he's yelling about," said Case.

"He says that he is the owner of the world and that you have no business in it," Genie replied.

"His title to the property is probably clearer than mine," put in Chester.

"How the heck do you know the language?" Case asked admiringly.

"Oh, I have full access to the memory banks," Genie said, "as long as I remain within the resonance field."

"Sort of a transmitter and receiver arrangement?"

"In a sense. Actually it is more analogous to an artificially induced telepathic effect."

"I thought that was only with people—uh, I mean, you know, regular-type people."

"Regular in what way?" Genie inquired interestedly.

"Well, after all, you *are* a machine," said Case. "Not that I've got anything against machinery."

"The owner of the world is coming this way," interrupted Chester. "And reinforcements are still arriving."

"Yeah, we're drawing a good crowd," Case said.

The troglodytes spread out in a wide half-circle. The leader called instructions, made complicated motions, turned to hurl an occasional imprecation at the three viewers on the slope.

"Looks like he's getting some kind of show ready. Probably a quaint native dance to get on our good side."

"He's disposing the warriors for battle," Genie said.

"Battle? Who with?" Case looked around. "I don't see any opposition."

"With us. Or, more properly, with you two gentlemen."

"Maybe a strategic withdrawal?" Chester offered.

"I wouldn't miss this for all the two-dollar bills in Tijuana," said Case. "Relax, Chester. It's only a show."

At a signal the half-ring of bearded warriors started up the slope, spears held at the ready.

"Boy, will they get a shock when they hit the wall," Case said, chuckling.

Yelping, the advancing savages broke into a run. They were fifty feet away, thirty . . .

"*I* know they can't get at us," Chester wailed, "but do they?"

"Perhaps I should mention," observed Genie above the din, "that a one-to-one spacio-temporal contiguity has been established."

Genie's voice was drowned out in the mob yell as the warriors pelted up the last few yards, converging on the rug.

At the last instant, Case tossed his cigar aside and leaped up, swung a roundhouse right that sent a hairy warrior spinning. Chester leaped aside from another, saw Case seize two men by their beards and sling their heads together, drop them as three more sprang on him, then go down in an avalanche of whiskers and bandy legs. Chester opened his mouth to shout an order to retreat, got an instant's glimpse of a horny foot aimed at his head . . .

Somewhere, a large brass bell tolled sundown. For a fading moment, Chester was aware of the tumble of dirt-brown bodies, distant cries, an overpowering odor that suggested unsuccessful experiments in cheese-making. Then darkness folded in.

3

The sun was shining in Chester's eyes. He opened them, felt sharp pains shooting down from the top of his skull, closed them again with a groan. He rolled over, felt the floor sway under him.

"We'll have to cut down on all this drinking," he muttered. "Case, where are you?"

There was no answer. Chester tried his eyes again. If he barely opened them, he decided, it wasn't too bad. And to think that this gargantuan headache had resulted from the consumption of a few bottles of what had always been reputed to be some of the best wines in the old boy's cellar.

"Case?" he croaked, louder this time. He sat up, felt the floor move again sickeningly. He lay back hastily. It hadn't been more than two bottles at the most, or maybe three. He and Case had been looking over the computer . . .

"Oh, no," Chester said aloud. He sat up, winced, pried his eyes open.

He was sitting on the floor of a wicker cage six feet in diameter, with sides that curved into a beehive shape at the top. Outside the cage, nothing was visible but open air and distant treetops. He pushed his face up against the openwork side, saw the ground swaying twenty feet below.

"Case," he yelled. "Get me out of here!"

"Chester," a soft voice called from nearby. Chester looked around. Twenty feet away, a cage like his own swung from a massive branch of the next tree. Inside it Genie knelt, her face against the rattan bars.

"Genie, where are we?" Chester called. "Where's Case? What's become of the house?"

"Hey!" a more distant voice called. Chester and Genie both turned. Across the clearing, a third cage swayed. Chester made out Case's massive figure inside.

"Couldn't get through the wall, eh?" Chester taunted in a sudden revival of spirit. "Just a show, eh? Of all the idiotic . . ."

"O.K., O.K., a slight miscalculation. But how the heck was I supposed to know Genie was cooking up a deal like that? How about it, Genie? Is that the kind of show you think an audience would go for at two-fifty a head?"

"Don't blame Genie," Chester shouted. "I'm sure she did no more than follow instructions—to the letter."

"We never asked for the real article," Case yelled.

"On the contrary, that's exactly what you demanded."

"Yeah, but how was I to know the damn machine'd take me literally? All I meant was—"

"When dealing with machinery, always specify *exactly* what you want. I should have thought that meat-eating reptile would have been enough warning for you. I told you the infernal creature was in the room with us, but you—"

"But why didn't Genie stop 'em?"

"Should I have?" said Genie. "I had no instructions to interfere with the course of events."

Case groaned. "Let's call a truce, Chester. We've got a situation to deal with here. Afterwards we can argue it out over a couple of bottles of something. Right now we need a knife. You got one?"

Chester fumbled in his pockets, brought out a tiny penknife. "Yes, such as it is."

"Toss it over."

"I'm locked in a cage, remember?"

"Oh. Well, get to work and cut the rope."

"Case, I think you must have been hit on the head

too—but harder. Have you considered the twenty-foot drop to the ground *if* I could cut the rope, which I can't reach?"

"Well, you got any better ideas? This bird cage is no pushover; I can't bust anything loose."

"Try hitting it with your head."

"Chester, your attitude does you no credit. This is your old pal Case, remember?"

"You're the ex-acrobat. You figure it out."

"That was a few years ago, Chester, and—hey!" Case interrupted himself. "What a couple of dopes! All we got to do is tell Genie to whisk us back home. I don't know what this setup is she got us into, but she can just get us out again. Good ol' Genie. Do your stuff, kid."

"Are you talking to me, Mr. Mulvihill?" Genie asked, wide-eyed.

"Huh? Listen, Genie, this is no time to go dumb! Get us out of this fix! Fast!"

Genie looked thoughtful. "I'm afraid that's beyond my capabilities, Mr. Mulvihill."

Chester gulped hard. "Genie, you brought us here. You've got to get us back!"

"But, Chester, I don't know how."

"You mean you've lost your memory?"

"Oh, no, my memory is excellent."

"What is this, a mechanical mutiny?" Case yelled.

"I think I know what the trouble is," Chester called across to Case. "Genie told us she was linked to the memory banks as long as she remained within the resonance field of the computer. But we must be a considerable distance from the apparatus now—and thus Genie has no contact with the machine."

"Some machinery," Case grumbled.

"As soon as we're back where we left the rug and chairs, I'm sure she'll re-establish contact," Chester said. "Right, Genie?"

"I don't know. But perhaps you're right, Chester."

"This isn't getting us out of here," Case cut in. "Let's cut the chatter and figure what we're going to do. Chester, you can use your knife to cut some of the lashings holding that cage together. Then you can crawl up the rope, make it to my tree, and let me out. Then we cut Genie down, and—"

"Listen!" Chester interrupted. "I hear them coming!"

He peered out at the bright morning-lit clearing below them, the surrounding forest, a trail that wound away between the trees. A group of savages appeared, moving along briskly, filing into the clearing, gathering under the trees. They looked up at the captives, jabbering, pointing and laughing. Two of them set about erecting a wobbly ladder of bamboo-like cane against Case's tree, jabbering as they adjusted it.

"What are they talking about, Genie?" Chester asked. "Or can't you understand them any more?"

Genie nodded. "I absorbed the language when we first arrived."

"In two minutes?"

"Oh, yes. That's one of the advantages of a direct telepathic contact with a data source."

"So you still know everything—except how to get us out of here."

"The actual environmental manipulation was handled by the computer. I was merely the mobile speaker, you recall."

"I guess so." Chester peered down at the natives. "What are they saying?"

"They're discussing a forthcoming athletic event. Apparently a great deal depends upon its outcome."

She listened further as the savages got the ladder in place. One of the bearded men scaled it, fumbled with the end of the rope supporting Case's cage.

"It is to be a contest between champions," said Genie. "A mighty struggle between giants."

"Hey," yelled Case, "if that knee-length Gargantua lets that rope go, I won't be around to watch the bout."

"It's O.K.," Chester called. "There's a sort of pulley-like arrangement of crossbars the rope is wound around. They can let it down slowly."

Case's cage lurched, dropped a foot, then steadied and moved smoothly down to thump against the ground. The savages gathered around, unlaced and opened a panel in the side, stepped back and stood with leveled spears as Case emerged. He looked around, made a grab for the nearest spear. Its owner danced back. The others shouted, laughed and jabbered excitedly.

"What's all the chatter about, Genie?" Case called.

"They are admiring your spirit, size and quickness of movement, Mr. Mulvihill."

"They are, huh? I'll show 'em some quickness of movement if one of 'em 'll get close enough for me to grab him."

Chester looked up at a sound from across the clearing. A second group of natives were approaching—and in their midst, towering over them, came a hulking brute of a man, broad, thick, hairy.

"Looks like they went for their big brother," Case said. "Quite a guy. He's got muscles like a waterfront bartender."

"This is one of the champions who will engage in combat," said Genie. "Their name for him seems to be translatable as 'Biter-off of Heads.'"

Case whistled. "Look at those hands—as big as a Chinaman's briefcase. He could squeeze one of these midgets like a tube of toothpaste."

"This should be an interesting battle," said Chester, "if his opponent is anywhere near his size."

"I'll lay you three to two on this boy without see-ing the challenger," Case called. "I hope they let us hang around and watch."

"Oh, there's no doubt that you'll be present, Mr. Mulvihill," Genie said reassuringly. "You're the one who's going to fight him."

"Chester, it's the best we can do," said Case. "We haven't got much time left to talk. The main bout's coming up any minute now."

"But, Case, against that man-eater you don't have a chance."

"I used to fill in for the strong man on Wednesday afternoons, Chester. And I'll bet you a half interest in Great-grandpop's booze supply that this kid never stud-ied boxing or judo—and I did. Leave that part to me. You do what I told you."

Half a dozen jabbering, gesticulating natives closed in around Case, indicated with jabs of their hardwood spears that he was to move off in the direction of the hairy champion.

"Poor Mr. Mulvihill," Genie said. "That brute is even larger than he is."

"Case knows a few tricks, Genie. Don't worry about him."

The two watched anxiously as the crowd formed up a circle about the local heavyweight and Case. One of the savages shouted for attention, then launched into a speech. The shaggy giant—all of seven feet tall—eyed Case, scowled, stopped to scratch, became absorbed in the pursuit of a louse, began to rotate like a dog chasing his tail, with one arm raised and the other halfway round his back.

"He doesn't look very bright," Chester said. "But what a reach! He's got hold of his own backbone!"

"I hope Mr. Mulvihill is noting the primitive's weak-nesses and planning his strategy accordingly."

A dozen yards from his opponent Case stood drawing deep breaths and letting them out slowly. He glanced up, caught Chester's eye, and winked. The speech-maker jabbered on.

"He's telling the people that Mr. Mulvihill is a demon which he summoned from the underworld," Genie said. "He refers to you as the Demon with Four Eyes and to me as the Naked Goddess. Mr. Mulvihill is under some sort of spell which will force him to fight fiercely against the large savage."

"Oh-oh," Chester cut in. "Here we go."

The native leader had stopped speaking. The crowd fell silent. Case pulled off his leather belt and wrapped it around his fist. The hairy seven-footer growled, eyeing the crowd, stalked forward, still slapping his chest. He stopped, turned his back to Case, and roared out a string of gibberish. Case took three rapid steps, slammed a vicious right to the kidneys.

"Go get him, Case!" Chester yelled.

The giant whirled with a bellow, reaching for the injured spot with a huge right hand and for Case with the left. Case ducked, drove a left to the pit of the shaggy stomach, followed with a right—and went flying as the giant caught him with an open-handed swipe. Case rolled, came to his feet. The native champion had both hands to his stomach now; his hoarse breathing was audible to Chester, forty feet away.

"Case hurt him that time."

"But Mr. Mulvihill—perhaps he's injured too!"

"I don't think so. His profanity sounds normal. In any event, he has their attention fully occupied. I'd better get started."

Chester took out the penknife, looked over the lacing that secured the woven bamboo strips and started sawing.

"I hope this blade holds out. I never contemplated

cutting anything more resistant than a cigar tip when I bought it."

"Please work quickly, Chester. Mr. Mulvihill may not last long."

Below, Case ducked aside from a charge, planted a hearty right in the big man's short ribs, danced back as the other changed direction.

"There's one," said Chester as the strands of lacing fell free. "I think three more may do it. Anyone looking my way?"

"No, no one. Ohhh, Chester, I'm frightened. Mr. Mulvihill tripped and barely rolled aside in time to avoid being trampled."

"Hey, don't revert to the feminine now, Genie. Keep the computer aspect of your personality to the fore; it has a steadying effect."

"Mr. Mulvihill has just struck the savage a very effective blow on the back of the neck," said Genie. "It staggered him."

"Two loose. I hope Case has a few more unorthodox blows in his repertoire. I'll need at least ten minutes . . ."

Chester worked steadily, freed a third joint, pulled a vertical member aside, and thrust his head through the opening. It was a close fit, but a moment later his shoulders were through. He reached up for a handhold, pulled himself entirely through, and clung to the wicker frame of the cage. He found a foothold, clambered higher, reached the rope from which the basket was suspended. A glance toward the fighters showed that all eyes were on the combatants. Chester took a deep breath, started up the rope.

The crowd shouted as Case hammered a left and a right to the giant's body, turned to duck away, slipped, and was folded into his opponent's immense embrace.

"Chester, he'll be crushed," wailed Genie.

Chester hung on, craning to see. Case struggled, reached behind him, found an index finger and twisted. The giant roared; Case bent the finger back, back . . .

With a howl the giant dropped him, twisting his hand free, and popped the injured member into his mouth.

Chester let out a long breath, pulled himself up onto the branch to which the rope was secured. He rose shakily to his feet, made his way to the main trunk, climbed up to the branch from which Genie's cage was suspended, started out along it. In the clearing below, the crowd yelled. Chester caught a glimpse of Case darting past the giant, whirling to chop hard at the side of his neck with the edge of his hand.

Then Chester was at the rope, sliding down.

"Chester, you'd better leave me. Save yourself."

Chester sawed at the bindings of Genie's cage. "Even if I were enough of a coward to entertain the notion, it would hardly be a practical idea. Just another minute or two, Genie."

The joints parted. Below, Case battled on. Chester pried the rattan aside, held the bars apart as Genie slipped through. She climbed up, reached the rope, shinnied up it easily. Chester followed.

Above him Genie gasped and pointed. Chester turned in time to see Case duck under a mighty haymaker, come up under his huge opponent and spill him off his feet. As the lumbering savage struggled up with a roar, Case caught him on the point of the jaw with a tremendous clout, knocking him flat again. The bigger man shook his head, stumbled to his feet and charged. Case threw himself against the oncoming behemoth's knees. Chester winced as the immense figure dived headlong over Case's crouched figure and smashed into the packed earth, face first. When the dust settled Case was on his feet, breathing hard; the giant lay like a felled tree.

"Unfortunate timing," muttered Chester. "He should have held their attention for another five minutes."

"They're sure to notice us now," Genie whispered, flattening her slender length against the rough bark.

"Don't move," Chester breathed. "We'll wait and see what happens next."

The crowd, standing mute with astonishment, suddenly whooped, surged in to clap Case on the back, prod the fallen champion, dance about jabbering excitedly. Chester saw Case shoot a quick glance toward the cages, then stoop suddenly, come up with two large, smooth stones. The crowd grew still, drawing back. One or two unlimbered spears. Case raised his hand for silence, then casually tossed one of the stones up, transferred the other to his right hand in time to catch the first with his left, tossed up the second stone . . .

"That's the idea," Chester whispered. "Good old Case. He'll entrance them with his juggling routine. Let's go, Genie."

They clambered silently to the ground. Chester looked back to see Case snatch up a third stone, add it to the act. The natives watched, mouths open. In the shelter of a giant tree bole Chester and Genie paused for an instant, then stole away from the clearing, found a rough trail among the trees, broke into a run. Behind them the cheers of the savages rose, growing fainter now, fading in the distance.

"In the clear," Chester gasped, pulling level with Genie. "Now all we have to do is search a few hundred square miles of woods until we find the rug and the chairs."

"That's all right, Chester," said Genie, running lightly at his side. "I think I know the way."

"Well," Chester puffed, "let's just hope that when we get there the computer is still waiting with its meter ticking."

4

Chester staggered the last few yards across the grassy slope to the rug and sank down in one of the yellow chairs. "Next time I go for a romp in the woods" he said, groaning, "I'm going to be wearing a good grade of boots; these melon-slicers are killing me."

"I see no signs of pursuit," said Genie. "Mr. Mulvihill is apparently still holding their attention successfully."

"Hold it, Genie." Chester pointed. "There's smoke rising from back there. You don't suppose . . . ?"

Genie looked concerned. "I don't think they've had time to start roasting Mr. Mulvihill—yet."

"Good Lord, Genie. You think—maybe . . . ?"

"It isn't impossible, judging from what I observed of the cultural pattern."

Chester got to his feet. "We have to go back, Genie. Maybe we can surprise them."

"As you wish, Chester. But I'm afraid we would accomplish nothing. Neither of us is sufficiently robust to overcome an antagonist by force."

Chester's shoulders slumped. "I've always led such a . . . civilized life. I never thought I'd have any occasion for muscles."

"We'd better go on, Chester. We'll obtain arms and hurry back."

"I suppose that's all we can do. Poor Case—he's probably broiling alive. He sacrificed himself for us. For heaven's sake, hurry. Genie! You *are* in contact, I hope?"

Genie considered, then smiled doubtfully. "Yes, I think so. I'll try. Stand close to me, Chester."

He gripped her hand. The sunny scene faded, to be replaced by a wide expanse of black macadam: a city

street. All around, tall buildings struck upward out of
shadow into high sunlight. A rumbling machine swerved
past on the left. Two smaller ones, snorting, veered by
on the right in a howl of brakes. An immense truck bore
down, air brakes hissing, ground to a halt, towering over
the brocaded chairs with its front tires resting on the
fringed edge of the rug. Behind the dusty windshield,
the drive yelled and shook his fist. The shout was
drowned in a torrent of horns, voices, engines. Chester
leaped up for the sidewalk, pulling Genie with him.

"Something's wrong!" he gasped. "Where are we,
Genie?"

"I don't know; there's some sort of imbalance in the
co-ordinates, Chester. Maybe it's because Mr. Mulvihill
was left behind."

A stout man with an open vest over a soiled shirt
discarded a toothpick and stepped from a doorway under
three tarnished brass spheres.

"Hey, sister, ain't you forgot something?" He leered
as he lowered his eyes to ankle level and came up
slowly. A man behind him jostled him aside.

"Hiya, babe," he said breezily. "A broad like you and
me could get along, kiddo. You're kinda skinny, but
Benny likes 'em thataway."

Chester stepped forward. "You don't understand.
We're involved in an experimental . . . " Benny glanced
at him, rammed stiff fingers into his sternum. "Get lost,
punk." Chester doubled over, gasping. The crowd ringing
the tableau separated as a wide figure in a pink uniform
and a chrome-plated helmet pushed through, nightstick
twirling. He looked Genie over, reached for her arm.

"Come on, sister, I'm takin' you in."

Genie swung a full-handed slap that sent the gaudily
dressed cop staggering back. "Chester, let's run!" She
seized his hand; he straightened painfully, scrambled
after her. The crowd parted again, gaping.

"Give it to 'em, kiddo," a drunk called cheerfully. The cop lunged, tripped over the drunk's outstretched foot, hit with a crunch.

A narrow alleyway opened ahead; Chester and Genie sprinted down it, rounded a corner, dodged garbage cans, emerged into a sheltered court hung with faded washing.

"I don't hear anyone chasing us," Chester gasped. "I don't know where you've landed us, Genie, but we're a long way from home. It looks like a parody of a twentieth-century scene—except for that pink policeman."

"I don't understand it, Chester," Genie wailed. "I was sure I used the proper angle of pi over rho squared . . . "

"The mob acted normal enough. Lucky they're spectator sports." Chester plucked a long-armed shirt from the lowest line, draped it about Genie's shoulders. "I've got to get you some clothes. Duck into a doorway and look inconspicuous. I'll be back as soon as I can."

Ten minutes later, Chester returned, arms laden. "I found a sporting-goods store," he panted. "This is a strange place you've brought us to, Genie. I had to open something called a charge account."

Genie wriggled into a pair of nylon panties, size 5, a 34B brassiere, a pair of whipcord riding breeches, a white linen shirt, a green tweed hacking jacket, and a pair of low-cut riding boots.

"You look charming, Genie," Chester commented. "Like a picture in an old book. Now we can—"

"Oh dear, someone's coming!" Genie exclaimed. "Shall we hide?"

"You take the doorway; I'll get back of the garbage bin!" Chester dived for shelter as a cop with a bruised eye appeared at the alley mouth.

"There she is, boys!" he called. "I told youse . . . "

Chester peered from hiding, saw a half a dozen cops fan out.

"Watch her, boys. She's some kind of wild dame from the circus. Now, sister, are you going to come along peaceable?"

"Hey, Sarge, I thought you said she was nood."

"So now she's got clothes on. It's the same broad."

The cops approached warily. "She don't look tough to me," a fat cop stated. From shelter, Chester thrust out a foot. The cop, moving briskly for the pinch, hooked an ankle, leaped face first into a patch of spilled garbage. The others charged as Genie darted from the doorway. Hoarse yells rang; cops struggled. Chester sprang to the rescue, put a foot in the garbage slick . . .

A shower of fire shimmered, fading into darkness.

Chester's head ached. He turned over, snuggled down to go back to sleep. He'd have to complain to the management about the mattress; and he was cold, too. He groped for a blanket, felt a rough wall, opened one eye and stared at iron bars and concrete. He sat up, fingering a large knot at the back of his head.

"Genie?" he called hopefully. There was no answer. He rose and went to the door. With his face against the bars, Chester peered along the corridor. The other cells in view were empty. Twenty feet distant, an unshaven man in blue overalls over tattletale-gray longjohns dozed at a desk under a bare sixty-watt light bulb. There was a curled calendar on the wall behind him, featuring a girl, stripped to a G string, hip boots and a deerstalker cap, holding a BB gun. Chester squinted, made out numerals: 1967. He groaned. Somehow, he thought, Genie had landed them in a grotesque parody of the simple halcyon days of a century before, when life had been leisurely and colorful. Chester called again, softly. Somewhere water dripped. There were faint street noises.

He went back to the gray-blanketed bunk, wincing

at the throbbing in his head, and sorted through the objects in the seal-away pockets of his sports jacket. Apparently the local cops hadn't managed to find them:

A permatch in a silver case.

A plastic credit card, showing a balance of twenty-one credits.

A half-used packet of Chanel dope sticks.

A buttonhole Tri-D pickup, with attached contact screens.

Not much there, Chester reflected sadly, that would be of help in forcing the steel door of the primitive cell. He twiddled the control of the Tri-D idly, winced at the sudden boom of cacophony, turned the volume low.

"Well, Jim," a tiny voice said. "Here we are in a spaceship, on our way to Venus."

"Yes, Bob," an even tinier voice replied. "We barely escaped capture by the corrupt Space Patrol, which fears we will reveal what we've learned of their illegal operations."

"Yes, Jim. However, if we can only reach the safety of Venus ahead of them, we can enlist the help of Professor Zorch, famed for his researches into abstruse scientific matters, and like that . . . "

Chester flipped the set off. Canned entertainment hadn't changed. On Tri-D, people were always able to adapt ball-point pens into Mark I blasters and fight their way out of any situation—but what could one do with a high-polymer credit card? Or a dope stick? The Tri-D was no better. As for the permatch . . .

Hmmm. Chester fingered the case, opened it and took out the slender two-inch tube of fused quartz with its cluster of components in a quarter-inch bulb at one end. Hadn't he read somewhere that it was dangerous to tamper with a permatch, since it was easy to throw the delicate lens alignment out of adjustment?

Carefully, Chester pried off the tiny protective cap, exposing the factory-set adjusting screw. Now he needed a tool.

The stiff corner of the credit card served nicely. Chester thumbed the permatch alight, then minutely turned the screw. The flame darted out in a thin blue streamer. He turned it farther; the flame winked out. He stared at it unhappily. A two-inch flame wasn't going to help. A faint acrid odor made Chester snort. Someone was burning dog hair. The odor grew stronger. Across the room, a tiny brown dot appeared on the scaled paint of the wall, grew larger, turning black at the periphery. A lazy coil of smoke ascended. Chester gaped, then flicked off the match; the smoke faded.

Back at the barred door, Chester squinted along the tiny tube, pressed the stud. The man in the chair slept on peacefully. A half-inch spot on the desk near his elbow bubbled, smoked. Chester moved the beam cautiously across until the long hairs over the dreamer's ear curled suddenly. The man's nose twitched. He slapped at his temple, sat up snorting, looked around. Chester jumped back, dived for the bunk, scrambled under it and huddled in a deep shadow against the wall. The unshaven face appeared at the door, blinking into the gloom. There was a muttered exclamation, then a clash of keys. The door opened. Chester took aim, focused on the callused heel of a large bare foot. The man yelped and hopped, grabbing for the singed member. Chester leveled his fire on the other. The man danced, staring wildly around, then made for the door.

"A poltergeist!" he shouted. "Hey, Harney!"

Chester wriggled out from concealment, ducked through the open door, and slid into the shelter of a gray-painted wall locker as heavy feet pounded in the hall.

"Don't tell me," the barefoot cop was shouting. "I seen 'em before, plenty times. They got a kind of attraction fer me. This here one is a bad one. First it picked up m' desk, then it started throwin' things, then it give me two hotfoots."

"Hotfeet," someone snarled. "See if he's got a bottle, Lem."

"Looky here," the barefoot one started. "I guess you boys never heard the time I seen the saucer . . ."

"Don't see no bottle."

Three large backs loomed a yard from Chester's concealment. He aimed through a narrow opening between them, focused on a blanket dangling from a bunk in the cell across the corridor. Smoke rose promptly.

"Hey!" one of the cops barked. "They's su'thin in there!" He backed from view. "I'll go fer help!"

Chester listened as the three men competed for position; three sets of footsteps receded along the hall. Chester pocketed the permatch and headed for a side entrance.

Half an hour later, a shabby brown tweed jacket filched from the station covering his modishly cut but conspicuous plastic-appliqué sports jacket, Chester strolled past the stretch of street where he and Genie had first arrived, now obstructed by large wooden signs lettered DETOUR. Police squad cars were parked three deep at the curb. The area around the rug with its two chairs was blocked off by yellow-painted sawhorses hung with red obstruction lights. A crowd of idlers gaped.

"All right, move along," a cop bawled. "The bomb squad is goin' in now. You folks wanta get blown up?"

Chester paused, scanning the crowd for Genie. No luck. She hadn't been in jail—at least not in the part he had had an opportunity to check. Surely if she were free, she would have come here. Not that it would help. No one could get through that police cordon.

Chester tried hard to think. If only Case were here—or Genie. But unless he could get back to the rug, he'd never see either of them again.

Case would be thoroughly roasted by now, of course, it that *had* been the purpose of the fire he'd seen— but perhaps that was being overly pessimistic. Perhaps Case was still juggling away, casting anxious glances down the jungle path from time to time, waiting for rescue.

And Genie, being grilled under the hot lights by policemen, who, in spite of their pink coats, were cop all the way through . . .

One of the cops seemed to be looking Chester's way. He sauntered on, whistling, stepped into the first doorway he saw, found himself in a shop plastered with SALE notices and crowded with flimsy tables stacked with gaudily colored merchandise among which bored-looking customers milled, picking over the bargains.

Chester tried to think. He couldn't just stand around; in time, the cops would be sure to notice him. Perhaps if he tried a sudden dash for the rug . . .

He glanced through the window. The cops were large and numerous, the sawhorses closely spaced, the squad cars ominously ready. He could never hope to penetrate that barrier by a surprise move alone; he would have to do something to distract attention and then slip through quietly.

"Git outa da way, ya bastid," a corpulent lady with a mustache and runover shoes said conversationally, nudging Chester aside.

"Oh, excuse me, Madam . . ." Chester moved on to the next counter, found himself nervously fingering a stack of clear plastic bags.

"That's the two-quart size," a salesman said to a man on Chester's left.

Chester picked up a bag. It was good, tough stuff.

"Seals with a hot iron," the salesman was saying.

Chester felt in his pocket. Hmm. His credit card was no good here, of course. He'd have to—

A large placard caught his eye: DON'T ASK FOR CREDIT!

"How do I know what you use 'em for?" the clerk was saying. "You want 'em or don't you?"

The customer mumbled. The clerk turned away. Chester slipped a two-inch sheaf of the plastic bags from the counter and under his coat and headed for the door. As he reached it, a hoarse voice called, "Hey, you. The guy with the funny pants!"

Chester hurled himself between two matrons in garish prints with uneven hemlines and set off at a run. Heads turned to stare. A whistle shrilled behind him. He rounded a corner, saw a short flight of steps with an iron rail. He took them four at a time, banged through a massive glass-paneled door into a dim hallway that smelled of stale vegetable oil, fly spray and deodorant. Carpeted stairs rose into a canyon of yellowed wallpaper. Chester went up, whirled through the landing as the door below banged open.

"In here!" someone yelled.

"Take the back. I'll check upstairs!"

The staircase ended three flights up in a narrow hallway leading to a gray window behind limp curtains. Feet were thudding on the stairs. There were three doors with brown porcelain knobs along each side of the hall. Chester jumped to the first on the left. It rattled but held. The second opened and a blat of sound emerged. Chester sprang for the third door, threw it open, whirled and slammed it behind him. In two jumps he was in the bathroom, pulling open a tarnished mirror. He seized a can of shaving cream, blasted a gob into his hand, slapped it across his face, under his chin. In a quick motion, he pulled off the coat, the sports jacket, tossed them aside, grabbled a bladeless safety razor from the cabinet shelf and scraped a swath through the layer of white lather, then dashed for the door and flung it wide.

A cop thundered past, threw a glance at Chester. "Stay inside, buddy," he bawled.

Chester withdrew, closed the door gently, and let out a long breath. "Who says there's no point in watching the Late Late Late Show?" he murmured.

From the windows, Chester looked down on the crowded street. The rug looked pitifully small in the center of the barricade of sawhorses, cops, cars and curious citizens. The distance was, Chester estimated, fifty feet vertically, and an equal distance out from the face of the building. The sounds in the hall had gone away now. He went into the green enameled bathroom, wiped the lather from his face, recovered his shirt from the living-room floor, then checked through the closet shelves, the bedroom and finally the kitchen. He found an electric iron in a cabinet under the sink. The ironing board was propped in a corner. Chester set it up, plugged in the iron, then counted his plastic bags. Forty-two of them. Still, there was no use starting on the bags unless he could work out the delivery mechanism.

A thorough search of the apartment turned up a ball of stout twine, nails, a hammer, a heavy-duty stapler, several hundred back issues of *Crude*, The Magazine for Male Men, and a small plastic wastebasket. Chester set to work.

Pounding cautiously, he drove two stout nails into the window sill eight inches apart, and a matching pair into the wall across the room at a level four feet higher,

then strung heavy twine across between them in two
parallel strands. Next he cut the bottom neatly from
the wastebasket and nailed the container to the wall
above the previously placed nails, with the smaller, cut-
out end down. The next two nails went into the right-
hand wall, with two more matching them on the
opposite side of the room, just under the ceiling. Again
he strung cord between the paired spikes.

Chester paused to listen. There was a murmur of
sound from the street, the drip of water from the bathroom, the snarl of an engine gunning somewhere. He
went to the refrigerator, took out a can of beer, drank
half of it and went back to work.

He opened a copy of *Crude*, stared wonderingly at
a double-page spread in full color captioned "Udderly
Delightful" and fitted the magazine over one of the
cables at the window sill so that the string nestled
against the spine, at the center of the thin sheaf of
pages. He crimped the other edge of the magazine,
folded the creased edge over the other line and stapled
it in place to form a shallow trough between the two
supporting lines.

The next *Crude* was positioned above the first.
Working rapidly, Chester extended the chute across the
room to terminate directly under the bottomless wastebasket.

He stepped back to survey his work. The center of
the trough had a tendency, he noted, to droop, the
edges of the magazines coming almost together. He
went to the closet, extracted half a dozen wire coat
hangers and bent them into shallow U-shaped braces,
which he fitted between the lines at three-foot intervals. The trough now formed a smooth curve from the
wastebasket to the window sill.

Fifteen minutes' work completed the other leg of
the trough, extending from the left-hand wall in a

shallow curve to end above the open top of the waste-basket.

There was a three-inch roll of masking tape on the desk; Chester used it to attach extra sheets bearing photographs of shirtless women to the floor of the trough, lapping the joints between magazines.

Back in the kitchen, he finished the beer, then filled a plastic bag with water, used a length of clothesline wire to assist in folding the top edge over evenly, then applied the warm iron, sealing the plastic. He went to the living room, stepped up on a chair and placed the plastic bag of water in the wastebasket. It dropped an inch or two, then wedged tight in the tapered passage. Chester went back to the kitchen, located a pint bottle nearly full of vegetable oil, returned and poured a generous helping around the plastic bag. It eased down, plopped into the trough below, where Chester caught it and set it aside.

He went back to the kitchen and carefully filled and sealed the remaining forty-one bags. Next he used the ice pick to make a hole in each side of the wastebas-ket, near the bottom, through which he threaded a length of string. He tied a knot at one end, drew it up snug, then looped the other around a large wooden match which nestled against the outside of the waste-basket, holding the string in position, blocking the bot-tom of the container. He used a chair to reach the top of the upper trough, into which he poured a liberal dollop of vegetable oil, smearing it out well so that the entire surface of the chute was lubricated. He repeated the operation for the steeper lower section.

Chester went back to the kitchen, where the water bags lay like a clutch of limp dinosaur eggs, selected one, and placed it in the upper end of the higher trough. It slid gently down the long chute and dropped into the wastebasket, easing down to rest against the obstructing string. Then he loaded the magazine trough above with the other bags. The forty-one rounds just filled the available space, lying bulging, end to end.

Chester crossed the room and looked out. The police below were striding about with tape measures, standing with folded arms, posing for photographers, and waving back the crowd that seemed about to engulf the tiny arena of official activity. Cautiously, Chester raised the window twelve inches. Oil dribbled from the end of the trough into the window sill. He went into the bathroom, ducking under the chute, washed up, smoothed his hair, straightened his shirt, donned his jacket, then removed his heavy silver ring and placed it on the medicine-cabinet shelf beside the shaving cream.

He opened the hall door and looked out. All quiet. The box of matches lay on a table by the door. He lighted one, touched it to the match securing the string which blocked the wastebasket, then sprinted for the stairs, leaped down them five at a time, rounded the landing, took the second flight, pounded down to ground level.

Breathing hard, he paused to glance out the street door. The fringes of the crowd were strung out near the corner. He stepped out, strode along quickly, pushed through the spectators to a position from which the third-story windows were visible. The one directly above the center of activity was open. The curtain billowed slightly; the end of the trough was clearly visible.

Nothing happened.

Chester swallowed. It hadn't taken him more than thirty seconds to make the three flights down to the street. Had the match gone out?

Something flashed in the window, glinted in an arc out over the street, dropped. A strangled yell sounded. The crowd simultaneously surged forward and recoiled, as curiosity struggled with discretion. Chester pushed his way through the press as a second almost invisible missile leaped from the window. "It's radioactive!" someone yelled. The mob churned. A woman screamed. Cops appeared, beating a strategic withdrawal from the field of fire. A third bomb flew from the window, splattered against a tall policeman who yelled and sprang for cover. A fourth bag of water soared out, down and exploded.

"A little under a second apart," Chester muttered, weaving between fleeing citizens. "A little too much oil in the wastebasket."

Four cops remained in the rapidly expanding clearing centered on the rug. One drew his pistol and fired into the air. The other three, eyes on the growing blots on the rug, dropped flat. Chester reached open ground, skirted the first rank of squad cars, seeing the flash of another round, then another. The next fell short, splashed off a police car, sent spray high in the air. Two fat women darted from forward positions, screeching and slapping at water droplets. Chester ducked aside, took an elbow in the ribs, stumbled out into the clear.

"Hey!" a shrill voice sounded behind him. "Ain't you the guy . . . "

Chester threw his leg over the sawhorse.

"That's far enough, Buster," the cop bawled. He took a step forward, bringing the gun around as a bag of water took him in the face. He went down backward. Chester scrambled over, took two steps to the rug.

An immense padded mallet slammed against his head. The world rose up and hit him in the face.

Curious, Chester thought dreamily. *I always pictured H-bombs as being noisy.*

Someone was hauling at his arm.

"This is the bastid, I seen him," someone was screeching. Chester shook his head, pulled free from the grip and struggled to his feet. A hatless cop wavered on all fours between Chester and the rug. The fat woman raised a rolled umbrella. "I'm claimin' the reward," she shrieked. A bomb splattered. The cop focused his eyes on Chester and lunged. Chester ducked away, managing a return jab at the fat woman as he bowled her aside, and sprang for the rug. He skidded to a halt midway between the two brocaded chairs, ducked a bag of water and yelled, "Computer, get me out of here—fast!"

5

The tall buildings, the street, the cops, faded, winked out of existence. The sounds died, cut off abruptly. Chester stood in the center of a wide square paved with varicolored cobblestones and lined with small shops and merchants' stalls. Beyond, a green slope dotted with dazzling white villas swept up to a wooded skyline. People in bright colors moved about, examining tradesmen's wares, stopping in groups to talk, or strolling at ease. Above a silversmith's shop, white curtains fluttered at open windows. The aroma of crisping bacon drifted across the square. In the distance a flute played a lazy melody.

Chester groaned. "Ye gods, where've you brought me this time, Computer?"

"Your instructions were," the computer's voice spoke from mid-air, "simply to—"

"I know. I always seem to phrase things badly. Every time I make a move, I'm worse off than I was. Now I've lost Case, and Genie, too. Where am I this time?"

"According to my instruments, this *should* be the Chester residence."

"You'd better have your wiring checked."

A brass plate set in the paving underfoot, half concealed by the edge of the rug, caught Chester's eye.

The inscription read: "IT WAS ON THIS SPOT THAT THE LEGENDARY KEZ-FATHER, HERO AND TEACHER, TOOK HIS LEAVE OF THE PEOPLE AFTER BRINGING THEM THE GIFT OF WISDOM. THIS MYTH, WHICH DATES BACK TO THE CULTURE . . ."

"Ye gods," Chester muttered. "I've already violated the local shrine." He moved quickly clear of the spot.

Two men in loose togas, one old, one young, stood nearby, looking earnestly past Chester. He cleared his throat and stepped forward. Nothing to do now but brazen it out.

"I white god," he said. "I come, bring magic stick, go bang, all fall down!"

The two men ignored him. "Remarkable!" the older exclaimed, turning to the younger man, in green. "Did you observe this phenomenon, Devant?"

The other, a well-muscled man with clear blue eyes and flashing white teeth, nodded. "Two curious chairs and a rug. I glanced away for a moment and when I turned back—there they were. I find it difficult to reconcile the manifestation with my world-picture. A very interesting problem."

"Possibly my senility is getting the better of me." The old man glanced at Chester. "Young man, did you observe the arrival of this furniture?"

Chester cleared his throat. "Not exactly, sir; I have been participating in an experiment, and I seem to have lost my bearings. Could you tell me—"

"No," the old man said, shaking his head resignedly. "That would have been too much to hope for. Why are there never any witnesses to these apparently supernatural manifestations?"

"Is it possible," the man in green cut in, "that this could be the probability crisis that Vasawalie has been predicting?"

"It's not supernatural," Chester said. "Merely a misguided piece of mechanical ineptitude. You see, I—"

"Please, young man; no mechanistic platitudes, if you please."

"You don't understand. This is *my* furniture."

The old man held up a hand. "I fear I must insist on my prior claim. I distinctly observed you to approach from—ah, I'm not sure of the direction, but it was well after I had pointed out the anomaly. In fact, I'm sure you were attracted by my cry of surprise. Correct, Devant?"

"I didn't notice just when he came up," Devant said. "But it was at least five or possibly ten minutes after you and I, Norgo."

"Actually, I was here first," Norgo said. "*You* followed by several minutes, Devant."

"Oh, never mind," Chester said. "Can you just tell me the name of this town?"

"I'll get a crew down right away," said Devant. "I want to examine this *in situ*. Molecular scan, fabric distortion, chronometric phase-interference, Psi band—everything." He waved a hand at Chester. "Please step aside; you're obscuring my view."

"This will be a serious blow to Randomism," said Norgo happily.

"What I wanted to ask was," Chester pressed on, "what year is this? I mean, ah, this isn't by any chance the future, is it?"

The old gentleman looked at Chester squarely for the first time. "Let us define our terms," he said, folding his arms. "Now . . ."

"What I mean is, this scene here—" Chester waved a hand—"is something my computer invented—just as a harmless sort of joke, you understand. The problem is . . . "

Norgo blinked. "I shall do a paper," he said, "on pseudorationalization in response to rejection of—"

"You don't seem to understand," cut in Chester. "I'm lost and my friends are relying on me."

"It will be the sensation of the Congress," Norgo droned on, rubbing his hands together. "Great Source of Facts. What if I should actually derive germane substantive data from this? That will dispose of the Ordainists, once and for all."

"Blast the Ordainists," Chester burst out. "I'm in serious difficulties. My best friend is being roasted alive, a young woman of my acquaintance is under detention by primitive police, and you—"

"Dear me, a well-developed delusional system," said Norgo. "Doubtless arising from frustration at having been anticipated in detection of the chair phenomenon. This will be most interesting to the Congress."

"You're the delusion!" Chester shouted. "I'm getting back on my rug; I'll dissolve this whole fantasy back into the computer banks it came out of!"

Norgo sprang forward. "I must ask you not to disturb the artifacts; they may be highly important scientific exhibits."

"They happen to belong to me." Chester turned, rebounded from the broad, muscular chest of Devant. Five more well-developed locals moved into position around him.

"You'll have to move on," the big man said. "Only technicians will be permitted in this area while the specimens are under study."

Norgo tsked. "We simply can't have these distressing exhibitions by frustrated partisans of misguided philosophical splinter groups. I shall propose to the Congress—"

"I've got to get back to my rug!" Chester made a dive for a gap in the ranks, felt iron hands clamp on his arms.

"Hey, Computer!" he yelled. There was no reply. The hands propelled him quickly along to deposit him well outside the growing circle of spectators.

"Any more disturbances," Devant said coldly, "and I'll have you locked up."

"But . . . how long before you'll be finished?"

"Just run along and amuse yourself. We'll have a great deal to do. It may take a while."

Chester gazed listlessly at the swimming pool rippling in the late-afternoon sun. A pretty brunette in a diaper crossed the terrace and offered a frosted glass. Chester shook his head.

"Shall we go for a swim, Chester?"

"No, thanks, Darina."

"Poor Chester. Can't you cheer up?"

"You don't seem to understand." Chester's voice held a plaintive note. "I've been idling here for weeks now while my friends suffer fates I shudder to contemplate. My computer's probably been dismantled. And those idiotic scholars still won't let me near my rug."

Darina made a sympathetic sound. "The rug is a powerful security symbol to you, isn't it, Chester? I remember a blanket—"

"There's nothing secure about it! It's probably nonfunctional now. And at best, I'll just find myself trapped in another of the computer's preposterous settings. But even that would be better than lounging here, completely ineffectual."

"Chester, have you thought of finding work to do?"

"What kind of work? I just want to get away from here. I've tried five times to creep up on my rug under cover of darkness, but that fellow Devant . . ."

"What were you trained in, Chester?"

"Well," said Chester, considering, "I . . . ah . . . majored in liberal arts."

"You mean you paint pictures?"

"No, nothing like that. Business administration."

"I don't think I've heard of that. Is it a game of skill or chance?"

"Both." Chester smiled patiently. "No, in biz ad we're taught how to manage large commercial enterprises."

"I see. And after receiving your training you went on to actual management of some such organization?"

"Well, no. Funny, but I couldn't seem to find any big businessmen who were looking for a fresh college graduate to tell them how to run their companies."

"Perhaps we'd better try something else. What about the arts?"

"I did do a painting once," Chester said hesitantly. "It had numbers that you compared with a chart and then you matched that up with the little cans of paint and colored in the spaces."

"I'm not sure there'd be a large call for that type of skill here."

"Don't disparage it. President Eisenhower—"

"What about handicrafts? We value the manual skills highly here, Chester."

"Oh, I've done a lot of that. Built a plastic boll weevil only last month. Over two hundred interlocking parts."

"You made the parts from plastic?"

"No. I bought a kit. But . . . "

"Perhaps in the field of sports?" Darina suggested.

Chester blushed. "Well, of course, in school I was a great fan of outdoor activities. I never missed a game the entire four years."

"Splendid!" Darina looked interested. "We'll be

happy to receive instruction in any new types of athletic competition of which you're master."

"Well, I didn't actually *play*, of course. But I was
there in the stands, rooting. And I know some of the
rules."

"You didn't play?"

"I was on my fraternity's bridge squad," Chester
offered.

"How is that played?" asked Darina, brightening.
Chester explained. There was an awkward silence.

"Chester, have you ever performed any useful labor?"
Darina asked.

"As a matter of fact, I worked one summer in a factory. I was an instrument spot-checker. I made sure
the controls that worked the automatic machinery were
functioning properly."

"This involved mechanical skills?"

"If anything had gone wrong with the TV scanner
that actually did the inspecting, I was on the spot to
see that the back-up scanner took over."

"You activated the emergency equipment, in other
words?"

"No, it was automatic. But I assure you, the union
regarded my job as essential."

"What about hobbies, Chester?"

"Oh, my, yes; I had a stamp collection."

"Hmmm. Perhaps something a little more active?"

"I built model airplanes as a boy. Of course, I gave
that up when I was twelve."

"Why?"

"Well, it seemed a trifle immature. All the other lads
my age were already learning golf." Chester broke off
as a white-haired elder took a table a few yards distant. "Say, there's that old fool who's behind all this."
He rose and crossed to the other table.

"Look here, Mr. Norgo, how long is this absurd

business going on? I've been here a month now—and I'm no closer to getting back on my rug than I was. You don't seem to understand—"

"Calmly, Chester," Norgo said, signaling a waitress clad in a wet handkerchief. "It is you who fail to understand. Important work is in progress. Meanwhile, just keep yourself amused."

"I'm in no mood to be amused!"

Norgo nodded thoughtfully. "Perhaps you'd like to participate in an experiment?"

"What is it—vivisection?"

Norgo considered. "I don't think that will be necessary." He hitched his chair around. "Chester, do you know what our most important natural resource is?"

"What has that to do with my problem?"

"Do you know how often a truly superior intellect is born?"

"Not very often. Look, I—"

"Once in four million, five hundred and thirty-three thousand, two hundred and four births. With a world population of half a billion, the present figure, the rules of probability allow for the presence among us of only one hundred such gifted persons. And do you know what percentage of these superior individuals are fortunate enough to encounter conditions conducive to the full stimulation of their latent abilities?"

"I'd guess about—"

"Not one percent," Norgo said flatly. "With luck, one individual."

"Very interesting. But to get back to—"

"If we were content," Norgo pressed on, "to allow unrestrictive increase in the population, we might, one could reason, improve this situation. With a ten-fold increase in population, the number of superior intellects should increase to a thousand, you say."

"I didn't say, but—"

"Not so! Environmental factors would deteriorate due to overcrowded conditions. The latent geniuses would find less opportunity to evolve their talents."

"That hardly seems—"

"The true function of the mass of the population is the production, by their sheer numbers, of the occasional genius. It is the objective of our educational system to identify and train such talents—and this can only be done by the realization, in each individual, of the maximum potential."

"Why? So they can grow up and talk like you?"

"Now, life is not an engineering project, Chester. It is a work of art."

"And while you're lecturing on art, my friends are—"

"I have long been interested," Norgo went on imperturbably, "in the purely theoretical problem of the reactions of a mature but untrained mind exposed to a full modern education, in concentrated form, after perhaps twenty-five years of indolence, laziness, carelessness, minimal demand. The pressure, of course, would be tremendous. Would the mind or body break under the stress? Believe me, Chester, the results of such an experiment would be of the most profound importance."

"Not to me. I—"

"Now you, Chester, while possessed of a normal potential, are, beyond the simple abilities to talk and feed yourself, plus a few fringe accomplishments such as playing the game you call bridge, totally untrained. Your body is weak, your will untried, your mind unused—"

"Maybe I don't get out a lot."

"All of which makes you an ideal subject—if you wish to volunteer for the experiment."

"I wish to get back to my rug."

Norgo nodded. "Exactly."

Chester's mouth opened. "You mean—why, this is blackmail!"

"Let us simply say that by the time the experiment is concluded, your—ah—rug will have been released by our research groups."

"How long will that be?"

"I shall attempt, Chester, to impart the equivalent of a twenty-year course of development in a single year."

"A year! But . . . "

"I know; you're concerned for your imaginary playmates."

"I told you . . . "

Norgo turned as a laden tray was placed before him. "Let me know your decision, Chester."

"If I do it—you'll let me back on my rug?"

Norgo nodded, sniffing a dish appreciatively.

"Of all the underhanded, unethical, unwarranted piracy I've ever encountered, this is undoubtedly the most unbelievable," Chester said bitterly.

Norgo blinked. "You mean you're refusing?"

"When do I start?"

6

Chester and Norgo clambered down from the open cockpits of the heli in which they had flown out from the Center. Chester looked around at the sweep of meadow, the wooded hills, and a low white building that covered a quarter acre near the crest of the slope. Cut in the white stone above the entry were the words: IS NOT IS NOT NOT IS

Norgo led the way across the grass and into an airy hall where mosaics stood out in brilliant color against white walls.

"Ah, here's Kuve now," Norgo said.

A tall young man with pale blond hair and a square jaw approached through an open archway. He greeted Norgo, studied Chester appraisingly.

"So this is to be my subject," he said, circling Chester. "Remove your shirt, please."

"Right now? I thought I'd have time to unpack, take a shower, stroll around, look over the campus, and then maybe have coffee, get acquainted with the other students, discuss the curriculum, plan a schedule . . . "

Kuve broke in. "There will be no opportunity for coffee or strolls. Your schedule has been planned in advance. You will become acquainted with the plan as necessary."

Chester slowly pulled off his shirt. "It sounds like a strange sort of school. How often will I be able to get back to town?"

"The trousers, please," Kuve said.

"Right here in the lobby?"

Kuve looked at him, surprised. "It is comfortably warm, is it not?"

"Sure, but—"

"Tell me," Kuve said interestedly, "are you under the impression that you are in some way unique?"

"I'm perfectly normal!"

Kuve looked Chester over carefully. "You're going to make a fascinating project," he said approvingly. "Norgo wasn't exaggerating. Almost complete atrophy of the musculature, obvious limited articulation, minimal lung capacity, poor skin tone, barely sub-parthenogenic posture . . . "

"Well, I'm sorry if I don't come up to your expectations."

"Oh, you do indeed. You even exceed them. But don't be concerned. I've worked out a complete developmental scheme for you."

"That's fast work. It hasn't been three hours since I volunteered."

"Oh, I started on it a month ago, when Norgo told me you'd be volunteering."

Chester trailed Kuve along a wide corridor to a small room lined with wall cabinets. Kuve pointed to one. "You will find garments there. Please put them on."

Chester squeezed into a pair of trunks, laced on sandals, and stood. "Is this all I get? I feel like the New Year."

A shapely young woman in a white kilt entered the room. She smiled at Chester, took a case of instruments from a cabinet, and reached for his hand. "I'm Mina. I'm going to trim your nails back and apply a growth-retarding agent," she said cheerfully. "Hold still now."

"What's this for?"

"Excessively long hair and nails would be a painful nuisance in some of the training," said Kuve. "Now, Chester, I want to ask you something: What is pain?"

"It's . . . umm . . . uh . . . a feeling that comes from damage to the body."

"Nearly right, Chester. Pain is based on *fear* of damage to the body."

Kuve went to a wall shelf, brought back a small metal article and held it up.

"This is a manual shaving device, once in daily use. This sharp-edged blade was drawn over the skin of the face, cutting the hairs."

"I'm glad I live in modern times."

"Under optimum conditions, the process of removing a single day's growth of facial hair with this instrument

occasioned a pain level of .2 agons. Under merely average conditions, however, the level quickly rose to .5
agons, roughly equivalent to the sensation produced by
a second-degree burn."

"It's amazing what people will put up with," Chester
said.

"Are your feet perfectly comfortable, Chester?"

"Certainly. Why shouldn't they be?"

"You have callus tissue on both feet, as well as defor-
mities caused by constricting footwear."

"Well, melon-slicers may not be the most—"

"In order to have produced these conditions, you
must have endured pain on the order of .5 agons continuously, for months and years. Yet probably you seldom noticed it."

"Why notice it? There was nothing I could do about
it."

"Exactly. Pain is not an absolute; it is a state of mind,
which you can learn to disregard."

Kuve reached out, pinched the skin on Chester's
thigh. "You can see that I'm merely pressing with very
moderate force. You are in no danger of injury."

"Is that a promise?" said Chester nervously.

"Now close your eyes. Concentrate on the sensation
of undergoing an amputation of the leg—without
anesthetic. The knife slicing through the flesh, the saw
attacking the living bone . . . "

Chester squirmed in the chair. "Hey, that hurts!
You're bearing down too hard!"

Kuve released his grip. "I squeezed no harder,
Chester. The association of the idea of injury intensi-
fied the sensation. You paid no attention whatever to
Mina when she applied a measured stimulus of .4 agons
to the exposed cuticle of your finger while I held your
attention. You accepted the twinges of a manicure as
normal and non-injurious."

Chester rubbed his thigh. "The leg still hurts. I'll have a bruise tomorrow."

"You may." Kuve nodded. "The control of the mind over bodily functions is extensive."

Mina finished, flashed a smile at Chester and left the room.

"Let's move along to the gymnasium." Kuve led the way along a corridor to a larger room, high-ceilinged and fitted with gymnastic equipment. He turned to Chester. "What is fear?"

"It's . . . uh . . . the feeling you get when you're in danger."

"It is the feeling that arises when you are unsure of your own capability to meet a situation."

"You're wrong on that one, Kuve. If a Bengal tiger walked in here I'd be scared, even if I knew exactly how incapable I was."

"Look around you; what would you actually do if a wild beast did in fact enter this room?"

"Well, I'd run."

"Where?"

Chester studied the room. "It wouldn't do any good to start off down the hall; there's no door to stop whatever was chasing me. I think I'd take that rope there." He pointed to a knotted fifty-foot cable suspended from among high rafters.

"An excellent decision."

"But I doubt if I could climb it."

"So you are unsure of your capabilities." Kuve smiled. "But try, Chester."

Chester went to the rope, looked at it doubtfully. Kuve muttered into a wrist communicator. Chester grasped the rope, wrapped his legs around it, wriggled up six feet.

"This is . . . the best I can . . . do," Chester puffed. He slid back to the floor.

There was a sound like water gurgling down a drain. Chester turned quickly. An immense tan mountain lion paced toward him, yellow eyes alight, a growl rumbling from its throat. With a yell Chester leaped for the rope, swarmed halfway to the distant rafters, and clung, looking down. Kuve patted the sleek head of the animal; it yawned, nuzzling his leg affectionately.

"You see? You were capable of more than you imagined," Kuve called matter-of-factly.

"Where did that thing come from?" Chester called.

"He's a harmless pet. When you mentioned a tiger, I couldn't resist the opportunity to make an object lesson."

Chester slid down the rope slowly, eyes on the cat. Back on the floor, he edged behind Kuve, who slapped the animal's flank. The animal padded away.

"If I called him back, you wouldn't panic now, because you know he's harmless. And if a really wild animal were released here, you'd know what to do—and that you were capable of doing it. You could watch the Bengal tiger you mentioned quite calmly and take to the rope only if necessary."

"Maybe—but don't try me. That cost me some skin."

"Did you notice that—at the time?"

"All I was thinking about was that man-eater."

"The fear and pain reactions are useful to the unthinking organism. But you have a reasoning mind, Chester. You could dispense with the automatic-response syndromes."

"It's better to be a live coward—"

"But you might be a dead coward, when mastery of fear could have saved you. Look down, Chester."

Chester glanced at the floor. As he watched, the milky white surface cleared to transparency, all but a narrow ribbon on which he stood, scarcely four inches wide, spanning a yawning abyss below his feet set with jagged black rocks. Kuve stood by unconcernedly, apparently suspended in mid-air.

"It's quite all right, Chester. Merely a floor of very low reflectivity."

Chester teetered on the narrow strip. "Get me out of here," he choked.

"Close your eyes," Kuve said quietly. Chester squeezed his eyes shut.

"Forget what you saw," Kuve ordered. "Concentrate on sensing the floor through your feet. Accept its solidity."

Chester swallowed, then opened his eyes slowly. He looked at Kuve. "I guess it will hold," he said shakily.

Kuve nodded. "Working here for a few weeks will help dissipate your irrational fear of heights."

"When weather permits," said Kuve, "you'll do your workouts here on the terrace in the open air."

Chester surveyed the hundred-foot-square area, floored with dark wood and surrounded by a five-foot wall of flowering shrubs. A cluster of tall poplars shaded a portion of the floor from the high morning sun. Racked against the low wall was an array of weights, bars and apparatus.

"Perhaps I should explain that I have no aspirations to the Mr. Universe title," Chester said. "I think perhaps a couple of Indian clubs would be more than adequate for me."

"Chester," said Kuve, motioning his pupil to a padded bench. "I've taken the first steps toward dispelling your certainty that pain is unendurable and that fear is both useful and overmastering. Now let us consider the role of boredom as a hindrance to the control of the intellect over the body. What is boredom, Chester?"

"Well, boredom sets in when you have nothing to occupy your mind."

"Or when instinct says, 'the activity at hand is not

vital to my survival.' It is a more potent factor in influencing human behavior than either fear or pain." He handed Chester a small dumbbell. "Do you find that heavy?"

Chester weighed the five-pound weight in his hand. "No, not really."

"Have another." Chester hefted a dumbbell in each hand. "Now," said Kuve, "please stand and place the two weights at shoulder height. Then press them alternately to arm's length."

Chester thrust the weights up, puffing. A minute passed. His pace grew slower.

Kuve seated himself comfortably in a canvas chair. "You'd like to stop now, Chester. Why?"

"Because . . . I'm getting exhausted . . . " Chester gasped.

"Exhaustion would result in your failure to press the weight up, but it fails to explain the mere desire to stop while strength remains."

"I think I've injured myself," Chester gasped. "I've overexerted."

"No," said Kuve, "you're bored. Therefore you feel the impulse to stop—nature's automism for conserving energy vital to the hunt, flight, combat, or mating. From now on I'll expect you to reject its control of your motivations."

It was late afternoon. Chester let his hand fall from the hand grip of the machine which he had been squeezing, twisting, pulling and pushing at Kuve's direction. He groaned.

"I thought you were exaggerating when you said you were going to test a hundred and seventy-two different muscles, but I believe you now. Every one of them is aching."

"They'll ache even more tomorrow," Kuve said

cheerfully. "But no matter. They'll soon accustom themselves to the idea that you intend to call on them henceforth."

"I've changed my mind, Kuve. Nature meant me to be the frail, sensitive type."

"Put tomorrow's ordeals out of your mind. At the proper time you'll go through the schedule I've laid out for you. When it's over forget it until it's time to work again."

"I haven't got the will power," Chester said. "I've tried diets and daily dozens before, to say nothing of night classes in which I was going to learn flawless French, or accountancy. It never lasted."

"The secret of winning disputes with yourself is to refuse to listen. By the time you've perfected your argument you'll be well into your routine. Now let's move along to the dining room. I have a briefing on mnemonics for you, after which I'll start you on pattern theory. Then—"

"When do I sleep?"

"All in good time."

"Not bad," Chester said, finishing off a bowl of clear soup. "What's next on the menu?"

"Nothing," said Kuve. "But as I was saying, the association of symbol with specific must relate to your personal experience—"

"What do you mean, nothing? I'm a hungry man. I've worked like a draft horse all day!"

"You're overweight, Chester. The soup was carefully compounded to supply the needed nutrients to maintain your energy level."

"I'll starve."

"You've been eating from boredom, Chester. When your attention is occupied elsewhere, you forget food. You'll have to master habit."

"This whole day has consisted of your telling me to mortify the flesh, mind over matter."

"The mind is the supreme instrument in nature; it must establish its supremacy. I asked you earlier what pain was. What is pleasure?"

"Right now, it's eating!"

"An excellent example: the satisfaction of a natural impulse."

"It's more than an impulse. It's a necessity! I need more food than a bowl of egg-flower soup without egg flowers!"

"All pleasure impulses, when oversatisfied, become destructive; controlled, the instincts can be very useful. Anger, for example. Here nature has provided a behavioral mechanism to deal with those situations in which aggression seems indicated. It can override other impulses, such as fear. When you are angry, you are stronger, less sensitive to pain, and immune to panic. You desire only to close with your enemy and kill. Before combat males of many species customarily set about working themselves into a rage."

"I'm well on the way."

"You'll learn to control the anger impulse, and evoke it at will without losing control. Now we must move on to the next training situation."

"More?" Chester protested. "I'm exhausted."

"The laziness instinct again," said Kuve. "Come along, Chester."

The sun was setting. Chester and Kuve stood at the base of an eighty-foot tower beside a pool. A steep flight of steps led to a lonely platform at the top.

Kuve handed Chester a small locket. "Climb to the top of the tower. This will enable me to talk to you at a distance. Tomorrow a similar device will be surgically implanted. Now, up you go."

"Let's just go back to that glass floor and pretend some more."

"Simply climb slowly and steadily."

"What's the point in risking my neck up there?"

"Chester, intellectually you are aware that you should co-operate with me. Ignore the distractions of instinct and follow your mind."

"I'll freeze on the ladder. You'll have to send three men up to pry my fingers loose."

"Last week I watched you at the dancing terrace. You sat at a table and ate a large amount of food. You watched the dancers. A girl called to you to join in. You patted your stomach and shook your head."

"What's that got to do with flagpole sitting?"

"The dance they were performing requires great skill and strength and endurance. Had you joined in, would you now enjoy recalling it?"

"Of course, I'd like to be able to—"

"Remembered moments of high achievement satisfy; remembered excesses disgust. Next week will you look back with pleasure on having refused the tower?"

"Not if I fall off and break my neck."

"You have the power to mold your memories—but only before they become memories. This is your opportunity to endow yourself with a recollection worth having."

"Well, just to humor you, I'll start—but I won't guarantee I'll go all the way."

"One step at a time, Chester. Don't look down."

Chester mounted the stairs cautiously, gripping the slender handrail. "This thing wobbles," he called back from ten feet up.

"It will hold. Just keep going."

Chester moved higher. The steps were of wood, eight inches wide and four feet long. The handrail was aluminum, bolted to uprights every fourth step. Chester concentrated his attention on the wood and metal. A buzz sounded from the locket at his throat. "You're going very well. Halfway up now."

The sunset sky flared purple and orange. Chester paused, breathing hard.

"A few more steps, Chester," said the tiny voice in the communicator. He went on. The top of the tower was before him now. Clinging to the rail, he made his way up the last few steps. Far away a twinkle of light showed against the dark forest on the skyline. Red light reflected from a river winding down the valley. The low white building of the Center glowed peach-colored in the fading light. Chester looked down at the pool below.

He dropped flat, eyes shut. "Help!" he croaked.

"Move to the steps, feet first," Kuve said calmly. "Lower your legs, then start down!"

Chester felt the first step under his foot, edged down, one step at a time.

"Halfway down," Kuve's voice said. Chester was moving faster now. At ten feet from the bottom, Kuve halted him.

"Look at the water. Can you jump in from there?"

"Yes, but . . ."

"Go back up a step. Can you jump from there?"

Chester balked three steps higher.

"Jump."

Chester held his nose and sprang into the water. He surfaced, climbed out of the pool.

"Do it again."

After three jumps, Chester went a step higher. Half an hour later, in bright moonlight, he made the jump from twenty feet, whistling down to splash tremendously, then paddling, puffing, to the ladder.

"That's enough for this session," said Kuve. "In a week you'll jump from the top—where you couldn't stand upright today. Now, back inside. While you're getting into some dry garments, I want to talk to you about the nature of reality."

"This is the time of day I usually retire," Chester said, panting. "Couldn't reality wait for tomorrow?"

"You'll have no trouble with insomnia here," Kuve assured him. "By the time you go to bed, you'll be ready to sleep."

In a narrow room with a high window, Chester looked critically at a padded bench three feet wide.

"I'm supposed to sleep on that?"

"There is no mattress like weariness," Kuve said.

Chester kicked off his sandals and lay down with a sigh. "I guess you're right at that, Kuve. I'm going to sleep for a week."

"Four hours," said Kuve. "In addition, you'll have a two-hour nap daily at noon."

There was a buzz from the communicator still on Chester's neck. "Not-is is not is-not," said a soft feminine voice. "Is-not is not not-is. Is is not not-is-not . . . "

"What the devil's this gibberish?"

"The basic axioms of rationality. You'll interpret this material at a subconscious level while you sleep."

"You mean this is going on all night?"

"All night. But you'll find it doesn't interfere with sleep."

"What does it mean—is-not is not not-is?"

"This is a simple statement of the nonidentity of symbolic equivalents."

"Um. You mean 'the map is not the territory . . . '"

Kuve nodded. "An apparent banality. But by dawn you'll have grasped the implications at a basic level."

"I won't sleep a wink."

"If not tonight, then tomorrow," said Kuve, matter-of-factly.

"Not-is-not is not is," the soft voice insisted gently.

"Only three hundred and sixty-four days to go," answered Chester.

7

The first gray of dawn had not yet lighted the sky when Chester tottered into the softly lit gymnasium. Kuve, fresh and immaculate in white, looked up from a small table set up in the middle of the room.

"Good morning, Chester. You slept well?"

"Like a four-day corpse. And I feel equally lively now. I just came to tell you that I'm permanently crippled from yesterday's overexertions. You'd better get a doctor out here. I ought to be in bed, but . . . "

Kuve held up a hand. "Chester, you're expecting me to make much of you and urge you on with inspirational talk. However, I'm afraid we can't spare the time for a pep rally."

"Pep rally? I'm a sick man."

"Still, you're out of bed at the appointed time, dressed for work. And since you're here, you might just take a look at this."

Chester hobbled over to the table. Under a surface of beaded glass, pinpoints of red, green and amber light winked off and on in an unpredictable sequence.

"I want you to analyze the pattern here. When you're ready, put your finger on the button here at the edge which matches the color of the light which you think will blink on next."

Chester studied the light board. A red light blinked, then a green, another red, another, an amber, a green . . . He touched the red light. The board blanked off.

"That means you chose wrongly. Try again with a

new pattern." Chester followed the lights. Green, red, amber, red, amber, green, red, green, red . . .

He touched the amber light. The board blanked.

"Never accept the first level of complexity as a solution to a problem, Chester. Look beneath the surface; find the subtler patterns. Try again."

The lights blinked in steady sequence. On Chester's fifth try the entire board lit up. Chester looked pleased.

"Good," said Kuve. "When you have three correct solutions in sequence, we'll move on to patterns of a higher complexity."

"I had to think three lights ahead on the last one, Kuve. The patterns seem to change while I'm watching them."

"Yes, there's a simple developmental progression involved in this set."

"I have more the poetic type mind. I'm no electronic calculator."

"You'll think you are before the year is out. This training, in its advanced phases, by applying pressure of a type never encountered in ordinary experience, will develop cortical areas hitherto unused."

"I don't think I'm going to enjoy that last part," said Chester dubiously. "What does it mean?"

Kuve pointed to the far wall. "Look over there. Keep your eyes rigidly before you." He held up a hand at the edge of Chester's field of vision.

"How many fingers am I holding up?"

"I don't know; I can just barely tell there's a hand there."

Kuve waggled a finger. "Did you notice that movement?"

"Certainly."

Kuve moved a second finger, stilling the first, then a third finger, and a fourth.

"You saw the movement each time," he summed up,

"which indicates that all four fingers are within your field of view." He extended two fingers. "Now how many fingers am I holding up?"

"I still can't tell."

"You can see the fingers, Chester; you've proven that. And yet you are, quite literally, unable to count these fingers which you see. The message sent to your brain through the portion of the optical mechanism concerned with peripheral vision is channeled to an undeveloped sector of your mind, a part of the great mass of normally unused cells in the cortex. The intelligence of this portion of your intellect is about at a par with that of a faithful dog which recognizes a group of children but is unable to formulate any conception of their number." He lowered his hand. "It is that portion of the brain which we shall train. Now, try this next pattern."

Chester leaned against the rail at the top of the eighty-foot tower, feeling the sun hot on his shoulders, watching as Kuve adjusted the ropes stretched across the pool below.

"This gives you a four-foot target," Kuve's voice said from the rice-grain-sized instrument set in the bone behind Chester's left ear. "Remember your vascomuscular tension patterns. Wait for the signal."

A beep sounded in Chester's ear—and he was in the air, wind shrieking past his ears, his chin to his chest, arms extended with hands flat, feet pointed.

He struck, twisted, shot above the surface, swam to the edge, and pulled himself up with a single smooth motion.

"You've come along well these first two weeks," Kuve said, motioning Chester to the table where a small steak waited. "You've explored the parameters of your native abilities; you've established an awareness

of the values we're dealing with, and overcome the
worst of the metabolic inertia. Your musculature is
in good tone, though you still have a long way to go
in developing bulk and power. Now you're ready to
attack the subtler disciplines of balance, timing, precision, endurance and pace."

"You make it sound as though I haven't done anything. What about the high dives? That four-foot target isn't very big from eighty feet up."

"That exercise was designed to develop your self-
confidence. Now you'll begin the real substance of your
studies. We'll begin with simple games like fencing,
riding, rope work, juggling, dancing and sleight-of-hand,
and proceed by degrees into the more abstract phases."

"What are you training me for, a side show?"

Kuve ignored the interruption. "Your academic studies will be concentrated on dual attention, self-hypnosis,
selective concentration, categorical analysis, advanced
mnemonics, and eidetics, from which we will proceed
to autonomics, cellular psychology, regeneration,
and—"

"Let's go back to fencing. At least I know what that
is."

"After you've dined we'll begin. In the meantime,
tell me what the word 'now' means."

" 'Now' changes," said Chester, chewing. "It moves
along with time. Every moment is 'now' for a while,
and then it isn't."

"For a while? How long?"

"Not very long; an instant."

"Is 'now' a part of the past?"

"Of course not."

"The future?"

"No, the future hasn't happened yet. The past is
already finished. 'Now' falls between them."

"How would you define a point, Chester?"

"The intersection of two lines," Chester said promptly.

"The *position* of intersection, to be more precise," said Kuve. " 'Line' and 'point' are terms referring to positions, not things. If a sheet of paper is cut in two, every molecule of the original sheet is contained in the two halves. If the cut edges are placed together, every particle is still to be found in the two parts; none fall between them. The line we see dividing the halves is only a position, not a material object."

"Yes, that's obvious."

"Past time may be considered as one of the parts of the paper, future time as the other. Between them is . . . nothing."

"Still, I'm sitting here eating my lunch. Now."

"Your ability to conceptualize falls short of the ability of the universe to proliferate complexities. Human understanding can never be more than an approximation. Avoid dealing in absolutes. And never edit reality for the sake of simplicity. The results are fatal to logical thinking."

Mina appeared on the terrace, wearing a close-fitting pink coverall and carrying foils and face masks. Chester finished his steak, pulled on a black coverall of tough resilient material, took the foil that Mina handed him.

Mina took her position, gripped her slender épée, arm and wrist straight, feet at right angles, left hand on hip. She tapped Chester's blade, then with a sudden flick sent it flying into the pool.

"Oh, I'm sorry, Chester. You weren't ready."

Chester retrieved the foil, assumed a stance in imitation of Mina's. They crossed blades—and Chester oofed as Mina's point prodded his chest. Mina laughed merrily. Chester blushed.

On the third try Mina locked Chester's blade with hers, then, with a twist, plucked it from his hand.

"Chester"—she laughed—"you couldn't be trying." She laid her weapon aside and strolled off. Chester turned to Kuve, face red. Kuve stepped forward, motioned Chester into position.

"We'll have half an hour each morning and another after lunch," he said. "And," he added softly, "perhaps you'll have a surprise in store for Mina one of these days."

Chester circled Kuve warily, bare feet shuffling on the padded mat. Kuve stepped in, his right hand flashing past Chester's ribs and up to grasp Chester's right wrist, forced back by Kuve's left hand. Chester twirled, caught Kuve's left hand, forced the wrist down. Kuve leaned to relieve the pressure, shifting his hold to Chester's neck, then threw his hip against Chester's side and heaved. In mid-air Chester brought a leg up, clipped Kuve's jaw with his knee, twisted to land on all fours as Kuve's grip slipped free. Kuve shook his head, looking surprised. "Was that an accident, or . . . "

Chester hit him low, dodged left to avoid a head-lock, clamped an arm over Kuve's head and reached for an ankle—

And was upended and slammed on the mat. He sat up, rubbing his neck. Kuve nodded approvingly. "You're coming along, Chester. If you hadn't been careless with your footwork just now, you might have pinned me."

"Maybe next time," Chester said grimly.

"I seem to note a certain suppressed hostility in your tone," Kuve said, eyeing Chester with amusement.

"Suppressed, hell. You've worked me like a rented heli for nine months."

"Cheer up, Chester. I have a new compound-reaction test situation for you. It's a very interesting problem group—but I warn you, it can be painful."

"In that respect it fits in nicely with the over-all program."

Chester followed Kuve across the terrace, through an arch, along a corridor, and out into an open court. Kuve pointed to a gate in the wall beyond which a patch of woods pressed close.

"Just go through the gate, Chester, and have a stroll in the forest. You'll find paths; whether you use them is left entirely to your own discretion. This is a tongue of the forest that runs up into the hills. I don't think you'll be in danger of straying too far, for reasons which will become apparent once you're in the forest—but nevertheless I'll caution you to stay close. As soon as you've made what you consider to be a significant observation, return."

Chester glanced toward the shadowed depths of the wood. "My first trip outside the prison grounds. Are you sure I won't run away?"

"Impossible via this route, I'm afraid. If you get into trouble, remember I'll be monitoring your communicator. Be back by dark."

"When in doubt, I'll remember the old school motto: Is-not is not not-is." Chester turned down the path. "Don't wait up for me. I may decide I like it out here."

Chester moved along the path at a steady pace, his eyes roving over his surroundings in a wide-scope comparison pattern.

A movement caught his eye; Chester threw himself backward, feet high. A rope whipped across his calves; then the noose was dangling high in the air. Chester came to his feet carefully, searching for a backup trap, saw none. He studied the tree to which the rope was attached, then moved off the trail to a nearby oak, scaled it quickly, moved out on a long branch, then dropped into the trapped tree. He untied the rope, a tough quarter-inch synthetic, coiled it around his waist, then slid back to the ground.

He moved into the underbrush, froze at a sharp pain in the back of his hand. Carefully he disengaged himself from a loop of fine-gauge barbed wire. Selecting a strand between barbs, he bent it backward and forward rapidly until it parted. He repeated the process with other strands, then went to hands and knees and eased under the barrier.

Half an hour later Chester stood on the brink of a sheer bluff. Fifty feet below, a stream glinted in a shaft of sunlight that fell between great trees. Upstream, a still pool showed black among smooth boulders. Chester noted that its placement was identical with the four-foot target area into which he had been diving daily—an open invitation.

He lay flat and examined the cliff face. The broken rock surface offered an abundance of hand- and foot-holds. Perhaps too many . . .

It was forty feet to the spreading branches of a large elm growing on the opposite side of the stream. Chester uncoiled the rope from his waist, found a five-pound stone fragment with a pinched center, and tied it securely to the end of the supple line. He stood, whirled the stone around his head four times and let it fly. It arched across the branch, dropped and hung swinging. Gently, Chester pulled as the stone swung away, relaxed as it returned, pulled again. The oscillation built up. As the weight started its inward swing, Chester pulled sharply. The stone swung up and over, once, twice, three times around the branch. He tugged; all secure. Quickly he knotted his end of the rope about a length of fallen branch, then man-handled a two-hundred-pound boulder over it. He tested the attachment briefly, then crossed, hand over hand. He left the rope in place, descended to the edge of the quiet pool.

Lifting a hundred-pound rock, he tossed it into the center of the black water. Instantly a large net, apparently spring-loaded, snapped into view, dripping water, to close over the stone. Chester smiled, raised his eyes to study the base of the cliff. Snarls of fine barbed wire guarded the lower six feet of the vertical rock face. It would have been an easy climb down, he reflected, but a long way back up.

The communicator behind his ear beeped. "Well, Chester, I see you've sprung the net at the pool. Don't feel too badly; you did very well. I'll be along to release you in a few minutes."

Chester smiled again and turned back into the forest.

Chester studied the sun, briefly reviewed the route he had followed in four hours of detecting and avoiding Kuve's traps. Sunset was just over an hour away, he judged, and he was three miles northwest by north from the Center. He halted, sniffing the air. The odor of wood-smoke was sharp among the milder scents of pine and juniper and sun-warmed rock. He had been climbing steadily for fifty minutes and was ready now to angle to the left to clear the upper end of a ravine. With each step the odor of smoke grew more noticeable. Now a soft gray wisp coiled from the shaded trunks ahead and above. Chester crouched low, moved on quickly. If there was a forest fire ahead, it would be necessary to get past it at once—before he was cut off from his route to the valley. He moved silently through sparse underbrush, saw through a gap in the trees a pale flicker of orange on the heights a hundred yards above. It would be close; he broke into a run.

The trees thinned. The tumbled rocks that marked the head of the gorge showed pale against the dark background of pines. A billow of smoke rolled toward him, carried by a down draft flowing into the canyon. Chester lay flat, drew a dozen deep breaths, then jumped up and scrambled over the broken rock. Ahead, fire twinkled among massive boles, flickered in whipping underbrush, leaped high in the crown of a pine. Hot sparks fell around him. He could hear the roar of wind-driven flames now. A sudden gust blew a wall of smoke toward him. It might be possible, he calculated, to round the knoll at the head of the rampart that edged his route on the right, then descend safely to emerge into the valley a mile north of the Center. There was no hope now of making it before dark. Chester worked his way higher. Another hundred yards—

Twenty feet upslope a heavily built man stepped into view. He was brown-bearded, dressed in patched pants and a loose jacket of faded plaid with three of the four buttons missing. His right hand was at his chin, two fingers hooked around a taut bowstring. The arrow notched in the string carried a four-inch head of polished steel, and it was aimed at Chester's navel.

"I know yew Downlanders move like the snake Demon when the Kez-favver tricked him into the fire pit, but Blew-tewf leaps faster van fought," the bearded man drawled in a barely intelligible dialect. "What yew want here in Free Places? Was life too tame down below?"

Chester frowned, running the sounds of the stranger's barbaric speech through his mind, noting sound substitutions and intonations; the pattern of the dialect was simple.

"If yew don't mind, I'd ravver Blew-tewf pointed over vere somewhere," Chester replied, motioning toward the deep woods, his eyes on the arrowhead. "Yew might just have greasy fingers or somefing of the sort."

"No need to mock the cant," the man said in clear

English. "I was ten when I left the Downlands. Now, what do you want here?"

"I was rather hoping to discover a route back to the valley, but I'd settle for merely remaining unskewered and unbroiled. Do you mind if I press on? The fire is blowing this way, you know."

"Don't worry about the fire. I set it myself to run game. It'll burn out against the escarpment above. Now move off to your right and up past me. Blue-Tooth will be watching every move."

"I'm heading in the other direction," Chester said.

"You better do what I told you. Like you said, the fire's gettin' hot." The arrow was still aimed unwaveringly at Chester's stomach. The bow creaked as the bearded man set the arrowhead on the handgrip. "Make up your mind."

"But what in the world do you want with me?"

"Let's say I want news of the Downlands."

"Who are you? What are you doing up here in the hills? If you want news, you could come down to the Center."

"My name's Bandon, and I wouldn't be happy in your blasted Center. Don't turn around, just keep movin' along—and if yew're finkin' of the little trinket tucked away back of your ear, forget it. Yew're out of range."

"You're planning on holding me here for ransom?"

"What treasures could Downlanders offer to equal the life of the Free Places? Bandon laughed.

"You'll let me go in the morning?"

"Not in the morning or for many a morning vereafter. Forget the tame valleys, Downlander. Yew'll be here until yew die."

8

Twilight was fading from the peaks as Chester and Bandon clambered over the stones of a fallen wall to the level surface of a road that curved between tall poplars toward low buildings silhouetted against the peach-colored sky.

"This is our town, Downlander," Bandon said, breathing hard after the climb. "There's food here, and a fire against the night chill, and strong ale, and the fellowship of free men: all your needs between dusk and dawn."

"Very poetic," Chester said, noting the potholes and weed clumps in the road. "But you left out a few things I've grown accustomed to, like literature, celery, dentists and clean socks. And it looks like some of your houses lack roofs."

"What's a few leaks to a free man?" Bandon snapped.

"Every man to his own little eccentricity," Chester said. "But why do I have to join your club? I'll go quietly."

"Yew came here uninvited," Bandon said flatly. He lowered and unstrung his bow. "Don't be fool enough to try to leave. There's sentries posted to guard our approaches."

"I know; I saw them."

"In this light? Our best woodsmen?"

"Just joking," said Chester.

"Maybe you did, at that. You Downlanders are keen-eyed as the Kez-father himself. Tell me, where did you learn the cant?"

"Your dialect? Oh, I . . . ah . . . studied it. A hobby of mine."

"Then it's not true what some say, that you Downlanders can learn our speech in the wink of an eye?"

"A baseless rumor."

"I thought so. Come along now an' we'll see what the brothers make of you." They made their way in the deepening gloom toward the nearest of the buildings. Chester made out the details of chipped carving around doorways, fallen trellises, collapsed porticos. A broken statue lay in the road.

"This must have been a pretty nice town, once," Chester said. "What happened to it?"

Bandon snorted. "We threw off all those slave notions about drudging away to put on a show for the neighbors. We're free here. No one to tell us what to do. Folks that didn't like the idea moved out. Good riddance. We don't need 'em."

"Swell," Chester agreed. "But what happens when it gets cold?"

"Plenty wood around here. We build fires."

Chester eyed the blackened foundation of a burned-out house. "I see . . . "

"That was an accident," Bandon growled. "Plenty more houses where that came from." He stopped. "Hold it right here." He threw back his head and whistled shrilly. From doorways and dark hedges and the shadows of ragged trees, men appeared.

Chester estimated the crowd of unshaved, hide-clad hill-dwellers who surrounded him at fifty individuals, all male—none of them, he reflected, of the kind who would arouse a desire for further acquaintance.

"Vis Downlan'er's a guest," Bandon was saying to the assembled brethren. "We'll treat him as one of us— unless he tries tew go somewhere. Now, I'm takin' him in the palace wiv me—jus' until he can get a place of his own fix' up. I warn yew now: if he comes tew harm, I'll hol' the lot of yew personally responsible."

A tall, incredibly broad man in striped coveralls black with dirt swaggered forward. "We heard a lot about how tough vese Downlanders are," he growled. "Vis one don't look so tough."

"Maybe he's smart—vat's better yet," Bandon snapped. "Leave him alone, Grizz. Vat's an order."

Grizz looked around at his fellows. "Funny none of us is good enough tew get tew sleep in the palace. But vis spy here walks in an' right away he's treated like the Kez-favver hisself when he went tew fetch the king hat back from the sea bottom."

"Never mind vat. Now yew boys get a fire goin' in the Hall and roast up some venison and break open a few kegs of ale. We're goin' tew have a real celebration here tew show the new man what kind of jolly free life we lead."

A few shouts rang out, a faint yippee sounded from the rear. Grizz stared at Bandon. "We got no venison. Plenty canned beans and stale crackers. Only ale we got is a couple cases of near-beer Lonny stole last week."

"Dew the best yew can," Bandon snapped. "Look lively about it. I want tew see yew lookin' cheerful around here." He turned to Chester and motioned toward an imposing façade featuring chipped columns and broken glass. "Come along tew the palace; yew'll have a chance tew get cleaned up before the feast."

"Jus' a minute," Grizz said. He stepped up to Chester, brought an iron bar into view.

"I warned you, Grizz," Bandon started.

"I won' hurt him—yet." Grizz growled. He gripped the bar at either end, hunched his shoulders and strained. The metal gave, bent to a crude U. He let out his breath, shoved the bar at Chester.

"Straighten it, Swamp-walker."

"Not in the mood," Chester said mildly.

Grizz barked a laugh, dropped the bar with a clatter, stepped to the roadside and came back with a massive chunk of carved stone. "Here, catch." He heaved the boulder toward Chester, who moved his foot barely in time as the rock crashed down.

Bandon strung his bow with a quick motion. "Vat's enough, Grizz," he snapped. "Come along, Downlan'er."

"I'll be seein' yew, Swamp-walker," Grizz called after them.

Chester followed Bandon across a littered stone terrace, past gaunt paint-peeling doors into an echoing interior that smelled of stale hides and forgotten food scraps. A broken-down sofa leaned in one corner beside a table with a bandaged leg. A heap of bedding sprawled by a wide fireplace stacked with splintered chair rungs. A staircase with a broken banister curved up past a glassless window to a gallery.

"The place looks a little run-down," Chester commented. "Who used to live here?"

"Dunno." Bandon took a lighter from his pocket, snapped it until it caught. "'Bout out of fluid," he said. "Used to be some boss types lived here, but when we wouldn't take orders, they just moved out—had to get down in the flatlands to get fitted for chains, I guess."

"What kind of orders?"

"Oh, you know. Always wantin' to set up a committee to patch roofs or clean gutters or string wire. Dirty work."

"I think perhaps they had some reason on their side," Chester said, looking around at peeling wallpaper and decayed curtains.

"Heck, they should've done all that themselves. But no, they ran off and left it. We locked up a few of 'em and tried to make 'em work, but they got loose somehow."

"The boss caste is sneaky, all right," Chester said.

"Always fooling us fun-loving folks by knowing something we don't."

"Durn right," Bandon agreed.

"Why don't you gather firewood in the forest instead of burning the furniture?" Chester asked. "There's no place to sit."

"Sure there is. Just look under that pile of hides there. We tried burning sticks, but they don't burn so good. This stuff's nice and dry. Now, soon's we have a cheery blaze goin', we'll have a talk about conditions down below. Still the same old slave life, I suppose: everybody minding everybody's else's business."

"Uh-huh," Chester said, glancing over the assorted debris scattered on the floor. "They're still burdened down with swimming pools and laundries and picnics and concerts and all manner of frivolity. By the way, where do the canned beans and crackers come from?"

"Plenty of stores here," Bandon said, dipping water from a barrel and pulling off his shirt. "Lots of stuff in 'em. The boys could turn up some good eats if they half tried." He splashed water on his face and chest, snorted, dabbed at himself with the shirt, then pulled it back on.

"O.K., it's all yours," he said. Chester eyed the brown water dubiously. "What happens when the stores are looted clean?"

"We've got plans," Bandon said darkly. "We won't starve." He shoved rubbish from a slack-twisted chair and seated himself. "I happen to have a couple of bottles of Tricennium brew tucked away," he said. "Soon's you're washed up, we'll have 'em. Wouldn't do to let on to the boys; not enough to go around."

"That's the spirit," Chester said. "I think I'll defer bathing until later."

"Huh! I thought you Downlanders were great ones

for washin' off. Heck, I wash off myself all the time, like you just saw me do."

"You have a great instinct for personal daintiness," Chester said tactfully. "An admirable quality. Tell me, why all the emphasis on rugged individuality? Did someone take away your pet goat when you were a lad?"

"Worse'n that," Bandon said. "They used to try to make my pa do their dirty work for 'em. He didn't take kindly to it. He organized the Resistance. Now look." Bandon waved a hand in a proud gesture. "It's all mine—mine and the boys'."

"I can see you're not one to keep off a lawn just because somebody else planted it and keeps it mowed," Chester said admiringly. "Strictly self-sufficient. You just live in these old houses that happened to grow here and you eat wholesome, natural canned beans, the way the Lord intended, and you loot your clothes right out of Mother Nature's own abandoned dry-goods stores. To heck with maintenance. When this town wears out, there's always plenty of others."

"You can lay off the smart talk," Bandon said. "We've got as much right as anybody to live soft."

"Sure—just because some smart-aleck invented something and some exploiter built a factory to make it and some wisenheimer did the engineering, that's no reason you shouldn't wake up from your nap long enough to get your share. And now let's have that ale you were talking about. If I'm going to spend the rest of my life here, I'll have to start getting used to drinking it warm."

"Yew'll like it fine, after you get used to it," Bandon said. He went to a doorless refrigerator, lifted the lid and rummaged, came up with two brown bottles. Chester wandered around the room, noting the remains of a grandfather's clock, a gutted washing machine filled with firewood, a coil of clothesline, some picture wire, a scatter of rusted nails, bent coat-hangers, burst cardboard boxes, wadded clothing.

"What have you got against the conveniences of life, Bandon?" he asked, accepting a bottle. "What would be wrong with, say, cleaning this room up so it smelled as good as the woods outside of town? Is there anything particularly independent about keeping your discarded junk in the living room?"

"We don't care anything about setting up fancy places to live in. We prefer a kind of nice informal look."

"You're echoing a long line of philosophers who concluded that the secret of the universe consisted of sitting around in your own dirt—all the way from early Christians to twentieth-century beatniks. I can be just as self-righteous as the next fellow, while I'm sitting in an air-conditioned restaurant ordering *haute cuisine* with one hand and lighting up an expensive dope stick with the other, with a well-stacked young lady occupying the rest of my attention. The point is, why not be virtuous in comfort?"

"Look here, don't go trying to spread discontent around among my men."

"Your men? I thought you were all free as bedbugs in the railroad men's Y."

"We are. But any outfit needs a little organization. Don't you get the boys upset—otherwise I might just give Grizz the go-ahead."

"I have a disturbing conviction that Grizz may not wait for the go-ahead. He seems to resent me."

"Don't worry; I'll keep an eye on him." Bandon finished off his bottle. "Let's join the boys. I guess things ought to be rollin' pretty good by now. Just stay close—and yell if you need help."

Chester followed Bandon down the wide, rubble-littered front steps into the street and across into a large, garishly lighted ex-restaurant, to survey a scene of half-hearted festivity. A blaze in the fireplace dispelled the evening chill. Around it, the brothers stood, hands in pockets, muttering. At sight of Bandon and Chester, the massive figure of Grizz detached itself from the bar.

"Well, the new man's been makin' hisself comfortable," he said loudly. "Say, I hear yew Downlanders are fast. I wonder if . . . "

Grizz made a sudden movement. Chester put up a hand and the bone handle of a hunting knife slapped his palm, fell to the ground.

"Here, Grizz, yew had no call tew frow a knife at our guest!"

"Never mind, Bandon," Chester said easily. "He was just kidding."

"Lucky yew happen' tew stick out yewr han' jus' when yew did," Bandon said. "It was comin' butt first, but it would have hurt. Grizz, leave him alone." Bandon slapped Chester on the back. "I've got tew circulate around a little, talk tew a few of the boys. Yew get acquainted tew." He moved off.

There was a step behind Chester. He eased aside and half turned. Grizz thrust heavily through the spot he had just vacated. The nearby men moved back, fanning out. Chester stood looking up at Grizz. The mountaineer was at least seven feet tall.

"We don't take much tew spies," Grizz growled.

"I can see why," said Chester. "If the other half knew what you boys had all to yourselves up here, they'd leave home tomorrow."

"Vere's a way tew handle swamp-walkers," Grizz stated, rubbing his right fist in his left palm.

"Vat's right, Grizz," a voice called.

"Show him, Grizz," another suggested.

"Now, Bandon says treat vis swamp-walker like one of the boys." Grizz looked around. Heads nodded reluctant agreement.

"But what if maybe vis guy jumps me? I fight back, right?"

"Shewre yew dew!"

"Yew ain' a man tew back down, Grizz!"

"I seen him dew it!"

There was a sound behind Chester. He stepped casually to one side; a man stumbled past the spot on which Chester had been standing, blundered into Grizz. With a snarl, Grizz pushed aside the man who had jostled him, stepped to Chester, and threw a tremendous punch—as Chester looked the other way, leaned toward the fire. The blow brushed his neck. Chester seemed not to notice. He rubbed his hands together. "Nice blaze," he commented brightly. He took a step away from Grizz, still not looking at him, moved a chair aside with a deft motion.

Grizz stumbled over the chair leg, fell full length. Chester looked startled, bent to help Grizz up. "Excuse me, Grizz old boy." He made ineffectual brushing motions at Grizz, who came to his feet, hamlike fists doubled, as Chester stooped, came up with Grizz's knife.

Grizz froze, eyes on the blade.

"Guess you'll be needing this," Chester said, holding it out.

Grizz hesitated, then snarled and turned away.

"Nobody could be that clumsy—and that lucky," a voice said softly. Chester turned. Bandon stood eyeing him uncertainly. "But on the other han', nobody could be that fast and that smooth—if they were doin' it on purpose."

"A grand bunch of fellows," said Chester. "I'm feeling right at home."

"You're a strange one," Bandon said. "I've got a feeling maybe it's Grizz who better be careful."

"I hope he never gets a good grip on me," Chester said. "I'm afraid I'd bend into a U before Grizz realized the danger he was in. I think I'll take a stroll outside."

Bandon grunted and turned away. Chester went out into the street, his shadow pushing before him. A man stepped from the shelter of an ornamental fountain, bow in hand. Chester angled off to the right; a second man appeared, weapon ready.

"Just checking, fellows," Chester said. He sauntered back, strolled fifty yards toward the dark woods before sentries appeared silently. He stopped, admired the view while the guards waited, then retraced his steps to the Hall.

"Time to eat," Bandon called. "Grizz was just talkin' mean," he confided when Chester came up. "We've got plenty of good stuff here. Try these sardines."

Chester eyed the soggy fish. "I'm afraid they're not a favorite of mine. I'll wait for the game course."

"Salami on crackers?" Bandon suggested. "We cut off the bad part."

"Any fruit—or berries?" Chester suggested. "Or nuts?"

"That's stuff for squirrels and rabbits," Bandon said shortly. "Hey, after the feast, we're all goin' to have a little shindig. You'll enjoy it."

"Ah, the true joys of the free life at last. What do you do, sing rousing songs, dance horn pipes, exchange buffets, all that sort of thing?"

"Heck, no. We view television. There's some dandy historicals about the old times, when men were men."

"I see. It's a sort of indoctrination program."

"Look here, you might as well quit smartin' off. I tell you, this is the life. After a few years, you'll start to see what I mean."

"It's not the years, it's the next few hours that bother me. I dislike Tri-D intensely. Suppose I go back and tidy up your quarters for you while you enjoy the free life."

"Suit yourself. You can't get away. I'll see that Grizz stays at the show so you can relax."

"Thanks. I'll try to arrange things at your place to give a more fitting reception to any unexpected callers who might drop in."

9

It was three hours since the last sounds of revelry had died. In the palace, Chester sat awake, watching the red glow of the fireplace, and listening. In the corner Bandon snored softly on his pallet. Far away, a night bird called. Something creaked faintly near the door.

Chester crossed the room to Bandon, called his name softly. He grumbled, opened his eyes. "Hah?"

Chester put his face close to Bandon's. "Quiet," he breathed. "Grizz is at the door."

Bandon started up. Chester held him by a hand on his arm. "Let him in. It's better to take him here . . . alone."

"He wouldn't dare push his way into the palace," Bandon whispered.

"Stay where you are." Chester moved silently to the door, stood beside it in the dark. There was a rasping sound, very faint. Then the door moved an inch, paused for a full minute, moved again. From his place behind the heavy door post, Chester saw Grizz's small eyes and bushy beard. Then the door moved wider; Grizz stepped inside, closed the door soundlessly. As he turned back toward the bed where Bandon lay, Chester rammed the stiff fingers of his left hand into Grizz's stomach, then, as Grizz jackknifed forward, struck him backhanded under the ear with the side of his fist. Grizz fell with a heavy slam.

Bandon was on his feet now. "Don't give the alarm, Bandon," Chester whispered. "There's nobody to hear it but his henchmen."

Bandon said hoarsely, "What did he want here? How do you know—"

"Shhh. Grizz was after both of us, Bandon. If he knifed me, he'd have to finish you, too—or face Blue-Tooth later."

"You're ravin'. My people are loyal—includin' Grizz."

"Grizz was listening this evening when we were talking. He was afraid you'd be influenced. That gave him all the excuse he needed. So . . . here he is."

"You come here to make trouble," Bandon grated. "Like Grizz said."

Chester pointed to a heap of uncured hides behind the crude table. "Conceal yourself over there and listen."

Bandon reached up suddenly, took his bow from its peg on the wall, nocked the steel-tipped arrow. "I'll hide," he said. "An' this will be pointed straight at you—so don't try any tricks."

"Be careful with that. I'd hate to be skewered by accident."

Grizz was beginning to stir. Bandon stepped from sight in the shadows.

Grizz sat up, shook his head, got clumsily to his feet. He stood swaying, looked around the silent cabin and saw Chester, almost at his feet, curled up in the bed of rags, snoring lightly.

Grizz half crouched, pig eyes darting around the room. He took a knife from his belt, dug a moccasined toe into Chester's side. Chester rolled on his back, opened his eyes and sat up.

"Where's Bandon?" Grizz growled, the long blade tilted toward Chester's throat.

"Oh, hi there," said Chester. "Say, I hope you're O.K. now after your fall."

"I said where's Bandon?"

Chester looked around. "Isn't he here?"

"He slugged me and got away. Now, talk, Swamp-walker. What are yew tew love birds plannin'?"

Chester chuckled. "He's the chief here; I'm just a captive Downlander, remember?"

"Yew're a liar on bofe counts. Yew fink I'm dumb enough not tew see frew vis setup? The tew of yew are in somefing tewgevver. Where's he gone?"

"If I help you, will you let me go?"

"Shewre."

"You promise? I'll have safe-conduct back to the valley if I tell you where Bandon is so you can kill him?"

"Yeah, I promise. Safe-conduct. Yew bet."

"How do I know you'll keep your promise?"

"Are yew sayin' I'm a liar?" Grizz leaned closer with the knife.

"Careful. I haven't told you yet."

"Yew got my word on it: yew go free. Where is he?"

"Well . . . " Chester came to his knees. "He's on his way back to my Tricennium. He discovered you were taking over here, so he—"

"Fanks, sucker!" Grizz lunged with the knife. Chester threw himself back, yanking at a tripwire; a bucket of sand dropped from a rafter and took Grizz in mid-leap. He slammed the floor face first. Chester came to his feet holding the knife Grizz had dropped. Grizz moved groggily, shaking his head.

"Looks like you're a promise-breaker after all, Grizz," Chester said, moving in with the long blade ready.

Grizz scrabbled backward, one hand up to ward off a thrust. "Don't dew it, don't dew it!" he squalled.

"Keep your voice down. If anyone barges in, you'll be the first to go." Chester stood over Grizz. "Now, what about that promise you made? You were going to give me safe-conduct."

"Shewre. I'll see yew get away clean. Just leave it tew me."

"I could kill you, Grizz. But that wouldn't get me out of here." Chester looked worried. "Suppose I let you go. Will you give me an escort down to the valley?"

"Shewre I will, yew bet I will, fella. I just got excited when yew said Bandon was on his way down."

"Well, I guess I'll give you another chance." Chester put the knife in his belt. "But remember, you've given me your word."

"Vat's right, my word on it, fella."

"I've got to get a couple of things . . . " Chester turned away. In a lithe movement Grizz rolled to hands and knees, snatched up a rusted hatchet lying conveniently by, sprang at Chester's back.

And slammed face first into the hard-packed earth floor as his toe hooked the wire Chester had stretched across the room at ankle height.

Chester turned, looked down sadly at Grizz. "You did it again, Grizz. Dear, oh dear. I'm afraid I have no choice but to cut your throat, since you're not to be trusted."

"Look," whined Grizz, scraping dirt from his face. "I figured you wrong, see? I made a mistake."

"You certainly did," Chester said coldly. He moved closer, reached out and set the point of the blade under Grizz's chin. "One sudden move, and in it goes. How would it feel, Grizz? They say a really keen edge feels cold as it slices through. There wouldn't be too much pain, but breathing would get rather difficult, and, as the blood drained out of you, you'd get weak. In a few seconds you'd be unable even to stand. You'd just lie there and feel the life dwindle in you."

"Don't hurt me," Grizz gasped. "I'll dew anything."

"Who sent you here?" Chester snapped.

"Joj did. He's the one. He planned it all."

"Tell me about it."

"Vere's over a fousand of us. We've got steel crossbows, even chemical bombs." Grizz outlined plans for a raid on the nearest Tricennium. "It's planned for free days from now," he finished. "Vey haven't got a chance against us. But yew . . . yew let me up now, no hard feelings, and I'll see yew get yewr share. Whatever yew want—slaves, women . . ."

"No point in my going back now," said Chester thoughtfully. "I don't want to be there when the massacre takes place." He straightened, the knife still ready. "My best bet is to go along with you. I'm pretty good with a knife, Grizz. If I join you, do my share of the killing, will you pay off as you suggested?"

"Absolewtly. Yew can trust me now. I've learned my lesson." Grizz eyed the knife as Chester tossed it aside and put out his hand.

"We'll shake on that, Grizz."

Grizz came to his feet, reaching for Chester's hand, and with a tremendous surge spun him around, threw a whistling left at the back of Chester's neck that somehow failed to connect solidly, followed up with a right cross that Chester somehow managed to avoid. Chester went down and Grizz was on him, his two hundred and forty pounds of muscle and bone crushing Chester flat, while two thumbs like bolt-cutters probed Chester's Adam's apple.

"Now, Swamp-walker," Grizz breathed, "what was vat about lettin' blood out of me? Cut my froat, would

yew? Feels cool, hey? How dew yew reckon it's gonna
be when I put the fumbs in hard?"

"You gave me your word," Chester wheezed. "I kept
my part of the bargain." He groped, found the loop of
clothesline he had prepared and flipped it into position.

"I don't bargain wif Downlander spies. I tear 'em
intew strips, barehanded."

"I let you go when I could have killed you," Chester
got out. "Now let me up and give me my escort." With
a quick flip, he dropped the loop over Grizz's head.

Grizz hardly noticed in his enthusiasm. "Yew fink
I'm stupid? I've got plans for yew, Swamp-runner," he
said, releasing his grip with one hand to tug at the loose
noose. "Ever felt a bone break—slow?"

"You mean you're breaking your promise?"

"Yew catch on quick."

Chester looked up at Grizz's puffed face, the wide
mouth among the wiry whiskers, the small eyes. He
tugged on the line. An expression of surprise crept
over Grizz's face. His back straightened, his head
rising. He dug in his thumbs frantically, but Chester
twisted away. Then Grizz was struggling to get his legs
under him, his hands raking at the wire that was
hoisting him up neck first.

Chester slid back, keeping pressure on the wire
which ran over a rafter to the loop on Grizz's throat.
Grizz scrambled to get his feet under him. "You're a
very slow pupil, Grizz." Chester jerked the wire. Grizz's
head bobbed. Chester hauled on the wire, then twisted
it around a stout peg set in a massive post. Grizz stood
on tiptoes, breathing rapidly, his eyes bulging, his head
tilted sideways by the taut wire, his fingers groping
fruitlessly at the noose buried in the fleshy neck.

Chester stood before him, hands on hips. "I guess
I'll just hang you, Grizz," he said. "Less messy than
cutting your throat."

"Please," Grizz whispered past the constricting wire. "Give me another chance."

"Have you learned your lesson?"

"Yeah, cut me down."

"Remember, it's no use trying to double-cross me. Now just give me an escort like a good fellow . . ." Chester released the wire. Grizz clawed the noose free, threw it aside, stood rubbing his throat and staring at Chester. Chester stood six feet from him, hands empty, looking at him casually. "Well, you're free now, Grizz. What about your promise?"

Grizz felt carefully about his head and neck, ran his hands over his arms, leaned to check his ankles, his eyes fixed on Chester.

"Oh, it's quite all right now, Grizz. There are no more wires attached to you."

Grizz glanced down, pushed out a foot to check for trap wires. He licked his lips.

"Don't do anything foolish, Grizz. I've warned you. I'm in control of you, not the other way around. The sooner you accept that . . ."

Grizz leaped, caught a tight-stretched wire square in the mouth and did a complete back flip.

"Get up!" Chester snapped. Grizz got to his feet, hands hanging at his sides, staring at Chester.

"Yours is the typical bully attitude," said Chester. "Anyone you consider to be stronger than you is your master; anyone who seems to be at your mercy becomes your victim. You've had a little trouble classifying me: I seemed to be a victim but repeatedly demonstrated that it was you who was being victimized. Are you ready now to accept reality?"

Grizz stood dumbly. Chester reached out, gripped the other's nose and twisted hard. Grizz gulped. Chester prodded him in the stomach, thumped his chest, kicked him lightly in the shin. "Well, care to try again?" Grizz swallowed hard, mouth opening and closing.

"I think perhaps you're properly oriented now, Grizz. You may go. Tell everyone that the attack has been postponed and that they're to stay clear of the palace. Don't tell anyone what happened here. Understand?"

Grizz nodded.

"And, Grizz, don't try to cheat on me."

There was a sound. Bandon stepped into view, the arrow aimed at Grizz's chest. "You intend to let this traitor walk out of here and warn 'em?"

"Hold on, Bandon. He won't give any trouble."

"Not if I can help it." Bandon made a sudden move and Chester whirled, snapped a hand out—

And stood gripping the shaft of the arrow, caught in mid-flight.

"You—you grabbed my Blue-Tooth's dart out of the air!" Bandon stared at Chester incredulously. "It's not possible!"

"Accept reality," Chester said. "It's simply a matter of trained reflexes and self-hypnotic alert conditioning."

"But then—when I brought you in—you could have . . . "

"That's right—but I wanted to see what was going on up here. Now we both know. We'd better move out now—fast. Grizz will snap out of his daze in a few minutes, and you'll discover how loyal your boys are."

"But . . . why should they want to turn on me? All I've done's been for their own good."

"Maybe—but the one thing your little group has in common is a yearning for more free goodies and less work. All anybody has to do to enlist their enthusiasm is promise them some easy loot."

"Hold on; I don't know what Grizz has said to them, but I can—"

"Promise them more," Chester finished. "But can

you deliver? This is a dead end, Bandon. Come on with me."

"I'm still boss here," Bandon said. "Come on; you'll see." He started for the door.

"Do me a small favor," Chester said, tucking the rusted hatchet into his waistband. "Sneak out the back way and look the situation over before you do anything foolish. I'm leaving now. I have a trail of unfinished business to see to. I hope you won't try to interfere."

Bandon hesitated. "I guess I owe you something," he said. "Grizz was out to get me, sure. But you're makin' a mistake. The free life is the only way."

Chester coiled the clothesline and looped it in his belt. "If you were smart, you'd head for the nearest Center and get used to clean clothes and a good bed again. You don't belong here with these wood lice. Leave this routine to Grizz and the other wild life."

"I'm safe enough. Come on with me. I'll give you a safe-conduct through the lines."

"Sorry, Bandon; I don't think you could guarantee that. I'm taking the back way."

"There's nothin' back there but the cliff face. You can't get through my sentry lines. There's too many men out there. You can't catch five arrows at once— and some of the boys have powder guns."

"I know—so that just leaves me one way out."

"Up the escarpment? You can't climb that—it's straight up."

"I don't have a lot of choice. Sorry you're not going with me. But if you change your mind, there's a cleft just behind the third house from the corner. I'll start from there."

"Got it all figured out, eh? You Downlanders beat me. Well, suit yourself."

"Thanks. And keep your head down until you see which way the wind is blowing."

10

In the blackness of Bandon's back yard, Chester paused, listening. A soft wind moved in the tall pines. Small frogs called; a bird shrilled again and again. Chester moved across the weed-choked garden, worked his way through a wild-grown hedge and over a fallen fence, started up a gravelly slope. Starlight gave a faint illumination. Behind him there was a sudden voice in the street, an angry retort. Chester recognized Bandon's voice. He reached the base of the cleft, found hand-holds, started up. Yells sounded from below now and Grizz's bull roar. Chester pulled himself up to a ledge and turned, waiting. The voices went on; then the thump of running feet sounded, coming nearer.

"Over here," Chester called softly. He picked up a fist-sized rock, hefted it. Hoarse breathing sounded below, the scrabble of feet on gravel.

"Bandon?" Chester said softly.

"It's me," a choked voice came back. "Why, those lousy, miserable, ungrateful skunks!"

"Uh-huh," Chester said. "Hurry up." He tossed the rock aside, unlimbered the coil of tough clothesline. Other feet sounded now. A torch flared behind Bandon's house.

Grizz's voice bellowed commands: "Beat vat brush, boys. Ve turncoat can't be far off!"

There was a sound of sliding, followed by a thump. Below, Bandon cursed in a strained whisper. "How in the name of the Kez-father do you get up there?"

"Hey, I heard somefing over vere," a voice called. A second torch flared.

Chester tied a loop in the end of the clothesline,

lowered it down the cleft. "Grab this," he whispered. "And keep it quiet."

Bandon muttered softly to himself; Chester felt the rope move as Bandon fumbled with it. "Hurry up!" Chester called.

"Haul away," Bandon said softly. Chester braced his feet and pulled. Bandon's feet scraped, sent small stones rattling down the rock face.

"Over vere!" two voices yelled at once. Pounding feet approached. There was a yelp and one torch went out.

"Somebody found my coon trap," Bandon grunted. With a final heave, Chester hauled him up high enough to grip the edge of the ledge. A moment later, they stood side by side.

"I'm going on up," Chester said. "Don't make a sound. As soon as I reach secure footing again, I'll lower the line."

"Don't waste any time," Bandon said. "Grizz may not be able to climb up here, but he's a pretty good hand with a long bow. A pure shame I didn't have time to gather up my Blue-Tooth."

"All you'd do is get us spotted quicker. Stand fast now." Chester reached up, found a grip, pulled himself up. The going was easy enough; the fingerholds were all of a quarter of an inch deep, and the climb was not even quite vertical; there was a slope of at least three degrees. As for the height, it was negligible: a mere sixty feet or so now. A few months ago, it would have been a different story, Chester thought suddenly, smiling. In the old days, he would have clung to the cliff, bleating for help.

Abruptly, the precariousness of his position dawned on Chester. What was he, Chester W. Chester IV, doing here, climbing up the face of a vertical precipice in the dark, with a crew of ferocious back-to-nature cultists at his heels? Suddenly, the meager handholds seemed grossly inadequate. Chester froze, digging with his toes for a secure footing. The light breeze seemed to batter at him like a gale. His shoulder blades drew together in anticipation of Grizz's long-bow bolt.

"Hey," Bandon's voice whispered anxiously from below. "Don't forget me."

Chester drew a deep breath and let it out slowly, feeling his fear-tensed muscles loosen. He was glad Kuve hadn't been around to see how easily he'd forgotten his training in a moment of panic. He went up another ten feet, found a foot-wide ledge and lowered the rope. There were three torches below now, near the foot of the cliff.

"Here's some footprints," someone shouted.

"Hey, look up vere," another voice shouted. "Did you see somefing move?"

"It's him!"

"Who's got a bow handy?"

"Bandon," Chester called softly. "Gather up a handful of rocks, then tie the rope around your waist. You pepper 'em while I pull you up. Maybe it will be enough to spoil their aim—or at least make them nervous."

"Sure."

Chester heard the rasp of stone, then a grunt as Bandon pegged one. There was a loud yell from below.

"Got the skunk!" Bandon whispered loudly. A moment later a second cry rang out.

"What's goin' on?" someone wanted to know.

"Rocks fallin'."

"Ohhh, my head!"

"Bandon, hurry up! Get that rope tied!" Chester felt the rope vibrate.

"All right," Bandon called. Chester heaved at the rope. It was hard work this time, with Bandon too fully occupied to assist by clawing his way up as Chester pulled. The rope cut into Chester's hands. An arrow clanged against the stone ten feet to one side, striking red sparks. Chester grunted and hauled. More arrows struck, one no more than a yard away. One of the torches below went out as its bearer yelled.

"Don't throw at the torches," Chester gasped. "All they do is blind them."

"Oh, sorry," Bandon said cheerfully. "The varmints are thick as fleas in a bearhide down there. Can't hardly miss."

He crawled up beside Chester. "Whoosh! That rope cuts! And we've still got a ways to go." An arrow ricocheted off the rock wall a yard from Chester's head.

"Let's get out of here. They'll bracket in on us before long. If you're hit, try not to yell."

"I'll keep 'em busy," Bandon said. He stooped, came up with a head-sized stone, and dropped it down into the darkness. It hit once with a crash; a moment later three hoarse yells sounded almost together.

"Ha!" Bandon exulted. "That's showin' 'em."

Three painful climbs and half an hour later Chester and Bandon lay stretched full-length on a wide ledge. The noise below had dwindled to an occasional half-hearted curse and a few groans. The arrows had stopped coming.

"Looks like we got away clean," Bandon said. "The skunks sure gave up easy."

"We'll rest a few minutes," Chester said. "Then we'll go on to the top and head back toward the Center—"

"Oh-oh," Bandon said.

"What's the matter?"

"Reckon I forgot somethin'."

"Well, I don't think we'd better go back for it, under the circumstances."

"It's not that. But I forgot to tell you. This cliff we've gone and climbed up on: no wonder the boys aren't too worried about getting after us."

"Well?"

"There's no way down. If you'd seen it in daylight you'd know what I mean. It's a mesa, and the side we're climbing is the easy one."

Hot morning sun beat down on Chester's short-cropped head as he walked along the cliff edge to the boulder against which Bandon sat waiting.

"It's like I told you," Bandon said. "We're stuck."

"Why didn't you mention the topographical peculiarities of the place to me last night, when I first announced I was heading this way?" Chester asked.

"I figured it wouldn't matter, 'cause I didn't figure you'd be able to get up here anyhow. I figured you'd be back in a few minutes, beggin' my pardon and askin' for that safe-conduct. I guess I made kind of a fool of myself."

"I won't be so uncivil as to argue that point." Chester peered over the precipice. It dropped vertically for fifty feet, then shelved back. The base was visible a hundred yards below, plunging sheer into a green blanket of treetops.

"Grizz'll have the boys spotted all the way around, and trip wires rigged," Bandon said. "Even if we had a way to get down, they'd be on top of us like flies on a beer keg before we got out shirt tails tucked in."

Chester scaled a rock out over the forest, watched it curve and drop down, down . . .

"Poor Genie," he said. "And Case."

"I don't know who you're grievin' over," Bandon said, "but you can add your own name to the list. If we don't starve up here, it'll be because we climbed down and broke our necks—or got plugged full of arrows. One thing we don't have to do is get heat stroke. Let's get over under the trees."

They walked across the stony ground toward the rising mound of wooded land that occupied the center of the ten-acre island of the mesa top.

"We'd better look around and see if there's anything edible growing up here," Chester said.

"And water," Bandon added. "I'm already gettin' thirsty."

"Maybe we can find some game. Why don't you set to work and make yourself a new bow? I'll start on a shelter, in case it rains—and we'll have to rig some sort of catch-basin, if we don't find a spring."

"What's the use? It'll just stretch out our dyin'. Maybe we ought to just take a flyin' jump. Maybe we'd land on a couple of Grizz's skunks."

"Here, none of that," Chester said sharply. "We may find that we can live quite comfortably here— in spite of the lack of canned beans and television. This is your opportunity to try the free life you're so fond of."

"Sure, but . . . " Bandon muttered.

"You start off in that direction." Chester pointed toward a stand of slender, bluish-needled conifers. "I'll check over there. We'll meet back here at the edge of the woods in an hour."

Chester laid aside the rusted hatchet with which he had been pounding in a stake.

"Any luck?" he called as Bandon tramped from the underbrush.

"I guess so," Bandon said dispiritedly. "There's a good stand of ash back there I can make some kind of bow out of. And I found some kind of an old tent—"

Chester came to his feet. "You mean the place is inhabited?"

Bandon shook his head. "Not any more. Come on. I need help to get it out. We can use the material to build that catch-basin, and I guess there's enough over to put a roof on that hut of yours." He nodded toward Chester's embryonic framework of sticks bound together with lengths of clothesline wire.

Chester followed Bandon back into the woods, pushing through tangled underbrush, squeezing between interlaced saplings. The taller trees became thicker and the ground more open as they progressed. Ahead, draped in the branches of a dead pine, Chester saw a billow of grayish-white, a snarl of lines trailing down almost to the ground.

"There it is," Bandon said. "Don't know what it's doin' in a treetop. But there's plenty of stuff there to make a hut and whatever else we need. And some good rope, too. Not that it's goin' to do us any good," he added.

"It's a parachute," Chester said in wonder. "I was under the impression that there were no aeronautics here, other than helis, and you don't need parachutes with those. They let themselves down gently if the power fails."

"What other kind is there?" Bandon inquired.

Chester explained to Bandon the function of a conventional flying machine.

"I never heard of any such thing," Bandon said, shaking his head. "But it seems like I remember some kind of big gas bag some fellows put on some kind of show with, once when I was a kid back in the Tricennium. They went sailin' right up into the sky. Damnedest thing you ever saw."

"I wonder what happened to the pilot who came down in this?"

"Oh, him," Bandon said. "He's right over here." He led the way across the carpet of leaves under the giant trees to a thicket. "In there."

Chester parted the brush and looked into a bower

of woven branches thatched with dried grass. On the dirt floor were three hand-made earthenware pots and a woven basket with the desiccated remains of what might have once been fruit. Beside the basket lay the skeleton of a man.

"Good Lord!" Chester muttered. "Poor devil."

"Can't figure what killed him—'less it was old age," Bandon said. "No arrows stickin' in him, no broken bones. Plenty of food and water, I'd say."

"He must have bailed out of his balloon, landed here and found himself marooned," Chester said. "But surely he could have signaled in some way . . . "

"Must have been a long time back—before our town was built. And there's no other Tricennium for twenty miles."

"What about the Center? It's not more than five miles."

"They just built that a year or two back. Nope, he was stuck, all right. Just like us. We might just as well hunker down beside him—"

"But why didn't he use the parachute? He could have rigged it somehow and jumped!"

Bandon eyed the sagging yellow-white cloth above. "Jump off the cliff with that trailin' behind him, hey? I dunno. I'd hate to try it."

Chester hitched up his belt. "You may just have to. Come on, let's get it down from there."

Chester and Bandon stood gazing sadly at the broad expanse of weather-spotted and puckered nylon stretched on the ground before them. Two long, dark tears in the material ran from edge to edge.

"I see why he didn't use it," Chester said glumly. "Well, that's that. The material's still sound, though. We might as well cut it up in sections for easy hauling and get back to work on our hut."

"Don't reckon we could sew it up," Bandon said doubtfully.

"Not a chance. We might manage to work some threads loose and lace it back together, but it wouldn't hold air. And with a double load—well, we'd splash when we hit."

Bandon winced. "Let's get busy. I'll salvage those pots and the basket. Must be water near here, 's the reason he camped here."

An hour later, having used Bandon's bone-handled hunting knife to dissect the parachute, Chester folded the sections, coiled the lines and settled down to wait for his companion's return. He could hear him crashing through nearby underbrush.

Bandon emerged, red-faced and scratched. "Found it," he said. "Little pothole, damn near buried in prickle bushes. We'll spend half our time just getting' enough water to stay alive on."

"I'll use the hatchet to clear it away," Chester said. "Let's be going."

"Why not built right here?"

"I like the open glade near the edge better. Then, too, this place has certain morbid associations."

"You mean him?" Bandon nodded toward the dead man's hut. "Shucks, he can't hurt us."

"I'd like to be able to look out and see the rest of the world. Let's be moving. We have a lot to do before we can consider ourselves settled in."

"Squirrel food," Bandon said, spitting blackberry seeds. "Only three days on squirrel food, and my britches are so loose they'd fall off if I didn't have 'em roped on."

"Why don't you finish up that bow? Then maybe you'd be able to eat rabbit for a change," Chester said cheerfully. "Personally, I like berries."

"Bow's made," Bandon said shortly. "But I can't string it till I get a rabbit to gut. And I can't get a rabbit to gut till I—"

"Why don't you use nylon?"

"That stuff? Stretches like rubber. You couldn't throw an arrow fifty feet with that. And besides, I need arrowheads and feathers and glue. Now, I can make up a swell glue—just as soon's I can shoot a few critters."

"Chip some heads out of stone," Chester suggested. "And you ought to be able to find a few feathers around an old nest or some such place."

"I've got plenty of nice arrow shafts ready. Good tough, springy wood. And light."

Chester fingered an arrow. "You do nice work, Bandon. Too bad you left the part of the world where it would be appreciated. You could have fitted in nicely as an archery expert."

"I wouldn't have been an archery expert if I hadn't thrown off the shackles first."

"Still, if you go back . . . "

"Ha!" Bandon looked out over the airy vista of distant ridges. "Unless we turn into birds, that's not likely."

Chester sat up suddenly, flexed the arrow shaft in both hands.

"Bandon, what kind of wood is this? Is there a good supply of it?"

Bandon raised an eyebrow at the excitement in Chester's tone. He waved a hand. "The woods are full of it. What—"

"You say you can make glue?"

"Glue? Sure I can make glue. All you have to do is boil down a few carcasses . . . "

Chester was on his feet. "Bandon, you get that bow of yours working. I don't care if you string it with shoelaces. Bring me in a brace of rabbits and boil up a pot of stickum." He picked up the hatchet, its blade bright now from use. "I'm headed for the tall timber."

"Hold on, here. What's goin' on? We've got plenty of firewood; and I've lost too much weight to go traipsin' off on a rabbit hunt."

"For what I've got in mind, the lighter you are, the better. And I'm not hunting firewood; I'm after what they call aircraft spruce."

"Chester, just what *have* you got in mind?"

"We're going to leave here, Bandon. It will take a few days, but we'll travel in style."

"In style?"

"To be precise—in a home-built glider."

"She'll be built along the lines of an old-time training ship," Chester said. "Neat and simple."

"Simple? We've already got more junk lined up to go into this contraption than it would take to stock a store. Five kinds of wood, cloth, wire, string, glue—"

"And we're still grossly understocked, believe me. But I think we can do it."

"I don't see the need of usin' my knife to make that thing," Bandon said, watching Chester take long, curling shavings from a spruce spar with a jack plane made from a chunk of wood and the knife blade.

"It's a lot more efficient than a knife for trimming up structural members," Chester said. "How's the glue factory coming?"

"Oh, I've got enough glue to feather a million arrows. Can I quit boilin' down rabbit now and fix a couple to eat?"

"Sure. But don't overdo it. I wasn't kidding when I said the lighter we are, the better. Then I wish you'd go to work stripping down that clothesline; there's ten strands of steel wire under the plastic cover. We'll use that for diagonal frame-bracing. And I'll need lots of the nylon parachute lines unraveled, too. Reel it on a stick as you get it worked apart."

Bandon set to work. "I still don't see how you figure to flap the wings, Chester. To hold us up, you'll have to have a spread of maybe ten, twelve feet."

"Thirty," Chester said. "And a five-foot cord. Not a very efficient layout, but I'm afraid it's the best we can do with the materials at hand. Figuring us each at one-fifty—or a little less, if we eat sparingly for another week—and the airframe at two hundred pounds, that works out to three pounds per square foot. And we won't flap our wings—unless I've miscalculated badly."

"Well, I guess you know what you're doin'."

"Certainly. In my youth I was a fanatical model-plane builder. Free-flight, control-line, RC, hand-launch—the works."

"You done much flyin' off cliffs?"

"Well, if you mean in full-scale aircraft—"

"I do."

"Actually, none."

"None? But you've built a lot of them, hey?"

"Well, not actually anything big enough to carry a man—but I did put together a seven-foot multi-engine control-liner."

"You mean we're goin' to jump over a cliff in a contraption you've never tried out before, and that you maybe don't know how to work even if it doesn't come apart?"

"The alternative," Chester pointed out, "is sitting up here in the eagle's nest until we get too old to pick berries."

Bandon shouldered his bow. "I'm goin' out and get us a couple of eatin' rabbits," he announced. "We might just as well eat and drink and enjoy it while we can."

"That's right," Chester said. "Because tomorrow—who knows?"

✦   ✦   ✦

"It looks like a coffin for a tall, skinny corpse," Bandon said, eyeing the twenty-foot openwork structure of spruce strips propped on sawhorses made from peeled logs.

"Two tall, skinny fellows," Chester said. "You stretch out here." He indicated a section floored with woven strips of willow bark. "I take up the right-hand position beside you. I'll have to have room to edge forward or back to correct the trim. Now, I want you to go along wrapping each joint with nylon patches, and working in glue. What I wouldn't give for a few square feet of one-eighth birch ply and a pound or two of wire brads."

"While you're wishin', you might just as well wish for a concealed staircase leadin' from here into that air-conditioned restaurant you were talkin' about. You can have the blonde. Just leave me to the steaks and chops."

Chester jumped as a sudden *whop!* sounded behind him. He whirled. A long steel-tipped arrow quivered upright against the sod.

"They're shootin' at us," Bandon blurted. "Where are they?" He stared wildly around.

Chester swept the scene with a glance. "That arrow came straight down—and from not very high up." He pulled it from the ground. "It wasn't buried more than a few inches."

As Chester looked toward the cliff edge, a second arrow shot up into view, curved and fell twenty feet away.

"Ah-hah! They're pegging them up here with an arbalest of some sort." A moment later a round stone the size of a grapefruit sailed into view, slowed to a stop and dropped back out of sight. "They've got a catapult working, too. I hope that drops back on someone's toe."

"I thought it was awful quiet these last few days," Bandon said. "They've been a busy bunch down there, getting' ready to lay down a barrage on us."

Chester watched a second stone fly into view and drop with a thump fifty yards away. Other arrows nipped up; some fell back, other clattered to earth at distances from ten to a hundred feet.

"How do they know where to aim?" Chester asked. "They're hitting pretty close."

"There's a couple pairs of binoculars in the town," Bandon said. "I reckon a few of the skunks are staked out on the next ridge watchin' every move we make." He shook a fist in the presumed direction of the spies. "See if you can figure it out, blast you!" he yelled defiantly. He turned to Chester. "Maybe we'd better move 'er back to the edge of the woods."

"I don't think we're in any real danger, short of an accident," Chester replied, watching a rock clatter down thirty feet distant. "There are as many falling behind us as in front. Let's just keep at it and hope for the best. I wonder why they're so persistent? They should be content to let us starve up here in peace, one would think."

"It's not that easy," Bandon said. "Grizz can't afford to let me get away—or die off."

"Why not?"

"Well, I've been thinkin'. He doesn't know where the treasury is—and he's not the kind of fellow to forget a thing like that."

"Treasury? I hadn't heard about that before. What does it consist of, a hoard of salami, canned crackers and replacement tubes for the Tri-D?"

"Nope. Guns and powder, mostly."

"Hmmm. I was about to suggest that you might throw a note over the side giving directions to its location, but under the circumstances that would be unwise."

An arrow dropped five feet from the edge of the wing.

"Oh-oh. We can't have any punctures now that we've started covering. Bandon, maybe you'd better start a counter-barrage while I work on the gluing. When I need you to stretch the next panel, I'll call you."

"That's a mighty flimsy-looking thing." Bandon studied the nearly completed project. "How long before we have to try it?"

"Not long. There are the tail surfaces to cover and install and the controls to link up. I'd say by sundown we'll be about ready—but of course, the glue needs overnight to set up thoroughly."

"That tail's not very big." Bandon gestured toward the stabilizer and rudder frames propped against a tree. "Why not just leave 'em off?"

"Impractical, I'm afraid," Chester said. "No tail assembly, no flight. We'd drop like a stone—tail first."

Bandon jumped as a rock crashed down at his feet. "Maybe we'd better head for the tall brush before Grizz gets lucky," he suggested nervously.

"And let them knock the glider apart at their leisure? Not—"

With a crash, a four-inch stone slammed through the woven floorboards of the pilot's compartment. Chester stared at it in dismay.

"We were lucky," he said. "It missed the keel. Bandon, get busy on that counterattack. We can't let them stop us now!"

11

A ruddy dawn was breaking over the distant eastern hills. Clutching an improvised cape about his shoulders against the early-morning chill, Chester examined the nylon-covered wing, glistening with dew.

"It looks as though she's survived the night intact."

"Here, look at this," Bandon called. He held up a paper-wrapped stone. "Looks like it might be a message." He stripped off the paper, glanced at it and handed it to Chester.

Kum don now and sav yerself frum gitin yer brans bust in. Bandon, it ant yu, jus the spi wer after. Grizz, bos.

"Well, that's an attractive offer," Chester said. "If you trust him."

Bandon snorted. "I heard him makin' promises to you a few days back. I reckon I'll take my chances with the flyin' machine. But, say, Chester, how do you figure on gettin" it over the edge? If we're both sittin' in it . . . "

"That's easy. We'll set up a pair of peeled willow rails; we'll use the poles we skinned for their bark. The glider will have to be anchored in position with a length of nylon line. When we're ready to go, I'll cut the cable. The rails will be laid up the slope at an angle, so a fifty-foot run ought to give us a good enough send-off. Of course, I'll have to put her nose down as soon as we're over the edge, to gain flying speed."

"Maybe if we rigged a weighted line and hung it over the edge, it would give her a little extra kick-off. We'd have to fix it so it'd drop off when we went over the edge."

"Good idea. You find us a suitable ballast stone—as big as you can lift. We'll try to get off before the morning barrage starts. I'll be ready to move her upslope and set up the track in about ten minutes."

Bandon nodded and moved off. Chester climbed into the pilot's compartment, stretched out face down and fitted his toes against the rudder bar. Looking over his shoulder, he could see the rudder wag in response to his foot movements. He tried the stick; the elevators flopped up and down correctly. A side pressure warped the trailing edge of the left wing panel up and down.

"Pre-flight check complete," Chester murmured to himself. He crawled out, moving carefully as the open-work fuselage creaked under his weight. Upslope, Bandon levered a boulder with a pole. It lifted, teetered, started a slow trundle downhill.

"Bandon!" Chester called, running forward. "Stop that!"

Bandon stood frozen, watching the massive rock gather speed, aimed directly for the glider perched at the cliffside. Chester slid to a halt, turned and dashed back for the ship. He skidded around under the wing, seized the tail post and hauled. The glider slid back with a grate of wood against soil, then jammed—just as the boulder took a mighty bound and leaped over it to drop from sight over the cliff. Chester slumped against the frail craft.

"Hey, Chester, I'm sorry about that."

A mighty crash sounded from below, followed by faint yells. Chester went to the edge and looked over. A great gap showed in the mass of foliage far below. Through the opening Chester saw men darting about among the splintered remains of a wooden structure. Bandon arrived at his side and stared down silently.

"Well, blast those skunks, Chester. You see that? They were buildin' an almighty big catapult down there. See the throwin' arm layin' off there to the left? Pretty smart, hey, sneakin' around under cover of those trees and fixin' to let fly with the big stuff. By the nine tails of the hill-devil, it's a good thing that stone got away from me."

"Maybe—but I'd just as soon we didn't do anything so dramatic again. Let's get that track set up."

Chester studied the panorama. "We'll angle it to the right to avoid that depression near the edge. I'll aim her right off there between those two knolls. With luck, we can stretch our glide to half a mile. That ought to give us all the start we need on our welcoming committee."

"Wonder what's happened to the artillery this morning? I guess maybe that little pebble we dropped on 'em shook 'em up a little."

"I hope so. It would be a shame to suffer a hit now."

Chester and Bandon set to work pegging wooden rails in place. They finished, then took up positions on opposite sides of the craft and lifted it clear of the ground.

"Hey, it's not so heavy," Bandon commented.

"Watch your footing," Chester said.

Together they toiled up the slope, maneuvered carefully, then settled the ship in place on the track.

"Hold her while I chock her," Chester called. He wedged a sizable stone fragment in place under the down-tipped nose. "All right, now we rig the restraining cable."

Chester payed out a length of nylon to the nearest tree, tied it securely, then attached the other end to the keel of the glider between the two pilot positions.

"All set," he said, removing the chock from the track. "All that's holding her now is the cable. When I cut that—off we go."

"It sure is quiet," Bandon commented, looking around. "I wonder . . . "

"Let's just be grateful," Chester said. "I wasn't looking forward to having to launch right out through a hail of arrows. I'll lay out the ballast line now while you bring in a stone."

At the edge of the precipice, Chester dropped the coil of nylon line and tied a secure noose ready to receive the weighting stone. As he rose to turn back, an unshaven face rose into view not ten feet from him; two grimy hands scrabbled for a grip.

Chester jumped, put a foot square in the face and pushed. With a yelp, the man dropped back; a tremendous crash followed. Chester looked over the edge. Twenty feet below, a rickety platform thrust up; three men crouched atop it, while another sprawled on his back, half through the shattered decking. One of the three brought a bow into position and launched an arrow in one motion; it whistled past Chester's ear. He whirled, grabbed up a hundred-pound rock and eased it over the edge. There was a noisy crunch. Now two of the men clung frantically to the shattered remains of the platform, while the third scrambled agilely down the rickety structure. The fourth man was gone. Looking to the left Chester saw a second platform and beyond it a third. And there were more to the right.

Chester was up and running. "Bandon! Forget the stone! Get to the glider!"

Bandon stared, then dropped the rock and headed for the craft at a run. From the woods behind the glider a man in a soiled shirt and torn pants emerged, his bow at the ready. Bandon, in mid-stride, nocked an arrow and let fly. The newcomer fell backward, feathers at his throat.

"Into your seat, fast!" Chester yelled.

"Say, I'm not really sure I want to risk this," Bandon exclaimed.

At the cliff edge, two men came into view simultaneously, scrambling up, starting for the glider at a run. Bandon whipped his bow up, set an arrow, twanged it on its way, sped a second. One man whirled and fell; the other dived for cover. Bandon dropped the bow and slid into his place, face down. Chester jumped in after him, wriggled his feet up against the rudder bar. Reaching down with his right hand, he sawed at the tether with the knife blade. More men appeared. One raised a bow and let an arrow fly. It struck the nose block with a *whack!*, stood quivering in the wood. The rope parted. With a lurch, the little ship started forward, grinding and bumping along the green-wood tracks. Wind whistled in Chester's face. The running men had halted, staring. The bowman raised his bow, loosed an arrow, missed by yards. As the glider bore down on him, he turned and fled. More men were coming over the edge now.

"The skunks stayed up late last night plannin' this one," Bandon yelled in Chester's ear. "They—"

"Quiet!" Chester choked.

The glider seemed to move forward with infinite leisure. The grass and gravel moved past in a ribbon that blurred slowly. The cliff edge was ahead now, coming closer.

"We're not going to make it!" Chester mumbled. "Not enough speed."

An arrow slammed off the framework above Chester's head, knocking off splinters. Ahead was blue sky and distant, hazy hills.

"Now!" Chester gasped. Abruptly the grate of wood on wood ceased—and the bottom dropped from under them. Chester shoved forward on the stick convulsively, his breath caught in his throat, his heart slamming madly under his ribs. Down, down, falling, the wide spread of green rushing up, wind screaming now in the wires at Chester's side, buffeting his face. Lying prone, he pulled back on the stick, neutralizing it, then farther back . . .

He could feel the air pressure resisting the stick. He pulled harder, felt pressure build against his chest, saw the green below tilting away, flattening, saw the hills sliding down into view, with sky above them. He looked over the side. Treetops rushed past a hundred feet below.

"Hey!" Bandon yelled. "We're flyin', Chester!"

The nose rose, aiming now at the distant sky. Chester pushed the stick, felt the ship slow, hesitate minutely, then drop her nose. He swallowed. "Whip stall," he muttered. "Pilot-killers."

"Say, Chester, this is great!" Bandon called.

Chester inched forward, applied a little right rudder. The ship turned sloppily.

"A little aileron," Chester told himself. He edged the stick to one side, felt the ship tilt sharply. Air currents buffeted the glider. Chester gritted his teeth, fighting the motion. "Let it fly itself," he reminded himself, consciously relaxing. A gust rocked the craft; it righted itself. The nose crept up; Chester eased the stick forward. The nose came down. The flank of a hill was approaching. Chester applied rudder, coordinating the ailerons; the ship heeled, curved away.

"Wheeeee!" Bandon cried. "Just like a bird, Chester!"

There was a valley ahead, a steep cleft between hills. Chester aimed for it, holding a straight course. He drew a deep breath and let it out slowly.

"Nothin' to it, Chester," Bandon said. "Here, have some nuts."

"Not yet, thanks," Chester called. "For heaven's sake lie still and let me fly this thing."

"Say, Chester, that's funny," Bandon said.

"What's funny?"

"We're gettin' higher instead of comin' down. Hey, Chester, how are we goin' to get down if this thing keeps goin' up?"

"You're raving," Chester said.

Wind screamed past his face, making his eyes water. He twisted his head and looked over the side. The trees below were a smooth blanket of green. He looked back. The mesa was visible a mile away.

"You're right!" Chester said. "I can see the top of the mesa. I guess we've snagged a thermal!"

"Is that good or bad?"

"Good. Now don't bother me for a few minutes, and I'll see if I can stretch our glide to a new Tricennium record!"

"Five miles," Chester called. "That was the Center back there."

"What keeps her in the air, Chester, without flappin' her wings?"

"We're riding rising air currents off these slopes. We've got a very poor glide angle, I'm afraid, but the updrafts are so strong we're gaining altitude in spite of our inefficiency. I'm hoping to catch some true thermals over the plains ahead. I'd estimate our altitude at about three thousand feet now. I'd like to work her up to about five and then set out west toward the Tricennium of the Original Wisdom. If we can make a few miles it will save us a long, hot walk."

"I'm all for it, Chester. I like it fine up here."

"That remark seems to indicate you've abandoned your simple-life philosophy. An aircraft—even a primitive one like this—is a far cry from chipping flints."

"Why, what do you mean, Chester? We made this ourselves, out of plain old wood and rabbit glue."

"Plus a few bits of nylon and some steel wire. But after all, every manufactured item is made from simple raw materials—even a Tri-D tube. All materials are natural, if you trace them back to their beginnings. There's nothing wrong with rearranging nature to give ourselves a few more comforts—it's misusing what we make that takes the savor out of life."

"Maybe so. But it's not really the *stuff*; it's the *people* that gravel me. I don't want anybody tellin' me what to do, tryin' to push me around. Soon's we land, I guess I'll head for the hills again."

"Bandon, learn to do something that other people want or need and you won't have to worry about being stepped on. Most of the shrill cries of social injustice come from people who contribute nothing to the scene that a chimpanzee couldn't do better. Why do you think people treasure the few really talented singers, actors, ball players, medical men, engineers that crop up? Because there are far too few of them—every one is a treasure. And if a new man comes along and writes a song that reaches out and touches something in everybody, he doesn't have to worry about being picked on. His fans won't let anything happen to him."

"Well, maybe I could start up an archery class, like you said. You suppose folks would come and want to learn?"

"Try it and find out. If there's something in archery that makes you love it, there'll be others that will get the same thrill. Be best at something—and let the world know it."

"Hey, Chester, look down there. A line running right across the countryside."

"A road," Chester explained. "That's good. We can follow it right back to town."

"And way up ahead—looks like buildings, away off."

"That's possible. From this altitude, the Tricennium should be visible; it's only about fifteen miles."

Chester squinted overhead for cumulus clouds, steered for the shadow of the nearest. The updraft rocket the tiny craft. "All right, Bandon, here we go." He banked the glider to the right and struck out for the distant city.

✧   ✧   ✧

Half an hour later the glider whistled in past a row of tall trees, cleared an outlying house by inches, settled in over a broad green lawn. It skimmed for a hundred yards, then dropped with a mild jar to skid for another fifty feet before heeling over with one wing tip scooping up turf, describing an abrupt arc and coming to rest.

"Whew!" Chester sighed. He rose to hands and knees and looked around at the well-manicured greenery, the peaceful rooflines and the half-dozen men coming across the lawn at a jog trot.

"Get ready for a rude reception, Bandon. I'm not certain these fellows quite appreciate *my* little contribution to society. They may be the pushy kind."

"Well, I'd like to see 'em try it with me," Bandon growled.

"Don't leap to any untenable conclusions: they're a mild-looking lot, but they're full of surprises."

The leading greeter came up. "Extraordinary!" he commented, looking at the glider, Chester, Bandon and the long groove in the velvety lawn. "Where in the world did you come from?"

A second man came up. "Now, Gayme, what did I tell you? A stiff-winged, manned aircraft. Look at these two chaps. As ordinary a pair as you'd care to meet. So much for your talk of the supernormal."

"The manifestation is, I insist, supernormal, in the sense that it surpasses the ordinary run of events. Note the lack of motive power. How did such an assemblage of artifacts and personnel come to be up there to begin with?"

"Look here," Chester said.

"Tut, tut, Gayme. I'm sure there's a simple, rational explanation. I suggest we start at the beginning by asking a few questions." He eyed Bandon. "You, sir. Do you mind telling me just how you came to descend from an empty sky?"

"Sure, easy," Bandon said. "I live on a cloud, and I just came down to get a refill on moonbeams. Any other questions? If not, how about a few eats? I'm hungry."

"Ah-hah," Gayme crowed. "Just as I suspected. We'll consult Norgo."

"This is where I came in," Chester said. "Look, Bandon, I'll just slip over to the town square and see to a few things. I may not see you again. If I don't, I hereby will you full rights to the glider. Don't let them euchre you out of it; they're good at appropriating things in the name of science. And work on your archery."

"Hold on, Chester. Say, I figure we get on pretty good together. I figured you and I'd stick together."

"Sorry, Bandon, old chap. It's been a most rewarding experience, but I have some unfinished business to attend to—if it isn't altogether too late. I'm going to find an inconspicuous corner and lie low for a few hours. Good luck."

Bandon took his hand. "Well, all right, Chester. Sorry about getting' you into that fix back there."

"Thus," Gayme droned on, "the phenomenon is related to the spontaneous precipitation of frogs sometimes reported from outlying areas."

"Who is outlying whom?" his friend inquired archly. "Now, I . . . "

Chester moved off quietly across the lawn. No one called after him.

In gathering twilight Chester moved across the square toward the shadows of the cupola, the scene of his arrival ten months earlier. As he reached the flower bed ringing the monument, a tall figure stepped before him, peered at Chester's lithe, broad-shouldered figure, his tanned face, sinewy arms, short-clipped sun-bleached hair and tight-fitting Tricennium costume.

"Oh, sorry," he said. "I was waiting for the poor little nincompoop who had the fixation regarding the rug. They say he slipped away from the Center right in the middle of the experiment. You're one of Norgo's crew?"

"I'm the poor little nincompoop," Chester said flatly. "Get out of my way, Devant."

"Wha . . . ? Is it really you?"

"It's really me—and I'm reclaiming my property now."

Devant laughed. "Still the same pathetic line, eh? Well, Norgo warned that you'd probably head for here. I'll take you back now to finish your course of experimental study."

"I graduated."

"Oh, really?" Devant laughed again easily, reached for Chester. There was a brief flurry of motion and Devant hit the pavement—hard.

"Glad I ran into you, Devant," Chester said, stepping over him. "That's one piece of unfinished business out of the way. If I find I'm too late to help my friends, I'll be back to finish the job."

Devant scrambled up with a shout. There were answering calls, the pad of running feet. Chester sprinted for the rug, veered around a stone bench, made out the dim outline of a chair. An overhead light glared suddenly, showing Chester a ring of men closing in, Norgo in the lead, holding up a hand. The posse halted.

"Computer, are you there?" Chester called urgently. There was a long pause.

"Chester, you know you aren't allowed on the rug," Norgo called. "Just come along quietly now."

"Watch him," Devant cautioned, dabbing at his cheek. "He's learned a few tricks."

"Ah, Mr. Chester"—the familiar voice spoke from mid-air—"I had a little difficulty in locating you."

"Stand by," Chester said. "I'll be with you in a moment."

He turned to face Norgo. "I'm sorry to rush off," he called, feet planted on the rug. "I'd have enjoyed staying longer, but personal affairs demand my attention. Give my regards to Kuve—and watch out for a rabble-rouser named Grizz. He lives up in the hills, but he's planning on moving into town soon."

"I had hoped your delirium would clear up once you were separated from your fetish object," Norgo said sadly. "Too bad." He signaled; the posse closed in.

"Goodbye, Norgo," Chester called. "Thanks for everything. And after I'm gone, remember: accept reality. Is-not is not not-is.

"All right, Computer," he added, "take me back to Genie."

12

Misty twilight turned to the glare of day on a city street. Chester looked around. Nothing had changed from his last glimpse of the scene ten months before, except that the crowd had dwindled to a few die-hards. The street was still roped off, although the phalanx of squad cars had been reduced to two vehicles, each with a pair of heavyweights in the front seat, none of whom was looking his way.

"Don't go away, Computer," Chester said softly. "I'll have to try to find Genie, and it may take a while."

"Very well, Mr. Chester," the computer's voice replied loudly. "I'll occupy myself with an analysis of—"

"Quiet!" Chester snapped, too late. Four round cop faces turned to stare at Chester. Car doors swung open; flat feet scrambled. Two cops advanced on Chester while two more rounded their vehicles, hitching at red leather pistol belts.

"Hey, what's them chairs and rug doin' back here?" one cop demanded.

"Who're you, Bud?" another spoke up.

Chester folded his arms and glared at the lead cop. "I thought I left instructions that this area was to be watched closely," he barked. "Who dumped these things here? You men think this is a used-furniture store?"

"What's that?" the lead cop said, letting his mouth hang open.

"Button your coat," Chester snapped. "And see that you shave before coming on duty next time." He put his hands behind his back and strode along the line of cops. "Sergeant, those boots need attention. And your car needs a wash."

"Hey, who're you?" a cop said.

"Who're you, *sir!*" Chester roared. "Don't you know the field uniform of a Commissioner of Police when you see one?"

"Sure," the cop replied promptly. "And that ain't it."

"State Police, that is," Chester amended.

"State Police? Heck, I seen the State Police Commissioner at the race track just last week."

"State *Department* Police, you nincompoop!" Chester bellowed. "Don't you realize this is a matter of international import? Why," he went on in a confidential tone, "I have it on good authority that the affair ties in with a scheduled interplanetary invasion."

"Geez," a cop said.

"Now," Chester went on smoothly, "do you happen to recall the case of the unclothed young woman who was arrested in this vicinity some time ago?"

The cops looked at each other. One lifted his chrome-plated helmet and squinted upward.

"Well," he said. "Ahhh . . . "

"I *think* maybe I remember something about that," another cop volunteered.

"Ah, fine. Can you tell me what disposition was made of the case? It seems to have slipped my memory."

"Well, let's see . . . "

"Perhaps she served a brief sentence and was sent on her way," Chester suggested. "She might even have gotten a job—somewhere nearby."

"A job," a cop repeated, staring at Chester.

"Why don't you come on down to the station house . . . ah . . . Commissioner? Maybe we can fix you up down there."

"Why, she may still be right there in the women's cell block," another cop spoke up. "Maybe you can have a nice little chat with her."

"An excellent suggestion, men," Chester said crisply. "You may drive me down at once."

"Sure. Right this way."

Chester followed two of the officers to their car. He rode along in silence, turning over ways and means. It was unlikely that after ten months Genie was still in the local lockup. Still, she might have compounded the original offense by assaulting members of the police force, damaging public property, attempting escape, resisting arrest and failing to produce a driver's license. And, of course, she was penniless—always a disadvantage when reasoning with the law.

The car drew up to a side entrance to a red brick building with twin pillars surmounted by milky white globes lettered POLICE. Chester stepped out and followed the driver up the steps while his partner trailed. Inside, the cop motioned Chester along a short corridor and into an inner room where a thin man in a red uniform glanced up from behind a desk with an irritated expression.

"Okay, Buddy," the lead cop said, looking at Chester. "Look who we got here—the International Commissioner of Police. Get a load of the outfit."

"Now, I'd like to know—" Chester started, stepping forward.

"He shows up in the stakeout and wants to know do we remember the dame we picked up down there."

"And by the way, the chairs and rug are back," the other cop volunteered.

The man behind the desk jumped up. "Back, are they? Did you get whoever delivered them?"

"And he says it's an invasion from Mars," the cop finished. "Naw, they was too quick for us. They had this fast car, see—"

"You imbeciles! Kablitzki, I'll have your stripes for this! Now get back down there and keep that area under surveillance—and that doesn't mean sitting in your car listening to the latest jerk-and-twitch record!"

"But, Chief, what about our pinch here? He's a dangerous nut case."

The Chief threw a glance at Chester. "Probably an escapee from a TV commercial. Lock him up for obstructing justice."

"Look here—" Chester began.

The two cops turned to him with expressions of relief, reaching out large square hands. Chester leaned aside, caught an outstretched arm, flipped the hand back and applied pressure. The cop yowled and leaped, landed in a heap.

"I simply want some information," Chester declared. "The girl I asked about—is she still under confinement?"

The second cop growled and moved in. Chester stiff-handed him under the third button, clipped him on the side of the neck as he fell past.

"Here—" the Chief cried, reaching for a drawer. Chester was across the desk, his hands gripping the thin man's collar.

"Listen, you confounded idiot!" Chester barked. "Where is the girl—the one you picked up for indecent exposure?"

The Chief struggled manfully; Chester rapped his head against the floor. One of the cops staggered into view. Chester hit him with the Chief.

"Now look," he insisted, holding the unfortunate official in an awkward position over the back of his padded chair. "All I want is information on the young lady's whereabouts. Why not cooperate in giving a little help to a law-abiding citizen?"

"She's . . . in the women's wing—north side, first cell on the right."

"Where are the keys?"

"It's a . . . combination."

"What's the combination?"

The office door burst open. A fat cop goggled, tugged at a heavy pistol in a hip holster. Chester swung the Chief around as a shield. More cops appeared. In the corridor a bell clanged stridently. Feet pounded. Chester hurled the Chief from him, turned, crossed his arms over his face and dived through the wide double-hung window, landed on grass in a tinkle of glass shards, rolled and came up running. He leaped the hedge, heading for a dark alley mouth across the street. A man stepped into his path.

"Don't let 'em get away," Chester bawled. The man stepped aside, looking startled. Chester sprinted up the alley, emerged in a busy street, fell back to a brisk walk. The coup had been a failure, but at least he knew where Genie was. Poor girl! Almost a year in a cold, gray cell.

In the next block Chester skidded to a halt before a wide plate-glass window against which six-inch letters spelled out CATERPILLAR MOTORS. Beyond the glass crouched a giant yellow vehicle, aglitter with chrome, spotlights, aerials. A placard before the looming golden monster said:

THE NEW CATERPILLAR
CONVERTIBLE FOR '67
(White Sidewall Tracks Extra)

There was an inconspicuous door beside the picture window. Chester pushed it open. Inside, a man with greased hair and a smile leaned against the polished flank of the mighty machine, talking to a paunchy customer of middle age.

" . . . convenient monthly payments," he was saying. Chester eased behind the immense convertible, climbed softly up, opened the bubble canopy and settled himself in the yellow leather seat. Gleaming instruments winked up at him from a polished panel. Down below the salesman said, " . . . heat and music, window washers, back-up lights, power seats, windows, top, steering, brakes, clasho-mesh transmission, triple tank-drain carburetion, luxurious cardboard interior, garbage disposal, foam-rubber mats, TV screen . . . "

Chester looked over the panel, located the starter. " . . . jet-blast mufflers," the salesman was saying. "Not one but—get this—two, yes, *two* Last Trump air horns, a full complement of cheery flashing lights in place of tiresome dials . . . " Chester switched on, pressed the starter. The engine caught with a roar. He shifted into low, moved toward the show window. The startled salesman yelled and leaped clear; the customer scuttled for safety. The great polished blade hit the glass, sent it clattering in jagged shards. The convertible rumbled through the opening, pivoted to the right, bounced a diminutive passenger car aside, took the center of the avenue. Chester sounded the Last Trump horns as the clasho-mesh shifted into high with a squeal of treads.

The crowd scattered before the onrushing monster. An alert patrol car started up, gunned back into the car's path. Chester swerved, felt the rear quarters of the smaller vehicle crunch as the treads mounted it. He swerved to avoid a Good Humor man, clipped a beer truck with the tip of the blade, dumping it on its side. A head formed in the street.

Chester rounded into the street where a scattering of excited office workers clustered on the courthouse lawn. The north wing, the Chief had said. Chester squinted at the sun, steering for the opening in the hedge. North was to the right.

People were staring, pointing, then turning to run as the giant machine clattered across the curb, trampled the hedge and struck out across the lawn. A petunia bed disappeared under the relentless treads. High in the red brick side of the building, narrow barred windows were set at ten-foot intervals. Beneath them, the caterpillar ground to a halt. Over the rumble of the engine Chester heard excited cries. Faces appeared at the cell windows.

Chester opened the cab door and leaned out. "Genie!" he called. "It's I, Chester!"

There was a boom, and a bullet whined off the flank of the convertible. Chester ducked back inside. Above, he saw a familiar oval face appear at a window. He waved frantically. Genie waved back uncertainly. Chester threw the clasho-mesh in reverse and gunned back, pivoted, then moved forward. He set the corner of the blade against the brick wall and pressed the accelerator. The treads ground; the caterpillar bucked, then the treads spun helplessly as the turf gave way. A mighty stream of soil boiled out behind the machine.

Chester backed, lowered the blade, then raced the engine. The massive machine leaped forward and crashed against the brick wall with a thunderous impact.

Chester felt the seat lurch; then bricks and mortar were falling, bounding off the polished hood, clattering against the plastic canopy. Clouds of dust rose. Timbers dropped, bent nails showing, where broken two-by-four studding dangled.

Chester backed off, looked over the situation. The gun boomed again, four times, rapidly. Two stars appeared in the plastic dome near his head. The cell-block wall showed a six-foot-high, ten-foot-wide gap, through which office furniture was visible. As he watched, another section of mortared bricks dropped. He moved in, hit the wall again. When he backed out from the load of debris, the upper floor joists were visible, sagging under a horizontal steel member. Chester moved in, jarred the wall again. A large section fell, exposing the open sides of two cells. He could see the iron-legged cots aslant on the tilted floor.

Chester maneuvered the caterpillar close to the shattered wall, raised the canopy and shouted to Genie. She appeared, on hands and knees, looking down over the edge at the huge, rumbling machine.

"Come on, quickly, Genie!" Chester beckoned urgently. He took a look over his shoulder. The fat cop was struggling to stuff cartridges into the cylinder of his foot-long revolver. Other cops were running in various directions.

"Is it really you, Chester?" Genie's voice quavered.

"Hurry!" Chester held up his arms. Genie moved then, turning to lower her trim, booted legs over the side, then slide down, hang by her hands and drop. Chester caught her, bundled her inside and slammed down the bubbletop just as the cop's gun went off. He backed quickly, turned, gunned off across the lawn. There were more shots. A bullet clanged off the canopy.

"Chester—it *is* you! You look so different—so handsome!"

"Genie, I'm sorry. I didn't mean to run out on you; I got back as soon as I could. But—"

"Why, Chester, you were marvelous! I knew it was you as soon as you said 'it is I' instead of 'it's me.' Wherever did you get this marvelous machine?"

"Nice, isn't it? Just the thing for traffic. Air conditioning, soundproofing—and bulletproof glass, luckily for us. But what I wanted to say was, I'm terribly sorry about you having to spend almost a year in jail."

"A year? Why, Chester, it hasn't been more than two hours since the policemen took us away!"

Chester blinked. "But . . . but . . . "

"Where will we go now, Chester? And where did you get those clothes, and that suntan, and those big, strong arms?"

"I . . . but I mean—you . . . Well, never mind. We'll figure it out later. Right now we have to clear a path through to the rug."

Chester swung the caterpillar into the street where the cop-guarded rug waited. A fire engine, approaching at flank speed, swerved, mounted the curb, clipped off a fire plug and came to a halt in a striking display of waterworks. Chester slowed, crimped the wheel, lumbered past a police car and crunched to a stop. He opened the canopy and, amid shouts, assisted Genie out. She leaped lightly across the remains of splintered yellow sawhorses to the rug. Chester followed. A pair of the ever-present pink-coated policemen charged, sticks ready.

"Now!" Chester said, seizing Genie's hand. "Take us back to where we left Case, Computer! And don't make any mistakes on your coordinates this time!"

13

The shadows of the tall buildings dissolved into sunny skies. Chester and Genie stood on the grassy slope in the shade of the spreading branches. She turned to him, put soft arms around him.

"Oh, Chester. This is such fun!"

"Fun? Great heavens, Genie! Those people were shooting real bullets at us!"

"But you wouldn't let anything happen, I know."

"Well—at least it's a great relief to know you didn't actually spend a year in that cell. If you knew how I've been picturing you, languishing in durance vile—and Case! I assumed I was far too late to help him—but now, if we hurry—"

"I'm sure he'll be all right." Genie looked anxiously toward the ridge. "Still, I don't see the smoke any longer. I hope the fire hasn't burned down to the proper size for Mr. Mulvihill already."

"If those blasted natives have singed one hair of Case's head, I'll mow the whole tribe down!"

Twenty minutes' brisk walk brought them to the edge of the forest. On the trail ahead, two clean-shaven, sarong-clad men and a beautifully proportioned woman appeared. They paused, then flung up hands in greeting and began to dance and sing.

"Looks like a different tribe," Chester said. "Much better-looking people."

"They seem to want us to follow them."

With excited beckoning gestures the natives had turned and were darting away along a path.

"Well, we happen to be going in that direction anyway."

Chester and Genie moved on along the rough trail, came to the clearing where they had watched Case battle the giant.

"Not a sign of them," said Chester, looking around. "The cages are gone, everything." They pressed on, climbed a wooded slope and emerged from the forest into a wide village street, tree-lined and shady, bordered by beds of wild flowers behind which neat huts of brick, boards or split saplings dotted a park-like lawn. From a large house halfway along the street an imposing old man emerged, clad in neatly cut shorts and vest of coarse cloth. He pulled at a vast white beard as he came toward them.

"Good Lord!" said Chester, bewildered. "This is the wrong place, Genie! What kind of setting have you landed us in this time?"

"I don't know, Chester."

"Look at the old man with the beard. He's immense. I'll swear he must be an early Mulvihill; he looks enough like Case to be his grandfather."

The old man came up, looked piercingly at Chester, then at Genie. He pulled at his beard, nodding to himself.

"Well," he said. "So you came back after all."

Chester and Genie sat with Case on benches under a wild-cherry tree at the crest of a rise that fell away to a blue lake under steep pine-covered hills. A native girl poured brown wine from a stone jar into irregular mugs of heavy glass.

"Tell me that again, slow and easy, Chester," said Case. "You say it's the same day as when you left here?"

"For Genie it is. I lived through ten months."

"You *do* look different, Chester. I guess there's more to this business than meets the eye. That damn computer must have its time meters scrambled."

"Case, we thought they'd be roasting you alive. How did you manage to get into their good graces?"

"Well, let's see. The last I saw of you two, you were sneaking off behind a tree. I kept juggling for an hour. Then I did a few back flips and handstands, and then I got them to give me a rope and rigged it and did some rope-walking. By that time they'd noticed you were gone. I made a few motions to give 'em the idea you'd flown away in good demon style. They didn't care much; they wanted to see more ropework."

"By that time you must have thought we'd abandoned you."

"I admit I was a little mad at first when you didn't come charging over the hill with the Marines in tow. I guess it took a couple of years to get used to the idea I was stuck here. I figured something had happened to you, and I'd better just make the best of it. By that time I rated pretty high with the locals. They let me have the best den back in the thicket, and brought me all the food I wanted. It wasn't fancy but it was an easy life. Course, after thirty years . . . "

"Thirty years!"

Case nodded his white-maned head. "Yep. Near as I can tell. I used to cut notches in a tree for the years, but sometimes I was so busy I forgot."

"Busy? Doing what?"

"Well, there I was laying around all day, doing nothing, watching the natives scratch for a living, dirty, hungry, ignorant, dying of diseases, getting chewed up by bears or wildcats. And the food they gave me—half-raw dog meat, pounded raw turnips, now and then a mess of sour berries. Every now and then I'd have to put on a show, a little juggling or acrobatic work, just enough to keep the evil spirits out of town.

"Then one day I got to thinking. The country around here was the kind of real estate some smart developer

could make a fortune out of back home. All it needed
was the brush cut back and the trees trimmed and the
lake shore cleaned up and garbage piles carted off somewhere and some fruit trees and flowers planted . . .

"Well, before I could do any tree-trimming I had
to have an ax. That meant I needed some iron. By that
time I could get by O.K. in the native language. I asked
'em if they knew any place where there was red dirt;
told 'em it was important magic. A few weeks later a
hunting party came back from the other side of the
lake with some pretty good samples. The witch doctor had some coal—used it to carve gods out of, 'cause
it was easy to work. I built a furnace and piled it full
of lumps of ore and chunks of coal and set it off, and,
sure enough, after a couple of hours melted iron started
running out the bottom of the furnace."

"Case, what do you know about smelting iron?"
Chester interrupted. "You didn't happen to bring along
The Handyman's Home Smelter's Handbook, did you?"

"I used to blacksmith for the show in a pinch," Case
said. "I didn't know much—but I learned.

"I cast half a dozen ax and hatchet heads in clay
molds the first time. They came out pretty good. I
sharpened 'em up on a flat stone, and then heated 'em
and dunked 'em in a pot of water. They hardened
pretty good. Later on I got the formula down pat. It
depends mostly on how much coal and stuff you've got
in with the ore."

"A carbon content of between .7 and 1.7 percent
produces the optimum combination of hardness and
malleability," said Genie.

"I wish you'd been here, kid," said Case with a sigh.
"You could have been a big help. But we managed. I
pounded out a knife blade and fitted a handle to it and
used that to cut ax handles. Then I put the natives to
work clearing land—and it wasn't for show. The local

wild life couldn't sneak up on the village any more—
no cover. I had 'em root out all the bushes and coarse
stuff, and the native grasses took over. We undercut
all the trees as high as a man could reach. Then I had
'em shape the trees, pull down all the vines and stuff.
Made it look like a regular park around here.

"Then we went to work on the lake. We made up
some flat boats and got out and cleaned up the dead
branches and cattails and then did a little dredging;
built up a nice beach along this side. I rigged some
fishing gear out of leather strips, showed 'em how to
catch trout, and then staged a big fish fry. They didn't
want to touch the fish; wasn't what their grandpaws
ate, I guess. These kids were as conservative as a bunch
of Ivy League alumni. But I gave 'em the old magic
routine and they tried it. Now they spend half their
time out on the lake. We made up a couple of saws
and I showed 'em how to slice a tree into boards, and
we built a few rowboats. Funny thing was, before long
a couple of boys were ahead of me on boat-building—
and fishing too. I made 'em up some bows and arrows
and cast some iron arrowheads. Made up skinning
knives and showed 'em how to scrape a hide and work
it till it was soft.

"There were a lot of wild sheep and cattle around.
We made up a batch of braided ropes and went out
and brought in a couple of young goats and a half-
grown critter that looked like an overgrown Texas
longhorn. Later on we got a couple of newborn calves,
a male and a female. In a couple of years we had a
nice herd going. We let 'em graze the park here to keep
the grass down. And o' course I showed 'em how to
milk and we experimented around and made some
cheese."

"I didn't know you knew that much about animal
husbandry," Chester put in.

"Anybody that's worked around a circus knows which end of a critter to feed. That was the least of my problems. I was getting a lot of pleasure out of admiring the beach and the park, and thinking what a pile of dough I could make out of it if I had it all back home. Then I'd see a couple of the local gals come trotting by, buck naked, grimy, fat, with stringy hair, and pretty gamy, if you got too close to 'em." Case sighed. "And I wasn't much better, I guess. I'd kinda got out of the habit of shaving, and there wasn't too much point in taking a bath if you had to put the same old leather drawers back on. So I decided it was time to give a little thought to developing the feminine industries."

"The first thing I needed was some cloth, to get away from the smell of hides. I tried some wool off these goats we keep. It wasn't much good. We scouted around for some wild cotton, but couldn't find any. Finally discovered a kind of flax. Went to work and rigged up a spinning wheel. That took the best part of a year, but we finally worked it out. We spun up a big batch of yarn. I had a loom ready; that wasn't so hard. We set it up and wove us a blanket.

"Well, I trained a few of the girls, and set 'em to work spinning and weaving. Made up some needles out of bone; couldn't manage it in steel. I wasn't much of a seamster, but I had lots of time. I cobbled up a pair of breeches for myself first, then a shirt. But heck, it's too warm here for sleeves, and anyway they're hard to make. I settled on a vest; it's just right to keep the chill off on a cool morning."

"What about the winter?"

"Funny thing, there don't seem to be any seasons here. Stays about like this year around."

"Pre-Ice Age," Genie murmured.

"Then I had to make soap. I messed around with animal fat and ashes and finally worked out a pretty good formula. I had to make 'em wash, at first, but I gave 'em the old Great Spirit routine, and pretty soon they were down at the lake scrubbing something every time I turned around. They're as bad as a bunch of Methodists when it comes to trying to make points upstairs with something easier than laying off sin. And once you get clean, you itch if you start letting dirt pile up again—and you start noticing your roommate— so the last few holdouts got dunked and scrubbed.

"Then I saw the need for a little civic improvement. The dump where we'd been living all this time was alive with fleas and rats and the damnedest collection of chewed bones, worn-out hides, magic frogs' innards, mummified totem animals, and other junk—just like Grandma's attic back home. They were a little mad at first when I burned it down. I told 'em it was the word from on high and that the place had to go, but there was a crafty little devil of a witch doctor that had the confounded gall to stand up and call me a liar. Imagine!"

"Well, after all, Case, you had been telling them everything you'd been doing was divinely ordained."

"Worked pretty good, too. It might even be true. Anyway, after I took the witch doctor down and dumped him in the lake, nobody else complained."

"You were lucky he let it go at that. From what I've read about shamans, they can be dangerous enemies."

"Oh, I hadn't taught anybody to swim yet."

"You mean you drowned him? Case, wasn't that a little drastic?"

"Maybe. But I figured that if I was setting up a society, I might as well do it along realistic lines. There's no point in letting somebody half your size push you around— especially when you're right. A weakling makes as bad a dictator as anybody else. The way I saw it, it was up to me to stand up for my ideas."

"The next big man might not be as interested in the public welfare as you were, Case. What then?"

"To tell you the truth, Chester, I wasn't interested in the public welfare. I was only interested in making a comfortable place for me to live in. I wanted clean, healthy people around, because I don't like smelling dirty, sick ones. I wanted them to live good so they'd have the time and inclination to learn the things I was trying to teach them, like fishing—so I could eat fish; raising beef, so I could eat steak—and, later on, painting pictures that I could look at and making music for me to hear and taking an interest in cookery so they could lay on a good feed for me and being happy so there'd be a nice atmosphere in the village. In the end I discovered that I got a lot more pleasure out of associating with a nice bunch of people than out of anything else.

"I started some of 'em wood-carving, and other ones farming, and some of them making glass. I scoured the woods for new plants we could raise for food, and I kept trying out new dirt samples for other metals. Now we've got copper and lead and a little gold—and I've trained people to go on looking. I've started 'em thinking about things and trying new ideas. And ever since I drowned the witch doctor, I've played down the spirit angle. The younger generation doesn't need the threat of spooks to do things; they've got an interest that keeps them busy. A lot of them are way ahead of me now. They learn fast. I wouldn't be surprised if one of 'em doesn't invent chemistry any day now, or fire up a steam engine, or discover medicine."

"But a tyrant . . ."

"Any tyrant that sets up shop around here better be damned sure he doesn't develop any unpopular taste," said Case. "These folks put up with me because I bring 'em good things. They're selfish, just like me. I've established a precedent. The next boss better keep it up, or he'll be joining the witch doctor."

"It seems to have worked out well," Chester said, looking around at the peaceful village in the gathering twilight. "Still, I can't help feeling you should have instilled a little more idealism in them. Suppose they fall on hard times? What if the climate changes, or an epidemic strikes, or even a forest fire?"

"I don't think phony idealism would help. As far as I can see, all these schemes to make people squeeze into somebody's Grand Plan for Elevating Humanity usually end up with the elevatees on the short end of the stick. Everybody has his place in this village and a job to do that he's good at. My shoemakers can hold their heads up and the same goes for the fishermen and the hunters and the miners and the weavers and the vintners and the potmakers."

"What about the arts? With this materialistic orientation . . . "

"Everybody dances and everybody sings. They all play games and they all make statues out of mud and they all paint. Some are better than others, but it's doing it that counts. In our setup everybody's an artist, not just a few half-cracked far-outers."

"There don't seem to be many people here," said Genie. "Not more than three hundred, I'd estimate."

"Too many people in one place mean problems. Sanitation, transportation, noise, conflict of interests. There's plenty of wide-open real estate. I've got twelve other villages going within fifty miles of here—and none of them have over three hundred people. Everybody can have all the kids they want, but if you put the village over the three hundred mark, off you go to start your own. There's always plenty of volunteers to go along—people that want to get a good spot right on a lake or river, or hunters that like the idea of a virgin territory. There's a lot of trade among the towns, and the men usually get their wives from another village. Seems like it's human nature to prefer to go to bed with a stranger."

"It makes the Internal Revenue Bureau seem very remote," Chester said. "Why do we surround ourselves with unnecessary complexities?"

"Chester, this is a pretty good place here. Why don't you just settle down and forget all that?"

Chester shook his head. "I started off by trying to wiggle out of my tax problem with illegal schemes to make money. Then, when I landed you in trouble, I sneaked away and left you."

"But we agreed—"

"Genie tried to help me, and I left her stranded, too," Chester went on. "I'd just about hit bottom when Kuve took me in hand. When I broke out of the Research Center, I made up my mind I'd settle my score. I helped out a fellow named Bandon, and I paid Devant for a couple of undignified incidents. Then I was lucky enough to find Genie. I'm sorry about your tough time, Case. I've cost you thirty years."

"Best thirty years of my life, Chester. And now you're even."

"No, I still have the circus to think about."

"Hey, that's right, Chester. If it's really thirty years ago—I mean if thirty years haven't gone by—then maybe it's not too late to salvage something yet!"

"And," Chester went on, "there's Great-grandfather's invention to see to. He spent his life on it—and he's left it in my hands. It's up to me to save it. And there's something else, too."

Case got to his feet. "Well, no time like the present, Chester. Let's get going."

Half an hour later, Chester, Case, and Genie and

a chattering group of villagers stepped under the trees toward the rug and the two brocaded chairs.

"Case, I suppose you'll want to make a speech, appoint a successor, make a few prophecies, whatever white gods do before sailing off into the sunset."

Case sighed. "I've got a lot of friends here, Chester. I'll hate to leave 'em. But there's no point in making a national holiday out of it. I've been trying to teach 'em how to run things for thirty years. I don't guess any last-minute instructions are going to change anything."

"Then let's go, Genie," Chester said. "But be sure you put us back in the right spot: specifically, Great-grandfather's underground control room."

Genie had a faraway look in her eyes. "I'm in touch with the computer," she said. "But . . . "

"What is it, Genie?"

"It appears," she said, "that the world we started from no longer exists."

14

"A number of awful suspicions are beginning to crystallize into convictions," Chester said. "Your villages, with their population limit of three hundred, and the Tricennia, where I spent a year. Could that have been *this* society at some remote time in the future?"

"Beats me, Chester. I've given up trying to figure out anything that has to do with that blasted computer."

"If so, that would mean we've tampered with actual reality. We asked the computer to show us scenes of the past in the simplest possible way—"

"You mean that infernal contraption came up with the genuine article instead of a good honest fake?"

Chester nodded. "I'm afraid our hoax has backfired, Case. The computer really is a time machine."

"When we were bodily transferred into the past," Chester said, "our presence there altered the future. I recall now that the computer seemed to imagine that the Tricennium was Great-grandfather's basement."

"But what about the city with those awful pink policemen, Chester?" Genie asked. "It was very similar to home, except for being a little out of date—and I imagine that was because Mr. Mulvihill's absence unbalanced things a little."

"Case had only been here a short time then; he hadn't yet altered things completely out of recognizable shape."

"So I guess we settle here after all."

"Let's ask the computer a few questions. Are we completely cut off from getting back home, Genie?"

"A wide spectrum of entropic streams was rendered invalid by factors at the eighth level of complexity stemming from Mr. Mulvihill's introduction . . ."

"Yeah," Case cut in, "but what about Chester's estate?"

"It has been relegated to the status of an unrealized pseudo-reality."

"Why didn't that moronic aggregation of war-surplus parts mention this in the first place?"

"It's a machine, remember," Chester said. "No initiative. We didn't ask."

"Well, if the house is gone, then where's the computer?"

"Shunted to a temporal vacuole," Genie said.

"Hey, Chester," Case said. "I've got a crafty notion. He raised his voice. "Computer, could you . . . ah . . . show us what Great-grandpop's place looked like—if it existed?"

"Oh, yes, easily." There was a moment of delay; then glassy walls shimmered into view around the group.

"I must caution you that this is a mere optical effect," Genie said. "It represents no substantive referent."

"You may have something here, Case," Chester said. "Computer, I'd like this view firmed up a little—more detail, greater verisimilitude. More realism."

"I'm not at all sure I can manage it, Mr. Chester. It involves readjusting my parameters drastically, which induces a severe electronic itch."

"Try."

"The effort may leave you isolated in a mass-probability environment whose very existence I have every reason to doubt."

"We'll take the chance."

There was a moment of silence. Then:

"There, I've managed tactile quality. You could feel the wall now if you touched it."

"Now add in taste, smell and sound effects. And daub in some externals, too."

After a moment the computer said, "I've extended the effect to include a pseudo-house, with pseudo-grounds, surrounded by pseudo-atmosphere."

"Breathable, I hope?"

"Oh, of course. All my illusions are of the finest quality and extremely accurate."

"In that case, you may proceed to supply the rest of the planet. Take your time and do a good job now."

"That last admonition was hardly called for, Mr. Chester."

"Sorry. But can you do it?"

"Oh, I've already finished."

"So now there's an apparent world outside, resembling the real one in every respect?"

"Yes, indeed; except that it isn't real, of course."

Chester crossed to the door, flung it open. The

familiar dusty wine bottles lay quietly in their cradles opposite the reels and flashing lights of the control panel.

"This may not be home," Chester said, "but I think the point is academic."

There was a peremptory rap at the door.

"What's that?"

"A Mr. Overdog of the Bureau of Internal Revenue," the computer answered.

"Well, you asked for realism," Case said. "Shall I let him in?"

"How does he know about this place?" Chester asked.

"Oh, I informed him of it by letter," the computer spoke up. "Retroactively."

"Why? Haven't we got enough trouble?"

"You indicated that you wished the tax problem dealt with. I took appropriate action."

"Say, how much time's passed here while we were out building universes?" Case inquired.

"Seven days, two hours, forty-one minutes and two seconds."

"Shall I let him in, Chester?"

"You may as well."

The door was opened to reveal a lean, red-eyed man with an old-fashioned hat of orange fur covering his hairless head. He eyed Case and Genie.

"I received your letter," he snapped. "Where's Mr. Chester? I trust you're ready to get on with it. I'm a busy man."

"Why . . . ah . . . " Chester started.

More footsteps sounded. A portly man with ice-blue eyes under shaggy white brows puffed into the room.

"Mr. Chester," he began without preamble, "before concluding any agreement with the IRS, I hope you will entertain my offer."

"What are you doing here, Klunt?" Overdog snapped.

"Who's this?" Chester whispered urgently to Genie.

"He's from the Bureau of Vital Statistics," she whispered back. "He got a letter, too."

"When did all these letters get written? There hasn't been time since we remanufactured the world."

"It's remarkable what you can do with temporal vacuoles," Genie said. "The letters were postmarked three days ago."

"What kind of offer did you have in mind, Mr. Ahhh?" said Case.

"Assuming your . . . ah . . . information storage device functions as I've been informed, I'm prepared to offer you, on behalf of the Bureau of Vital Statistics . . . "

"I'll settle for half the tax bill," Overdog cut in. "And we'll entertain the idea of a liberal settlement of the balance, say, over a two-year period. Generous, I'd say. Generous in the extreme."

"Vital Statistics will go higher. We'll pay two full thirds of the bill!" Klunt stared at Overdog triumphantly.

"It's a conspiracy! You're playing with prison, Klunt!" He turned hard eyes on Chester. "Final word, Mr. Chester. Complete forgiveness of the entire tax debt! Think of it!"

"Chicken feed!" snorted Klunt. "I'll have a check for five million credits ready for you in the morning."

"Sold!" Chester said.

"On an annual lease basis, of course," Case added.

"Giving us full rights of access," Chester amended.

"A deal, gentlemen! I'll revolutionize Vital Statistics with this apparatus! With the increased volume of information, I should say a staff increase of fifty persons would not be excessive, eh, Overdog?"

"Bah! I'll expect your check tomorrow, Mr. Chester—

and another next March!" He stalked out. Klunt followed, planning happily.

"Well, that's taken care of," Case said, beaming. "Nice work, Chester. I guess the Wowser Wonder Shows won't have to worry for a while."

Chester opened the door and looked out. "You're sure it's safe out there, Computer?" he called.

"The question seems to have become academic, Mr. Chester. A reappraisal indicates that the present scene is substantive after all. Mr. Mulvihill's village was a figment of the imagination, I now perceive."

"Oh yeah? What about this beard?"

"Psychosomatic," the computer said without conviction.

"What about Genie?" Case asked. "Do we leave her stored here, or what?"

"Genie's coming with me," Chester said.

"Well, I figured maybe she was part of the lease."

"Lease? Nonsense. Genie's as human as I am."

"Don't kid me, Chester. We were both here when she was built—right, Computer?"

"You asked that I produce a mobile speaker in the configuration of a nubile female," the computer replied. "The easiest method was to initiate the process of maturation in a living human cell."

"You mean you grew Genie from a human cell—in a matter of hours?"

"The body was matured in a time vacuole."

"But . . . where did you get the cell?"

"I had one on hand—one of yours, Mr. Mulvihill. I took a blood specimen for identification purposes, if you recall."

"But that's impossible. I'm a male!"

"It was necessary to manipulate the X and Y chromosome balance."

"So I'm a mother," said Case wonderingly, "and an unwed mother at that. It figures, though—growing a real girl was simpler than building one out of old alarm clocks."

"In that case," Chester said, taking Genie's hand, "I hope you'll consent to give the bride away in your capacity as both parents—assuming Genie agrees."

"Oh, Chester," Genie said.

"Well, folks," Case boomed, "let's have a drink and get used to the idea."

"I'll be along in a few minutes," Chester said. "I want to have a talk with the computer first."

"What about?"

"I've spent twenty-five years in society and contributed nothing. Now I'm going to start a school—just a small institution for a few selected students, at first. I want to see what I can do to straighten out a few of the world's irrationalities. The computer has the facts—and, thanks to Kuve, I've learned to think."

"Yep, you've changed, all right, Chester. Well, take your time. We'll wait."

Chester settled himself in the brocaded chair. "All right, Computer. Here we go with your first lesson: Isnot is not not-is. Not-is is not is-not. Not-is-not is not is . . ."

AFTERWORD

❧

The next volume of Baen Books' reissue of the writings of Keith Laumer, the fourth in the current series, is entitled *A Plague of Demons & Other Stories*. In that volume, we'll be presenting some of the best stories Laumer wrote centered around the theme of the threat to human beings posed by hostile aliens.

This venerable sub-genre of science fiction, of course, was hardly invented by Keith Laumer. It dates back at least as far as H.G. Wells' *War of the Worlds*, and has never ceased being one of the staple themes of SF writers. But Laumer brought his own unique style to that kind of story.

And nowhere, I think, is Laumer's style better exemplified than in the novel which will lead off the volume: *A Plague of Demons*. A novel which, over the years, many people have come to regard as his finest. (I confess that I'm not *quite* among them. For what are perhaps simply reasons of personal quirk and taste, I have a slight preference for *Galactic Odyssey* and *Dinosaur Beach*. But I would definitely agree that *A Plague of Demons* is one of the *three* best novels Laumer ever wrote. Well . . . one of the four. I'm also very partial to *Catastrophe Planet*.)

It's a little hard to describe Laumer's "style" in the abstract. The closest I can come is simply to say that, at his best, Laumer could rip off a story with more verve and energy than any science fiction writer I can think of. The headlong pace of Laumer's best novels is something that you'll find very rarely—anywhere, not simply in science fiction. Where other writers might rely on the intricate structure of the plot to keep a story going, Laumer would generally rely on pure bravura—something which very few authors can manage to carry off successfully.

But, Laumer could, and that's why his best stories work so well. To be honest, the plot structure of his novels often doesn't bear too close an examination. Laumer was cheerfully willing to advance his plots by the hoariest devices. Four in particular:

The Friend Who Conveniently Shows Up At Just The Right Time.

The Unknown Girl Who, For No Discernable Rhyme Or Reason, Saves The Hero.

Going Back To Square One By Having The Hero Get Bonked On The Head. Or the slight variant, used in *Galactic Odyssey*: Screw Up Royally. (Which, of course, usually results in the needed Bonk On The Head.)

And, always his favorite, which he borrowed—giving full credit, and in public—from the great detective writer Raymond Chandler:

When All Else Fails, Have Somebody Come Through The Door And Throw A Punch.

It's all very shameless. Oh, yes, indeed it is—and, for the public record, I hereby officially cluck my tongue.

I will also state—and also in public—that I couldn't care less. Mind you, when Laumer didn't quite "hit it right," these plot devices have a tendency to stick out like sore thumbs. But when he did—which happens more often than not—the momentum of the story itself makes it all a moot point. Whining about the jury-rigged plot is like complaining that the drivers at the Indy 500 are racing at dangerous speeds. Or—gasp—that there is *gambling* in Rick's casino!

Well, yes—that's why you go there in the first place.

Probably none of Laumer's novels illustrates my point better than *A Plague of Demons*. Leaving aside every specific use of the device, the plot of the *whole novel* can be described in terms of the classic Raymond Chandler ploy:

Aliens—really nasty ones, too—come through the door and throw a punch.

Alas, they slugged the wrong guy. And we're off to the races!

And race it does. Like *Galactic Odyssey* and *Dinosaur Beach*, the pace of *A Plague of Demons* is that of Laumer at his best. It's the literary equivalent of running the rapids on a raft. Exhilarating, for those of us who enjoy such thrills. I will, clearing my throat, warn those who prefer a more sedentary tale to look elsewhere. Coupled together, the terms "sedentary" and "written by Keith Laumer" would be the silliest oxymoron ever invented.

I'm tempted to leave it there, but I fear my fellow Laumer fans would scowl upon me if I didn't also make the point that, when he wanted to, Laumer was quite capable of crafting a tightly-plotted and well-structured tale. And, indeed, in the very same volume, you will find examples of such stories as well. Laumer's well-known "Thunderhead" comes immediately to mind. And so, for that matter, does "Doorstep"—a story which has what I think may well be one of the half dozen greatest closing lines in all of science fiction.

Enough. Afterwords also benefit from hoary plot devices, not the least of which is: End It.

Eric Flint
October 2001

CLASSIC MASTERS OF SCIENCE FICTION BACK IN PRINT!

〰〰〰

James Schmitz's stories
edited by Eric Flint

Telzey Amberdon	57851-0 ♦ $7.99	___
T'NT: Telzey & Trigger	57879-0 ♦ $6.99	___
Trigger & Friends	31966-3 ♦ $6.99	___
The Hub: Dangerous Territory		
	31984-1 ♦ $6.99	___
Agent of Vega & Other Stories		
	31847-0 ♦ $7.99	___

Keith Laumer's writing
edited by Eric Flint

Retief!	31857-8 ♦ $6.99	___
Odyssey	0-7434-3527-3 ♦ $6.99	___
Keith Laumer: The Lighter Side	0-7434-3537-0 ♦ $6.99	___

〰〰〰

for more books by the masters of science fiction and fantasy,
ask for our free catalog or go to www.baen.com

Amazons 'r Us

The Chicks Series, edited by Esther Friesner

Chicks in Chainmail
87682-1 ◆ $6.99

"Kudos should go to Friesner for having the guts to put together this anthology and to Baen for publishing it . . . a fabulous bunch of stories . . . they're all gems."
—*Realms of Fantasy*

" . . . a romp that certainly tickled this reviewer's funny bone."
—*VOYA*

Did You Say Chicks?!
87867-0 ◆ $6.99

Those Chicks in Chainmail are baaack—and They Are Not Amused! Sure, you're entitled to a laugh or two . . . while you're chuckling show some respect. You can start by buying this book. Pardon us for a moment . . . have to wash the bloodstains off these swords before they set. . . .

Chicks 'n Chained Males
57814-6 ◆ $6.99

Continuing a great tradition, *Chicks 'n Chained Males* is not what you think. Never would such as they stoop to the exploitation of those poor chained males who have suddenly found themselves under their protection and succour. No-no—these chicks are here to rescue these victims of male-abuse from any number of Fates Worse Than Death. . . . Right here. Right now.

The Chick Is in the Mail
31950-7 ◆ $6.99

From the silly to the simply smashing, the Chicks in Chainmail are back to save us once again! Whether weekending in the woods to get in touch with their Inner Warrior or showing giant reptiles that Tokyo's not gonna take it anymore, these female fighters will always have what it takes. So what are you waiting for? Pick up your male—er, *mail!*

And don't miss, also by Esther Friesner:

Wishing Season
87702-X ◆ $5.99

Available at your local bookstore. If not, fill out this coupon and send a check or money order for the cover price + $1.50 s/h to Baen Books, Dept. BA, P.O. Box 1403, Riverdale, NY 10471. Delivery can take up to 8 weeks.

Name: _____

Address: _____

_____

I have enclosed a check or money order in the amount of $